THE HISTORY OF
HONEY SPRING

DARIN COZZENS

ZARAHEMLA
BOOKS

Cover designed by Jason Robinson
Design and layout by Marny K. Parkin
Fence image designed by brgfx / Freepik

ISBN 978-0-9993472-6-3

Zarahemla Books
869 East 2680 North
Provo, UT 84604
info@zarahemlabooks.com
ZarahemlaBooks.com

"Part post-Vietnam meditation, part Old West saga, *The History of Honey Spring* tells the story of Jim Ray, fresh from war, who finds himself the last surviving relative of the mysterious loner, Goss Harvey. With that designation, Jim inherits not only land but a longstanding feud between founding families. Cozzens' Wyoming characters are as richly drawn as Dickens' inhabitants of London, his descriptions as physical and present as the Wyoming landscape he evokes. This novel rests easily alongside the works of Wallace Stegner and Annie Proulx.

— Paul Bowers,
author of *Ten Acres of the Universe*

"Cozzens' vision of humanity in Balford is as expansive as the population is small. More than just a gifted chronicler of rural Mormonism, Cozzens is a chronicler of grace."

— Christopher T. Lewis,
Associate Professor and Chair, World Languages & Cultures,
University of Utah

"A young man back from war finds healing in a place and among a people who must let go of the past to make him one of their own. You will find yourself fully immersed in *History of Honey Spring*, its compelling description of life on a Wyoming farm in a Mormon community in the 1960s—a life-affirming tale of recovery from loss."

— Rita Lawrence Rogers,
Retired English/Literature Instructor,
North Carolina Community College System

"In the vein of Wallace Stegner, William Kittredge, and Annie Proulx, Darin Cozzens' *The History of Honey Spring* depicts a place and its people that tourism and social media influencers have passed over. This novel is a rich and knowing psalm to the true, unadorned American West."

—Todd Robert Petersen,
author of *Picnic in the Ruins*

Other Books by Darin Cozzens:
Light of the New Day
The Last Blessing of J. Guyman LeGrand

To my uncle
John Cozzens
1930–2016

CHAPTER 1

WHEN LANCE CORPORAL JIM RAY CAME HOME FROM war in mid-April of 1966, the only people in the world waiting for him were two strangers—the lawyer Rickett, whose letter had found him one month earlier in a sandbag bunker somewhere in Chu Lai, and a distant and dying cousin named Goss Harvey. And they were waiting, not in Jim Ray's hometown of Mapleton, Utah, but five hundred miles away, in a nursing home in Cody, Wyoming.

"Lord *knows* I didn't want my half of Honey Spring to go to a Mormon, blood or not," the eighty-six-year-old Harvey whispered from his nursing home bed, clenching his pale fists. "But better you than those damn Vanderfisks!"

The nursing home visit took place on a Sunday evening. When Goss died in the early hours of the next morning, his body, in accordance with an adamant final instruction, was not taken the thirty miles back to Balford to be buried by a church he had parted company with many years earlier. Better, he had insisted, to let the worms have at his flesh in the comfortable anonymity of the Cody cemetery, away from the hypocrisies of a pioneer Mormon town.

"I can't say I blame him," said the lawyer Nolan Rickett, who was only ten years younger than his just-deceased client. "Having grown up Catholic in a little corner of the Latter-day Saint Zion known as Luna Valley, New Mexico," he said, "I am well familiar with the idiosyncrasies of the religion and its people."

After a brief and unseasonably cold graveside service Wednesday morning, Rickett settled accounts with the mortician, the cemetery groundskeeper, and an open-minded Methodist minister—the only other people in attendance. The instant the lawyer turned away from his last transaction, one hand fished inside his overcoat and came out with a pack of Pall Malls. The coat, like the hat on his head, had been in style twenty or thirty years earlier. With a flick of the wrist, a single cigarette suddenly protruded from the pack's open corner. From there, the butt end went directly to his lips. The other hand—patting, reaching, digging—came out with a lighter whose silver plating was worn to the brass in several places. Rickett flipped open the lighter's cap and, tilting his head so as to make a windbreak with his hat brim, thumbed the flint mechanism. In the chill breeze, the tiny flame guttered, but did what it was intended to do.

After a long first drag, Rickett turned to Jim. "As you may or may not recall from my letter," he said, "the bequeathed acreage comes with 'sundry possessions.'"

These possessions included, first of all, a 1941 Ford pickup. "Big engine, low first gear, heavy-duty leaf springs," Rickett said. "It'll haul like a dump truck and tow like a freight train. Not to mention," he added, "a functioning radio and heater *and* a gun rack."

The sundry possessions also included a bigger and even older farm truck for crop hauling, two hard-used tractors—a McCormick and a Case—and enough worn-out machinery to make a crop.

As for property "improvements," the letter had listed a tool shed, chicken coop, grain bin, various outbuildings, corrals, barn, and a furnished single-wide trailer house shaded by several mature cottonwoods.

"The cats ran off," Rickett said, "and good riddance; they weren't much as mousers anyhow. And I gave the hens away. But the two dogs I took home. Nothing special in the looks department, but you should see them with cattle." He said, "They'll earn their keep."

"You want them?" Jim Ray asked. "You've been feeding them."

Rickett hesitated. "They've been good company, sure enough," he said. "But they're your dogs. And I'll see them often enough."

From a lawyer who had just buried his client and was tying up that client's final loose ends, the last statement was cryptic.

"Last but not least," Rickett said, "you've got a decent Angus bull and thirty-some head of good mixed-breed cows. Given Mr. Harvey's illness last winter, we left them to fend for themselves on riverbottom pasture. They've grown quite comfortable down there and will not take kindly to being driven toward a more restrictive enclosure. Without the dogs, we wouldn't stand a chance."

We?

If Rickett wasn't going to offer an explanation, Jim was going to have to ask. "What exactly was your arrangement with Mr. Harvey? I mean, how long were you planning—"

"Long enough," Rickett said. "That's nothing for you to worry about right now." With the fingers of one hand, he managed his cigarette. With the fingers of the other—one of them bearing a thin, silver wedding band—he slipped the lighter into an overcoat pocket, then pulled out a wadded handkerchief. Still using just the one hand, he very dexterously blew his nose.

"Now," he said, "what could *not* be communicated in my letter was the grief you would have caused an old man on his deathbed, not to mention the considerable headache for me, had you come back from over there in a box."

As it turned out, the legal agreement for dividing Honey Spring—drawn up sixty years earlier, when the two landowners were friends—also stipulated that if either died without an heir, his half would revert to the survivor. For Goss Harvey, finding that heir became the last, most desperate quest of a long, hard life. He had been wifeless for over three decades and childless for over four. He had no siblings. On his paternal side, there was no family tree to shake. His father was an orphan from Lampeter, Wales—a knacker's apprentice. It wasn't even certain that this orphan gave the missionaries his real name when he was baptized in late 1855. On the ship the next spring and then pulling a handcart across Nebraska and Wyoming, he was known to his fellow converts only as Boy Harvey. He was fifteen years old.

By default, then, the search for an heir had to focus on the other half of the lineage. Goss's mother did have a sibling—a sister. But in all his years in Wyoming, Goss had not had any contact with that sister's descendants. The only thing to do was go to her last known location, which happened to be central Utah, and start poking around in towns with names like Spanish Fork and Payson and Nephi.

"And that," Rickett said, "is how I stumbled on your little hometown and the name of that sister's great-granddaughter— one Minnie Ray."

The letter delivered to the sandbag bunker had made it clear that the heirship came through Jim's maternal line. Still, at the mention of his mother's name, Jim's throat tightened.

Rickett took another pull on the cigarette, then turned his head aside to blow smoke into the cold wind. "I soon discovered, however, that this Minnie Ray was herself a long-time widow who had died three years earlier—from heart problems stemming from a childhood case of rheumatic fever. I don't mind telling you, Cousin Goss was getting frantic. But fortunately, Minnie Ray's young husband, who *did* eventually come back from war in a box—courtesy of the Japanese—had managed to beget a son just before shipping out." He paused. "The fact of the matter is, the final leg of my search took a lot longer than it should have because I thought I was looking for someone named *Theron*."

The two men studied each other.

It took just a moment for Jim Ray to decide that now was as good a time as any for an explanation: "My mother read the name in a book somewhere and liked it—at least long enough to saddle me with it. But I don't think she wound up liking it as much as she thought she would. She never used it much when I was little and none at all by the time I got in high school. The only people who *did* use it were people who didn't know me—somebody reading me off a list. Like a teacher. Maybe a nurse. Or a drill sergeant." He paused. "Or a lawyer."

A hint of a smile played across Rickett's face. Very discreetly, he dropped his cigarette butt onto the cemetery turf, then toed it into grass blades showing, toward their roots, the first hint of green. He said, "We'll have to see which category the Vanderfisks fall in."

"That's the bunch Mr. Harvey mentioned."

"It is," Rickett said, pulling on a pair of black leather dress gloves. "We kept you a secret as long as we could, but they were bound to find out. They kept pretty close tabs on Goss, even when he got so he was hiding from the world. And even before that, old Enoch Vanderfisk had never completely given up on a redeemable friendship with the man." Rickett paused and looked at Jim. "One thing you got to understand: in the old days, they were very close."

When Jim didn't say anything, Rickett tugged his hat brim down and coat collar up. Then he looked him in the eye.

"Son," he said, "Goss Harvey's half of Honey Spring now belongs to you. You can do with it as you wish—sell it or keep it or donate it to charity—and I will help you in any way I can. I'll start with some unsolicited advice: I wouldn't rush a transaction, which is exactly what the Vanderfisks want. Wave a wad a money in front of a young lad just home from war in one piece and hope he'll take it and sign on the dotted line."

"How *much* money?" Jim asked.

"Hard to say," Rickett said, "but certainly enough to pose the one temptation your religion has not fortified you against."

"And if I don't sell?"

"If it was January," Rickett said, "you could find a renter. But it's too late in the season for that now."

"So what do I do?" Jim asked.

The lawyer hesitated. Then, tentatively, he said, "You could always farm it yourself."

Jim stared at him. "Are you kidding?"

"Try it for a year," Rickett replied, very quickly, "just to get a feel for the place and the work, then decide if renting better suits you."

"I wouldn't know a plow from a pie tin."

"Just out of curiosity," the old lawyer said, "what *do* you know—besides humping the boonies?"

"Delivering newspapers. Bagging groceries. Last half of high school, I worked one summer at a sawmill and another on a guardrail crew. Neighbor orchards always needed apple pickers in the fall. In junior high wood shop we had to build a bootjack. Mine came apart the first time I stuck my heel in it." Jim paused, waiting for Rickett to concede the absurdity of his proposal. And when there was no such concession, Jim said, "But *none* of that is farming your own farm."

"No," Rickett finally said, "but you can learn."

"From who?"

A hint of guilty presumption crept into Rickett's face. He didn't say anything.

"*You?*" Jim asked.

Rickett didn't say anything.

"You're a lawyer!"

"I am that."

"Wouldn't that be a little like the blind leading the blind?"

"Probably," Rickett said. "But look at it this way: You got any *better* prospects waiting for you back in Mapleville?"

"Maple-*ton.*"

"Maple leaf, maple syrup, maple taffy—whatever. Mormons and their names! You got a job waiting down there? Girlfriend? Pot of gold?"

Jim had none of those. After a moment, he said, "You don't want the Vanderfisks to end up with Goss's place, do you?"

"I wouldn't want to bias you," Rickett said.

The wind blowing over the gravestones had a raw edge.

"Too late," Jim said.

The graveside service took place on Wednesday of Jim Ray's first full week in Wyoming. Nine o'clock the next morning found him, by invitation, in the office of the man who was married to Enoch Vanderfisk's oldest daughter.

"Well, isn't this a fine bloody how-de-do?" said Big Frett Maxwell. "With no more thought than you'd give to picking chocolate or vanilla, that's your answer?"

Thanks to his marital credential, Big Frett was also managing vice-president of Balford Savings and Loan. From behind his managing vice-president's desk, Big Frett said, "Ten years my Bernene has had her eye on the half of Honey Spring with any decent soil. And now she loses out to a Johnny-come-lately G.I. Joe who turns down an offer of thirty thousand dollars cash money because he thinks he wants to be Old McDonald." Only at this point in a rather one-sided conversation did coercion finally defer to entreaty. "She has grand plans for that acreage, son. A whole lot grander, anyway, than pinto beans."

"I *can* call you Theron, can't I?" Bernene herself asked early Thursday afternoon, during a second well-orchestrated interaction with Goss Harvey's heir. Following her into the front room of a big house at the edge of Balford, Jim appreciated the aptness of Rickett's reference: Big Bernene. (According to Rickett, the reference helped an outsider like him keep track of who was married to whom among the town's Latter-day Saint population.) Her impressive girth and stature were crowned, symbolically and otherwise, by her hair. As Jim took the seat she invited him to take, he estimated that her bouffant would easily fill a bushel basket.

"Or," she said, taking a seat across from him, "are you more comfortable with 'James'? Or maybe 'Jimmy'?" She didn't wait for an answer. Nor, in the remainder of their brief meeting, did she find any reason to address her guest by any name at all. "I do wish you'd reconsider," she said, when it became clear that her guest's polite refusal of cookies and lemonade wasn't going to be his only refusal of the day. "Can you imagine what a young man of your background and circumstances could *do* with thirty-five thousand dollars?"

"That *is* a lot of money to someone of my background and circumstances," Jim said in a pay-phone conversation with Rickett, who had instructed him to call with a report.

"It's a low-ball, Mickey Mouse, bullcrap offer," Rickett responded. "That property's worth at least three times that, and they know it."

"Is this more of your unsolicited advice?"

"If it's money you're after, at least hold out for an offer that's not downright laughable."

"I don't know what I'm after," Jim said into the telephone receiver.

Friday morning, old Enoch himself took a turn. Despite his role as Vanderfisk patriarch and honorary bank president, he neither coerced nor entreated. But he did increase the offer to forty thousand dollars.

When Jim declined, the old man sighed from behind his aged oak desk in an office beside the vault. For a long time he sat in his matching oak swivel chair without saying anything.

Jim shifted in his visitor's chair.

"You have inherited a property," old Enoch said finally, "without knowing its history." Whether the statement was accusation or allowance was hard to tell. He then leaned forward in his chair—it squeaked—and lifted from the desk's surface a saucer-sized frame. For a long time he gazed at the photograph it circumscribed. "She was a beautiful woman, my wife. In my opinion," he mused, without showing the photo to Jim, "these old black and whites capture the truer image."

Checkering the wall behind him were many such images and their color counterparts. There were groundbreakings, ribbon cuttings, Chamber of Commerce and Rotary awards, prize-winning, bank-sponsored lambs and steers at the county fair. Punctuating the community-relations gallery were other photos. Enoch the hunter triumphantly grasping the antler of an impressive buck or bull. Enoch the fowler kneeling in autumn stubble behind several brace of pheasants. Enoch the fisherman displaying the splendid trout. Below all these, in the bottom left corner, a wallet-sized photo showed two young men in white shirts and ties, standing side by side, each with an arm around the other's shoulders. It, too, was black and white.

When Enoch finally spoke, his voice was thick with emotion. "She got tired of telling people that, yes, Honey was her real name. She didn't wait for me and Goss to ask. First thing she said when we met her, 'We'll all three get along a lot better if you know from the start that's what my parents actually wanted on Church records and every other kind of record—because they thought I was sweet.'" Enoch smiled as he remembered those words, or perhaps the way his wife had said them. "And for a while we all *did* get along," he insisted. Several moments passed. Finally, he rubbed his eyes wearily and said, with just a hint of exasperation: "How was I to know there'd be money in rock?"

CHAPTER 2

RICKETT SAW NO INDIGNITY IN FARM WORK. AS HE never tired of repeating, his intimate acquaintance with Mormons came, during the formative seasons of his youth, from hiring out to farmers and ranchers around Luna. "Decent enough men," he granted, "although in any kind of money dealing, they could give lessons to a Jew." But that chapter of his life was long past, and now, at age seventy-six, whatever his personal interest and role in the future of Honey Spring, he preferred tutoring to doing.

Beginning that first Monday in late April, he came dressed like no farm tutor Jim could have imagined. On his feet were high-top sneakers that had once been white. On his head was a frayed newsboy hat. Beneath an old tweed coat he wore cotton coveralls that had come green from a store shelf a decade or two earlier but were now faded white at the seams and patched at the knees.

"You got to start somewhere," Rickett said, walking Jim over to the McCormick and pointing to a cushionless, cup-shaped metal tractor seat beaded with cold dew, "and this is as good a place as any."

He began his tutoring as he began most things—with a cigarette in his hand or mouth.

"If my tobacco bothers you," Rickett said, "just say so. It never did Goss. Not in all the time I knew him, which would be the better part of ten years, I guess. In fact, he once told me he thought seriously, after he dropped out of your church, of taking up the habit. In spite of my encouragement, he never got around to it."

Comical as the old lawyer looked, there was nothing comical about either his knowledge or his commitment. During the next month, six days a week, he devoted every daylight hour to his teaching. During the first acres of tilling, he rode the tractor's wheel fender, beside what he kept calling the tractor's cockpit long after the misnomer had lost its charm. From his fender perch, he directed and reminded, pointed and warned, guided and chided. Sometimes, out of urgency or convenience (when he didn't want to bother with an explanation), he skipped words altogether and simply executed the needed maneuver or adjustment himself—nudging the throttle handle one way or the other, fingering a hydraulic lever, stomping the brake pedals. Occasionally he commandeered the steering wheel altogether.

In the Nolan Rickett approach to teaching, all risk and accountability fell to the student. In the tightening of nuts or collars or couplings, for instance, he equated caution with fecklessness, urged more and more force—right up to the instant the bolt snapped or the threads stripped. Then this: "I could see you were overdoing it." Jim found himself blamed for cobblings and improvisations that predated him by years. The choke cable on one of the tractors, for example, had long since been replaced by a strand of baling wire. When, on Jim's first tug, that wire broke, Rickett sniffed and said, "What'd you expect?"

Rickett's most indelible teaching was in the art of ditch irrigating. The idea, he explained one bright, chilly morning, was to get the water from ditch to field. That transfer first required the raising of the ditch's water level. The raising was achieved with checks (barrel lids or scraps of tin or some such) angled so as to impede the current and supported against a portable weir frame of sticks, boards, posts, pipe—the more mismatched and unwieldy, it seemed, the better. After the flow was checked at several intervals, as needed, it was stopped completely with a portable dam (a rectangle of canvas made rigid along one long edge with a board or rod threaded through a stitched sleeve).

The setting of the dam was a lesson all by itself. For this task, especially, Rickett preferred lecture to demonstration. At his age, he said, he couldn't risk falling or getting soaked because the last thing Jim needed was an invalid on his hands. First, therefore, Rickett had him straddle the ditch facing downstream. Then he had him center the rigid edge of the dam against another set of weir sticks. Then: spread and stretch the canvas over the water, anchoring the two loose corners beneath the well-worn soles of knee-high rubber irrigating boots inherited from Goss Harvey. Then: with a shovel tip, push the tight-stretched hem down into the ditch's current until the fabric fills like a sail, conforms to the ditch's interior surface, bellies against the weir. Then: with the edge of the shovel blade, gently pinch the hem into ditch mud and weight the bottom with slices of sod. At that point, with the water backing up and building pressure and threatening the lip of the ditch bank, the only remaining step—to be carried out with frantic haste—was to channel it into the field through aluminum siphon tubes shaped, according to Rickett's description, like question marks without the dot.

With each new "set," every piece of irrigating gear had to be moved—which meant stumbling atop a grassy and uneven ditch bank or at its rutted base, carrying armloads of weir sticks and tubes that blocked a clear view of the path immediately ahead. Rickett helped by admonishing Jim, most of the time *after* a flailing fall, to watch his step.

Jim discovered a few things on his own. The same armload of tubes that was slimy cold in the early morning became sizzling hot at midday. Mole tunnels were a lot easier to find at one end than the other. And setting a canvas dam in the wind was a comedy act in which the hapless irrigator was repeatedly

bested by an eight-foot-by-six-foot piece of canvas flapping wet
and muddy in his face.

"Hasn't anybody in this valley ever heard of sprinklers?" Jim
asked after about the third day of moving (or "changing") water,
when the relentlessness of the chore was already beginning to
wear a groove.

"We're just not as enlightened as you Utah folks," Rickett said,
"spiritually *or* agriculturally."

Submitting to the tutoring of such a man had its benefits, though.
In the month following the meeting with old Enoch Vanderfisk—
during the loading and spreading of barn manure, the replace-
ment of plowshares (which were considerably thicker than pie
tins), the filling of seed hoppers, the mounting of corrugating
shovels for making irrigating furrows in the newly planted barley, and session after session of changing irrigating water—Rickett the lawyer instructed Jim Ray the former Marine in much
besides farming.

"The history of Honey Spring can teach you a lot," he said
one morning as Jim changed the McCormick's hydraulic fluid.
Discolored from overlong use and fouled with moisture, the old
fluid streamed thin and foamy from the reservoir's bunghole
into a five-gallon bucket. "For one thing," Rickett observed, "it
proves that the Latter-day Saint brotherhood is not so unassail-
able after all."

The lawyer's interest in the estrangement of two Balford pioneers was widely shared. During this same period, late April and
all of May of 1966, the townspeople went out of their way to
apprise newcomer Jim Ray of the finer points of the friendship's
dissolution. That apprising was anything but impartial. From
behind the counter at the post office, for instance, henna-haired

mail clerk (and Sunday school chorister) Dorcas O'Bannion pursed her lips and said, "Goss Harvey did all he could to sully the Vanderfisk name." And Hap and Percy Croft, who shoed the many cherished horses and mules of those bearing the supposedly sullied name, stopped just short of cursing Goss. "Only because he's already dead," Hap said.

On the other side of the division stood someone like ditchrider Eb Godwin, who reflexively claimed solidarity with every other Jack Mormon in the world. "It's all who you know around here," Eb concluded on the morning he opened the property's headgate to let the season's first irrigation water into Goss's main ditch. And at the grocery story, Tom Criswall, avowed Mormon hater, stopped Jim in the bread aisle to correct the presumed misconceptions a newcomer was bound to fall prey to. "There might not've been much to like about Goss Harvey," he said, "but even he wasn't low enough to stab an old church buddy in the back."

After a few weeks of such apprising, Jim began to wonder if there was anybody in town who *hadn't* taken a side in the matter of Honey Spring.

"I know all about the sexual temptations of military life, son," Bishop Clive Sebright said almost as soon as he sat down behind the little desk in the office assigned to him as lay leader of the Balford Ward. "If there's anything you need to tell me, I promise there's not much I haven't heard in nine years of warming this chair."

It was the last Sunday in May, and Jim was in that office by invitation. While the directness of the interview's beginning impressed him, it also caught him flat-footed. For a moment he and Bishop Sebright just stared at each other. The quiet in the little office was profound. On the closest side wall hung a painting of Jesus in Gethsemane. The same painting hung in the children's Primary room of the Mapleton Fifth Ward's meetinghouse. In childhood, Jim was fascinated with the trunk of the olive tree on which Jesus rested his elbows, hands clasped in prayer. The trunk, gnarled and misshapen, grew out of the ground at a forty-five-degree angle.

"I'm bad to assume the worst," Clive Sebright said. "Nine years of bishoping will do that to you. You deserve better. But if there *is* anything you need to put right, I'll do my best to help you."

Bishop Clive Sebright was a farmer himself and had been for over twenty years. For Sunday attire, he wore unpolished Wellingtons, faded brown corduroys held up by a worn workaday belt with a tarnished buckle, a green suit coat and white shirt, and a bolo tie with a turquoise clasp. Anywhere indoors, especially behind the little desk in this cubby of an office in the Balford meetinghouse, his voice seemed unnaturally subdued, as if it threatened its own containment.

But the man's manner was so affably genuine and decent, Jim was won over. He looked Bishop Sebright in the eye and said, "If you only knew how many things I wish I could put right."

The bishop seemed grateful to hear a voice besides his own, as if now he could be of some use. "I may know a few of them," he said. "They put us ashore in North Africa, a place called Oran. We were some of the first ones in, just like you, except we were Army—which I know is third string to your bunch." He smiled.

"I don't know about that," Jim said. "I met plenty of Army guys who could clean my clock." He paused. After a moment, he said, "I almost wish I had something like that other to tell you. Maybe it would be easier to live with."

"Don't bet on it."

The stillness in the little office seemed almost liquid.

"It's not just sexual wrongdoing I know how to hear about," the bishop said. "Even I'm more versatile than that. I remember when I first got home, it was hard to sleep sometimes. I couldn't always get the things I'd seen—and *heard*—to stay in their box. Especially at night. Any of that sound familiar?"

Jim nodded.

"Are you sleeping okay?"

"Mostly. Work helps."

"Yeah, it does," Bishop Sebright said. "That's good."

The man's face was wind-burned, his hair thin and not overly submissive to a comb. Compared to other bishops Jim had known, this one was pretty rough around the edges. But his eyes were almost mesmerizing. They showed more than just empathy. It was a kind of charity Jim had never known he needed.

"If any of it ever gets to where it won't stay put away," the bishop said, "you call or come see me—here or out at the place. I mean it."

Jim found himself nodding again, flooded with a relief he hadn't expected to feel in this meeting with a man he hardly knew.

"Now then," Bishop Clive Sebright declared, by way of transition, "I imagine it might have helped your adjustment to civilian life not to be waylaid by the town's oldest rift."

"*That* may be the thing that starts keeping me up at night," Jim said, smiling.

"I've wondered," the bishop said. "Should've got you in here earlier. I'm sorry. I try to talk to newcomers, especially young ones like you, as soon as I can. I blew it this time."

He loosened the bolo tie's turquoise clasp and undid the collar button of his white shirt. Then he rocked back in his chair and stretched, as if its proximity to the desk was suddenly constrictive. He gazed for a moment at the Gethsemane painting, then rocked forward and looked back at Jim.

"Listen," he said, "I've known both sides in this thing a long time and have always been torn. Enoch didn't wrong Goss

Harvey, not really. But when you look at everything that happened, can you really blame Goss for feeling different?"

"And everything that happened," Jim said, "who would come closest to knowing that?"

Bishop Sebright pondered for a moment. "Arvy Bingham," he said, "if he wasn't ten years in the grave. And Foley Haws, if he wasn't nine parts senile. They both homesteaded not too far down the road from your place. The truth is," the bishop said, "there are plenty of old timers around who will gladly give you their two cents' worth. And their descendants more than that. But the only person who went to the trouble of writing anything down is Enid Cottrell." The appeal of the recommendation seemed suddenly and convincingly obvious to the bishop. "Everybody knows her as a petite little piano teacher and wife of the town jeweler—which she is. But she also happens to be a pretty darned good history keeper of this particular patch of the earth's surface. She's the one you want to talk to."

Jim did not have to seek her out. He had only to attend the ward picnic in the town park five days later, which was June 3, a Friday. When the softball game finally broke up about nine o'clock—on the strength of a winning homerun by Millard Vanderfisk, from the insurance and real estate branch of the family—Sister Enid Cottrell, all five feet-two inches of her, was waiting beside the 1941 pickup, holding a manila envelope.

"Brother Ray," she said, looking around furtively, "I know you've probably heard all you want to hear about your property and its history. And I know you don't know *me*, to feel any different about what I might tell you. But I grew up here, married my Hardin here, raised our only son here." Her eyes misted. "For a long time after Wesley went down with the *Arizona* at Pearl

Harbor, the only thing that sustained me from day to day was knowing that he was all right and that, for his loved ones left behind, God would keep sending sunrises over the Bighorns." She stopped, as if cautious of how quickly words can get ahead of discretion. "It's just sagebrush and wind, but I love this place. And, despite their shortcomings, I love the people."

She gripped the envelope resolutely. "I started this during the war," she said, "to take my mind off a grief that was going to swallow me if I let it. And it worked. It was good therapy. I covered up through 1945 and then set it aside. I thought it was finished. I had no desire to see it widely published; it wasn't that kind of record. But I couldn't let it go. It had gotten hold of me. Things were still happening that needed to be told. Told to whom, I didn't know. But ten years later, after yet another war, I took it out of the drawer and added to the story. And I've kept adding, right up until Brother Goss's death. At some point I realized that my history of the place had really become a history of people, especially the relationship between two men." Enid Cottrell paused for moment. "But when I realized that, I also realized something else: people make better history than places."

For a moment, Enid Cottrell searched Jim's eyes with unnerving scrutiny. Then she said, "I've showed other folks bits and pieces, but never the whole thing. Why? I didn't know. And then you came. I don't think your being here is accidental."

With great determination, she now proffered the envelope. As Jim received it with both hands, she grasped his forearm.

"I've tried to get the facts right," she whispered, "but then there was the question of what to *do* with the facts. What people expect from an old piano teacher is a pretty story. She's not supposed to hurt or offend or ruffle feathers. She mustn't stir things up. Oh, no. She has to be much too tactful for that." Enid Cottrell uttered these words with an irony that belied her height and hair bun. "But that's exactly what this book would do in the hands of almost any other person in this valley. Why do you think I've kept it in an envelope for twenty years? I *tried* just facts, and it wouldn't work. There's always more than that. So I can't show it to anyone whose roots are here; I can't do that. But I feel as though I wrote it for a purpose, to show to *somebody.*" She hesitated, then with daunting conviction said, "Now I know: You're that person."

In the peripheral glow from the softball park's four light poles, Balford's historian appeared younger than she was. For a moment Jim was able to picture her as she must have looked forty years earlier to a suitor named Hardin Cottrell. "The driving force behind the Vanderfisk interest in Goss's place is *not* Enoch," Sister Cottrell said, as if disclosing a deep secret. "It's Bernene! She is not a bad woman, but over many years she has gone to considerable lengths to get her hands on property that now belongs to you. And if I know her half as well as I think I know her, those efforts will not stop."

With Enid Cottrell still clasping his forearm, Jim listened. During the most recent rebuilding of the highway, it was Enoch's picture that had appeared in the *Balford Clarion*, along with stories about the family's ambition to honor the sacrifices of the area's Latter-day Saint pioneers. But it was Bernene who actually lobbied the Highway Department for the turnout and historic marker.

"But that is not Bernene's only ambition," Enid Cottrell warned. "As you have no doubt noticed, the turnout and marker just happen to be located directly above Goss's little pond and apple orchard—which are on *your* side of Honey Spring. And I don't need to tell you that the turnout is five times bigger than it needs to be. Maybe if there was a bathroom, she'd need all those parking places right now. But there isn't—yet. No, Brother Ray, she's got something else in mind. This is just phase one. Bernene Vanderfisk Maxwell is not what you'd call reticent. And word gets around. You need to know she intends to make a tourist stop out of your Honey Spring—walking trail, flower garden, reflective fountain—right there on the main route to Yellowstone. And she intends to call it Vanderfisk Park!"

By the time Enid stopped for a breath, her eyes were shiny and imploring. The slight tremble in her countenance and frame traveled through her arm to the hand clasping Jim's forearm. After several seconds, the trembling calmed.

"So the Vanderfisks have definitely had *their* reasons for doing what they have done," she said finally. "But Goss Harvey had his, too. Don't you see? And unless you account for the reasons on both sides of a thing like this"—she looked at the manila envelope—"you don't have a story."

In the last half mile of the drive home that night, with very little traffic on the Balford-Cody Highway, Jim pulled off at the paved turnout. Beside him on the seat rested the manila envelope. Enid Cottrell had generously assumed he knew more than he knew. In six weeks, he had not even acquainted himself with phase one of Bernene Maxwell's ambition. Old Enoch wasn't particularly tactful, but he was right: Jim had indeed inherited a property without knowing its history. He shut off the engine and climbed out of the cab.

The moon was full. Hanging high and lovely in a sky brilliant with stars, it illuminated the surrounding topography. Flanking the highway to the north was a slope. Along the crest of that slope, in a channel dug through veins of sandstone, flowed the canal. On a terrace, halfway down the slope, ran the railroad. Farther down still, at the slope's base, lay a strip of the original boggy trough from which the roadbed had risen. The road engineer's profile and cross-section for this particular trough in the terrain had called for massive quantities of "fill" and "ballast." Until tonight, the feat of such a man-made elevation had meant nothing to Jim.

In the bright moonlight, everything was beautiful, and Jim surveyed it all. Stretching roughly east and west, the highway's handsomely cambered asphalt gleamed as if coated with lacquer. To the south lay both halves of the Honey Spring property stretching to the Shoshone River. Across the river the McCoullough Peaks rose in clear outline on the night horizon. The night air carried the smell of canal water and alfalfa.

Jim stood on the seam between highway and turnout. Only slowly did he bring his attention to bear on the latter. As to shape, it was simple—a flat, paved semicircle built onto the south side of the main road. As to size, it surely did seem disproportionate. On their way to or from Yellowstone, how many cars and campers actually *would* stop at any one time without a restroom to supplement the lure of a historic marker?

Yet when he regarded the marker at the apogee of the turnout's far edge, its lure was pretty powerful to him. Approaching slowly, across the ample parking space, Jim noted the sheen of a pair of painted six-by-six posts and, mounted between them, a plaque the size of half a sheet of plywood. Standing before the marker, under the unusual brightness of the night sky, he could even make out the bas-relief lettering of the plaque's headlines:

HONEY SPRING
SITE OF THE FIRST MORMON ENCAMPMENT
IN WYOMING'S BIGHORN BASIN

Below those headlines, the plaque's lettering grew smaller. Even under this night's extraordinary moon, it wasn't quite legible. And Jim didn't have a flashlight with him.

"What's Mormon?" some travel-bored teenager from Scranton or Knoxville or Austin was bound to ask. "Oddball religion,

I think," the father would say. Then he would say, "And some of the bishops in that religion know all about the sexual temptations of military life."

Along this edge of the turnout ran a galvanized guardrail. In the moonlight, it gleamed like a new nickel. Jim knew a well-made guardrail when he saw one. Not an off-plumb or misaligned post in the whole arc. Only now did he notice, behind the historic marker, the gap in that rail. Five feet wide and barred by a thin chain, it opened directly onto the embankment's steep slope.

Do you have any idea, son, how much gravel it takes to raise a roadbed fifteen or twenty feet?

That was almost the last thing Goss Harvey had said on that cold Sunday evening six weeks ago. Then, after mustering strength for one more utterance, he had said, "But she ain't gonna get my spring."

Thanks to Enid Cottrell, Jim now understood that last line.

The moon over Balford and the surrounding valley was as bright as any Jim had ever known, brighter even than a couple of nights in Chu Lai. He stood centered in the opening in the guardrail; he felt the thin barrier chain against his thighs. From the shoulder of the embankment, he looked down on what he had inherited. Demarcating that inheritance was Honey Spring, a silver strand winking its way to the river. At the top end of the spring was a pond encircled by half a dozen apple trees. Through apple boughs, the pond glinted, its surface dappled with light and shadow. Up-slope from the pond, at the base of the highway embankment—immediately below where Jim stood—was a willow thicket. And somewhere amid that thicket lay the spring's mouth. That's what Rickett said, though he admitted to having never seen it with his own eyes. Just beyond the willow thicket loomed a grove of cottonwoods. From a branch somewhere aloft came the resonant night cue of an owl's hoot.

For a long time, Jim stood looking down at Honey Spring. Enid Cottrell was right: the alignment of the spring's mouth and the gap in the guardrail could be no accident. He imagined the pond and orchard gone or changed beyond recognition, replaced with fountains, flowers, hedges. He imagined an ample path, zigzagged to mitigate the incline, conducting throngs of tourists from here to there, perhaps past a dispenser of coned paper cups for sampling spring water. Then he imagined, over the very spot where he stood, an archway bearing the name *Vanderfisk Park*. For reasons unexplainable by just six weeks of stewardship over a property whose history he did not know, the prospect troubled him.

Later, back at the inherited trailer house, showered and ready for bed, Jim opened the manila envelope. It contained a type-script—single-spaced, eighty-three pages long, with amazingly few erasures. It was held together with red yarn double-wrapped length- and widthwise, and bow-tied in the center of the title page: *The Settlement of Balford, Wyoming, and Surrounding Areas*. The manuscript was dedicated "to the loving memory of Wesley Hardin Cottrell."

Sitting on his bed, his back propped against two pillows, Jim turned to the first page and began to read.

CHAPTER 3

THE HONEY SPRING PROPERTY WAS DEFINED BY FENCES. Most prominent was the one that divided it between two owners. The divider fence paralleled the channel of water for which the place was named and thus ran north to south, almost two miles from highway to river. Not too far south of its midpoint, that fence intersected a second fence. This second fence line hugged the edge of the concaved bluff overlooking the river bottom and separated each man's cropland from his pasture. Below the bluff, on Goss's side of the spring, the riverbottom pasture was rich swamp grass and cattails. On the Vanderfisk side, the swamp soon gave way to alkali and scrub. That difference explained the composition of the divider fence: woven wire, then three closely spaced strands of barbed wire, *then*, running from insulator to crowning insulator, along the tops of the posts, an additional, electrified strand. On a farm where much else was patched or lately neglected, the divider fence did not have to concede a single rotted-off post or missing staple. It kept even the hungriest neighbor cow from greener grass.

It was here, in a sagebrush clearing at the intersection of fences, that Goss chose to locate the rough square of his farmyard. Within that square, on the west side, was the cluster of his corrals. Bordering the east side of the square was the divider fence. At the south end, near the bluff, was corral fence; at the north end, more corral fence, then windbreak made of sawmill slabs nailed upright. Except for several corral gates, the only way into or out of the yard was an opening in the slab fence. That opening accommodated the road that ran along the bank of Honey Spring.

Despite the natural appeal of two or three more comely and convenient sites for a dwelling place, Goss had chosen this remote corner because of what Enid Cottrell's history called an "affinity for seclusion." But as that history also made clear, seclusion wasn't the whole story. Long before there was a single-wide trailer, the corrals were built here to put their smell at a wise downwind distance from Goss's original house. And the original house was not secluded at all. Goss had built it in the cottonwood grove, a short path away from the orchard and pond. Only when the house burned—a few years after his wife's death—did he move a single-wide into the farthest corner of the farthest corner. In the years after the locating of the single-wide, that chronology was widely forgotten.

The first step in setting up the single-wide was to level it on cinder-block piers. The last step was to skirt it with sheets of tin and straw bales. In between those two steps, Goss had cable-anchored its beams to deadmen as if to keep the trailer from blowing off the edge of the bluff. Only a stone's throw from the trailer's south end, that bluff overlooked riverbottom swamp. The only notch in that bluff, the only traversable slope down its face—except for what Rickett called a gopher trail, on the other side of the property—followed the spring's channel.

To the immediate north and west of the farmyard stood a rise thick with the sagebrush from which the yard had been cleared. This was no ordinary variety of the plant. In this particular soil, it grew seven and eight feet tall, with heavy boughs and stalks. It made of this thirty-acre patch in the mid-section of the property a kind of forest. The slab fence, in turn, gave the farmyard the look of a stockade. Between them, the slabs and sagebrush blocked any view from the highway. Here the only prying eyes would belong to magpies and rabbits.

It happened that the trailer house stood close enough to the divider fence to supply the current for its electric strand. And it stood close enough to the bluff fence that a breakfaster sitting at the unpainted plywood table in front of the trailer's east-facing kitchen window had a clear view of the long concave of the bluff's edge on the neighbor's side of the property. That view included the grazing ground far below. Mostly that grazing was little more than scrub, and toward the property's far southeast boundary, even that petered out.

But the Vanderfisks' far section of bluff could be credited with another resource. And that other resource made up for all the barrenness in the world. *Do you have any idea, son, how much gravel it takes to raise a roadbed fifteen or twenty feet?* The question, as Rickett had explained, referred directly to the most recent rebuilding of the Balford-Cody highway.

More important was the question's indirect reference—to a source of cobble rock that defied depletion. The trailer's east-facing window looked across the neighbor's riverbottom land and, thanks to the bluff's concave, directly framed a view of two great shelves dug into its far face. Twenty months after the last load had gone out, the marks of bulldozers and loaders were still clear.

On this morning after the ward picnic and softball game, the first Saturday in June, Jim Ray sat at the plywood table eating toast and a bowl of cornflakes. Not so many hours after finishing Enid Cottrell's manuscript, he had awakened to the sound of raindrops on the trailer's roof. Now, as he ate, he watched through the steady drizzle, on the lower shelf of the distant gravel pit, a lone cow scratching her flank on an abandoned section of a crusher conveyor. She scratched a long time.

Until the day six months earlier when he finally got sick enough to let Rickett take him to the hospital, Goss would have had to look at the Vanderfisks' gravel pit every time he ate a meal. According to Enid Cottrell's history—corroborated by all Rickett had said about Jim Ray's benefactor—such forced proximity would have been an unremitting offense. During the height of road construction, with work going on around the clock, he couldn't have retreated anywhere on his property to escape the sounds of machinery and transport. But nowhere were those sounds closer and more clearly audible than in his intentionally secluded farmyard.

The washing of his breakfast dishes positioned Jim at another window. This one was smaller and faced south. But it afforded a view of the notch through which Honey Spring descended the bluff. And, from this window above the kitchen sink, the notch itself afforded a clear view of the segment of divider fence running across the riverbottom swamp. As Jim rinsed bowl and glass and spoon, his eyes were drawn to some cattle on Enoch's side, close to the fence.

That Goss would drive a rusty eight-penny nail into the finished outer surface of a kitchen cupboard did not by now surprise Jim. Nor did the use of that nail to hang a pair of binoculars. But for six weeks he had wondered why the nail and binoculars were located *here*.

Suddenly he understood.

Down in the swamp, next to the divider fence, stood a cow. With dripping hands Jim brought the binoculars to his eyes. The cow had taken another step toward the fence and was sniffing the lower squares of the woven wire. Slowly, cautiously, her nose explored upward, along the woven mesh, then higher still, to the strands of barbed wire. Finally, standing knee-deep in swamp water, she stretched her moist muzzle, closer, closer, toward the wire carrying electric current.

At the moment of contact, Jim flinched. Between his upper lip and nose, he felt a phantom arc and tingle, even as he witnessed, a third of a mile away, the cow's shock—the recoiling and rearing, the soundless floundering and splashing and falling back on her haunches. For Goss, such a scene, regularly replayed, must have been a refreshing delight—for reasons beyond mean amusement. It was comeuppance. It was compensation. It was penance. Impressing comeuppance and compensation and penance on cows was as close as he would ever come to impressing the same on their owners. With his own nose rubbed daily in the disparity of fortune, it would have become almost a reason to live.

There didn't seem to be much else to keep him going. Certainly the trailer's furnishings—unchanged for how many years?—suggested no such purpose. In the whole dwelling, there were only three chairs—a ladder-back and a lawn chair at the homemade eating table, and a rocker in the corner of the living room between a small bookcase and reading lamp. For overflow crowds, there was a folding camp stool in the closet. The bedroom held a cot and a dresser, and on that dresser rested a cookie tin that still contained Goss's wallet, pocketknife, loose change, pencil stub, and a folded sheet of paper bearing scribbled notes and numbers. On the kitchen counter sat a radio. On an average day, it picked up a station from Cody and one from Balford. On a good day, it picked up Garland, too. The only wall decoration, besides the binoculars, was a 1965 calendar hanging from another nail. There was not the least knickknack or keepsake. And not a single photograph anywhere.

For the first morning in six weeks, thanks to the rain, Rickett's Chrysler had not made the trip down from wherever its driver lived up above Cody. The trailer's thin door had not been pounded on with the side of a fist, nor had the pounding been accompanied by the usual shout: "Hey, G.I. Joe! Your inheritance is waiting!"

At first Jim Ray had been suspicious of farm tutoring at the hands of a lawyer, especially one who never got his fill of saying, "We're more like the hind leading the hind!" The first time he uttered the line, he laughed at his own word play and at Jim's puzzlement. "Look it up," Rickett said. "That's what farmers over in England call their hired hands. Ha-ha-ha. Ha-ha-ha!"

But after the first morning, the Monday after the funeral, Jim was grateful enough to ask only one question: "How you getting paid for this?" Though munificent in many ways, the inheritance had not included any cash, which explained the condition of most of the sundry possessions. Every tire on the place was bald, every brake shoe worn thin. On the inside of the driver's door of the 1941 Ford pickup, a pair of Vise-Grip locking pliers served as both latch lever and window crank.

"I mean, don't take this the wrong way," Jim had said, "but what's in it for you?"

Rickett had smiled and said, "The dogs." That was the extent of his answer.

The barley drilled in late April now carpeted several fields. Corn sprigs had broken the harrow's crust, but were too tender yet for the first pass with a tractor-mounted weeding rig known as a cultivator. Elsewhere, the beans were just barely in the ground, and the alfalfa, soaking up the third irrigation of the season, still lacked ten days until its first cutting. So, drizzly or not, this first Saturday in June was Jim's to spend as he pleased. He had not known such a luxury since coming to Wyoming—or since returning from war. He might have inherited a property without knowing its history, but every day remedied that ignorance a little more.

According to its plat, Goss's property comprised over half a section—a bequeathal of about 385 acres. With the 140 acres of crop land at the north end, Jim was now passably acquainted— from having driven a tractor over all but the hay ground. But the riverbottom at the south end—half again as many acres—still needed to be walked and studied, as did the sagebrush forest occupying the property's middle section.

But first things first. And the first of all, after the reading of Enid Cottrell's history, was an exploration of the spring itself. Because the divider fence ran along its east bank, the spring fell, over the entirety of its length, on Goss's side. The logical place to begin was at its source.

After drying his dishes and sweeping the kitchen floor, Jim Ray stood in the trailer's doorway and pulled on the inherited irrigating boots. ("At least you won't have to buy any gumboots," Rickett had said, using his preferred name for such footwear.) Even with thin socks, they were half a size too small. From the back of the rocking chair, Jim took a hooded poncho rummaged from Goss's closet. It was the first day in Wyoming wet enough to warrant it, the first time since Chu Lai that he had smelled and fingered oilcloth. This poncho was faded yellow, not military green. And it smelled like a closet in an old trailer house, not like another day of patrol.

Yet he hesitated.

Finally he said, to no one in the world except himself, "This is just dang silly," and in one practiced move, flipped the poncho, hood-forward, shook it open like a sack, and ducked into it. Nevertheless, in the instant it took for his head to reach the hood opening, he had the weird sensation that, upon reaching that opening, his eyes would look out again on jungle. The sensation was so strong that for several seconds after the hood cowled his forehead and cheeks, he kept his eyes closed. And when finally he opened them, he was immensely relieved to see nothing but Wyoming on a rainy day.

The gumboots were too small, and the poncho too big. Through the trailer's door Jim Ray stepped carefully, as he had learned to do, onto a tiny stoop clapped together long ago from cinder blocks loosely stacked. From the stoop, he placed a foot onto the first of three unmortared cinder block steps. Even for someone just home from hiking some hellacious terrain, this descent every morning threatened the twisting of an ankle or knee. Goss Harvey surely must have been the nimble old cob Rickett said he was.

The trailer needed a proper stoop and stairs, but that was another job for another day. In a squat, open-ended welding shed, Jim hunted what he would need for this one. From among a bouquet of tools standing handle-down in a thirty-gallon drum, he pulled a leaf rake and pitchfork. From nails driven into rough-cut studs hung a bow saw and a sickle. From a crooked shelf above a very old air compressor, he pulled a rusted oven pan. It held half a dozen beet knives. A beet knife was as close as he was going to come to a machete, but the claw riveted to the blade's square end would be, for the work ahead, nothing but a snag and a hindrance.

The sickle's blade was dull. Six weeks of familiarity with Goss's bench grinder—of the same vintage as the air compressor—had bred contempt. The grinder's power cord was frayed, its toggle switch fickle, the twin wheelstones worn to the hub. Its mounting plate was secured, with loosely cleated-over nails, to the slightly canted surface of a cottonwood block. During operation, the whole machine crept clockwise, then counterclockwise, back and forth, back and forth.

One morning several weeks back, after trying to put a better edge on a cold chisel, Jim had said, offhandedly, "What we need is a *level* mount and some dang lag screws."

"What we need is a lot of things," was Rickett's rather testy reply.

Yet on this morning in early June, if not for kneeling to try to shim up the cottonwood block, Jim would not have spotted, against the wall beneath the sagging workbench, the best tool of all for the work ahead.

"Never seen one of these, no lie?"

The question had come from a guy named Fritchey, when they happened upon the same kind of tool left behind at the edge of a landing zone. "The bush axe will win us this here war."

Most guys chose their good luck charms from a pretty predictable list: ace of spades, perfumed page from a girlfriend's letter, crucifix, ring or medallion, polished stone or odd coin or other such amulet. For Fritchey, from Arkansas, the charm was a bush axe. Everybody had a machete. Machetes were commonplace. But a bush axe? With a piece of rope, Fritchey even fashioned a carrying sling for it.

Standing in Goss's shed, holding the tool that was going to win the war, the very specimen bequeathed to him, Jim saw something other than luck. He saw a broad blade shellacked almost black from sap and a cutting edge notched and pitted along its whole length. The handle was well weathered. An old fracture was bound with several wide bands of friction tape. It occurred to Jim that the last person to touch that handle was Goss Harvey.

After nursing the grinder through one more sharpening, Jim loaded the tools in the bed of the Ford and climbed in. To the right of the steering column, he turned the starter key to the *On* position. To the left of the column, he pressed the starter button with his thumb. The button and everything else in the cab showed more wear than even a quarter century of hard use should have been able to inflict. Like the hard-shell plastic of the steering wheel fissured, in places, all the way to the metal core. Like shredded upholstery. Like a silver-dollar-size rust hole in the passenger side of the naked metal floorboard. Like the played-out ratchet and pawl of an emergency brake that evidently had seen too many emergencies. But the heater worked, and it had a fine gun rack.

Jim turned the pickup around, pulled away from the corrals and outbuildings, and passed through the opening in the slab fence. As he drove, the windshield wipers squeaked. The rubber blade on the driver's side was coming apart in such a way that it trailed the wiper arm across windshield glass like a little black snake—crawling up, then down; up, then down. As he drove the narrow road between the spring's west bank and the sagebrush forest, big silver boughs lashed the side of the pickup. Even with his window rolled almost all the way up, Jim could smell the wet sage. The road was rough, too. "This track can get pretty messy in the winter," Rickett had said, "but Goss could never bring himself to lay down any gravel. And Enoch offered. More than once."

After one last bumpy stretch, the road cleared the sagebrush, smoothed out, and became the border of an alfalfa field. At the head of that field, Jim stopped to change water. "Don't let a rainy day lull you into neglecting your irrigating," Rickett had cautioned back in late April, when reservoir water was first turned into the main canal. "Under the next blazing sun, all your sins will be made manifest. You'll be able to tell right to the row what's been irrigated and what hasn't."

On this rainy morning after the softball game, during the moving of tubes along this field's ditch, the slicker protected against wet aluminum. And there was no wind nor much of any sound at all. Just a lovely muffling haze and mist. Behind the newly set dam, the backed-up water looked like cocoa. Color and consistency indicated origins. Ditch drew from canal. Canal drew from reservoir. Reservoir drew from rivers with headwaters on the continental divide. Raindrops like those kissing the ditch water's surface must have fallen during the night along all tributaries. Rivulets and streams and freshets brought with them particles of all the soils they flowed over. So the water soaking Goss Harvey's alfalfa roots probably contained grains of mountaintop a hundred miles distant.

Jim climbed back in the truck. He drove slowly. The spring ran between the road on one side and the divider fence on the other. Almost to the top end of the property, the three stayed parallel. Then, abruptly, the spring diverged from the arrow-straight line of the divider fence, and the road followed. Both doglegged twenty yards to the northwest, up a rising slope, to the pond and orchard. From there, the spring doglegged back, ten yards up an even sharper slope, toward its mouth, where no road could follow. At this second dogleg, the road turned sharply west, curving with the head ditch of the closest field, around the grove of cottonwoods. Just past that turn, Jim clutched and let the truck roll. When he saw what he wanted, he stopped, shifted into reverse, and backed into a treeless gap between the orchard and grove. With one last, hard pull on the hand lever—to urge the pawl beyond the worst of the worn ratchet teeth—he set the emergency brake against the incline of his parking space.

He sat for a time listening to the flip-flap of the wipers, watching the up-and-down crawling of the little black snake. Then, peering in his rearview mirror, he tried to orient himself in accordance with last night's moonlit view from the highway turnout. There was the willow thicket.

Jim killed the pickup's engine. When it died, so did the wipers, frozen in the middle of their arc, with the snake wriggling upward. In five seconds, droplets blurred the windshield; in ten, they obscured it. He worked the Vise-Grip door latch and slid out of the cab. From out in the middle of a harrowed bean field came the cry of a killdeer. The cry of that particular species of bird always suggested a level of alarmed skittishness unwarranted by circumstance. A shift in breeze, a cloud's brief mitigating of the sun's glare, the distant, muffled slam of a pickup door on a rainy morning—the least provocation sent the bird skirring from one spot to another to resume bug and worm pecking.

Pulling on a pair of yellow cloth gloves—also rummaged from Goss's closet—Jim reached into the pickup bed and gathered his tools. After shouldering the rake, pitchfork, and bush axe, he gripped the sickle and bow saw in his free hand and started through the little orchard. For a moment he stopped to watch raindrops dimpling the pond's surface. No grains of mountaintop clouded this water. Just above the farthest apple tree, he came on the one odd surviving fork of a cherry tree's trunk, its twin somehow amputated in times past. He had never noticed this trunk and its lopsided branches, and wouldn't have noticed it now except for its profuse blossoms.

From the trunk of the cherry tree, Jim followed the spring up the sharp incline of its second dogleg. "The slope underfoot," Fritchey always said, quoting the wisdom of his pa or granddad or uncle, "is always steeper than the slope on the map." But this last, steep segment brought Jim finally to the willow thicket. It stood just inside the right-of-way fence, below and a little to the west of the gap in the guardrail. Under a full moon, the highway embankment's whiskering of erosion-control rye grass had seemed more lush. And the willows had seemed less dense and tangled.

The willows not only hid the spring's mouth, but at their lower edge, they diffused its flow so as to make guesswork of tracing a main channel. That concealment benefitted, even this early in the season, from Johnson grass, ragweed, thistle, and wild currants.

Ten feet downstream, where the rivulets reconverged, Jim picked a likely spot on the bank, stuck the pitchfork upright in the spongy sod, then dropped on the ground beside it everything but the bush axe. The awkwardness of working against the incline was aggravated by the poncho. Still, the drizzle was too steady for him to go without. Jim splashed into the water and took a couple of cold steps toward the thicket's lower fringe. Settling for the least unsuitable posture for swinging, he gave both hands to the axe.

"I don't reckon there's a soul in all the Ozarks what hasn't cut his teeth on a bush axe." From the mouth of Ardizzoli from New York City or Lester Croom from Texas, any declaration related to native place would have been pure cocky bravado. But not from Fritchey, whose mail from home bore the postal seal of Pea Ridge, Arkansas. He didn't have a cocky cell in his body. Not Fritchey—who considered military life a step up. Not Fritchey—who bought the farm late last fall. And sold the ranch. And bit the dust. Anything but the actual words for the effect of the sniper's round, for the helmet askew and the glazed eyes that were never going to see Pea Ridge again. Not Fritchey—who said of the noble bush axe, "It'll pure-tee do a number on bamboo."

It did a pretty good number on willows, too. Between swings, the blade's beak could be used to gather felled stalks and withes. From time to time, for weeds and grass, Jim swapped the bush axe for the sickle. With the pitchfork, he stacked the accumulation of brush and cuttings—to be burned on a dryer day.

The poncho *was* cumbersome. But later, as hunger or fatigue dictated, he would return to the trailer, pull it off, would not be constrained, as when sleeping in a hole dug by an entrenching tool, to use it as both bug cloak and blanket.

A half hour into the willow clearing, one of the withes offered so little resistance to the axe's blade that the momentum of the swing almost toppled Jim headlong into what had gradually become identifiable as a cleft in the slope. Wouldn't that stir the town's chatter? Upstart owner of the place, survivor of war, found injured—or, better yet, dead—from a freak broken neck. "It was that yellow poncho caught my eye," some truck driver would say. What he wouldn't say was that his interest in stopping at the turnout in the first place was not the early history of Mormon settlers in these parts, as summarized on a varnished plaque, but a bulging bladder and the privacy promised by a little apple orchard.

Regaining his balance, Jim repositioned to allow for the cleft's deceptive depth. At slow intervals, tires hissed by on the wet pavement above. A goose honked. Jim looked up into the misty gray drizzle. Against a headwind undetectable at ground level, the V of the flock seemed hardly to move at all. The geese were trying to go north but, for the moment, had all they could do to stay aloft. By any judgment, their predicament qualified as the serious business of life, yet the honking of a gander leading fifteen mates through hostile air currents was as disproportionately calm as the convulsive cry of a ground-level, safe-and-sound killdeer was frantic.

After two hours, more willows were cut than standing. After three, Jim stood between the newly cleared banks of the cleft. Even in June, the water was cold. Thin boot rubber did nothing to insulate his toes. From the clear purling and burbling, he knew he was close to the spring's opening. If Rickett hadn't seen it, who *had*? Who else, during Goss's long stewardship of the place, would have stepped foot on this soil, especially during the period of the owner's estrangement? Enid Cottrell's typescript didn't say. Wading closer to the sound, Jim swung the bush axe again, and again, then swept away felled brush and limber willow shafts. He squatted. With cold water eddying ankle-level around boot rubber, he held his rump just above the current. Bending neck and head downward, he saw, at last, part of a horizontal slit in the earth. Hanging from the ceiling of the slit, threads of root danced atop the water's surface.

He cupped a hand, dipped, lifted, drank. No bitter purification tablets necessary to make this water potable. As with so many times in a dripping jungle, it seemed odd to be so thirsty on a rainy morning. Maybe Fritchey was right. Maybe wearing a poncho tricked the body's gauges. Jim stretched out at the edge of the spring and lowered his mouth to the current. To satisfy thirst, chickens pecked only drops at a time. Cats and dogs somehow took in enough by lapping. But horses and cows had it right. Rest the muzzle on the water's surface and tank up. As Jim drank, the cold wetness tickled his gums and palate. And when he had drunk his fill and raised his dripping chin and nose from the water, an itchy numbness marked the wetted area.

One more willow stalk, and the whole spring opening would be exposed. But this stalk was two inches thick—the biggest so far. The blade on the bow saw had proved warped, dull, and mostly useless. But with some hacking, a bush axe could manage two inches. Fritchey wouldn't have hesitated to attempt such a diameter. Jim raised the tool high overhead and brought it down at a slicing angle.

Nothing about that final stroke went as planned. The blade glanced off the willow trunk's slick underbark and plunged into sod that might as well have been cotton candy. Still, at a certain depth, something checked the blade with a muffled clunk. The blow jarred teeth and wrists and snapped the handle at the ferrule. Blinking the drizzle from his eyes, Jim stood looking at the bladeless, friction-taped handle still gripped with both cloth gloves. The break was so clean it looked almost sawed. Whatever was down there, under six inches of soil and roots, had pure-tee done a number on this bush axe.

Jim dropped to his knees and pulled from the sod the dismembered blade. Then he gripped it, tip-end and handle-end, and began working it like a drawknife against the bank of the spring. Starting at the gash of his errant swing, he gouged and scraped, gouged and scraped some more. The ground was soft. Stroke by stroke, the blade cut a little pit to the necessary depth. Then came more scraping. Inch by square inch, the scraping revealed, beneath roots and soil, a slab of sandstone. The slab turned out to be roughly oblong, about the size of a wall clock. Besides the fresh nick inflicted by the bush axe blade, the slab's surface bore grooves discolored by the minerals of its long sod covering.

With a gloved hand, Jim swept the stone's surface. With an ungloved hand, he ladled spring water to flush away mud and grit. Now he took off the other glove and twisted one of its fingers into a swab. Groove by groove, he dislodged soil to clear the lines of what were more and more obviously rough-etched letters of the alphabet. Swab and flush. Letter by letter. The process fretted the tips out of two of the glove's fingers, but finally the whole inscription was readable:

HONEY SPRING

GH

EV

MAY 1900

The drizzle had thickened. Jim was hungry, and, under the poncho, his upper clothing was soaked with sweat. He was ready for a break. But still he knelt, unable to take his eyes off the inscription. The rain droplets hitting the sandstone slab seemed both absorbed and repelled.

What had happened to these two men in sixty-six years?

After a long time, Jim stood. As if the answer might be found in fences, he followed the new right-of-way fence line a short distance, to the exact point where it intersected the divider fence line—at the northeast corner of Goss's property. He looked down the divider fence, toward the river. In the morning's misty overcast, the tops of the posts ran together and disappeared. In its entire length, there was no gate, not even a stile.

Then Jim turned and looked down the right-of-way fence, along the base of the highway embankment, in the direction of the property's other north corner. If this particular section of highway showed Bernene Maxwell's influence—turnout, historical marker, gap in the guardrail—the corresponding section of fence showed Goss Harvey's. Everywhere else along the newly widened corridor between Balford and Cody, mile after mile, the Highway Department standard on its right-of-way fences was four strands of barbed wire. Yet this stretch bordering Goss's property featured the same woven-barbed mix as the divider fence. And nailed to each post top was a homemade fifteen-inch extension. These extensions were equipped with insulators to support, not one, but three electrified strands. In fact, the only Highway Department specifications unaltered were the type and spacing of the posts themselves—milled and creosoted pines set a rod apart as opposed to the divider fence's knobby, sharply tapered, hand-chopped cedars set at half that distance.

As if sixty-six years would reveal their mysteries through some other number, Jim began counting posts. After a moment, so as not to lose count, he commenced walking the fence. He stayed close, kept the woven wire always within reach of his right hand. His post-by-post progress along the base of the highway embankment soon took him beyond the pond and orchard, beyond the gap in the guardrail above, beyond the stumps of the willow thicket and the cleft marking the spring's mouth, beyond the cottonwood grove. He kept going. Post by post, he measured Goss's estrangement and isolation; post by post, his defiance and ingenuity.

Spaced a rod apart, fence posts number three hundred twenty to a mile. From the northeast corner of Goss's property to the northwest, there were one hundred and nine. That number did not include the H-brace midway or the one at the far end. The end-brace stood, as Jim now did, at the top end of the ramp leading down to Goss's access road. It was the only turn-off into the property—marked, in turn, by the only gate.

In his early eighties, when most men contented themselves with a soft chair and warm fire, Goss Harvey had fabricated over a hundred extensions for a brand new livestock fence already officially altered to satisfy his wire preferences. He had cut old steel T-posts into fifteen-inch lengths, to be easily fitted with clip-on insulators sold by the dozen at the Co-Op. He had

welded each length to a torch-cut pedestal of thin sheet metal
the diameter of a tuna can, had then drilled four nail holes in
each pedestal. According to Rickett, no one actually saw Goss
add the extensions or string the electrified strands. One morning, in the light of the rising sun, they were just there.

And fence modifications were not all. At Goss's insistence, his
one allocated turn-off had been built in the property's farthest
upper corner, a location that made it necessary to overshoot, by
more than a third of a mile, the line of the spring and the road
beside it. The overshooting, in turn, required an obviously incon-
venient doubling-back to get Goss on that road and, from there,
to his farmyard and dwelling. People attributed the highway gate's
strange location to eccentricity and cussedness, the same qualities that explained, in their minds, the location of the single-wide
trailer in the property's most remote lower corner (not counting
riverbottom swamp). But people were wrong. The insisted-upon
location put Goss's one gate to the outside world as far as possible
from Bernene's turnout and historical marker, and thus from any
implied cooperation with Vanderfisk designs on Honey Spring.

To compensate for its generosity in granting Goss's unorthodox preferences, the Highway Department leaned the other way
in paving the apron of his turn-off ramp. Such aprons are supposed to extend through and well beyond the gate opening. Yet
when the day's last hopper of asphalt hot mix petered out three
feet *short* of the gateline, the highway boss yelled, "Close enough!"
Nor did he see to it that the apron's bottom edge was properly
beveled. The unbeveled edge was left to cool and harden into a
raw, four-inch ledge. The jolt from that ledge would ever thereafter mark passage into and out of Goss's half of Honey Spring.

The gate itself—made of standard Highway-Department
orange tubing fourteen feet long and five feet high—bore two
more of Goss's dark-of-night alterations. For one thing, it was

completely overlaid with catwalk metal extending below the bottom spar, almost to the packed gravel of the rampway. Even less hospitable was the extra, welded-on spar on top, unpainted and bristling with four-inch spikes, like short punji stakes. No doubt it was the shaping of so many tips that had worn the grindstones to their hubs.

"No *No Trespassing* sign?" Jim had asked a few days after the funeral.

Rickett had looked at him quizzically. "Do you really think he needs one?"

Managing a gate like that, with every coming and going, was no small chore. Even before the catwalk metal and the top-heaviness of the small-scale abatis, the hinges were too flimsy for their load and set slightly off-plumb to boot—which made every opening a free fall and every closing a wizard's trick. During closing, the gate tender not only had to brace a shoulder against the downhill drift of the monster gate, but do the shouldering while straining and fumbling to thread the padlock's shackle through the end links of the chain. For the sake of sanity, another half a link would have been nice.

The drizzle had become a soaking rain. Listening to drops on his poncho hood, Jim stood surveying the lay of his property from the top of the turn-off ramp. Not until this rainy morning did he realize that the new highway and the new right-of-way fence each had a predecessor. The first stretch of Goss's access road, made necessary by the location of the turn-off, started at the base of the turn-off ramp and followed a two-hundred-yard arc of old pavement. The carefully engineered curve and dip of that old stretch were dealt with, in the straightening and elevating of the new roadbed, by simple abandonment. Less than half a decade into that abandonment, the old pavement was masked by a creeping layer of silt, rain-washed and wind-blown, and weeds poking up from every crack.

Running along the stretch of old highway was a stretch of old barbed-wire fence. Starting at the hinge post of the abatis gate, Jim began walking it. This time he didn't count posts. Like the old highway, this fence curved down and away from its successor. Then, as with the highway, that curve brought it back. The last stretch of original fence ran through the cottonwood grove and ended at an original brace post, only half a rod from the new fence line. The abandoned fence had fared better than the abandoned pavement. Aside from a few missing staples, it was in good shape—wherever it was standing. And the only place it wasn't standing was a twenty-yard gap just before the grove. There, during the early stages of putting down underlayment for the new highway, when five minutes' work with a pair of wire cutters would have made an opening for Goss's rerouted access road, a bulldozer was called in.

Jim had made a full circuit. Between the cottonwood grove and apple orchard sat his pickup. From where he stood now, beside the old brace post just inside the grove, he could see the pile of felled willows. He looked for a long time at the end brace of the abandoned fence, then up-slope to the new fence line, then back again. How did a man get from initials etched in sandstone to electric strands and abatis and padlock—none of which had anything to do with livestock? And all of which bespoke more than the alienation of a bitter hermit. No, every fence feature on this place was a declaration of ownership. Or a denial of it: while the Vanderfisks owned much, they didn't own *this*. Without ownership of the land on which the spring actually flowed, there could be no pebbled serpentine trail, no tropical fronds, no reflection benches, no flowers, no fountain, no botanical garden. And without any of that, what was there to see besides the historical marker?

A pretty pond? Apple and cherry blossoms in season? The long, thin line of cattails marking the spring's channel southward to the river bluff?

Turning toward the pickup, Jim confronted a huge lightning-blasted cottonwood log that had to be crawled over. The rough bark made easy handholds. Climbing down the far side put his back to the pickup. As he turned, he abruptly checked his movement. Gaping before him was a pit, full almost to the brim with decaying brush and debris. Then he realized it was no pit at all. Framing the brush and debris were concrete walls and, in one corner, a steep and narrow concrete stairway. What he had almost stepped into was a small basement—all that remained of what had once been Goss Harvey's house.

CHAPTER 4

THAT FIRST PIONEER COMPANY CAME FROM UTAH—
all of them from Provo except one person. And that one person, a man named Goss Harvey, hailed (Enid's word) from just down the road in Mapleton—the town where, two decades later, a distant cousin named Minnie Dillon would be born; where, two decades after that, Minnie Dillon would become Minnie Ray and give birth to a son; a town where, after the better part of two more decades, she would die and the son, shortly thereafter, would enlist in the Marines.

Departing in late March of 1900, the wagons traveled eight weeks. At dusk on their last day on the trail, just after the scout's bleak report of no drinkable water anywhere closer than the too-distant Shoshone River, Goss and a by-now-fast trail companion named Enoch hallooed (also Enid's word) the weary travelers with tidings to the contrary. Despite the blurring and distortion of a hazy twilight, they had somehow spotted a little stand of willows and had found that stand to mark the mouth of a freshwater spring with an abundant flow. The friends were both twenty-one at the time and of stout heart and spine.

They were instant heroes. After a long, dry afternoon, the discovery answered an urgent need. The people could have made do with what was left in the barrels—but not the livestock, including the small herd of cows and trail-born calves the two friends had coaxed so many miles. The group, which just minutes earlier had been travel-worn, regretful of snug homes left behind, dispirited by sagebrush and rattlesnakes, could now cook and wash and camp contented, amid a landscape devoid as yet of canal and railroad—and highway. As a lucky complement to the celebratory mood, Goss even killed a yearling buck. After a supper of roasted venison, a vote determined that, on the morrow, the wagons would travel no farther, that this very spot would serve as the hub of the group's settlement labors.

A few days later, their leader and future town's namesake— Bishop Wagon-Boss Balford, as he was known—told the two friends that, as its finders, they could name this spring that had constituted such a blessing to so many thirsty mouths. Give the matter some thought and prayer, he admonished them. The name would endure through generations.

Despite the solemnity of the christening duty, Goss and Enoch couldn't at first get past the predictable—Sweet Spring, Clear Spring, Destination Spring. Or the biblical—Massah and Meribah, Jordan, Eshcol, Gihon, Cherith. Even adding Book of Mormon water names to the mix—Sebus, Sidon, Irreantum, Ripliancum—didn't help. True inspiration didn't bless their efforts until the arrival, two weeks later, of a young lady from over on the Idaho-Utah border, a place called Bear Lake. She was part of that big Utley clan divided ten years earlier with the Manifesto ending polygamy.

"Not Honey like 'Honey Pie' or 'Honey Dear,'" she explained to her two new admirers. "It's my *name*."

She was almost seventeen. Friendly, lively, pretty as a peach. And sweet beyond sweet. While no photograph would ever do full justice to her youthful countenance, there was one, eventually displayed in a saucer-shaped frame, that would come close. The evening of the very day the two friends met her, they found, on the far side of a boggy sink, toward the crest of a steep rise above that sink, an oblong slab of sandstone. The slab would serve as both marker of the spring and tribute to their new acquaintance, one purpose now clearly more compelling than the other. Taking turns with an old hitch-pin, they went to work. Plied with such eagerness and devotion, that pin must have been worn to a fine point. Yet all through that first summer in the Bighorn Basin, Honey Utley betrayed no particular interest in either admirer, treated them both as older brothers.

By early June of 1900, not even a month after the Utah group's arrival—and exactly sixty-six years before the breaking of the bush axe—the great sagebrush plain spreading from the spring had been surveyed and divided into lots, to be parceled out through a drawing. Because of the consensus that married men would draw first, Bishop Wagon-Boss Balford, for the only time in his tenure, pulled rank to reserve the spring (and adjacent property) for the pair of bachelors who had found it. The two had long since won his favor for bringing his milk cow five hundred miles over hill and gully, and seeing her trail-born twins safely to this destination.

The most practical split, Bishop Balford decided, was along Honey Spring itself. In that split, the west tract came out smaller, but with better soil and pasture. The east tract was bigger, but much of its area went to scrub alkali and badlands—and, of course, the rockiest segment of river bluff. To be fair in the matter, Bishop Wagon-Boss authorized a coin toss to decide who got to pick. That pick fell to Goss. After only a moment's thought, he chose quantity over quality. "Now I've got rocks on my property," he said good-naturedly, "to match the ones in my head." Whether he chose what he chose out of self-interest or generosity would be a matter of conjecture for decades to come.

CHAPTER 5

NOWHERE DID THE PICKUP'S BRAKES STIMULATE adrenaline as they did on the highway turn-off into Goss's property. The jolt of the asphalt apron's unbeveled edge was accompanied by a downward plunge of the front tires. With that plunge, the bug-specked windshield seemed aligned for collision with the gate's abatis. Such alignment invested every approach—before the front bumper finally came to a stop inches from the gate's catwalk metal—with the relief of averted disaster.

This sunny morning in mid-June of 1966 was no different. As the metal punji sticks rushed toward him, Jim stomped on the brake pedal, then stomped again. At the second action, the brakes caught *too* well. The suddenness of the stop dislocated everything in the pickup's bed. A clutter of siphon tubes and weir sticks banged against the bed's front panel. One of a half dozen bundles of baling twine—two spools per package—thumped the back of the cab, just beneath the rear window.

"Don't say it!" Jim said. "'The heater works, and it's got a fine gun rack.'"

"No, smart ass," Rickett said, "that's not what I was going to say. I was merely going to recommend a little lighter touch on the brakes."

Jim hauled on the hand lever of the emergency brake and jiggled the pawl until it caught. He eased his foot off the brake pedal, waiting for the wheels to creep. He sat for a moment, aware of his pulse and breathing. Finally, resting both hands on the fissured steering wheel and looking straight ahead, he said, "Would the sky fall if we just left the dang thing open?"

Through his own smoke, Rickett was squinting, almost cross-eyed, at the nearly inch-long ash drooping from the cigarette in his mouth. On cooler days, when his window was up, he often used the rust hole in the floorboard for an ash dispenser. But today the weather was warm, and his window was down. The ash grew even longer while he considered Jim's question. His shrug, when it finally came, was hard to read. Indifference toward the gate proposal? Or caution toward the slippery slope of change? Rickett took another deep pull on the cigarette, then held the fragile and impressive ash out the open window and, with a tap, sent it into the summer air.

"It's your place."

"Goss Harvey wanted to be left alone. Okay. He had his reasons. I get it." Jim gripped the steering wheel, then released it. "But I'm not him. And opening and closing this freak gate every time we go anywhere is getting to be an A-1 pain in the butt."

Gradually Rickett looked his way and took another pull on his cigarette. "If you decide to leave it open," he said, "you got to be prepared for all the folks who take an open gate as an invitation."

"What do you mean?"

"A lot of people drive this highway on their way to work. And while they're driving, they're dreaming of not working, dreaming of the weekend and vacation time. Then they come by this property in the pretty morning haze, and it looks like paradise. On their own little plots in town, they know right to the inch where their lawn meets the neighbor's and would fight about it. But out here? Who can claim deed to fresh air and blue sky? Which, translated, means *they* assume the right to come and go as they please."

"What have I got that they could possibly want?" Jim asked.

"You'd be surprised."

Rickett blinked slowly and contemplatively and paused for a long time before he went on.

"And, too," he said, "keeping your gate shut will go some distance toward mollifying Bernene—as long as she can't buy you out."

"What would she care either way?" Jim asked.

"It's true, there's not much on the Vanderfisk side of the farm land that takes people's eye, and what there is can be gotten to only from the bottom end, through the gravel pit, by a road very few folks passing by would even know to look for. But they've got *some* swamp and river frontage—not nearly what you've got, but some. And swamp and river are very attractive to hunters and trappers." Rickett took a last drag on his cigarette, let the smoke seep from his nostrils. "The point is," he said, "*whatever* they might want to get to on the Vanderfisk side is best gotten to from your side."

"What about the fence?" Jim asked. "It's a pretty solid barrier— no gate anywhere, too high to hop over, and I've seen what that electric strand can do to a cow."

"They have their ways," Rickett said. "Pull a staple to make a space to crawl between the woven and the barbed wire. Or ground out the electric. Or rig some kind of portable stile. It gives drivers something to think about all the way to Cody or all the way to Balford. They'll map it all out—take your irrigating road to the far side of the place, out of sight of the spring and your trailer, park in the sagebrush, and then take that gopher trail down the bluff. Unless you heard gunshots—and in certain weather, even that sound doesn't carry—you'd never know they're there."

"So you're saying keep the gate closed?"

"No, that's not what I'm saying," Rickett said. With a deft fillip, he sent the cigarette butt sailing over the abatis. "Goss Harvey picked a mighty hard way to live out the end of his life—on guard day and night against the whole human race. You'd do well not to subscribe to that approach. And," he added, with a faint smile, "since the opening of the gate would *so* frustrate Big Bernene, it's hard *not* to love the idea for that reason alone." He paused one last time. "But the question will be, as it always is, whether the good outweighs the bad—because once you open it, you open it to everybody."

Over the summer and into fall, Rickett's words were fulfilled.

First, regarding Bernene Maxwell. Almost as soon as the latch chain was left dangling, she knew about the open gate. *How* she knew was a mystery. She lived in a big house in Balford, miles from Honey Spring. How often did trips to Cody bring her this way? However she found out—spies, agents, elves?—it was clear that the open gate did not meet with her approval. After sacrament meeting the last Sunday in June, she cornered Jim at the back of the chapel and warned that an open gate would *entice* onto his property all sorts of undesirables. While he might not mind such people traipsing across *his* fields and pasture, such traipsing, she said almost exactly the way Rickett had foretold, would inevitably put them in close proximity to Vanderfisk property, a prospect she was not at all comfortable with. And she would have to live with that discomfort all the long months until fall, before Jim would again see fit to close his gate so his cattle could feed off his fields. "Or," she asked, "do you plan to abandon that practice as well?"

The first to cross the new threshold uninvited was a rodeo cowboy—on the eve of the Fourth of July. From the gate, he soon enough availed himself of an irrigating road bordering the closest hay field, then the culvert into that field. This particular patch of alfalfa and clover had yielded an even thousand bales, dropped just that afternoon from the plunger chamber of a very old John Deere baler. When Jim drove up in the hazy dusk, the cowboy had already lashed one of the thousand to the left fender of his horse trailer and was lashing another to the right. For a long and awkward moment after Jim got out of his own pickup, he stood watching the process, absolutely certain the cowboy *knew* the process was being watched.

The explanation, when it came, was more defensive than contrite. "I can live on Skoal and a prayer," the cowboy said, "but Hi Ho Silver in there"—he nodded toward the trailer's shadowy twelve-hundred-pound cargo—"needs something with a little more nutritional value."

The lady in the big Oldsmobile didn't venture so far off the highway. On an afternoon in mid-August, when Jim's first barley was finally ripe enough to cut into windrows—almost two weeks after everybody else's—she parked at the edge of the cottonwood grove, close to the bulldozed gap in the old fence loop. From his perch on Goss's ancient windrower, coming around the grove on his way to a far field, Jim spotted the open trunk and the flash of what turned out to be the blade of a brand new shovel. He knew what the Oldsmobile lady was after. In the process of knocking over the fence, the bulldozer blade had sliced through a hillock of wind-drifted soil. Jim maneuvered the windrower close to the car and stopped. In the trunk rested two cardboard boxes. The lady didn't look his way. With the shovel blade, she poked at the sliced surface of the hillock, turned to the trunk, flung her meager quantity of dirt into one of the boxes, and turned back to repeat the process.

Jim throttled down and killed the windrower's engine. The silence after the machine's hydraulic whine accentuated the day's breezeless heat. Between shovel strokes, the lady mopped her brow with the sleeve of a blouse not ordinarily worn for this sort of work. At last she looked up at him. She said she and her husband had just built a new house in Garland. She was worried she had too much mulch in her entryway flower bed and not enough soil. Begonias, she said, needed a little of the real stuff. She thought she would just stop and get a little of that real stuff here, where there was so much of it to be had for the taking. "Bernene Maxwell is a good friend of mine," she said. "Isn't this her family's property now?"

In late September, with all but the last ten acres of pintos raked and curing in windrows, the plunder was apples. This time there were two takers, a father and a daughter. The girl was maybe eleven years old. They were more productive than the Oldsmobile lady. The three lard buckets at their feet were heaped full, and they had a good start on the fourth. "Hello, there," Jim said, friendly as could be. "Do you know whose property you're on?"

"Couldn't tell you," the man said, smiling widely. "But whoever it is oughtn't to let this good fruit go to waste." Picking with both hands and using the pocket of a hooded sweatshirt as a holding chamber, the man blamed canned pie filling for any number of disorders and diseases, opined that the government had much to gain by lacing the country's canned food supply with subtly toxic chemicals. With a twitch of his jaw and chin, he directed his daughter's holding of the bucket, emptied his sweatshirt pocket, then wondered aloud how anybody in his right mind could resist the flavor of freshly picked, thinly sliced winesaps under a flaky crust.

That evening, the supper menu at the single-wide was crackers, cheese, and sardines—and canned soup undoubtedly full of dangerous chemicals.

"It's meals like this," Rickett said, "give me a hankering for some fresh garden tomatoes. You know, it wouldn't have been all that hard for you to put in a few plants."

"So I could have strangers stealing them, too?" Jim said, busy with his eating.

"It's something to think about for next summer," Rickett said. "That's all I'm saying."

Jim looked up. *Next summer?* He was both startled and comforted by the presumption. After a moment he asked the question that had been fermenting all *this* summer:

"Why don't they just *ask*?"

Rickett looked at him. "The lure of forbidden fruit," he said philosophically. "Old as humankind."

"I would've given any of them what they were after," Jim said. "Even that ten-gallon peckerwood last July, the one who said he was from Cokeville. I would've given him twice as many bales as he stole."

"Is that the one with the girlfriend who wanted to marry him to keep him out of the draft?"

Jim nodded.

"Would that work?" Rickett asked, lighting a cigarette.

"No." As he stood, Jim slid the empty sardine tin across the table to serve as ashtray. Then he stepped to the refrigerator, grabbed a carton of ice cream from the freezer compartment and the closest clean utensil for scooping—a ladle—and brought both back to the table. "I knew guys who were married," he said. "If the government needs bodies bad enough, nothing works except maybe being too blind to send rounds down-range or too flatfooted to hump. *Or* having connections to a high government official of some sort. But the cowboy," he went on, peeling back the lid flaps of the ice cream carton, "is both healthy *and* unconnected. So he's a goner, and he knows it. He said he was going to beat Uncle Sam to it, was thinking of joining the Marines."

"Did you give him the benefit of your wisdom?"

Jim let out a short laugh. "Me? The minute he saw me, he wrote me off as a duffer. I could see it all over his face. And what would I tell him anyway? The shortest life expectancy belongs to the man walking point? The M-16 is bad to jam right when you most need it *not* to jam? And the best C-ration combination is sponge cake and cling peaches in heavy syrup?" Using the ladle like a miniature backhoe, Jim filled a bowl with ice cream, then slid the bowl toward Rickett. "You know what he had the nerve to yell out his window right before he drove off with two bales of my hay? He asked if I needed a girlfriend," Jim said, answering his own question as he shoveled another bowl full of ice cream.

"I've wondered the same thing," Rickett said. "I'd be interested to know what you told him."

"You and all the gossips in the Balford Ward."

"Man does not live by crackers and sardines alone, Jim."

"And tell me when, exactly, I would fit in something *besides* crackers and sardines. Same spare time I should've used for tomato growing?"

"I managed during law school."

"Tomatoes?"

"A social life," Rickett said. "That's when I met my wife."

Early in their acquaintance, Jim had learned that Nolan Rickett was a widower. But in four months of voluble admonition, storytelling, and history lessons, the lawyer had said no more on the topic. And now, though he grew contemplative for a moment, the only thing he said was, "So what *did* you tell the cowboy?"

"I used your line."

Rickett's eyebrows rose.

"I told him I need a lot of things."

Rickett chuckled. For several minutes they ate without saying anything.

"I could press charges on all these people," Jim said. When Rickett didn't immediately confirm that possibility, Jim said, "Couldn't I?"

"Did you get their names and addresses?"

Jim shook his head.

"Do you want to spend months, maybe years on end in court?"

Jim shook his head again.

"Do you have a good lawyer?"

The younger man looked at the older man with skepticism.

"We'll call that a no," Rickett said.

For a minute Jim concentrated on eating his ice cream. Then he asked, "Are you sure keeping the gate open is bugging Bernene?"

Rickett grew very serious. "You can bet on it."

On a cold, overcast morning the week after Thanksgiving, during the combing of swamp reeds and frozen hummocks for two years' worth of half-wild calves, the forbidden fruit was pheasant. The hunter betrayed his presence when the boom of his twelve-gauge momentarily swallowed the shriek and wing-beat of the target rooster. Unharmed, the bird rocketed over the day's first muster of wild-eyed cattle. The noise gave them just the excuse they were waiting for to scatter to the four winds, their hooves flinging divots in the chilly mist.

In early October of 1900, Bishop Wagon-Boss Balford received a letter from Church headquarters in Salt Lake. In that letter, Bishop Balford was directed to extend a mission call to one of his congregants, a young man named Goss Harvey. Harvey was to proselyte in England for a period of two and a half years, that term to commence as soon as his personal circumstances would allow. Goss's personal circumstances, like those of all the settlers, lately had involved a frantic digging of potatoes before the onset of an early winter. There wasn't a team or wagon available to take a missionary the twenty-six miles to the Frannie station to meet the closest train. So, well before dawn on the first Monday in November, Goss closed the hewn door of his little log-and-sod hut on the rocky side of Honey Spring and, carrying only a small valise and satchel, set off walking. He hadn't gone a hundred yards when he met Enoch, who was riding one horse and leading another, saddled. Enoch leaned down and took the valise from him. "I'd thought I'd better see you to the station," he said. "I know how you like to dawdle."

On Thanksgiving of that year, with a sufficient harvest gathered and the walls of their shelters thickened in any way possible against the winter wind, the members of the new Balford settlement gathered at the community bower. Within the bower's three canvas walls and beneath its willow-lattice roof, the settlers met regularly for Sunday worship, weekday business, and for entertainment and refreshment. This cold, windless evening in late November marked their biggest social yet. Just beyond the bower's long, open side, two bonfires blazed. Inside the bower, people sat on split-log benches. Standing at one end of the bower, Bishop Wagon-Boss Balford gratefully acknowledged, again, the two young men who had herded the milk cows that made possible the luxury of cream. One of those young men, the bishop reminded his listeners, was now abroad serving the Lord in the mission field. "Remember him in your prayers," he said. After the blessing on the food, people fell to eating a supper of venison and baked potatoes, for which the bishop had generously provided butter.

After supper there was a dance. Even wrapped up against the cold, people were eager to move their feet in time to fiddle music. During that dance Enoch held Honey Utley in his arms for the first time and, for the first time from that proximity, looked into her eyes. And for the first time, she looked into his.

CHAPTER 6

I N THE HOURS AFTER THE PHEASANT HUNTER'S EARLY
disruption of the roundup—and an apology consisting mostly
of a backhanded gripe about the escape of a sure trophy bird—the
cattle were twice as hard to gather. After long months of roaming, they resented being driven anywhere, especially toward the
steep and narrow notch in the bluff. And they resented, even
more, all efforts to hold them together for the collective push
up the notch. Those efforts came to center on, as a conveniently
improvised marker, a lone aspen tree growing on the bank of the
spring. The tree became the center of the cattle's restless movement. For the most part, they defied—or ignored—yelling and
waving and brandishing of staffs (a Russian olive stick for Jim
and a broken hoe handle for Rickett). Instead, they milled and
mooed, balked and jinked. Over and over, a mother found this
year's calf only to lose it again in the press. She might pause long
enough to urinate, but the steaming puddle hadn't even soaked
into the frozen ground before she was moving again. The evacu-
ating of bowels occasioned not even that much of a pause. Both
loosened and strengthened by unrest, they erupted with complete unpredictability.

Peevishness was not confined to the cattle. When, after several lucky dodges of black-green slurry, Jim wasn't so lucky,
Rickett couldn't resist garnishing the insult. Above the din of the
milling herd, he yelled, "If you're wondering what makes it so
liquid—"

"I'm not!" Jim yelled back.

On certain days Rickett seemed to miss holding forth in front of a jury. Today was one of those days. He was in fine professorial fettle. "There are four chambers in the ruminant stomach," he explained loudly. "By the time forage moves all the way from rumen to abomasum, through who knows how many yards of gut—stewing every inch of the way in gastrointestinal juices that would peel paint—"

"I'm *not* wondering!"

"Bovine anatomy is all it is," Rickett said. "You know, you really could stand a little more study of what you've inherited."

"Ten minutes into this roundup," Jim said, "I knew all I wanted to know about cows."

On this particular day, Rickett also must have missed sparring with an opposing lawyer. "You know, it might help your attitude if you'd dress for the weather."

"What's my dress got to do with being painted up and down with cow crap?" Jim asked.

"If a judge will allow it," Rickett said, poking this or that cow with his hoe handle, "it's called establishing pattern. Patterns like negligence, indifference, flippancy, hardheadedness"—he looked pointedly at Jim—"*chuckle*headedness in some cases. What were you thinking, wearing summer gloves and gumboots on a day like this? This is Wyoming, fella. You can't forget that."

"You think I grew up in Tahiti?" Jim asked. "Hawaii? Cancún? Egypt? You and Ardizzoli ought to get together. 'You don't know from cold,'" Jim mimicked. "He was always saying that, bragging about New York people toughing out their bad weather—like nowhere else on earth has cold and wind and snow."

"I'm not bragging," Rickett said. "I'm just telling you you're not dressed appropriately for the conditions."

"Don't you worry about me and conditions," Jim said. "I've been through conditions. I'll survive your conditions. Cold day in a swamp? Piece of cake. You can't see my wool socks and long-johns. With them on, I maybe—just maybe—stand a chance of surviving the day here in the wilds of Balford, Wyoming."

Rickett looked as if he were trying to decide whether, and to what degree, he was being mocked. What he himself was wearing—frayed trapper's hat with a missing chin strap, calf-high rubber overshoes (half of whose buckles were defective), and *two* pairs of thin gloves (with the hope that the holes in the outer pair wouldn't align with the holes in the inner)—evidently qualified him to promote insulated snow packs, coveralls, mittens, and far more ear protection than the hood of "a silly beach bum's sweatshirt." And when Jim pointed out that no such cold-weather gear was hanging in the trailer's closet, Rickett asked if he'd ever heard of a store. Jim reminded him that store transactions require money and that, generous as it was in so many hard-to-measure ways, his inheritance had included none of that.

Rickett countered with the prediction that, if not for the bequeathed denim coat's quilted lining, Jim wouldn't last twenty more minutes before the onset of hypothermia. And when Jim didn't seem properly worried by that prospect, the admonition finally took on an edge of disgusted futility.

"You won't feel so brash," Rickett said, "when your every extremity is black and shriveled with frostbite."

Grievance begat grievance.

"Well, before I die of frostbite," Jim said, "do you mind telling me why you wouldn't accept the Sebrights' invitation to Thanksgiving dinner?"

"*That's* what you're so sour about today?"

"*Me?*"

"Look," Rickett said, "this Sebright is your bishop, not mine—in a religion that I have done well to keep a leery distance from for a long time."

"Except for Christian decency, there was nothing religious about it," Jim said. "It was food. It was a meal. And they invited us both. It was just him and his wife and kids being nice."

"I know about Mormons and nice. Underneath the nice—the nice turkey, the nice dressing, the nice pumpkin pie—they're always trying to reform you or convert you. I got a craw full of that growing up in Luna Valley. And have I ever mentioned to you that I then went and *married* one of them?"

"No, you never mentioned that," Jim said.

"Let's just say she liked the idea of marrying me a lot more than her family did," Rickett said. His next prodding of a cow was a good bit more forceful than it needed to be. "She was a very good woman, my wife," Rickett said. "Never pressured me once to convert, mind you, but I always wondered if she would've liked me *better*—or maybe liked our marriage better—if I had come her way on religion."

"Were you ever tempted?"

"No," Rickett said. "I was not."

In the end, the best remedy for surly cattle and even surlier herders was the pair of wonder dogs. By midday, they had more than justified Rickett's regard for them. They were artists. They stalked. They feinted. They pursued. As the moment demanded, they were stealthy or bold. They circled and flanked, urged and headed off. Dodging hooves, they nipped dewclaws, hocks, stifles. Dodging horns, they worried briskets and underbellies. And they did all this without barking. They were virtuosos.

By early afternoon, a herd of nearly fifty head—brood cows and this year's unbranded and uncastrated calves, all the unbranded heifers and uncastrated bulls from last year, and the old Angus bull that still enjoyed a corner on the siring—was laboring up the notch trail. Despite its many windings and switchbacks between sagebrush clumps, the trail stayed close to the spring and divider fence. The cattle could not see what awaited them at its top end, just beyond the lip of the bluff where Goss lived out his days in a single-wide trailer. They could not see, less than twenty feet from that lip, the portal in the south perimeter of the main corral, waiting open to receive them. Nor the low cedar-log barn roofed with chicken wire and barley straw. Nor, on either side of that barn, various smaller pens and the cutting chute and squeeze chute and, extending from one of those pens fifteen feet or so into the farmyard, a lopsided loading chute.

About a week after the pheasant hunter, Jim and Rickett— with the unexpected and very welcome help of Bishop Clive Sebright—finally saw to the long-overdue branding, castrating, and dehorning, a chore better suited to warmer days. Then came the cutting out of animals to be sold from those to be kept and turned into the fields to feed off stubble and straw.

The last of those bound for market were loaded on a cold morning just two weeks before Christmas. The sky was brilliantly clear, and there was no wind. Five inches of snow had fallen the night before, as if to re-coat crust and drifts unmelted since the last storm. On the loading chute ramp it was a lovely hindrance. Even with the cleats bolted crossways to the ramp's planks, the hooves scrabbled and slipped and soon churned the fresh white powder into green muck. That is how the last bunch of cattle made it up and into a crop-hauling truck fitted with a welded stock rack.

Like all Goss's creations, the rack was a product of thrift and ingenuity. Every frame piece, every slat and paling, was scabbed together from oddment and scrap. Round sucker rod was mated to square PTO shaft, rebar to faucet stem, angle iron to harrow spar or tie-rod or pitman arm. Gaps were filled with old bolts, railroad spikes, strap braces from the crosstrees of telephone poles. Almost anything—spoke of a mower reel, broken plowshare, clevis, skill-saw blade—could serve as a gusset. Even less important than uniformity of material was any symmetry of design. The whole thing looked as if it had been assembled with contempt for a tape measure and square.

Yet, season after season, it had hauled to market many loads of cattle. Dried splashes of slurry, from the abomasums of animals long ago ground into hamburger, encrusted surfaces inside the rack and out. Much fresher manure clotted the straw spread over the slick hardwood of the truck's bed. Following the last steer up the chute, wary every inch of the way of the point of origin of both both dried and fresh, Jim hurried to secure the cage's gate before that steer or any of his mates grew to resent tight quarters and decided against traveling.

Goss evidently had not wanted such securing to be easy. The gate neither swung on oiled hinges nor slid in greased tracks. It was nothing but a welded, roughly rectangular frame overlaid with a patchwork of catwalk metal and pieces of oil-drum lids. With a swipe of his gumboot, Jim cleared heavy, soiled straw from the threshold of the rack's doorway, then snugged the gate to the sill and uprights. When he had wired it shut, two places on each side, he hopped down.

No sooner had the soles of his boots touched the ground than Rickett said, "You sure two's enough?" He had asked this question after every loading in the past two weeks. Under its restless cargo, the old truck rocked and shifted.

"It's enough," Jim said.

Before climbing in the cab, he and Rickett stood looking into the empty corral. They both leaned against its perimeter fence, a work of art that bested even the stock rack. It had started with poles, five high, scarf-jointed and spiked to heavy posts. Then, between the poles, rough-cut planks. Then a layer of sheep wire and another of chicken wire. All that was reinforced with whatever could be supplied by more of Goss's frugality and ingenuity—pallets, panels, scraps of roofing tin, a couple of old doors, a set of bedsprings.

But there was an even more singular feature. All along the fence, like a kind of wainscot, ran a line of old pews set end to end and oriented so that worshipers would have faced the corral's interior. It was plain that these pews had doubled for a good many years as both fence reinforcement *and* feed bunk. The weather-dulling of varnish showed only on the pew ends and higher up on the backs. The bench surface itself, and the angle between it and the back, shone as if freshly finished. Those were the surfaces where the tenderest fodder settled and where long tongues, abrasive as sandpaper, made repeated passes during morning and evening feedings, years on end. Only under those pews, where it had blown and drifted, did any clean snow remain.

"Where did he get that many?" Jim asked. "That's more than half a chapel's worth."

"I don't know," Rickett said. "That was before my time."

Except for the swapping of mittens for gloves, each man was dressed exactly the same as during the roundup. But on this morning, neither was thinking of dress or mastery of bovine anatomy or refused Thanksgiving dinner invitations. Nor did they think for long on the origin of pews, which were by now a familiar novelty to them both. The sorting of cattle marked the end of Jim Ray's first farm season, and this last load marked the end of the sorting. This was a moment to savor.

After a time, Jim said, "I hate to bring it up, but when they're out in the fields, I'm going to have to start closing Goss's gate again, aren't I?"

Rickett had lit a cigarette and now finished a long pull and exhalation before he said, "Not necessarily."

Jim looked at him in surprise.Rickett let smoke out through his nose. "You know what a cattle guard is?" he asked.

"Yeah," Jim said, not quite certain whether he was being talked down to or not. "But where would I put a cattle guard? The Highway Department would never okay one on that main gate." He paused. "Would they?"

"Probably not. But I'm not talking about anywhere that needs the Highway Department's approval."

Jim waited.

Rickett tapped cigarette ashes into the snow at his feet. "What do you think about that bulldozed gap in the old highway fence," he said, "by the cottonwood grove?"

When Jim didn't say anything, Rickett went on. "It's the only part missing. Everywhere else the old fence is still up and in good shape—and it wouldn't take much to fill the gap. Just put the cattle guard where the road runs, there close to the grove. Build you a new fence brace on either side of it. That's really the only *hard* fencing required. Drive two or three steel posts to fill in the rest of the gap, re-stretch your barbed wire, drive a few staples, and you've got it. Your cattle are just as fenced in as they would be with the big gate shut—with just as much field forage."

He spoke the same way he smoked—deliberately, unhurriedly, and with immense satisfaction.

"As for the cattle guard itself," Rickett went on, "it needs a pit underneath it and a concrete box to sit on, if you're going to do it right. You might have to hire a backhoe for the digging. The box you can frame and pour yourself; you've got a cement mixer, you know."

"One of my sundry possessions?"

"Right."

Jim had seen it sitting in a corner of Goss's machinery yard. "Does it even work?"

"Yes, it works," Rickett said, mildly insulted. "Runs off your tractor's PTO. You just have to pick a day when it's supposed to get above freezing to do the mixing." Then he said, "If you're game, I can show you how to do all this in the next week or so, before I head south for the winter."

Jim looked at him. "When did you hatch this plan?"

"On the way out of the post office last week," Rickett said, "I ran into Bernene. She said if I wanted to give you some 'good' advice that you might actually listen to, I'd advise you to shut your gate."

"That's good enough for me," Jim said. "The only problem I see with an otherwise excellent plan is that I don't *have* a cattle guard."

Rickett smiled, flipped his cigarette butt into corral muck, and took off walking. Jim followed. When they came to the little alley between the grain bin and the back of the welding shed, Rickett turned in. Here Goss kept his scrap metal. But getting to the metal was complicated by more than knee-deep drifted snow. Over the summer the metal shared the alley with an amazingly prolific variety of pigweed. In every open space, it had sprung up thick as field corn. Even in unopen spaces, weed stems threaded their way through a clutter of scrap iron, through and around and between odd bits of equipment kept all these years on the off-chance they might supply a usable piece to someone handy with a torch and welder.

Now, amid stomping a trail and grunting, Rickett said, "You should've got back here once in a while last summer with a hoe or machete." After another couple yards, he stopped. He stood facing the only thing that approximated a storage rack. Here, on the cross-pieces of a pair of outward-leaning A-frames, rested longer pieces of sucker rod, square tubing, angle iron.

From Rickett's posture and expression, Jim got the feeling he was supposed to notice something he wasn't noticing. He looked more closely.

Then he knew what the A-frames were. Toeing through the snow at the base of one of them, he felt the rounded surface of a pipe. Kneeling, he shoveled with mittened hands to clear a larger area. One pipe lay parallel with many others. The even spaces between them were chinked with snow, but the more he cleared, the more recognizable the pipes were as spars of a cattle guard.

"And that," Rickett said at length, "is one of the many sun-dry possessions *I* didn't know about until I discovered it myself. Now look close," Rickett instructed, pointing to the pipe spars. "That's oil well casing. Thick as tank armor. In fact, that thing would hold a tank without a quiver. Just splice it into your fence line, and you're set."

Jim stood, brushed snow from his pants. "Goss never mentioned this to you? I thought you two were tight."

"Oh, no, kiddo," Rickett said, "not tight. We knew each other. We needed each other. We helped each other. And we got along okay. But we were not what you'd call tight. Mostly because, after Enoch Vanderfisk, I'm not sure Goss was ever again tight with anybody in the world. No sir, there was a *lot* he didn't mention to me."

"But you stayed around all this time," Jim said, drawn back to the same persistent question. "And don't give me that baloney about doing it for a pair of good cow dogs."

Rickett smiled but didn't say anything.

Jim had grown used to his reticence on the point, but it was harder and harder not to dig at its edges. Still, it was easier for both of them to puzzle over Goss's secrets than over their own. After a moment, he said, "So why go to all that work to build a cattle guard and then never actually use it?"

"Goss had more than a little martyr in him," Rickett said. "That was something he didn't *have* to tell me. I saw it for myself. Every time he opened and closed his big gate, he was reminded how life had wronged him. Strange as it sounds, strange as it *ought* to sound to someone of your religion, that reminder was vital to him. No matter how much he might've valued an open gate, he valued the reminder more."

Cold as the day was, the sun shone splendid in a clear blue sky. Standing in the alley between the grain bin and welding shed, Jim squinted at the sunlight reflected off the new snow.

"Wow," Rickett said, shielding his eyes with a palm. "I guess this is what I get for dreaming of leaving a white Christmas behind."

Rickett's words might as well have clicked a switch in Jim's brain. In that very instant, one of his own undisclosed secrets momentarily banished from consciousness cattle and cattle guards and Goss Harvey's martyrdom. Just about exactly a year ago, that was the song Private First Class Jerome Snow was humming not long before he hiked into a tripwire. Not even a month after Fritchey. A non-militant Detroit soul brother. By his own description. And amazingly good humored about the teasing his surname fated him to. Black as snow. Snowblack and the Seven Dwarves. I'm dreaming of a black Christmas. "Sing it that way," he was urged during a chow break in a fairly safe-looking place, before he took point. "You'll sound better than Bing."

From the direction of the truck and loading chute came a restless bawling. Jim took off a mitten and rubbed his eyes with a bare palm.

"You okay?" Rickett asked.

"Yeah," Jim said, still rubbing his eyes, "I'm okay."

So in the final week of 1966, Goss Harvey's little scrap metal storage yard, undisturbed in twenty years, suddenly had to be disturbed quite thoroughly to allow for the removal of the cattle guard. A tow chain behind the McCormick dislodged the welded grating of oilfield pipe. Under the snow, in the dirt floor of the little scrap yard, the pipe grating left, as an imprint, a matching pattern of molds in the frozen dirt. Most of the molds were leveled by the scooting, screeding movement of the heavy pipe. The few that were spared showed, in their shiny cupped surfaces, the grub trails and root tendrils of summer, and one mouse's nest.

From the scrap yard, the tow chain sledded the cattle guard through the slab gate and slowly up the snowy road along Honey Spring, past the orchard and then around the cottonwood grove. Under Rickett's supervision, the pit had been dug and the concrete box poured. And now, under his supervision, the pipe grating was placed and anchored, and the fence restored. And when the job was done, Jim said, "That is going to simplify my winter considerably."

"You plan on getting out a lot, do you?" Rickett asked.

"Groceries. Mail. Church." Jim's tone promised a longer list than the one delivered.

"That's not really the getting out I had in mind," Rickett said. "Isn't there anything *else* on your agenda?"

Jim stared at the old lawyer. "Not that again," he said. Then he said, "Where was this concern for my love life last summer?"

"You had more pressing obligations."

Jim laughed. "*Obligations!*"

"The underside of inheritance," Rickett said, "the part nobody wants to talk about."

"*I'll* talk about it with anybody who wants to talk about it," Jim said.

"Oh, yeah?"

"Yeah. And here's what I'll say. I'll say if a geezer lawyer in a worn-out overcoat comes up to you in a cemetery, run the other way."

"What do you mean?" Rickett said. "You're better off here than you would be pumping gas or frying hamburgers back in Mapleville."

"Maple*ton*."

"The point is," Rickett said, "while I'm off playing snowbird in New Mexico, maybe you could sneak down to Cokeville to comfort that hay thief's girlfriend while he's serving his country."

"You serious?" Jim asked. "In the Corps, we had names for guys like that."

"Maybe not so serious about Cokeville," Rickett said. "But you ought to be looking for *somebody* of the female persuasion to spend your life with."

"You sound like Bishop Sebright."

Rickett smiled. "If gentiles appointed bishops as freely as you folks do, I believe I might apply for the job."

CHAPTER 7

DURING HIS CHILDHOOD YEARS, JIM ATTENDED YEAR-end tithing settlement with his mother. December after December, he watched her sit across the desk from Bishop O. Weldon Partridge of the Mapleton Fifth Ward and declare, of her own volition—and with absolute honesty—that she had donated a full tenth of her annual income to the Church and thus to God. Like all bishops in that setting, Bishop Partridge took her word for it. He never saw a member's pay stub, never made a calculation.

Like all Latter-day Saint bishops and organists and nursery workers and Sunday school teachers and elders quorum presidents and Relief Society presidents and stake presidents, Bishop O. Weldon Partridge wasn't paid a farthing for his church service. Whether such payment, or the consciousness of its source, would have altered his manner in tithing settlement with Minnie Ray would have been hard to ascertain. What wasn't at all hard to ascertain was the manner itself. Despite an ordinarily unimpeachable endorsement of the requirements of discipleship, he nevertheless faltered when it came to Minnie Ray's tithing. Bishop Partridge had distinct eyes—heavy-lidded and moist, very kind but sad. They reminded Jim, in the most respectful sense of the comparison, of a hound dog's eyes. With such eyes there was no hiding the genuine reluctance to receive yet another offering envelope, the final one of the year, from a woman who was raising her son on a librarian's wage. But, as she deferentially insisted, it was her prerogative to give it and his duty to take it.

And when he did, year after year, with tears in his eyes, he could barely give voice to the promise that she would be blessed in accordance with her needs. Not because he didn't believe it, but because it was nothing *he* could guarantee. In that respect, the tithing promise was a lot like a second familiar promise—usually repeated in conjunction with the first—that one's private tribulations will never exceed the ability to bear them.

Fine sentiments, both, but in the end a little troublesome logically. Jim had contemplated the matter by the hour and had decided that the fallacy lay in the impossibility of *dis*proving either promise. So long as you survived—in fact, so long as you still drew breath—you could count both fulfilled. The only way to refute them would be to actually perish from neediness or tribulation. But then you'd be dead and not really in a position to enjoy the triumph of your reasoning. And even then the perishing could be called divine relief, thus corroborating God's hand after all. That was the thing about faith: it could be every bit as stubborn as doubt.

As to the needs of Minnie Ray and her son Theron James:

Food. Shelter. An old but functioning car. Good and dedicated school teachers. Sound health (a not-quite-accurate description in her case). A safe place to live. Charitable neighbors and attentive ward members. A testimony of the restored gospel. The promise of being together as a family in the hereafter. Over and over, his mother had cited such blessings. And Jim couldn't argue. But in the seventeen years between his dad's death and hers, were there needs tithing *didn't* cover? For talk and laughter? For companionship? For the other side of the double bed to be warm? Did his mother ever wonder, at all, if paying tithing or some other corner of her steadfastness was going to yield blessings to answer any of that? That was the question on Jim's mind when, on the eve of New Year's eve, he sat down for his first tithing settlement with Bishop Clive Sebright.

"So did you wind up farming your first year for money or just love?" the bishop asked from behind his desk in the little office with the Gethsemane painting.

When, after several seconds, Jim took his meaning, he said, "If those are the choices, then for love, I guess."

"Me, too," said this bishop who was also a farmer. "Crop prices were lousy, and my yields not much better. But the Lord's system of tithing is as simple as it gets. A tenth of not much is not much. So what you've paid this year—does it square you with him?"

"I wouldn't go that far," Jim said. "I risk blasphemy and irreverence enough as it is."

"You're right," Bishop Sebright said. "That was a lousy way to ask it." Then he said, "But I'm going to chew on that answer for a while anyway."

"Now if you're asking if I did my math right . . ."

"That's exactly what I'm asking."

"In that case, yes."

The bishop signed Jim's tithing form. "Just out of curiosity," he said, looking up, "did you pay during your time in the Marines?"

"In boot camp," Jim said, "they made you go to church, but for a lot of guys it was just an excuse to get out of regular duty. Catholics, protestants, Jews, a few of my own kind—a lot of them didn't care one thing about their religion. I was no model myself. But once we got in country, that all changed. When that first shell came whistling in—man, we *all* shaped up real fast into whatever our religions wanted us to be—choir boys, altar boys, deacons, priests, elders. Guys who'd never made a religious donation in their lives were suddenly sending a few bucks home to their pastor. A little extra protection couldn't hurt. That was the joke, but they meant it, too."

"Come to think of it," said the bishop, "I saw some of that in North Africa."

"But even before that," Jim said, "I liked tithing. It's a real clear commandment."

"Not near as tricky as loving your neighbor, that's for sure."

"Or maybe I just like feeling self-righteous about acing at least one little corner of obedience."

Bishop Sebright leaned back in his chair. The top button of his white shirt was not fastened. Several inches below the unfastened collar hung the bolo tie's turquoise clasp. "It's not so little as you think," he said. "You wouldn't believe how many people tell me tithing's harder for them than chastity. Maybe it's according to the individual, but I'd vote chastity every time. How about you?"

Jim nodded. Yes, that's exactly how he'd vote. Not all bishops were as comfortably candid with the topic. The one and only time Bishop O. Weldon Partridge mentioned it in a private interview was shortly before Jim left for San Diego, and then only to say, with great conviction in his heavy-lidded eyes—and awkward stiltedness in his voice—that a woman's body was a magnificent and hallowed temple, ordained against trespass and trifling.

Bishop Sebright's candor invited the same from whoever sat across the desk from him. "During boot camp," Jim began, "a billy goat could claim chastity. You're so wiped-out tired and scared and restricted, moving all the time and getting yelled at, what chance is there to do anything wrong? And for the next twenty months, until the war broke out, I just found something else to do with whatever free time we had. When there was somebody else who wanted to go to the movies or see the sights or whatever, good; if not, I went by myself. And nobody ever questioned my pastimes."

The bishop listened.

"But in-country was different," Jim said. "Back at base, after that first patrol—after a hot shower, clean clothes, cooked chow—this guy named Ardizzoli just could not fathom how anybody, even a guy from the other side of nowhere, from a religion he'd never heard of, could refuse the next logical item on the schedule."

Bishop Sebright didn't blink much. But his steady gaze was not scrutiny or a calling to account. It was not demanding or discomfiting. It was something else, something Jim had no words for. It was as if the bishop's eyes somehow turned Jim's own eyes inward. Yet even as they turned inward, he was more aware than ever of the gnarled olive tree in the Gethsemane painting.

"Ardizzoli was from the Bronx, die-hard New Yorker. He says to me, 'Dinks every day trying to blow you to bits, Ray, and you're sweating a little R and R nooky?'" Jim looked across the desk and said, "I should've at least told him why."

The bishop listened.

"He thought I was afraid of getting the clap," Jim said. "But I didn't even know what 'clap' was. So pretty quick he figured out this was just something else against my weird religion." Jim paused, shook his head. "But I truly don't know how much religion had to do with it. The only reason I didn't go was because I promised my mother."

For several moments the office was very quiet. Then Bishop Clive Sebright said, "What's the difference?"

Jim looked at him. "Ten thousand chastity lessons in church, but it was freaky how, for a minute there in Da Nang, Ardizzoli started to make sense."

"I know it, son," Bishop Sebright said, nodding. "Believe me, I know."

"In the Sunday school stories," Jim said, "guys are always valiant and converting somebody with their good examples. But that wasn't me. There was no example to it. Whatever guys were planning to do, they did. But I just couldn't get my mother's words out of my head." He stopped, scooted back in his chair, and looked down at the carpet. Then he looked up and again met Bishop Sebright's eye. "She's laying there dying," Jim said, "and you know what's on her mind—almost the last thing? She says, 'Promise me, Jim Ray.' I'll never forget the way her voice sounded.

She'd been so quiet, just barely breathing, I was sort of surprised she even woke up again. I really was. All of a sudden her eyes are wide open, and she's looking at me serious and a little bit frantic, like there's one more thing she's got to do. My mother really was a meek and quiet woman—all the time and not just at church—so that look on her face got my attention. I'm expecting *Good-bye isn't forever* or *Until we meet again*—or something like that. Heck, I didn't know what people say when they die. Not much, I found out later. Not like in the movies where they go on and on. Or maybe it's different dying in a bed. Anyway, out of the blue, with her eyes looking at me really bright, she tells me to promise her. Those two words. *Promise me.* Two or three times she said it. I felt bad. I didn't know what she meant. I wanted to know, but I didn't, and I didn't want her to die *without* me knowing. And then finally she got it out. She said, 'Promise me you'll stay close to the Church and mind what you've been taught. I need you to promise. No smoking, no drinking, no . . .'"

"No R and R nooky?"

Hard as he tried, Jim could not imagine Bishop O. Weldon Partridge uttering that phrase. But it seemed as natural in Bishop Clive Sebright's mouth as the response seemed in Jim's: "Well, she didn't call it *that*."

For a long time the bishop looked at him. Finally he said, "Your mother was a good woman."

The office was quiet. Jim nodded and, for the first time in a long while, sitting beside the Gethsemane painting, he felt the sting of tears.

Just after the ringing in of 1967, the widower Nolan Rickett left for Luna, New Mexico, to visit his deceased wife's kin, then on to Las Cruces to spend what he called the shank of the winter in a warmer climate. As a farewell, he warned Jim to be wary of any-body with the surname Vanderfisk or Maxwell and not to sign *anything*. Old Enoch and Big Frett Maxwell might be big fish in the little pond of Balford, but in the matter of Honey Spring, they were just doing Bernene's bidding. She was after Honey Spring, and Jim wasn't to forget it.

While Rickett was away, Jim looked after the wonder dogs, fed and watered the old Angus bull in its pen, and watched the cattle in the fields. With salvage lumber, he finally built a little eight-by-eight stoop for the single-wide. With a few sheets of salvage tin, he patched the roof of the tool shed. With some of last summer's barley straw, he replenished the roof of the cedar-log barn. For a week, he filled in as a plumber's helper. For three weeks, he filled in as a roustabout in the oil field.

Before long, the new year wasn't so new anymore.

"Young and single and eminently eligible," said Enid Cottrell, ladling red punch into a paper cup printed with hearts, "and you have the audacity to come *alone* to the ward Valentine's pot-luck." She said this, all five-feet-two-inches of her, from behind one of several folding tables set end to end along the edge of the Balford meetinghouse's small-scale gymnasium. Despite its genuine hardwood floor, despite the backboard and basketball rim at each end of that floor and the painted boundary lines, the gym doubled as a "cultural hall." The culture enjoyed in that space included youth dances, wedding receptions, baby showers, fundraisers (a fall bazaar and spring smorgasbord), and regular potluck suppers.

"I only heard the part about the meal," Jim said, taking the proffered drink.

With his full plate in the other hand, he turned to hunt a vacancy at the eating tables. Like most church get-togethers fea-turing food, this one had drawn a good crowd, most of whom had already made a good start on their meal. At that moment, he noticed, bringing up the rear of the food line, Enoch Vanderfisk and Big Frett, and, a minute later, the tardy arrival of Bernene, a woman who was never tardy and who never brought up the rear of a line. Slipping in behind her was a girl Jim had never seen.

Enid Cottrell had noticed her, too.

"Not that you're interested," she whispered coyly, "but that is Bernene's niece. Her name is Jocelyn, should you ever need to know."

Beginning last fall, with the urgency of the farm season finally eased, Jim had attended exactly three church get-togethers for "young single adults." The first was a Sunday fireside (as such a gathering was still called several generations after any actual warming fire had disappeared from the evening program of faith-promoting messages and refreshments). That fireside, hosted by the Garland Ward, drew eleven guys and three girls. At the second activity, a dance in Burlington—an hour away—there were six people total, two of them female. "I do believe this is what you call slim pickings," one of males had remarked. For the third gathering, a service project to spruce up the Balford Cemetery—trimming, raking, replacing a few pickets in the border fence—the attendees were Jim and a married chaperone couple from Cody. Now, in mid-February, the coldest time of year, most of the church girls anywhere close to his age were away at Ricks or BYU.

On this night, after the Valentine's potluck, Jim's help with the clean-up wasn't entirely service-minded. He had questions to ask the woman who would most likely have answers.

"Hardin and I will not have grandchildren in this life," Enid Cottrell said as she and Jim gathered tablecloths splotched with drips and spills from all kinds of casseroles and desserts and, of course, red punch. "Enoch and Honey have well over fifty. That young lady you saw tonight has the distinction of being the youngest of the lot—the youngest of the youngest. Agnes—her mother—is the baby of the family. A *surprise* baby, I think it's fair to say. There's nearly ten years between her and the next youngest. Honey was forty-two when she was born; the pregnancy and birth were very hard on her. She took a long time to recover and never did regain *all* her vitality. So Bernene—who was twenty, newly married, with a brand new baby of her own—ended up doing a lot of the mothering of her little sister. She and Agnes are very close." Enid paused to hold open a laundry bag for Jim.

"Now, what else will you need to know?" she said, as if asking herself. "She's from Bear Lake—that's where Agnes settled—and, from what I understand, is here staying with Frett and Bernene on a trial basis. I guess during her last year of high school, she got bored and restless, wanted to see the world. Some young people are like that." Still holding the laundry bag, Sister Cottrell paused and smiled wistfully. "My Hardin was like that. That's why he joined the Navy. He got as far as Pearl Harbor, Hawaii." Holding the bag's mouth with one hand, she used the other to pat each eye lightly. Then she resumed her two-hand hold on the bag and cleared her throat. "Anyway," she said, as if the word were a full sentence. Then she said, "Jocelyn—and that's the person you really need to know about—is now twenty, or close to it, and can do as she pleases. So if she's here with her aunt and uncle, it's because she wants to be or has at least agreed to the arrangement. She may *seem* a bit aloof," Enid said, "but don't let that fool you. She just doesn't know anyone yet—not anyone her own age, that is."

Enid Cottrell's coy tone was now accompanied by a coy smile.

"She's a sweet young lady," she said, "and, as you can see for yourself, she's quite attractive. I think the reason for the move to Balford was to get her away from some boy over there in Bear Lake. It might very well be, in fact, that they hoped for better prospects here." The coy smile gave way to Sister Cottrell's compassionate shaking of the head. "Whatever the case, I'm sure

Bernene doesn't want to risk the least circumstance that could lead to what Agnes went through."

For a moment after the last tablecloth was stuffed into the bag, neither of them said anything.

"I realize that's a gossipy-sounding teaser," Enid said, "but some of what I know, I know in confidence." Suddenly her eyebrows lifted. "But I know a way around violating that confidence. I don't have to *say* anything!" Her laugh was almost a girlish. "You still have in your possession my history, I trust."

Jim nodded.

"You'll recall a rather lengthy section devoted to the genealogy of this valley's founding pioneers, which you may well have skipped over—and I wouldn't blame you. There's nothing more tedious than looking at other people's vacation pictures unless it's their pedigrees." She placed a hand on Jim's arm, much as she had done eight months earlier under the lights of the softball field. "But if you study that genealogy closely," she said, "it will tell you a great deal."

Later that night, back at the trailer, Jim found the manila envelope containing Enid's manuscript. The first time through, he *had* mostly skipped the genealogy pages. Now, as he sat down in Goss's rocking chair, that was the very section he was after. Scooted close to the propane heater, shawled with a blanket, he thumbed pages and listened to the wind. With every moaning, buffeting gust, he was grateful for cables guying the trailer's beams to the edge of the river bluff.

And there it was—the page listing Enoch and Honey Vanderfisk's descendants: eight children and dozens of grandchildren, all the surnames typed in capital letters. The third of the eight was Bernene LeDawn, born 1905, married 1924 to Arthur Frett MAXWELL. In a column below their names ran the names and birthdates of *their* ten children. That was the pattern of listing—for the siblings older than Bernene LeDawn and for those younger. Until the very last one, the only other daughter: Agnes Ellen. Beside her name there was no spouse, no marriage date. But there was a daughter (surnamed VANDERFISK), born in 1946 and christened Jocelyn Bernene.

The morning after the Valentine's potluck, Jim got a call from Bernene Maxwell. Could he drop by the next morning? That's all she said to explain his second invitation to the big house on Balford Hill.

On a bitterly cold Saturday morning, he drove up the long lane, through grounds blanketed with snow, past the big mule barn, past the tennis court, to park in the expansive open lane in front of the house itself. Everything looked bigger and more imposing than he remembered it from his one visit ten months earlier.

Bernene answered the door. Bound with a sturdy scarf, her bouffant resembled an outsized broccoli floret rising from her head. "Good morning, Theron," she said with a politeness that didn't quite rise to warmth. She took Jim's coat, then directed him to a room different from the one in which she had offered him thirty-five thousand dollars for his property.

"Go ahead and have a seat," she said. "We'll be right in."

The room Jim sat in probably deserved to be called a parlor. It looked like something out of a magazine—several chairs that didn't get sat in much, a couple of couches facing each other, coffee table between them, fireplace blazing cheerily, a clock centered on the mantel. He sat in one of the seldom-used chairs. Before long, Bernene, now accompanied by her husband, came into the room. Big Frett shook Jim's hand, something Bernene had not done. As husband and wife sat down together on one of the couches, they motioned for Jim to relocate so as to sit more directly across from them on the other couch.

This visit included no offer of refreshment. The couple looked at Jim. Jim looked at the couple.

At length Bernene began. "We couldn't help but notice, Theron," she said, "that you have installed a cattle guard at the entrance of Mr. Harvey's property."

Yes.

"I'm just curious," she said. "Before you installed it, did you consider how that decision might affect us?"

If only she knew how thoroughly he had considered that very point. But Jim did not say this. Instead he said, "The gate was already open"—which, by the look on her face, was still a sore spot—"so I didn't see how the cattle guard could matter." In making this statement, he remembered Rickett's parting cautions and tried to sound more adversarial than he felt.

"Summer trespassers are one thing," Bernene said. "But autumn and winter bring hunters—with their guns." And even if a hunter had Jim's permission, and even if that hunter stayed on Jim's side—which was a very big *if*—what was to keep him from shooting in the wrong direction if the desired quarry presented itself? And if not hunters, she went on, what about trappers—of fox and bobcat, mink and muskrat, badger and beaver?

"According to Mr. Rickett," Jim said, "beaver are pretty rare in these parts."

"Your Mr. Rickett," Bernene said, "is no more familiar with the fur-bearing species of this area than he is with the people and their history."

She stopped. Her words had gotten ahead of her discretion, and all three people in the room knew it. All of a sudden, Jim felt more sympathy for her side of things than Rickett would have wanted him to feel.

Just then the mantel clock bonged. And it kept at it—*bong! bong! bong! bong!*—eleven times, as if to emphasize that the cattle guard, though an offense, was not the only reason for this meeting.

When the clock noise subsided, the room grew very quiet.

Big Frett started to say something. But that start from him was all his wife needed to take up where she had left off. "Traps are more than just a nuisance," she began. Yet she was cautious. She seemed to want to divulge only as much as she *had* to divulge to correct Jim's various misunderstandings, without knowing exactly what those misunderstandings were. "Has anyone told you," she asked, "about the pretty little heifer calf that some years back stepped into a beaver trap illegally set on our property?"

No one had.

"Well, it didn't kill the poor little thing, but it might as well have done."

As it turned out, the little heifer, by the time she was found, had been fighting that trap for two days. The jaws had gouged to the bone and, what with the gangrene, there was no saving the leg. And since a cow with three legs is worthless, there was no reason to save the calf.

For a moment they all sat contemplating the little heifer's tragic end.

"So you see," Bernene said, "we just want to protect our interests."

Jim cleared his throat and pointed out that there was a very sound woven-wire fence between their properties and that its function was reinforced, from river to highway, with an electric strand.

Since when, Bernene asked, did a fence deter a truly dedicated poacher or trapper?

At this point Big Frett, a man unaccustomed to being on the sideline of a conversation, uttered his first substantial lines in this one. "It's your cattle guard, Jim, and your property," he said. "But I can tell you, from long experience, that a lot of things can go wrong when any old yahoo can pull off the highway and right into a herd of foraging cattle. You might as well know: There *are* poachers around, and rustlers are not unheard of."

A burning log popped. The whole fire settled a little lower onto the grate.

"Look," Jim said, "I meant no harm or insult with the cattle guard. I just want to be able to leave my gate open. But," he said, "maybe it wouldn't hurt—just so we're all clear—to find out if there *is* any liability if a trespasser goes from my side to yours." He looked at his hosts. "Or your side to mine."

The second possibility seemed not to have occurred to them.

Just then they all heard a door at the back of the big house. From where he sat, Jim saw someone pass from one room to another. Presently that person was standing in one of the doorways of the parlor. Now, at a distance much closer than across the gym floor at the Valentine's potluck, he was looking at Jocelyn Vanderfisk.

"Sorry to interrupt," she said without the least hint of contrition, "but the lady at the post office said one of you is going to have to sign for the package. She wouldn't let me." She looked at her aunt and uncle, then, for a lingering instant, met Jim's eye. "I must look shifty. You know us Bear Lake types."

With that, Jocelyn withdrew and was gone. But she had distracted Bernene, who in turn distracted Big Frett. Whatever the meeting had or hadn't accomplished, it was over. Nothing more was said of either trespassing or the cattle guard. Though there was no hand-shaking as Jim stood, there was no real tension, either.

Besides, as he put on his coat and exited the big house, Jim Ray himself wasn't thinking about trespassing and cattle guards. He was thinking of a favorite baby sister who, many years earlier, had found herself pregnant and unmarried. Though Enid Cottrell's history made each of those conditions clear, it was too discreet to make them clear in any close and explicit proximity to each other. The narrative conveyed the fact of the pregnancy by speaking of the day when immediate family members learned that baby sister Agnes "was expecting"—written in exactly the same tone as might have been used to say that she had been diagnosed with asthma or bad tonsils. At the same time, the history dealt with the absence of a husband simply by not mentioning the absence. It calmly went on to the move to Bear Lake, Idaho, the relocation an apparently foregone conclusion. Here again a crucial fact was conveyed by omission. Without a single reference to Agnes's own mother—whose sentiments couldn't be recorded in a polite account?—the history gamely explained that it was Bernene who went along to help establish the younger sister with that mother's relatives, that she (Bernene) visited when the baby came and frequently thereafter, and that she (Bernene) became a very doting aunt.

Agnes Vanderfisk had never married. Which meant she had mothered without a husband even more years than Minnie Ray. With Agnes, even among strangers in Bear Lake, there would have been, along with fear and loneliness, a certain inevitable amount of scandal. To weather all that and more, had she had sufficient for her needs? Whatever those needs were, they became an abiding obligation to her older sister Bernene.

At the end of the sidewalk, Jim turned to look back at the house. As he did, his eye was drawn to an upstairs window. Jocelyn Vanderfisk was watching him. This time she did not withdraw. Jim paused, then waved. After several seconds, she waved back. The winter air was cold and clear. He didn't turn away for a long moment. And when he finally did, the cold was a different thing. Crunching toward his inherited pickup, he felt no snow under his feet. And as he drove away, he couldn't find, in the protecting of this *particular* interest—the one that had waved from that upper window—anything to fault Bernene for.

CHAPTER 8

I N THE WEEKS SINCE THE CATTLE HAD PASSED OUT OF corral gates to forage in the fields, their coats had grown shaggy. And a good thing, too. During the third week of February, 1967—the week after Jim's visit to Balford Hill—the temperature dropped to thirty below zero. Cottonwoods and orchard trees and the sagebrush forest could break the wind, but nothing save a very thick coat could protect against the cold.

In such cold, anything originating inside a cow's body—fluid, solid, gas—steamed as it cleared its orifice. That fact would have been amply confirmed when, unbeknownst to novice cowherd Jim Ray, one very self-sufficient Shorthorn chose the most frigid night of all to give birth. Beside a hollow on the lee side of a giant wind-combed sagebrush, she left a string of afterbirth that almost instantly froze so rock-hard that even coyotes didn't catch its scent. Yet, thanks to the astonishingly keen instinct guiding the mother's nuzzling and tonguing, the calf suffered only two lasting effects from coming into the world on such a night—a tail and a pair of ears docked by frost. From then on, the calf could be singled out, across field and pasture, by its uncanny facial resemblance to a Doberman pinscher.

The first singling out happened the morning after the birth. On that morning, the coldest of the year, Jim had scraped frost from the pickup's windshield, unplugged the engine heater from the drop cord running from the tool shed, and come up the Honey Spring road to chop drinking holes in pond ice. He got out of the truck and reached for his axe. That's when he looked across the nearest bean field, a hundred yards or so, and spotted a newborn calf. Even at that distance, Jim could detect something different about the ears. The day had warmed to ten below, and the calf frisked among the foraging cows, as if chasing June butterflies in a green paddock. Jim smiled and went to work with the axe. Every few swings, he adjusted his grip on the ice-glazed handle. And every few adjustments, he turned to check on the hardy little Doberman calf.

When he looked up from chopping the last hole, the calf was nowhere to be seen. What could be seen were several plumes of steam. The plumes came, not from feeding and cud chewing and bladder emptying, but from some*body*—a breathing human—wandering among the frozen tracks of rake and combine. Jim dropped the axe in the pickup's bed, hopped across the field's border ditch, and started walking toward the wanderer.

With every rod of closed distance, the wanderer became more of a curiosity. He held a curious stick and moved in a curious way, now standing, now crouching, poking, prodding, as if gathering clams on a beach. Behind him he dragged a curious gunnysack. And he had a curious rapport with cattle. Despite his proximity to tail ends and head ends and flanks, not one animal spooked. In fact, this clam digger wouldn't have seemed any *more* at home if he had dropped to his hands and knees, lowered his head to the ground, and taken up a mouthful of threshed pods.

Beyond the bank of the far border ditch, the clam digger's curious rig came into view. It was a very old pickup truck, and this very old pickup truck was hauling, not towing, a sheep wagon. It was as if someone had removed the wagon's tongue and wheels and dropped the whole dome-roofed structure, top-heavy and overhanging, into the pickup's bed.

At thirty feet from the closest cow, Jim stopped.

Most trespassers knew when they were caught. Like the rodeo cowboy last summer, they often pretended *not* to know by turning their back on the catcher, but the move only confirmed their awareness. But the way this clam digger meandered among the cows, singing and muttering to himself, it was hard to tell. Finally he let go the gunnysack, stretched and yawned as if just out of bed, and, without turning around, yelled, "The fields are white already to harvest!" He had a booming voice, each syllable accompanied by a puff of vapor. And it was clear that he knew his voice was heard by other than bovine ears.

Jim waited a moment, then said, "A little early in the year for harvesting anything, isn't it?"

"Not if that anything is chips!" the clam digger said. He didn't turn, but he did grab his sack and sidle in Jim's direction. "Best gathered, as you might have surmised, when Mother Nature has things sufficiently deep-frozen to prevent crumbling and to minimize odor on specimens not yet fully cured."

Until this instant, Jim hadn't surmised any such thing.

As the clam digger approached, dragging the sack along, he scoured the ground, with expert sidelong glances, for any particularly choice and well-frozen turd or pie or flop. Weaving his way between three or four cows at the fringe of the herd, prodding with his stick every now and then, he finally stood before Jim. "Cold as it is," he said in his booming voice, "these fine animals have granted me rich supply."

Up close, curious gave way to weird. The clam digger had a long, bushy beard hung with thin, amber icicles. Snugged tight over ears and jowls was a thick stocking cap. But a gaping hole in its crown allowed as much hair to extrude from its top as from its bottom. His hoodless coat looked like a tailored Army blanket. There were button holes but no buttons. It was held together, more or less, with a piece of string threaded, at one end, through a button hole and, at the other, through a slit made with a knife or scissors. Beneath the loosely fastened coat was a pair of insulated coveralls. Both were mottled with stains. The cuffs of the coveralls didn't quite reach the ankles of bell-toed, fudge-colored rubber snow boots laced with baling twine.

"They call me Beeswax!" the weird man said with much volume and vapor. "And what do they call you?"

"Jim Ray."

"Well, how do you do, Jim Ray?" Beeswax stuck out a mitten and delivered a stiff, one-pump handshake. Even in the outside air, he was pungent. He smelled like pelts and butcher rooms and wild onion. He smelled, too, like the plug of chewing tobacco that seemed to explain a nervous jaw. "I'm from over by Clarks Fork," he said. "When the weather's right, I come this way to replenish my supply. And, boy, has it been right lately!"

His oversized smile revealed a set of teeth unlike any Jim had ever beheld. Top and bottom, they called to mind the teeth of a two-man timbering saw—pointed and stained, leaning and overlapping, chinked at the gum line with what looked like pine pulp.

Through the saw-blade teeth, Beeswax took in a wheezy breath. It was hard to tell how old he was. Forty? Probably more than that. Sixty? Maybe. Neither number would have surprised Jim. Toeing the gunnysack gently, as if it contained diamonds and pearls, Beeswax said, "This is a good batch. And am I ever glad to get them."

"For what?" Jim asked.

"Pit roasting!" Beeswax said, cheerfully offended by the ignorance behind the question. When that announcement didn't seem to clarify much, he gave the sack an up-and-down shake—according to sound, it could have been half-full of frozen loaves of bread—then dropped it back on the ground. As he made ready to speak, he leaned on his stick as if it were a cane.

"Here's how you do it," he began. He lifted one hand from the stick so as to have an appendage for gesturing, which seemed to loosen his tongue even more. "You dig a nice, broad hole"—he spaded the air with mittened fingers—"maybe two, three feet deep. You line the bottom with live coals; fruitwood of any sort is this country's best substitute for hickory. Then you spread a nice generous layer of these chips—not too thick, not too thin—to temper and modulate the heat." The lining and spreading were also represented with hand gestures. "Oh, they work slick," Beeswax said. "They burn long and hot, with very little smoke and no odor to speak of. Now I would as lief have buffalo chips as the next pit cook, but they are a little hard to come by these days. And these"—he bent and tossed into his sack a specimen too good to pass over—"have proven to be a very serviceable substitute."

Beeswax interrupted his explanation with a sudden series of jaw and tongue contortions, all part of shifting his quid from one inner cheek to the other. Then he spat a brown stream, little of which cleared his beard.

"Once you lay down your base of heat," he continued, "it's whatever you're roasting. Turkey. Or goose. You can do goose. Goose is fine. Either one. 'Course there's pork shoulder and ham. You name it, I've cooked it: beef, mutton, venison, elk. Brisket, rump roast, ribs. Or loin, for that matter." Beeswax enlisted the handiest cow as an illustration, used his stick as a pointer to indicate her loin. "Actually loin is one of the cuts most amenable to this method of preparation." He paused very reflectively. "I have heard of folks down in the southwest roasting their native javelina in a pit, though that's a meat I've not experimented with personally. And to be frank," he added, "I'm not sure I want to. The javelina has a very potent musk gland. Puncture that when you're gutting or scraping"—he mimed an errant knife stroke— "and supper's over."

Beeswax paused again to spit. "As for me and my house," he said, "I am partial to fowl. But whatever floats your boat, so to speak. Just be sure to wrap it first. Banana leaves or palm fronds would be best, as the island peoples of the Pacific long ago discovered. Up here all's we've got is corn shucks, but they work just fine. It just takes more of them, on account of their size. And who besides the island people would know the difference, right?" He laughed at the cleverness of his reasoning. "Anyway, wrap it good in the shucks, then wet burlap, then tinfoil, and set it on your bed of coals and smoldering chips, then cover it back with loose dirt. And that's about it. Get you some sunflowers or piñon nuts and a jug of something compatible, and relax while the meat's own juices do the roasting. In due time—twenty-four to thirty-six hours, depending—it will melt in your mouth."

The thought of anything melting in Beeswax's mouth—amid those saw-blade teeth steeping in tobacco juice—didn't help the case for pit roasting.

"It's all in the chips," Beeswax said. "Pioneers on the treeless prairie might have first used them out of pure necessity and nothing more, but what they discovered was their superior utility as a fuel source. Something about ruminant digestion does it. Mark my word. Wherever there are ruminants—ox, camel, yak, giraffe—you will see the locals burning chips for fuel. You ever wondered why?"

Beyond hearing a reference or two to the chips produced by Great Plains bison, Jim had never thought much on the matter.

"You take Tibet, for instance," Beeswax said. "That cold over there makes ours look balmy. Nothing but wind and snow and ice eleven and a half months of the year. If it wasn't for their domestic mainstay, a creature known as the takin, those folks wouldn't have anything to keep their hut fires burning. Same with the Burmese and their gayal. I bet you've never heard of either animal." When Jim shook his head to confirm the assumption, Beeswax seemed supremely pleased. "You ever wonder *why* chips from a ruminant burn so good? Simple. Because of what their digestive system does to their food. It's pure fuel, like natural gas. They've got four stomachs, you know."

This time Jim could actually nod.

Beeswax stopped and looked at him suspiciously. "Did you really know that?"

"I can name them if you want."

"No, no," Beeswax said, still skeptical. "But you can rest assured you're one of a very small population of laymen who possess that knowledge. Most go along blithely ignorant of such matters. Humans have enough trouble with one gut, so I suppose they have a hard time fathoming four."

He shifted his quid again.

"*My* problem," he said, studying a specimen clutched in his mittened hand, "is pinto beans. Much as I admire that mighty legume, and much as cows like the taste of its vines and pods, the chips it produces just do not rise to the quality of those made of grass or alfalfa." He crumbled the specimen into the cold air and heaved a mighty sigh of resignation. "*But*—they will have to do."

Jim should have stopped with a general show of wonderment and admiration. But he made the mistake of saying, "I think I'll stick to an oven or frying pan."

Beeswax looked at him with genuine disbelief. "And give your meat the texture of *what*?" he asked. "Tire rubber! And with the *flavor* of what? Wall paste! Candle wax! Might as well broil your boot soles and baste them with sawdust, as much juice as an oven affords. You wait. After the first succulent bite of my turkey, you'll never again stoop to oven-cooked. I guarantee it." He spat again. And again the stream didn't completely clear his beard. "Just like old Goss. He took some convincing, too."

All debate over pit and oven fled Jim's mind. He looked at Beeswax. "You knew Goss Harvey?"

"You darned right I knew him," Beeswax said. "Many years. Fact is, there's folks think the name of the place has something to do with me."

"Why's that?" Jim asked.

"Honeybees!" said Beeswax. "Who do you think tends those dozen bee boxes in the lower corner of your fields? Technically, they're called supers. Did you know *that*?"

Jim was almost reluctant to nod. And when he did, Beeswax paused as if both skeptical *and* mildly resentful of an outsider's knowledge of his world.

"Well," Beeswax said after a moment, "I fill them every year. This place makes mighty good clover honey. 'Course the bees do all the work, but tending them takes a certain amount of smarts." He tapped his stocking-capped head with a mittened hand. "Anyway, me and Goss had us an arrangement: Come a cold spell, I'd bring him a little breast or brisket—whatever was fresh from the roasting pit—and he'd let me gather chips. In perpetuity, he said. To my knowledge, I was the only other person on this good earth he entrusted with a key to his gate padlock. With old Goss gone to his reward, I maybe should've asked somebody today before I crossed the cattle guard—a very nice convenience, by the way— but Goss said perpetuity. And perpetuity means what it means, right?" He paused. "Now if I *was* to ask somebody, would that somebody be Mr. Jim Ray?"

"It would," Jim said.

"You buy the place?"

"Inherited it."

"It and all its ghosts, I imagine," Beeswax said in a tone of sympathy. Then, as a reminder, he said, "*And* its promises, I hope. I'm the one person Goss let onto his place after that mess with the gravel trucks."

Jim looked at him. "What mess?"

Beeswax stared with the anticipation of disclosure. "When neighbor accused neighbor!" he said.

"Of what?" Jim asked.

"Malice. Perfidy. Slander. Greed."

"When was this?"

"Five, six years ago, just after they started the latest rebuilding of the highway. Do you know that made three times in a fifty-year stretch the government paid good money for Enoch Vanderfisk's rock? And this last time," Beeswax said, "they weren't just filling holes and crossing boggy stretches with it. No telling how many thousand tons it took to raise that roadbed high as they did. Now, a ton of gravel ain't worth much, but multiply not much by enough, and you still get rich."

"So what was the accusation?"

"I'm getting to it," Beeswax said, "I'm getting to it. You got to have the background, son, or the rest won't make any sense." With a nervous tongue working between nervous jaws, he dredged from the depths and caverns of his mouth some tiny splinters of tobacco stem and dabbed them from his lips with the seam of a mitten. He studied the splinters for a time and finally brushed them on the sleeve of his Army blanket coat. Then he looked in the direction of the Vanderfisks' gravel pit. "For that kind of hauling," he said, "the road crew had a wondrous fleet of dump trucks. Early on, before they started working around the clock, they parked them every night in Enoch's gravel pit. Fifteen or twenty of them lined up side by side—sitting-duck irresistible to somebody perched up on the bluff with a high-powered rifle. Shot out the windshield of every one of them—and a few tires for good measure. And it wasn't just windshields and tires. Whoever it was hit a cow, too. Maybe not intentionally, they said. But just as dead. So Goss faced two accusers—the construction company for the trucks and the Vanderfisks for the cow. Mostly it was Big Frett and his wife pushing the cow accusation. Not so much Enoch, from what I heard. All I know is it's a good thing Goss already had that lawyer from Denver."

Jim studied the man standing before him, so big and weird and weirdly knowledgeable. "Why did Goss need a lawyer before all this?"

"Wasn't enough they ended up with all the gravel on their side," Beeswax said. "*Mrs.* Big Frett got it in her head she wanted Honey Spring, too—or at least the top half of it. And I'm telling you," he said, clapping his mittens against the cold, "if it hadn't been for that lawyer, she'd a got it, too."

In the second half of his life, Enoch would trace the rift to that night in late November of 1900 when he first danced with Honey Utley, not even a month after Goss had left for his mission in England. But in the first half, there was no basis for blaming anything on anything, or anybody. Before Enoch acted on his feelings for Honey, he wrote a letter asking for—and, in due course, receiving—his best friend's blessing. By the time Goss stepped back onto the platform at the Frannie train station in the early spring of 1903, Enoch and Honey were two years married and expecting their second child.

Regarding the marriage, Goss couldn't have been more gracious. But the graciousness of one friend only evoked guilt in the other. Goss had been very fond of Honey, had spoken often, during that first summer in the Bighorn Basin, of a desire to court her when he got a little more established. Under the circumstances, then, how could a man, even one as good as Goss Harvey, resist the conclusion that his absence had been taken advantage of? So Enoch got it in his head to make right something that Goss insisted wasn't even wrong. Thoroughly familiar now with Honey Spring's endowments and knowing his good friend's ambition for farming, Enoch went to him in that spring of 1903 with the offer to swap sides—that is, to swap the better cropland and pasture on one side of the spring for the greater acreage of alkali and rocks on the other. "You're the one who needs topsoil," argued Enoch, a young man already showing promise in trade and business. Mostly to ease his friend's mind, Goss agreed. At Bishop Wagon-Boss Balford's suggestion, they put the agreement in writing. "Ink," the bishop counseled, "is a lot better record keeper than memory."

CHAPTER 9

IN LATE FEBRUARY JIM BEGAN SUPPLEMENTING THE herd's field foraging with a daily ration of hay. In none of his many parting instructions had Rickett explained how the field feeding of hay, a two-man chore, was to be managed by one. All he had said was: "It's pretty easy duty—a lot easier than visiting in-laws, I'll tell you that."

It turned out to be neither easy nor what anybody could call safe. It required hopping out of a slow-moving pickup (loaded with fifteen or twenty bales) amid a throng of hungry cattle. It required pushing through that throng so as to get a hop-up foothold on one end of the moving bumper (slick with frost), so as to mount the moving tailgate (also slick with frost), so as to cut twines and break bales on the moving pickup bed (slick with frost *and* hay leaves), while kicking flakes of those bales into the pickup's wake. After the last bale, at the end of a trail that confirmed the absence of both beacon and rudder, and was marked by clusters of feeding cows, it required dismounting and resuming the driver's seat.

It is true that the driverless truck moved in low first gear and, with no one to tend the accelerator pedal, it moved very slowly, sometimes haltingly. And when a tire encountered a rock or corrugation rut, the question was whether the truck would keep moving at all. So what was the risk? Only this: that at any given moment, one could trip, slip, stumble, fall and get kicked, trampled, crushed, dragged.

After three weeks of supplemented feeding, the fields were picked clean. It was early March. Jim corralled the herd (with his usual load of hay bales as bait and considerable help from the wonder dogs), closed the corral gates, and tied open the farmyard's slab gate for the new season. Day by day, the air warmed, the snow melted, the ground softened. Following other parting instructions, he changed the tractors' oil filters, charged batteries, and tilled thirty acres of last year's bean ground to be planted in this year's barley. At some point, Rickett was going to ask what had gotten done in his absence, and Jim wanted to have something to report.

But on the morning of his return from New Mexico in mid-March of 1967—almost exactly a year after the arrival of his letter at the sandbag bunker in Chu Lai—the old lawyer took his time getting to that question. Drinking coffee at the plywood table, he talked at length of the Chrysler's speed on clear roads, stability on icy roads, and widely unappreciated fuel economy on every kind of road. Then he described the flea market in El Paso where he had haggled with a shrewd Mexican merchant named Fernanda for the Hawaiian shirt he was wearing over his long-john top. Calling attention to his fresh shave and haircut, he extolled the social and psychological benefits of good grooming, especially in one's dotage.

"It's bad enough getting old," Rickett said, "without looking like a Neanderthal. And it's more than just a matter of what's still clinging to the scalp after threescore and ten—though I am grateful for what little there is of that." He said, "If I'm going to pay a barber good money, he's got to be willing to do the eyebrows and ears. I saw geezers in Santa Fe with more hair growing out their ears than on top. Not this kid! And that's not the only unlikely place hair goes berserk. It's like some of them got a pair of shaving brushes stuck up their nostrils—handle-first." He paused reflectively. "But for the trimming of that particular region, you're on your own, which I can't blame the barbering profession for at all. Can you?"

Jim shook his head.

From the big front pocket of his new flowered shirt, Rickett fished a pack of Pall Malls. He got one in his mouth, thumbed the worn lighter, touched flame to tip. He relished a long draw, then exhaled. Squinting through his smoke, he poured a second cup of coffee. Of necessity, he had brought his own thermos.

After a moment's reflection, he said, in the soberest of tones, "Can you tell me, Jim Ray, exactly what it is you Mormons have against the coffee bean?"

Jim was working his way through a stack of toast. Every slice got a curlicue of honey from a little jar shaped like a bear. Running his final bead along the edge of a slice, he said, "It falls under the 'hot drinks' category of the Word of Wisdom is all I know. And to us, that's scripture."

With the slice of toast clamped in his mouth, Jim half rose from his seat to reach the cleaned-out sardine tin that had been waiting on the counter since early January. He scooted it across the table, and sat back down.

"If that's scripture," Rickett said, "it's the nuttiest inconsistent scripture I've ever heard of." He knocked his first length of cigarette ash into the sardine tin and shook his head in wonder. "You drink cocoa hot. You drink Postum hot. You drink soup hot." He shook his head at the pitiable absence of logic in yet another of the religion's tenets. "I used to have this same conversation with my wife. And every time I'm around any of her people, even for the briefest periods—as I was here of late—I come away with all the same old arguments stirred up."

"Who's arguing?" Jim said. "You asked a question; I tried to answer it—but evidently not to your satisfaction."

"No, not to my satisfaction!" Rickett said. "What about hot Tang and hot cider? Hot lemonade, hot eggnog, hot julep? Even hot milk! Hot! Hot! Hot! Every kind of hot ingestible liquid known to mankind. So what in the world is so bad about coffee? Or tea, for Pete's sake! What could your Word of Wisdom possibly have against the lowly tea leaf?"

Jim shrugged. "I don't know what to tell you," he said, chewing toast. "Maybe you should write Salt Lake and protest. Tell them you're a lawyer. See if that carries any weight."

Rickett hardly heard him. "And it's not as if the coffee rule is consistently abided by," he said. "Down home in Luna, I knew one of your elders used to guzzle the stuff by the bucketful, and he didn't get kicked out of the Church for it; far as I know, he was never even reprimanded."

"It takes more than coffee drinking for that."

"Cigarettes?" Rickett asked, staring defiantly at the smoking specimen clamped between his fingers.

"Nope."

"Riotous living?"

"Maybe," Jim said, "if it's riotous *enough*."

"Like *how* riotous?"

"Wenching, whoredoms, felonies of one sort or another—embezzlement, extortion, treason, murder. That'd probably do it."

Rickett paused in his drinking of coffee, and Jim paused in his eating of toast. They regarded each other for a long time.

"And your mother wouldn't have liked any of that?"

Jim shook his head.

"To tell you the truth," Rickett said, "mine wouldn't have either."

Jim never got the chance to report on his winter labors.

At some point toward the end of breakfast, much cheered up, as always, by his airing of another grievance about the Mormon church, Rickett said, "Thanks to your late start last year"—which he seemed to suggest was Jim's fault—"we didn't get the ditches burned before we had to turn the water in. So," he announced, "we're going to make up for it this year."

An hour later, loaded with old tires taken from a supply behind the grain bin, the pickup pulled up at one end of a dry ditch. Pointing to banks thick with winter-killed grass and weeds, Rickett said, "Makes you wonder how any water made it through at all."

On this morning he was at his supervisory best. He directed Jim in the unloading of one of the tires, a big bald, truck-sized ten-ply—and in the making of a wire leash for that tire. "Better too long than too short," he stipulated. "You'll soon see why." Then he handed Jim a pitchfork and directed the piling of tumbleweeds. After the piling, Rickett stomped the dry, springy stalks and branches as flat as they could be stomped, then flipped his cigarette butt into the pile. At first nothing happened. But then the smallest of flames licked upward, and suddenly the weeds caught like a torch. Shielding his face with one arm, Rickett tossed the tire on top of the pile. "When I first witnessed this method of weed burning," he said above the crackle of flames, "I told Goss what he needed was a propane tank and torch wand like everybody else. Do you know what he said?"

Jim was pretty sure he knew the answer, but he shook his head anyway.

To be heard above the flames, Rickett had to speak with some volume. "He said, 'Torches and propane cost money; cast-offs from Bud's Texaco don't.'" Rickett smiled. "In some ways, posthumous acquaintance is more interesting than knowing people in the flesh."

For a moment they watched the tire atop the burning brush. Then Rickett said, "But I've decided the appeal was more than economic. If you've got the least little bit of pyromaniac in you, as most men do, you'll see what I mean."

Before long, the worn tread and sidewall were sweating smoke. After another few minutes, one small segment had caught. The flame crept both directions. When head met tail, it was a ring of fire. At first, the smoke billowing into the morning's crystal sky had looked like dirty fog. Now it was laced with black. Amid the shimmer of roaring flames, the stagnant rain water or snowmelt trapped inside the tire began to boil and give off a rubber-smelling steam. Crackling and snapping, the tire seemed to writhe. As its outer skin puckered and blistered, there was a sound of little balloons—some popping and others deflating with whooshes and burps and squeaks.

The tire was ready. Rickett handed Jim the leash and gave him the go-ahead: he was to step into the ditch's channel, tug the flaming ring down behind him, and, with a waist-high bank on either side—Go! Move! Don't look back.

The practicality of the method was soon apparent. The puller could hurry as fast as he could hurry. He didn't have to pause or wait even so long as it might have taken the main flame, erratically buffeted by the breeze, to touch off tumbleweeds or the winter-killed brome matting either bank. Because it wasn't the main flame that did most of the touching off. In proportion to the puller's speed, the blazing tire trailed gobbets of burning rubber, which then ignited whatever there was to be ignited. The fire spread. In no time, it consumed every bit of vegetation in the ditch and on the banks, burned it all right down to dirt.

But the method was not a light labor. Even in the best conditions, the burden at the end of the leash presented considerable resistance. And the best conditions were rare. The surface of the ditch floor was uneven, strewn with clods and clumps of sod, punctuated by sand bars and washes and bottlenecks. Often the tire snagged; just as often the puller stumbled. But especially when the wind whipped the tire flame in the direction of the pull, the motivation to keep moving was strong, and the virtue of the long leash did indeed become clear: it kept the puller one step ahead of singed nape hairs. With that one-step advantage, Jim dragged through narrows. He dragged through widths. He dragged through bends and straights. Occasionally, he dragged over streaks of unmelted snow, leaving burning gobbets to hiss and sizzle.

At last, panting and dry-mouthed, he came to an end culvert. On hands and knees, he climbed out of the ditch and stood up, slightly weak-kneed. Despite the morning's chill, he was sweating hard. A final jerk on the leash brought its much-reduced burden up and out as well. All that was left of the tire was its charred reinforcement wires and, clinging to them, one last chunk of burning rubber, about the size of a chuck roast.

And there, just beyond the licking, devouring flames, beyond the smoke and cinders, stood Rickett. Having driven the pickup from the ditch's other end, he held a second tire, already leashed. Without a word, he dropped it on the remains of the first. While the second tire caught fire, Rickett stepped across the culvert and pointed to the perimeter of the field of barley stubble. "Just follow the border," he yelled, tracing a loop in the air. "If you hustle, it should just take this one tire."

This one tire was soon ready. Outside the confines of a ditch, Jim could move faster, trailing a line of fire as he went. But he had a long way to go. He double-timed, then single-timed, then felt pretty accomplished to be doing any time at all. He pulled with his right arm, then with his left, then with both. There was no good way.

Spreading inward from the field's edge, the burning line became a swath, and the swath became a sector. Marked by a dense curtain of whitish smoke, the expansion was so rapid that even as Jim rounded the final bottom corner for the home stretch, the burned area exceeded the unburned. And not five minutes after he completed his circuit, back where he had dropped the first tire in the ditch, maybe forty minutes ago, the remaining unburned area of stubble was enveloped. Standing downwind from the white curtain, eyes smarting, trying to catch his breath, he watched the nucleus of stubble get smaller and smaller, until finally the great racing fire died as quickly as it had begun.

Rickett had moved the pickup again, had parked it away from anything burning or burnable, on the far side of the ditch. Again, just beyond the worst smoke and cinders, he stood waiting. This time he held a canvas water bag. Dragging the charred wire reinforcements of the second tire, Jim walked toward him. The field stretching below them was a scorched plain. Across its clean-burned expanse smoked a thousand chips. Beeswax would have looked on them with regret.

"Who needs a flame thrower, huh?" Rickett asked, offering the water bag.

"Or napalm," Jim said, gratefully accepting.

Since his first acquaintance with it during last summer's hay hauling, Jim had greatly admired the canvas water bag. He liked the smell of its soaked fibers, which cooled the water and, unlike the purification tablets dropped in canteens, gave it a pleasant flavor. He liked the neat aluminum collar and the cork stopper on its tiny chain tether. He liked the bail—a length of coarse, bristly rope passed at each end through a corner grommet and secured with a knot. Best of all, it didn't have to be carried on a utility belt, bouncing and chafing with every step.

When Jim had drunk his fill, he handed the bag to Rickett, in whom supervising always seemed to work up a mighty thirst. The old lawyer uptilted the bag and began to drink. With every swallow, his Adam's apple dipped. It dipped many times. As Jim had discovered last summer, the man had the stomach capacity of a Clydesdale. The overflow trickled from the corners of his mouth, cut little streaks through the residue of ash dust on his face.

At the pickup, Rickett hung the water bag on the side mirror, then sat down on the open tailgate. He waited for Jim to join him. Gazing toward Honey Spring, where a tire would also have to be dragged before the spring burning was finished, then gazing beyond the spring to the Vanderfisk half of the original property, he said, "Any interaction with your neighbors while I was gone?"

Jim's own gaze took in the cottonwood grove and the old fence. "Bernene doesn't like the cattle guard."

"I imagine she told you this one Sunday at church," Rickett said, "after a sermon on loving your neighbor."

"As a matter of fact, she invited me to their house for another little meeting."

The news worried Rickett. "Was Enoch there?"

"No."

"Big Frett?"

Jim nodded. "But only for moral support. He didn't say much."

"Did she make threats or what?" Rickett asked.

"Not really," Jim said. "She's just worried about trespassers on my side crossing over to her side."

"That's a lady with too much time on her hands," Rickett said. "If you can prove the trespasser is trespassing on both pieces of property, neither neighbor is liable—at least not in any state that I'm aware of. Did you tell her that?"

Jim shook his head. "Maybe she's worried about Beeswax."

Rickett glanced at him sharply. "Did *he* come around?"

"About a month ago."

"I should've warned you about him," Rickett said. "In light of Goss's death, I was hoping he'd found another source for his cow chips, had maybe moved to Alaska or Siberia."

"Does he have a real name?"

"A real surname, yes. Jones. That's all I know."

"That seems normal enough. Why'd he pick *Beeswax*?"

"I don't know that he picked it," Rickett said. "More like it evolved. But he doesn't seem to mind. He keeps hives on a dozen farms, I'd say—including this one. They're down there in the west corner, right at the bluff."

"He told me about them."

"Did he tell you about the five gallons of honey he brought Goss every year for a rental fee. That was part of their deal."

"No," Jim said. "He never mentioned that."

"Figures."

"Was their deal really wandering rights in perpetuity?"

"Is *that* what he claims?" Rickett asked, chuckling.

Jim nodded.

"I know Goss let him come on the place pretty regularly," Rickett said, "and even gave him a key to the gate lock. But perpetuity is a bit of a stretch."

"Would *he* worry Bernene?"

"He's a weirdo, no two ways about it," Rickett said. "But harmless. If his cow chipping and honey tending should bother anybody, it's you. *She* has no need to worry about him."

"But let's say, with my generous new attitude, I let somebody else come on the place and he *does* cross onto the Vanderfisk side and turns out *not* to be so harmless. Would she have a case against me?"

If Rickett had had a reassuring answer, he would have offered it.

Jim looked across the smoking field. By and by, he asked, "Are there really poachers and rustlers around here?"

"I suppose," Rickett said. "But I don't see how your cattle guard increases Vanderfisk vulnerability to either one. If somebody is bent on shooting a deer out of season or stealing a cow, a chain and padlock isn't going to stop him."

"That's what I was trying to get at with her."

"But you didn't sign anything?" Rickett asked.

"No," Jim said. Then, after a pause, he said, "But to be fair, she didn't ask me to."

"To be *fair*?" Rickett said. "You think it was fair of her to invite you over just to browbeat you about something that's none of her business?"

"I wouldn't call it 'browbeat.'"

"Okay—politely pressure and intimidate." Rickett waited for a response. When there wasn't any, he said, "Was there anybody else there? Did anybody else hear what was said?"

Jim thought of Jocelyn Vanderfisk. He remembered her face in the parlor doorway and in the upper window. He nodded.

"Who?"

"It's still way below freezing at night. You sure you didn't come back too soon from Luna Valley?"

"Nice try," Rickett said. Then he asked again, "Who else was there?"

It was odd to admit, but disclosing Jocelyn Vanderfisk to Rickett felt more confessional than anything said in Bishop Sebright's office. But after a moment's hesitation, Jim came out with it: "Bernene's got a niece from Bear Lake staying with them."

"Single?"

"I guess."

"I'd guess that's more than a guess," Rickett said. "And Bernene invited you over with her there? Doesn't that seem a little more than coincidental?"

"It wasn't anything like that," Jim said. "The niece came home in the middle of the meeting. Bernene didn't even introduce us. I'm not somebody she wants in their life any more than I already am."

Rickett studied him. "Are you interested in her?"

"Bernene?"

"The niece, wise guy!"

"I haven't said one word to her."

"That's not a no."

The day had warmed. The sun shone down on Honey Spring with such brightness and clarity that the view was hard to drink in without a kind of breathlessness. Already birds were alighting in the cooler sections of the burned-off field, feeding on something exposed or drawn out by the fire—worms, grubs, dung beetles. From off toward the orchard came the song of a meadowlark.

"If noticing the only girl your age in a room, standing ten feet from you, is interest," Jim said, "then okay, I'm guilty. It's not like there's a whole lot to pick from around here."

"Is this niece interested in you?"

"No-o," Jim said with a sound almost like a snort.

"That's a pistol-pat answer," Rickett said. "You sure?"

"I'm sure."

"Bernene may not consider you suitor material right now—"

"Thanks a lot."

"—but if she decides such a relationship would in any way be to their advantage, you can bet she will exploit it." The old lawyer drummed his fingers on the edge of the tailgate. "That's how they got their youngest daughter married off, you know. The one with the comic-book name I can never remember." The old lawyer rubbed his forehead as if the action could aid recall. "Patty Dew!" he exclaimed suddenly. "Patty Dew! What is it about that name? I always want to say Patty Cake, Patty Pie, Patty Muffin. But it's Patty Dew—Patty Dew—Patty Dew." Now the rubbing of the forehead seemed to suggest that the name could be massaged into memory. "Who gives a kid a name like that?" He shook his head, baffled. "Anyway," he went on, "this Patty Dew turned up pregnant. Then jilted. In that order. At that point, most parents in such a predicament admit defeat, circle the wagons, try to make the best of it. Not the Maxwells. They go out and *recruit* a husband, had her engaged in no time."

For a moment Rickett gazed over the smoldering field.

"The truth is," he continued, "I felt for old Winn. Folks sort of thought the Maxwells were scraping the bottom of the barrel with him, a reaction I know well. I encountered a version of it myself in the good Saints of Luna Valley when my wife scandalized them by marrying outside the faith." The finger drumming stopped, and Rickett grew quiet and defiant. "The difference is, my wife—as chaste a girl as ever walked the earth, I want you to know, one who brooked absolutely no hanky-panky before marriage—the difference is *she* could have had anybody she wanted. The Maxwells, by contrast, were in no position to be picky." After a few moments, defiance gave way to reflective humor. "Anyway, that's how Patty Dew Maxwell was spared the worst of her condition's reproach and how Wild Winn—who knew a thing or two himself about riotous living, by the way—suddenly got himself a wife."

"You're talking about Winn and Patty Bingham?"

"None other," Rickett said. "The happy couple who make their home not five miles from where we're sitting right here."

"I've heard he farms six hundred acres."

"He does now. So how do you think a dissolute bachelor who could hardly manage his widow mother's garden patch ends up, just nine years later, with six hundred acres and enough crew and machinery to work it all?" When Jim didn't respond, Rickett said, "Dowry, son! Courtesy of Big Frett Maxwell. Only dowry in this case was just another name for out-and-out bribery." Rickett waited as if to gauge whether the intended lesson had sunk in. Finally he said, "So beware of supper invitations. Next thing you know, Big Frett will be calling you Theron, and Bernene will be calling you nephew-in-law."

Jim was quiet for several seconds. Thinking what he was thinking, after the recounting of such a history, he felt slightly disloyal toward both Goss and Rickett to ask, "Do you really think Bernene's as bad as we're making her out to be?"

Rickett was hunting a cigarette. To reach the pocket of the Hawaiian shirt, he had to get through a coat and jacket. "I knew families like the Vanderfisks down in Luna," he said as he dug and fished. "High and mighty, always buying their way out of trouble."

"But can you *blame* Bernene for looking out for her daughter? Or for her younger sister, who was in the same situation? Or for her niece?"

Rickett cocked an eyebrow and said, "Did you do something besides feed cattle while I was gone?"

"Very funny," Jim said. "What I mean is a niece with no father."

"First rule of biology and paternity cases, Jim," Rickett said, managing finally to get a hold of a cigarette, "there's *always* a father."

"Not one who married her mother. I saw the family record."

"You don't say," Rickett said with an air of triumph. "Enoch must not have had Big Frett's stomach for bribery."

"However it happened," Jim said, "it wasn't *all* the younger's sister's fault."

"What did I just say?" Rickett asked. "Even when a girl from a high and mighty family jumps track, she doesn't do it alone. But the second rule of biology is just as immutable as the first: if the father is a bum, the girl is left holding the bag. For her and her family—if the family cares at all—there's no running from it."

"So Bernene cares," Jim said. "Sister Cottrell's history says she's a very doting aunt. She's not using her niece to scheme her way into Honey Spring. I know it's not easy for either of us to admit," he said, "but Bernene has a good side."

For several moments, Rickett sat on the tailgate holding the hard-won cigarette unlit. He log-rolled it between his palms; he wind-milled it; he balanced it upright on the back of his hand as if playing mumblety-peg.

At last he said, "Your charity does you credit, Jim Ray. But it's not people's good side I dealt with in court for forty years."

CHAPTER 10

D IG THE IRRIGATION CANAL, BUFFALO BILL CODY HAD advised the settlers early in the new century, and the road will take care of itself. That prediction proved only partially true. When, by means of teams and slips and Buck scrapers, the canal was gophering its way across the shimmering sagebrush plain, the "road" hugging its south bank was nothing more than a rut-ted access track. And for a long time it stayed that way. Only in 1916 was that track finally grubbed and graded. By then Balford and Ralston and Garland had all sprung up, with homesteads in between. And by then Goss Harvey had gotten married. Only in 1916 were the road's sinks and holes filled with whole rock and its surface spread with crushed rock.

When Goss learned one night at supper that much of that rock was coming from the face of the bluff on the other side of Honey Spring—the side he had originally owned—and that that rock was bringing in regular cash payments, his shock lasted only for a minute before it gave way to amused irony. He leaned close to his only child, a little boy with straw-blond hair. With clowning face and exaggerated voice, he asked, "Who'd a thought there'd be money in *rocks*?" And he was mostly happy for Enoch, who was already thriving as a businessman and, with the sale of this one resource, would thrive even more. "He deserves it," Goss could still say. "It never seemed quite right that I got the better grass and soil."

Who could have predicted where that canal road would lead? In 1936, in the bottom of the Depression, that same road was one of the few that came in for paving—the whole thirty miles of it between Balford and Cody. Paving required a roadbed, for which there was no better material on earth than gray gravel. Given the convenient location of Enoch's property, between the two towns, the Vanderfisk pit could supply the project for many miles in each direction—east toward the Bighorns, west toward Yellowstone—and would again secure steady government payments. Thus, at a time when nobody else had two dimes to rub together, Enoch Vanderfisk had a great many.

This time, when Goss Harvey learned of his old friend's good fortune, he could muster no well-wishing. He was almost fifty-seven. With the loss of his straw-blond son during the flu epidemic of 1918 and the loss of his wife not even ten years later, he had suffered profound grief and loneliness. And for three decades, he had *not* thrived as a farmer. He had tilled and tended and threshed, without ever making more than a bare living from his labor. Truly he had eaten the dust from the west side of Honey Spring. Now he had to eat the dust from the east side as well. Over in the Vanderfisk gravel pit, diggers and crushers and loaders kept the air filled with it. As he irrigated or hoed or mowed, Goss had to watch truck after loaded truck crawl onto the new roadbed and roar past to go dump rock worth more than his barley and beans. The irony was hard to bear. For the first time, Goss was heard to say, "I sure enough got the short end of that stick."

In the spring of 1958, Wyoming's governor attended the Rocky Mountain Governors Conference. The guest list included his counterparts from the six other states that actually encompassed portions of the Rocky Mountains, plus Kansas and Nevada. Kansas made it on the list because *its* governor was a personal friend of the president of one of the oil companies sponsoring the gathering; and Nevada, because the conference's host city was Las Vegas.

The theme of the conference was tourism. So, when they weren't enjoying the hospitality of their host city, the governors served as the choir for a great deal of preaching. To wit: Tourism was the sleeper resource, the unsung potential, the latent asset. Tourism required no drilling or pumping or digging or transporting. Tourism sat in plain view. Tourism turned a profit on God's most splendid and conspicuous handiwork—snow-capped mountains, pristine lakes and rivers, clean air and stunning vistas. Tourism would command an ever bigger piece of their business pie. Tourism would lead them into the twenty-first century. Tourism! Tourism! Rah! Rah! Rah!

The only downside of tourism as the theme of such an affair was that, unlike charity, it *was* inclined to vaunt itself; it *was* a bit puffed up; it *did* envy. Though Wyoming's governor would have been loath to admit this downside, he was that downside's embodiment. Despite his outward good cheer and geniality, he was racked inwardly by competitiveness and rivalry. To wit: Wyoming's splendid and conspicuous handiwork in the form of Yellowstone and the Tetons *had* to be more of an attraction than bat caverns in New Mexico. And certainly his state's assets could hold their own against Utah's rock arches or those moon craters over by Arco, Idaho, or even Glacier National Park up in Montana. But outshining Colorado and Arizona was another matter. With the Tetons and Yellowstone all but shuttered from October to May, it was hard not to begrudge the winter enticement of world-renowned ski slopes or the year-round draw of the Grand Canyon.

A day or so after his return to Cheyenne, the governor sat in his office staring at the big map of his state framed on the wall behind his desk. As he stared, he pondered. And by and by his pondering led him to concur, albeit reluctantly, with his counterpart from New Mexico. This counterpart had hogged the conference spotlight early on by donning a ridiculous pointy-eared mask and saying, "Just call me Batman, gentlemen!" With that, Batman had reported (with galling certitude) a plan to compensate for *his* state's winter lull in tourism by taking fuller advantage of the summer boom. Then came the smug announcement, cleverly timed, that the plan was already well underway—that very season, that very moment—in the form of a vigorous campaign to *double* the number of visitors to . . . the Carlsbad Caverns.

Carlsbad? Carlsbad was Batman's ace in the hole? His crown jewel? If caves full of guano could be hoked up to pull in more tourism, there was no telling what could be done with an *obvious* above-ground splendor like Old Faithful. Get the tourists that far, and they'd find themselves a mere hop and a skip from the Grand Tetons. And those coming from the east—which would be the lion's share of them—would come spending money all along the way, in places like Casper, Gillette, Sheridan.

And Cody. As the Park's gateway town, it was the linchpin to any plan to increase summer tourism. Any place named after Buffalo Bill was obliged to become *the* model Old West tourist town. Forget Batman's boasts about Santa Fe and Tucumcari. Forget other governors' lauding of Cave Creek and Coeur d'Alene and Kalispell. Forget Elko, Reno, Durango. In fact, forget Dodge City. As an Old West theme town, Cody would surpass maybe even Cheyenne itself. It had all the makings for the makings. Several city blocks given over to approximating a remote and dusty main street from the Old West era—hitching posts, clapboard facades, plank sidewalks, saloon doors, Boot Hill on an ominous rise in the distance. Jackson Hole had beat Cody to a wild west *Arc de Triomphe* fashioned from elk antlers, but Cody would compensate. Fast-draw reenactments at high noon. Muzzle-loader marksmanship contests. Daily chuck wagon.

Nightly rodeo. Hourly frontier history lectures from a Buffalo Bill look-alike holding forth on a prominent main-street balcony. Stagecoach tours departing at half-hour intervals from old-west Cody to travel a loop through new-west Cody, the half-asleep horses clopping amid hordes of pedestrians and bumper-to-bumper motor traffic. The town's intersections and side lots would feature the tallest teepees, the longest Conestogas, the biggest stuffed grizzlies. Its souvenir shops would outsell all others—more shot glasses and paperweights and penknives and headdresses and fringed buckskin and moccasins and plastic tomahawks and turquoise jewelry. Its dinner clubs would serve buffalo steaks thick as two-by-fours. Cody would be a tourist town on a hill!

Yet even as he dreamed of northwest Wyoming becoming the West's premier tourist destination of the second half of the twentieth century, the governor realized that, without a proper, modern road by which to get to that destination, its charms would remain under a bushel. If station wagons and Airstreams and cab-over campers and motorcycles were to materialize in numbers commensurate with his dream, they would have to materialize on a bigger and better highway.

The most important segment of the bigger and better highway would run right through the heart of the Bighorn Basin. Even for a town like Balford, which was not highlighted on the governor's map, the new highway promised to be a boon. With the widening and elevating of the roadbed well underway in the early 1960s, with the day-and-night movement of gravel trucks, the economic faith behind that promise—more traffic, more customers—inspired the refurbishing of several businesses along Balford's main thoroughfare.

No one had coupled that faith with more good works than the owner of the A&W drive-in at the west end of town. In phase one of *his* refurbishing project, he had enlarged his lot on the back-alley side so as to close the circle of canopied car stalls around the restaurant hub. Phase two was the remodeling of the hub itself. Since the remodeling couldn't increase the size of a building now enclosed by car stalls, it had to increase productivity and efficiency. That challenge required a careful study of the work of carhops. To speed up the movement of loaded food trays from hub to stall, the owner had to eliminate bottlenecking at the point of supply.

His solution? Refined coordination. In practical terms, such refinement mostly meant carhops and kitchen workers had to be able to *see* each other. That requirement meant, literally, more transparency, which in turn required, in the restaurant's outer wall, a great deal more glass. And to serve the greatest number of possible carhop routes, that glass was fitted all around with closely spaced wickets and slots, and several Dutch doors—all of which were supported, inside and out, by a cunning network of counters and nooks and chutes.

Though the refurbishing of the drive-in necessarily concentrated on customers in vehicles, it had also made generous provision for walk-ups. A vehicle that couldn't find an open stall, as during lunch rush, could still park comfortably out of the way on the expanded and newly paved lot, and order at either of two ample new customer windows, front or back. Then, order filled, the walk-up customer could go happily on his way or stay and eat at one of several picnic tables conveniently positioned between the car stalls and the building.

Impressive as they were, these improvements did not, in the ensuing years, bring in *quite* the hoped-for bounty of business from tourists hurrying on to Cody. Nor did they take into account the one detail that came to matter to Jim Ray: despite all the glass, a carhop—or customer—approaching the building on the street side could not see, for the kitchen furnishings, anything or anybody on the alley side. And it was the street side that Jim approached during noon hour of a warm day in April, on his first anniversary of not returning from war in a box.

Not that coming into town for hamburgers and rootbeer in any way marked that anniversary. What it marked was one of Nolan Rickett's dietary whims. After supervising the planting of barley all morning, the old lawyer had handed Jim a ten-dollar bill and said, "No offense, but I'm tired of your cooking." To which Jim had replied, "You're free to take over anytime." To which Rickett had counter-replied, "I'm tired of mine, too."

The place was busy. Waiting for his order, Jim sat at the only unoccupied picnic table. That particular table was situated next to a counter bearing squeeze-bottles of ketchup and mustard, along with a dispenser for drinking-straws and another for napkins. Radio music drifted from somewhere. Through the many wickets and slots came good grill and fryer smells.

In a strange twist of association, those smells evoked memories of remembering *them*. "Now take your hamburger," Fritchey had said very philosophically during chow one evening on their very first week of patrol. "I got nothing against it a-tall. Nice juicy beef meat, pickles, onions, maybe a slab of cheese—what's not to like?" But then he made the mistake of qualifying his endorsement: "But if I had my *druthers*, is all I'm saying, I would have to choose my ma's corn bread with pintos." Inspired by C-ration fare, most food dreams one-upped each other for extravagance. So Fritchey's had met with a chorus of chaffing. *Come on, Frit-chee! Pin-tos? For real? Why not some nice possum pie or fritters and hogback?* And Fritchey—uncowed, unperturbed, unswayed in his defense of the mighty legume—smiled, shrugged, said, "Just saying."

Now, too late, Jim wished he had opened his mouth and sided with Fritchey in his endorsement of pinto beans. If only out of loyalty to the underdog. If only to level the playing field. If only to make a fair fight. But there was nothing fair about any of it and no way to make it so. Pea Ridge, Arkansas, had given the war a good boy.

The girl at the customer window handed out Jim's order—one sack of hamburgers and french fries, another holding a cylindrical carton of soft-serve ice cream, and a gallon jug of root beer. Then she pointed to the napkin dispenser on the closest counter. Because of the rush, she explained apologetically, she hadn't had a chance to restock, so he would have to try the dispenser on the other side of the building.

On the other side of the building Jim saw, notwithstanding all the glass and transparency, what he otherwise would not have seen. Three of the restaurant's new stalls held big Harley-Davidson motorcycles. The gas tank on the one closest bore a shiny decal. *Make Love, Not War.* The three riders weren't locals. Headbands, sleeveless denim jackets, harness boots. Two had hair below their shoulders. The other had shaved his head, wore a knotted bandanna over his scalp, like a pirate. They sat at the closest picnic table, their backs to Jim. Across from them sat two girls. Between the riders and girls, in the center of the table, stood a transistor radio on high volume, surrounded by rootbeer mugs, a litter of food wrappers, and a lot of napkins. And at the counter by the customer window stood the third girl fetching more. After taking the last the dispenser offered, she turned.

It was Jocelyn Vanderfisk.

This time, amid the good smells of Balford's refurbished A&W, she waved first. And her wave was accompanied by the most amiable of smiles. For her ride on the pillion behind one of the bikers—whichever one he was—she wore a cotton jacket over a light blouse. Jim couldn't help wondering: how many rides and how far?

All this happened in two wordless seconds. Then, perceiving Jim's interest in the empty dispenser, Jocelyn Vanderfisk said,

"I'm so sorry," divided her handful of napkins, and offered half to him. "Will that be enough?" she asked.

Oh yes, oh yes, oh yes.

The last water channel burned back in March was Honey Spring itself. The job had required two tires. The first one lasted from the orchard pond to a point just about even with the slab gate in the farmyard fence. The second went from there, past the single-wide (protected by a margin of ground bare of all but the sparsest growth) and on down the notch in the bluff, all the way to riverbottom swamp. Far from being destructive of plant life, the burning of those banks—and all the others—had stimulated new growth, particularly the growth of wild asparagus. And asparagus, as Jim discovered in late April, enticed all sorts of people to cross the cattle guard uninvited.

There was, for instance, the insurance salesman with a mostly empty paper grocery bag and a necktie whose color pattern borrowed from the coral snake. When Jim refused a guilt offering of half the meager pickings (which would have amounted to about four spears), the guy tried to sell him a term-life policy. "Are you married?" the salesman asked, nervously running the tie between his thumb and forefinger (red touch yellow, kill a fellow), "or maybe expecting a first child?" Without waiting for an answer, he said, with a hint a desperation in his voice, "Even if you're only *thinking* about marriage—and it's never too early for that, you know—you'd do well to have some coverage." As they parted, the man was still playing with his coral-snake tie, still talking. His selling had turned to cadging. "Even as a bachelor, you don't want to take any chances," he shouted over his shoulder. "You never know what's going to happen."

And there was the 4-H advisor with very bright eyes and a big plastic bowl. She wanted her chapter's annual spaghetti supper to feed the mind as well as the body. But did she realize, Jim asked, that the asparagus on her menu for the feeding of the body was growing on private land? The 4-H lady's bright eyes blinked, but she ignored the question. Then she asked if he didn't think it downright embarrassing that today's young people didn't know the science behind their food. She laughed. They probably thought every item on their supper menu *grew* on grocery store shelves. She wanted to change that. She wanted the youth in her charge to know that pasta contained wheat and where that wheat was grown and milled, that the sauce *on* that pasta came from real tomatoes, and the meatballs from real cattle.

She said, "Envision this." Then she described a buffet table arrangement that, for one meal at least, would remedy ignorance of food origins. "In front of every dish on the serving table," she declared with precise finger gestures, "I'll have a little tent-card placard: *From the plains of eastern Colorado, semolina pasta flour made from the venerable 'Triticum durum.'*" She pronounced the Latin term with a special flourish. "Or this," she said: "*From pastures closer to home, beef of the grass-fed 'Bos taurus.'*" Then she pointed to the contents of her bowl. "Now envision this: Just down the table, before the desserts, will sit a chafing dish full of *'Asparagus officinalis.'* Of everything on the menu, people will feel the most loyalty to this because the tent-card will say, *From our own Honey Spring.*"

For other uninvited crossers of the cattle guard, asparagus was a secondary interest, a bonus on top of whatever else they had come to help themselves to. One fine Saturday, beneath the boughs of a giant sagebrush, Jim discovered a hardy husband and wife, kneeling and digging with hand spades. They were biology teachers at Cody Community College, hired as a pair when the school opened just a few years earlier. One of their favorite hobbies, they said, was fossil hunting. Yet their specimen pail was heaped, not with the petrified snails and clams they claimed to be looking for, but with asparagus officinalis. On their way to this spot in the sagebrush forest, they had crossed several ditches and had espied tender shoots *everywhere*. No sense letting such bounty go to waste, they said. When Jim ventured a polite challenge to that wearisome justification, they didn't want to talk about asparagus anymore. They wanted, instead, to explain the geology of Honey Spring. Ten or twenty billion years ago, the couple estimated with great authority, this land was all prehistoric ocean floor. "There's evidence of all kinds of marine life just waiting to be discovered," the husband said, "if you're willing to dig beneath the surface."

And finally, among those who helped themselves to Honey Spring's abundant asparagus officinalis, there was Beeswax Jones.

CHAPTER 11

EESWAX JONES'S SECONDARY INTEREST IN ASPARAGUS officinalis emerged on a cold afternoon, the first day of May of 1967, nine weeks after his primary interest in cow chips. But at dawn on that day in May, when, except for an unusually chilly breeze from the north, the weather portended nothing of what was to come, Beeswax's primary interest had lain in fishing the river below Goss Harvey's bluff. Like the gathering of chips and tending of bee supers, fishing evidently fell under his claim of perpetual access to the property.

Even if the claim weren't so dubious, Beeswax's manner of invoking it would have been annoying. For one thing, he didn't bother with even the most minimal protocol in the relationship between visitor and host: no driving into the farmyard to make his presence known, no greeting, no *divulging* of his primary or secondary interest on any given day. Instead of coming into the heart of the property by way of the main lane along Honey Spring, he kept to irrigating roads and seldom-used tracks and parked his weird sheep wagon pickup in the most remote and secluded spots on the property. Jim couldn't decide whether that habit was furtive or presumptuous, or which was more irksome.

The most remote and secluded spot of all lay on the far side of the sagebrush forest, where the bluff fence intersected the property's western boundary fence. One reason for parking there was obvious: that was the corner where his dozen bee boxes stood. But the other reason was not so obvious. That was also the corner closest to the one other way on Goss's place, besides the Honey Spring notch, to traverse the bluff from rim to base. Just across the bluff fence, hidden between two Russian olives, was the top end of what Rickett called the gopher trail. But it could also conduct a deer—or a daring man—down a sheer and seemingly impassable bluff face to a slow bend in the river.

But why risk the steepness and narrowness of the gopher trail when the notch was, by comparison, so much easier to get to and to get up and down? Maybe because the gopher trail posed some sort of wilderness-man challenge. Or because using that trail suggested a proprietary knowledge of one of the property's secrets. Or because getting down the bluff by way of the notch would require driving into the farmyard and being *seen*, which might, in turn, require human interaction from a man whose booming voice and fund of ready lectures on many subjects belied an aversion to such interaction. Maybe the preference for the gopher trail could be attributed to its convenience and nothing more. Its bottom came out within casting distance of deep river pools full of brown trout. On almost any spring morning— besides the first day of May, as it turned out—those trout would bite on any bait offered.

May first, a Monday, happened also to be the day Jim had set aside for branding calves. At a little before six-thirty on that morning, the sky over the Bighorns, lit by the rising sun, was splendid. Save for that chilly breeze from the north, the day promised fair weather.

Rickett was in fine fettle. "It'll be just like December," he said, drinking coffee from his thermos. "One guy showed up—*one guy*, Jim!—out of how many sitting there in Sunday elders quorum lesson blowing hot air about helping their neighbor?"

What Rickett forgot to mention was that, back in December, nobody at church *knew* about the off-season branding plan. Jim hadn't told anybody. Nor, in his complaint five months after the fact, did Rickett mention that the "one guy" happened to be the source of the Thanksgiving-dinner invitation he had spurned. Yet somehow, a few weeks after that dinner, that one guy, Bishop Clive Sebright, on another early morning, had just happened to drop what he was doing and pay a visit to the single-wide. That visit cost him a two-day ordeal helping an old man and a young man do what they would have had a hard time doing without him. The old man knew law, and the young one knew guard-rail construction and war, but neither knew branding. Like most people, Rickett practiced a selective amnesia. He could call to mind obscure legal precedents dating back scores of years but could not recall the exact number of church helpers dating back five months. On the second day of the December branding, the bishop had brought along his brother Roy, who, despite such short mid-week notice, stayed almost as long as the bishop, who stayed until the job was finished.

Back in December, the calves were resistant, as calves in such a circumstance usually are. But back in December, they were over-grown as well. It was a bad combination. For his trouble, Clive Sebright got kicked and bunted and stepped on and bled on and crapped on more than either of the two men actually affiliated with the long overdue project. When, at the end of the second day, they finally loosed the last newly minted steer in the chill of the fast-falling winter dusk, the bishop sighed with fatigue, then wiped his pocket-knife blade on his pants and folded it into the handle. "Next time, fellas," he said with astonishing good humor, "would you be against lining up a little more help?"

That subtle admonition didn't come up in Rickett's recollec-tions, either. Early on a morning five months after the off-season branding, what most occupied the old lawyer's mind was, as usual, his sentiment against Mormons—or Latter-day Saints, as he preferred to call them, with mock emphasis on the word *saints.* Only Goss Harvey could have boasted a more impressive grudge. But Goss was dead. Among the living, Tom Criswall, who still used every grocery store or post office encounter to try to rescue Jim from the perils of his faith, might rival Rickett for vehemence, but not for credibility. Thanks to a long marriage to a good woman of that faith and a long acquaintance with that good woman's huge family, not to mention all the other intermarried, interrelated folks in Luna Valley, Rickett *knew* Latter-day Saints. He was drilled in their beliefs, tutored in their exhortations and prohibitions, steeped in their pieties. At the same time, he was well acquainted with their quirks and shortcomings and out-and-out faults—and thus knew just how *un*saintly they could be.

But such intimate knowledge worked as much against grudge-holding as for it. Just about the time Rickett thought he had discovered, in Balford, the world's second richest mother lode of Latter-day Saint sanctimony—the first being Luna Valley—the purity of the vein was marred by this or that unbidden kindness, by compassion or generosity, by some genuine goodness associated with the faith.

Such was the marring at six-thirty on branding day. Rickett was only halfway through a soft rant about the foolish futility of the bishop's call for volunteers when the first volunteer's pickup rolled through the open slab gate, past the grain bin and welding shed, and pulled up next to the single-wide. That's when they learned that Bishop Sebright, gone to Oregon for a cousin-in-law's funeral, had enlisted another of his own brothers to help in his stead. This one was named Darl. When, less than five minutes later, Rowe Sloan's pickup pulled up, Rickett could only reiterate his reaction to his foiled prediction. "Well, I'll be double-damned," he muttered.

And there was a triple damning yet to come. At the arrival of the third pickup, coughing and gurgling from a missing muffler, Rickett's grudge-nurturing was spoiled for the rest of the day and maybe forever. This pickup was every bit as old as Goss's, and surely burned more oil. In the brief moments between the stopping and the shutting off of the engine, it became wreathed in blue smoke. Its tires were smooth as balloons, its fenders dented and rusted. With a vehicle like that, setting out for any destination was a leap of faith. Yet its driver, in response to an invitation made just yesterday in priesthood class, had made that leap to come and help with the branding of calves whose owner he had never actually conversed with.

"Penroy, I think, is his name," Jim whispered in response to Rickett's question.

"A year you've been riding the same pews with a man who's come to help you with your calves," Rickett muttered, "and you don't know him any better than *that*."

"I *know* him," Jim said, still whispering. "I see him every Sunday. I just can't keep all the names straight."

"Well, you ought to keep *his* straight," Rickett said in a strange and sudden reversal from skeptic to supporter. "Branding goes above and beyond the call of Sunday brotherhood, you know."

The third man's name *was* Penroy—Crue Penroy, short for Crufford. Whatever brass and cymbal Nolan Rickett looked for in Mormons, he probably could have found somewhere in Sunday priesthood class. But he would have had a hard time finding it in a guy like Crue Penroy. When the Monday morning branding party was announced, Brother Crue was the first to raise his hand. Unlike the majority of his quorum mates, he was not going to be out of town or on the road or vitally and indispensably busy elsewhere. And unlike those who said maybe, possibly, if the planets aligned, he attached not a single qualification to his pledge. Less than twenty-four hours later, he got in his junk bucket of a truck and, at the appointed time, showed up.

As if they resented their function, the hinges of that truck's driver-side door creaked loudly in the morning stillness, and, in closing, repeated the protest. It took two hard slams to make the latch do its job.

"I've got a can of spray lube," yelled Rowe Sloan, standing next to the trailer's stoop, where he and the others had congregated.

"Nah," said Crue Penroy, moseying toward the group, "the only thing would fix that door is a blowtorch, and I've half a mind to use it."

He had made his greetings all around when the hinges of the truck's other door announced their want of lubrication. Crue hadn't said anything to suggest the company of a passenger. And for a moment, there was no other movement to suggest it, either. Then out slid that passenger, hair uncombed, shirt untucked, belt unbuckled.

"That's his boy," Jim whispered to Rickett.

Hewell Penroy was thirteen years old. Still puffy from sleep, his eyes took no interest in his surroundings. Vaguely leaning and swaying at the waist, nodding and flopping at the neck, he seemed hardly able to stand upright, let alone walk, as if his spine yearned for the mattress and pillow too soon left behind. He pulled on a sweater, then shuffled forward. His jeans were patched at the knees, and his socks showed through toe holes in his untied work boots. Clutched in one hand was a half-eaten jam and butter sandwich.

"Stand up straight, son," Crue said gently as the boy approached, "and make yourself ready. There's work waiting."

In the rough circle of men gathered at the stoop, Crue and the boy stood across from Rickett. Rickett kept looking from father to son, from son to father. As he looked, his face showed a curious admiration. Crue Penroy was fifty-six years old, but he could have passed for seventy. He was stooped and stiff. The hair left to him was gray. His scalp and face and neck were lined from sun and windburn. Besides a significant portion of nasal septum, he was missing a top molar, a bottom incisor, and a third of one index finger. Surgery had excised the gall bladder he was born with and, a few years later, a thyroid cyst he wasn't born with. "Big as a plum," the doctor had said. "No telling how long that thing's been growing on your gullet."

And Crue Penroy bore other scars. Like Goss, he had never more than eked out a living on his rocky acreage over on Willwood. Over the years, frost and hail and wind had conspired, again and again, to thwart the dream of a bountiful harvest. To ballast that dream, his wife Edrus had long ago resigned herself to disappointment. Such a reaction was well developed from other disappointments in her life, the biggest of which had to do with the puzzling intervals at which their children had come into the world. In the first three years of marriage, Crue had begotten two daughters. Then, despite the couple's prayerful and resolute efforts, twenty years passed before the begetting of their son. From certain intimations, associated with his wife's long-suffering forbearance, Crue had always felt—without a shred of medical evidence—that the blame for this particular disappointment had been assigned to him.

Anybody who didn't know better would have naturally assumed Crue was the boy's grandfather. And knowing better only made Rickett stare harder. Standing next to the man who, in fact, wasn't his grandfather, young Hewell took a big bite of his jam and butter sandwich. Despite the age difference, the likeness in expression and posture and manner was uncanny. Rickett couldn't take his eyes off the pair. Finally, with an unpracticed softening of tone, he asked, "Is school already out for the summer?"

The question was intended for Hewell, but his father innocently missed the cue. "*Heck* no!" said Crue Penroy with a laugh. "There's three weeks left. But all's they do this close to vacation is kill time with picnics and parties." He tousled his son's unruly hair, patted his shoulder. "I can't say as I blame the teachers for that, but it's not the same as doing class. I figure old Hewell here will learn a whole lot more from a day of branding with men he's used to seeing in their Sunday best." He looked at the familiar faces around the stoop and said, "So, brethren, don't disappoint me by being *too* mannerly when the calves get ringy, will you?"

They all laughed. Then Darl Sebright said, "I think this is all of us, Jim. We'll go where you point us."

"I guess this way, then," Jim said. With that, he leaned away from the stoop and started toward the corrals. His first steps were slow, to give young Hewell a chance to tie and tuck and buckle.

When the boy stuck the last bite of the jam and butter sand-wich in his mouth so as to free his hands, Rickett's eyes actually welled. It was hard to tell if nostalgia was all he felt when he leaned close to Jim and said, "The first time I helped a branding crew down in Luna Valley, I was no older than that kid."

Then the group was moving at a diagonal across the yard, a direction that took them toward the bluff. "I sure appreciate you all coming," Jim said as he walked. Then he shivered, drew the hood of his sweatshirt around his head. "Is this chilly for May?"

"A little maybe," Rowe said.

"I've seen it snow every month of the year hereabouts," said Crue Penroy with a native's proud and rueful wisdom.

Whatever Rickett had felt in directing his first question to the boy, he was still feeling when he tried a second: "So, Hewell—do you expect there's going to be much vacation in *your* summer?"

Hewell smiled around the sandwich in his mouth. Like the other two church men, his father was a farmer, which was answer enough.

Jim's route led the crew around the cluster of pens and barns, beyond the segment of perimeter fence that hugged the lip of the bluff. That segment constituted one side of a long enclosure bisected to make the two biggest pens, both wainscotted with pews. In one pen, thirty calves milled and bawled; in the other, their mothers did the same.

In this carved-out corner of the sagebrush forest, Goss Harvey had located his corrals here, as close as possible to the bluff, as an economy of space. The even more important reason for the location, as Jim had realized the year before, was the downwind distancing of smell from the original house. According to Enid Cottrell's history, that house, built in the cottonwood grove beside the highway, burned to the ground when a lightning-stricken cottonwood fell on it not long after the death of Goss's wife. Only in the years after that fire would the actual chronology of things be muddled and the corral's location be interpreted as more evidence of hermitage. "Even his cows are recluses," someone once said.

From one end to the other, the margin between corral fence and bluff's edge nowhere measured much more than the width of a pickup. Much earlier on this morning of May first, before Rickett had arrived to help separate mothers and calves, Jim had backed the Ford midway along that margin, then parked close to two snubbing posts—two lengths of salvaged power pole solidly set so their tops stood thigh-high. Beyond the snubbing posts, a little farther along the bluff's shoulder, a hot fire burned. Between the tailgate and fire, the branding crew would do its work.

Today Jim intended to redeem himself for his December ignorance and clumsiness. Today he was ready. The pickup held plenty of firewood and all necessary gear—lariats, whetstone, ear punch, horn saw, a jug of disinfectant, and, to stop different degrees of bleeding, one tin of powder and another of tar-like salve. Laid out on the tailgate were three branding irons—a G and a ⊙ and an H. (G-Target-H was still registered under Goss

Harvey's name, which, according to Rickett, would bother no one in the brand registry office, for a while anyway.)

Goss had put some thought into his system. A gate in each pen opened onto the lip of the bluff. The gates were spaced so that the margin of lip between them could accommodate the fire, the snubbing posts, and the pickup; the gates were hinged so that calves could be brought out one—to be branded, tagged, doused, castrated—then funneled back through the other. There were only two flaws. After so many years, both gates sagged on their hinges and dragged along their bottom spars. And the latch chain for the north gate had long ago broken and been replaced with a doubled strand of baling wire top and bottom. Even if, for the sake of efficiency, the crew made do with just one of those doubled strands, the fastening and unfastening was bound to get old.

Leaning against the top spar of the gate with the broken chain latch, Rowe Sloan studied the eclectic corral fence itself, particularly the pews.

The church crew's motive for helping was Christian fraternity, plain and simple. But not one member of that crew could have denied some curiosity to see up close the world of a man who spent the last two decades of his life distancing it from as many eyes as possible. It was the gratification of curiosity that now led Rowe Sloan to remark, "I don't believe I've ever seen a corral fence quite like that."

"He about had to make it rabbit-proof," Crue said, taking in the lush pasture below the bluff. "If I was a cow, that's what it'd take to keep me from wandering."

"No," Rowe said, "I meant those benches. "

When Crue still didn't seem to fully take his meaning, Rowe asked, with subtle clarification, and no small amount of wonder and admiration, "Who would think to use a pew like a feed bunk?"

"Goss Harvey," Darl said, "that's who."

"Those have got to be from when they tore down the old meetinghouse," Crue said, clear now on the drift of the conversation. Then he said, "I didn't think Goss was still going to church at that point. I wonder how he came by them."

Rickett looked one by one at the other men and said, "Maybe he wanted a souvenir."

The statement had an edge to it, and the laughter it evoked was weak and awkward.

"Well, brethren," Darl said, so as not to permit the least lapse in goodwill, "how about we do what we came to do?"

"Ride 'em, cowboy," said Rowe Sloan, grabbing a lariat. He was as aware as the rest that there were no horses here. He was also aware that mothers and calves were already herded and separated and that the wonder dogs, unless their skills also included roping, would be of little use today.

Without a single word devoted to claiming or assigning chores, the men settled into a pattern. Darl and Crue did the actual branding, along with the ear-tagging and castrating and, as needed, the sawing off of nub horns. Rowe and Jim kept them supplied, which meant they did the roping and bringing out through the north gate, the throwing and trussing, and the releasing through the south gate. With the trussing of the first calf, a feisty black-white-face, Jim was pleased to remember, from five months earlier, Bishop Clive Sebright's lesson about slipping at least one foreleg in the head loop to prevent choking. In the presence of farmers who had managed to avoid choking thousands of trussed calves, the knowledge of that practice was a relief. It eliminated at least one deficiency to be corrected or allowed for.

For their part, old Rickett and young Hewell found many ways to make themselves useful. They kept the fire hot and the branding irons cherry red. During the tending of each calf, they fetched irons (whose handles they insulated with wet gunny sacks), ear punch and tags, powder and salve, occasionally the whetstone, once in a while the horn saw. After each calf, they untangled and recoiled lariats, tidied the tailgate, rearranged, replaced, replenished. Between these chores, one showed the other how to record in a stained ledger each calf's description beside its ear-tag number.

"Where'd you learn all this?" Hewell asked in wide-eyed wonder.

"Even a blind hog roots up a spud once in a while," Rickett told the boy.

Darl winced from the flaming smoke of the brand he was making. "I always thought it was an acorn," he remarked.

"Come to think of it," Crue Penroy added, "I one time heard it said a peanut."

"I vote yam," Rowe said. "Or maybe turnip."

"*Could* be a turnip," Crue said. "I didn't think of that. Or a radish, for that matter."

Rickett had borne the interruption to the limit of his patience. "Well, whatever the damn pig roots up," he said, "he does it *blind*! *That's* the point."

"You sure know a lot of things, Brother Rickett," Hewell said. "That's all I can say."

Much to Jim's surprise, the old lawyer didn't protest or correct the boy's manner of address.

And so it went. All through the morning, clouds gathered, and the temperature dropped. The calves exited one pen fighting the rope, planting their hooves like tilling chisels or exploiting the least bit of slack to buck and plunge and test their restraints.

Ten minutes later they entered the other pen favoring a scorched left hip and feebly shaking tagged ears. The new steers bore one additional indignity.

Late afternoon, Hewell pulled a dripping gunny sack from a bucket and, dodging smoke from the branding fire, stepped to the edge of the bluff to do his wringing. From that vantage point, he saw what none of the others could see—the west slope of the Honey Spring notch and someone ascending that notch.

"Hey, look," he said with a voice marked by the first tone distortions of puberty.

The crew paid no attention. They were too busy. The morning's breeze had matured into a cold wind, and the clouds over the Beartooths could no longer be thought, even optimistically, to hold rain. Down to their last calf, the men were hurrying to finish. Even if they had heeded Hewell's directive, they wouldn't have seen anything. Nature had terraced and contoured the notch's west slope in such a way that, for now, that one glimpse, from that one vantage point, was the only one afforded.

At the moment of Hewell's unheeded announcement, the pair in charge of roping and bringing out entered the holding corral one last time. In the center of the corral, the remaining calf stood looking at them.

"What happened to his ears?" asked Rowe Sloan.

"Frostbite," Jim said, holding the coil of the lariat in one hand and shaking out a loop with the other.

Rowe regarded the calf for a moment. Then he said, "It's a wonder more of us didn't come home from Chosin looking like that."

The ears belonged to the little Doberman calf, who wasn't so little anymore. In nine weeks' time, he had grown into a bull in miniature. He watched the approach of the two men, the shaking out of the loop, then the twirling of it. Yet he stood motionless, head high, unblinking. His docked ears twitched now and again, and the expression on his adolescent bull face bespoke an impudent dare, an expression maintained even as the loop was released and came sailing toward him. It was almost as if he *wanted* to be caught—because only if he were caught could he prove what a trifle it was to get free. About the time the Doberman calf worked out that line of reasoning in his bovine mind, the loop settled around his neck. There was one half second of calm. Then, in an explosion of motion, he reared high, pirouetted, almost went over backwards, then came down with a short, hoarse bellow.

Most roped calves run *away* from the roper, and most such running *takes up* slack in the rope. The reversal—the dock-eared face charging straight at him, the slack accumulating—paralyzed Jim. Moments later, he would remember what had been said of Jerome Snow, of the half second after he hit the tripwire, how he looked as if his boots were nailed to the trail. Just how far down a nail would have to go in corral muck to reach something solid was another matter.

Only at the last instant did the Doberman dodge. He was aiming, not for Jim's groin or gut after all, but for Goss Harvey's eclectic corral fence. The calf accelerated and, for a moment, looked as if he intended to jump it—and use the feed-bunk pew as a springboard. But instead he veered and settled for leaping atop the pew's bench. Racing parallel to posts and poles, his hooves drummed the smooth hardwood and left little dung crescents where churchgoers once sat.

Laid end to end, as they were, the pews must have looked like the straight and narrow toward escape. But now the Doberman calf *was* taking up slack, fast. And Jim's paralysis had passed. Practicing a technique learned that day from Rowe Sloan, Jim made a rump sling of the rope's tail and, with a hand planted at each hip, held it tight.

"Back!" Rowe shouted. "Lean *back!*"

As the Doberman approached the first set of pew ends, he didn't slow, didn't even hesitate, but with enviable muscle and tendon strength, sprung upward to clear the hurdle.

And then the slack was gone.

The docked ears snapped sideways and backward, and the manure-slicked rear hooves splayed and skated on the pew's hardwood before flying into the air. At his end, the abrupt tightening of the rope jerked Jim forward, and the rump sling spun him three-quarters of a turn before yanking his legs out from under him. He landed on his back about the same time the Doberman landed on his. Meanwhile, in the blink before the four legs at one end of the rope outscrambled the two legs at the other, Rowe Sloan was there, reaching down, catching hold of the lariat, first with one big gloved hand and then the other.

And just in time. With all four hooves under him again, the calf jigged and strained at the lariat. Up and down, back and forth. And what a chorus of gutteral bawling and blatting. "They didn't teach you calf-roping tricks in boot camp?" Rowe teased, setting his heels and hauling on the lariat to check the calf's movement.

The plowed tracks of the Doberman's balking became the longest and deepest of the day. He was hard to drag through the gate of the holding pen, hard to throw, hard to truss. Before his rear hooves were cinched together with a lariat loop and fettered with half-hitches, they made contact a notable number of times with shins and legs and knees and hips. By the next morning, every such point would be a bruise. One of the most colorful would bloom high on Crue Penroy's inner thigh, would prompt wife Edrus to ask if anything was permanently damaged, to offer a liniment rub, and to recall (with a tone that defied the default disappointment of her life by actually approaching playful innuendo), "Seems like we finally got Hewell after something like this."

For now, Crue knelt at the head of the trussed calf and strained to bring together the handles of the ear punch, remarking that these ears didn't give him much to work with—and such surface as there was was tough as a tin can. "Either that," he said, "or this punch is dull." After a moment, he added, "And to tell you the truth, there don't hardly seem to be a reason for tagging this fella at all. Just write *freak ears* in the book, and *anybody* could pick him out of a herd."

Despite being bound fore and aft and stretched tight between snubbing posts—with *both* forelegs in the neck loop—the Doberman calf didn't bawl or blat now. Despite the sequential searing of three glowing irons on three adjacent spots on his left hip, the only part that flinched at all was the docked tail. Despite the acrid smoke from flaming patches of his own winter coat billowing into his pop eyes, he didn't blink. Between convulsions of straining, he just chewed his lolling tongue and blew snot.

But one last procedure awaited him.

"Hewell, old friend," said Rickett, turning to the boy, "I need a favor." Somehow the Doberman's straining had found slack where all would have sworn there was none to be found. "Step on that back rope and keep this guy stretched tight, would you? This isn't something we need him thrashing around for."

While the boy did as bidden, Darl drew the blade of his big pocket knife across the whetstone. The last of his strokes coincided with a wind swirl that washed him in smoke and cinders from the branding fire.

"What makes bull calves so much more trouble?" Jim asked, directing the question to no one in particular.

"You never heard of testosterone?" Rowe said.

"Is *that* how you say that?" asked Crue Penroy. "For some reason I always thought it rhymed with *macaroni*—thought it was one of those words from France or Italy or somewhere like that."

"That's it?" Jim said. "That's the mystery? Testosterone?"

"Pretty much," Darl said.

"If you think about it," said Rowe Sloan, "it explains the whole logic of boot camp."

"However you say it," Rickett said, "it's the bane of the male in most species, especially ours."

"This one must have a big problem with it, then," Hewell said innocently. His comment drew smiles from all the men, including his father.

"Not for long," said Darl Sebright. Fanning smoke from his eyes, he dropped to his knees, next to the exposed underside, and went to work.

The hands at the end of his arms could have been his brother's—for size, for pigment, for texture, for deftness. The hands in May assumed exactly the same attitude as the hands in December, followed the same sequence of motions, were bloodied in almost the same places. They grasped and stretched, sliced and extracted, slit, peeled, thinned, finally detached. One done and tossed to the dogs. Then the second. With one of those hands, Darl wiped the blade on the Doberman's hair just below the crisp, charcoal-flaked lines of the brand. With the other, he patted the calf's ribs. With Rickett the medicine bearer standing close, Darl exchanged the knife for the jug of disinfectant, from which he dashed a generous quantity, then exchanged jug for shaker can. While he powdered, neither he nor any of the others noticed the look on the face of the man who was reminded earlier in the day, by the oddest combination of details, that he had no son and, now, by this combination, that he had no brother.

The last calf was finished. Darl stood. At that very moment, as if a giant shaker in the sky had been upended, just once, a dash of sleet came down on the snubbing posts and tailgate and everything around them. Darl glanced upward. Then he stood clear as the rope at each post was undone. Like the others, he expected an unleashing of violent movement. Yet even with the loops loosened and the hocks unbound, legs which just minutes earlier had been cudgels remained limp and motionless. With a sympathy that was mysterious to him, Hewell stared at the bloodied cod. The Doberman was listless. Only with toe nudging and a slap across the snout from Rowe Sloan's loose glove did the big calf finally raise his head, roll to his belly, find his feet and stagger upright.

The sleet fell steadily now. The three branding irons lay on bare ground at some distance from the fire, hissing and steaming whenever a sleet pellet made contact. Already the bottom third of each shaft, pitted and attenuated from many hot fires, was taking on the peculiar scorched hue of a cold furnace grate. Something in the direction of the single-wide caught Hewell's eye. Where the slope of the notch eased, a straw hat came into view. "Hey, look," the boy said with a hoarse, faltering blend of tenor and bass. But this time he added, confidently, "There's that man again."

Even now the men of the branding crew paid no heed. The gaze they followed was the gaze of the Doberman. He had taken a ginger step or two toward the open receiving gate, toward his anxious mother, then stopped. First he looked to his left across the floor of the receiving corral, at the bull pen twenty yards away. The bull's enclosure was a pen within a bigger pen. Its fence, made of bridge plank, stood six feet high. Through a gap between planks, the old Angus stared, his own testosterone disquieted by the scent of castrating blood. Dazed and subdued, the Doberman calf turned his head to the right and gazed along the bluff. Only then did the men finally look in that direction.

Forty yards away, a man was just cresting the notch. Through spitting sleet and wind-driven smoke from the now-abandoned fire, his stolid, step-by-step climbing brought him into view one detail at a time—after the misshapen straw hat, the beard, then bib overalls, then green hip waders folded down at the knee. And on this day, instead of a gunny sack, he carried a fishing pole. From one shoulder strap hung a canteen; from the other, crisscross to the first, a creel. Once on the flat at the bluff's edge, he paused for a few moments to tug his straw hat down tight on his head and catch his breath—and maybe rule out any last hope of escaping notice. Then he came straight on toward the pickup.

Rowe Sloan closed the gate of the receiving corral behind the Doberman calf, then said, "Is that who I think it is?"

To Jim, Rickett whispered, "You don't suppose he really has been over on Big Bernene's property, do you?"

"Afternoon, all!" Beeswax Jones called in his booming voice as he drew close. The ankles of his hip-wader boots looked too slender for their burden. He was a big man. His belly taxed the apron piece of his bib overalls such that only one of the two brass buttons at each hip could be fastened. Whereas Crue Penroy wasn't as old as he looked, Beeswax wasn't as young. He breathed hard from his climb. The hair and beard beneath his straw hat had more gray in them than Jim remembered. He looked at every face, lingered on Jim's. "And howdy to you, Jim Ray. It's good to see you again."

The men of the branding crew couldn't help but be impressed with the familiarity of the greeting. Nothing helped an outsider fit in quite like acquaintance with a local oddity like Beeswax Jones.

"If we was ever to run into each other in nice weather," Beeswax said, "we wouldn't have anything to talk about."

"I guess not," Jim said, smiling.

"It's sleet now," Beeswax said, looking heavenward, his gaping mouth revealing the timber-saw teeth, "but mark my words, gentlemen: We'll see snowflakes before this May Day is over."

Darl checked the sky again himself. "You might be right," he said.

"No 'might' about it," Beeswax said. His eyes took in the dying fire and cooling irons, the snubbing posts, the ground stirred and matted and blood-stained from tending the Doberman and

all his predecessors. Off to one side, the wonder dogs were licking their chops. He said, "Don't tell me you been feeding the
dogs what it looks like you been feeding them."

Jim smiled again, this time awkwardly.

"You do know, don't you," Beeswax said, "that if they're prepared right, they make good eating? Not so much from an old
bull, mind you. But from a young one, they're hard to beat. In
fact, a delicacy in some places. Didn't anybody here know that?"

In Beeswax's mind, proper preparation of the day's delicacies
undoubtedly called for wrapping in corn husks and roasting in a
pit of fruitwood coals overlaid with cow chips, a process that, in
turn, called for a long and thorough explanation.

So they all felt everlastingly grateful to Rowe Sloan when the
seed of that explanation found no soil. "To tell you the truth,
Beeswax," he said, "we haven't had time to worry about any delicacies today. How about you? How's the fishing?"

Beeswax's eyes brightened, and the first lecture was forgotten.
He leaned his pole against the truck and stepped closer, gesturing for them all to gather around. "Depends what you're after,"
he said, patting the stained and battered creel hanging from the
shoulder strap. "When one door closes," he said, flipping back
the lid, "the good Lord opens another."

Sleet was falling thick now, all around a creel bulging to the
brim with asparagus officinalis. Beeswax let his audience marvel
at the wonder of his bounty for a moment, then said, "When the
trout weren't biting, I decided, while I was here, I might as well
fill my canteen from Honey Spring—best water in the county.
So I crossed the pasture and came along the fence line running
up the notch. I never seen anything like it. Must be the water.
Clump after clump of asparagus, practically every post. I got to
picking and couldn't stop."

He paused, rolling around in his mouth a quid of tobacco, but
he didn't spit. He looked directly at Jim.

"When my creel wouldn't hold another spear, I started back the way I come, along the base of the bluff. But when I got to a clearing I needed to cross, what should I see blocking my way, looking lonely and surly as can be, but *your* bull." Beeswax's mouth curved into a grin, but with teeth like his, a grin was the same as a leer. When his top lip was drawn up in a certain way, he looked a little feral. In apples or cheese or fudge, the kerf of such teeth would be phenomenal. "I won't tell you how to manage your herd, Jim Ray, but I will tell you this: If your sire down there is going to do his job, he's going to need some female company."

Now that mothers and calves were reunited, the corrals were much quieter. After Beeswax's loud declaration, the only sound was the velvet pelleting of sleet on the lip of the bluff. Every member of the branding crew knew what Beeswax didn't know. The pelleting grew insistent before one of them found a way to tell him: The only bull in Jim Ray's inheritance stood twenty yards away, perturbed in his glands, balefully eyeing the world through a gap between bridge planks.

CHAPTER 12

WITH THE HAYSTACKS NEARLY GONE, THE HERD WAS set to go down onto riverbottom pasture right after branding. But it couldn't go down with a trespassing bull waiting. He and the Angus weren't likely to get along, and separating him from the herd would be even harder than trying to find him now and drive him back to wherever he came from. Such finding and driving awaited Jim in the waning afternoon of a stormy May Day.

Despite thwarted expectations of home and warmth and rest, every one of the church crew stayed on to go with Jim into the darkening riverbottom on a trail turning slicker by the minute. For Beeswax, the descent was the second of the day, and it meant forfeiting elevation just gained. But he was magnanimously willing. "I got me a good pair of peepers," he said, "and a good sniffer." He set his creel of asparagus on the stoop of the single-wide. "You might need both."

Jim's peepers met Rickett's. How could a person even *think* of rescinding wandering rights for a man thus willing?

While Rickett fixed a pot of hot chocolate and found drinking vessels, the others put on such extra jackets or sweatshirts as could be found in their pickups or borrowed from Goss's closet. But they were short on ear coverings. When Hewell Penroy pleaded to join the men instead of waiting behind in the single-wide, his father pulled a wadded red bandanna from a pocket, scarfed the boy's head, then knotted the bandanna's corners tightly beneath his chin.

Beeswax had striven for the same effect with a rag-bag T-shirt torn so as to make a piece long enough to enwrap jowls and ears and the crown of his straw hat.

"Nice ear muffs," Rickett said, handing him a pint mason jar.

"Laugh if you want," Beeswax said, holding the jar while the lawyer poured it half full straight from the steaming pot, "but I make do with whatever's handy." He looked down into the jar, then held its rim to his nose as if to confirm his suspicions. "Cocoa!" he said. "How's a man supposed to catch a wild bull on cocoa? A working crew needs *coffee!*"

"Not this working crew," Rickett said, in begrudging defense. "So drink up or pour it back."

As Rickett and Jim well knew, the bull could have come only from a neighbor pasture. And the only neighbor pasture belonged to the Vanderfisks. So, starting at the river, below the bee boxes, the men fanned out and worked eastward toward the divider fence and Honey Spring. With the help of the wonder dogs, they combed the Russian olives at the base of the bluff and a wide swale between trees and swamp. Halfway through that sweep, the wind grew even more raw, and sleet changed to wet snow.

Not quite two hours after learning the contents of the creel, they huddled at the base of the notch to report, every one of them, the same results: No bull. At just past five o'clock, under a foreboding sky, the bad news settled hard. The men stood close enough to Honey Spring to hear its gurgling current. For a moment no one said anything. Even the dogs seemed defeated.

Hewell Penroy's red bandanna scarf had slipped away from his ears. They glowed as bright as his cheeks. Now, as the men paused in indecision, Crue removed his own gloves, held his hands over his son's ears for a time, then re-scarfed and re-knotted the bandanna.

"I know where *I'd* hide if I was a bull," Hewell said, looking down and across the pasture.

From where they stood, the spring descended the sloped base of the notch, then leveled out to cross a spongy meadow and disappear into riverbottom bog. For the next three hundred yards, the only evidence of the spring's current was a serpentine hair-part through cattail reeds. The general line of its meandering oxbows hugged the divider fence until the channel straightened at the bog's far bottom edge.

"If he's in those cattails," Darl Sebright said, "it'll take more flushing than we can muster."

He had given voice to the common sentiment. And Jim heard. Trying again to find one other button on the long denim barn coat grabbed at the last minute from Goss's closet, Jim was as ready as any of them to call off the search. "Listen," he said, "I'm sorry to drag you all down here for nothing."

The men were commiserating when Hewell interrupted them. "Hey, look!" he cried, pointing through falling snow, toward the near edge of the swamp.

And this time the men did.

"Your eyes are playing tricks on you, sonny," Beeswax said, incredulous to think of his peepers being bested by a boy's.

Hewell pointed with all the more vigorous certainty.

"His eyes are just fine," said Rickett, the second person to see the bull for himself.

Then the rest saw him, too. He stood at the edge of the swamp, out about seventy-five or a hundred yards from the divider fence, and facing that direction. His coat matched the dun of a mule deer buck and almost perfectly camouflaged him against a patch of last year's cattail reeds. Mud-slicked to the knees, snow-fringed along his spine, the bull stood looking at them. From his boss rose a pair of massive horns curved like scimitars. His tail swished.

Until that moment, strangely enough, the dogs hadn't seen the bull, either. Or smelled him. But a wind shift changed everything. And now that they had smelled him, they needed no command. When the tail swished a second time, they bolted, in a pursuit that didn't seem at all to surprise the bull. He watched them race toward him across the snow-spackled meadow and made no move. Then, as ably as any cutting horse, he pivoted away from the fence, away from his home pasture, and started in the opposite direction. For a distance, he merely pranced along the swamp's edge, as if to even the dogs' odds. Only when they had halved the distance did he break into a run; only when they had halved it again did he start galloping, tail high, divots flying. When they were closing on him, he suddenly ducked into the cattails and disappeared.

When Jim took off after him, Rickett yelled, "That swamp is no man's land." And Jim, running clumsily in heel-worn gumboots and the bulky, knee-length, poorly buttoned denim coat, yelled over his shoulder, "That's where I do my best work."

He planned to swing wide around the fleeing bull and drive it back toward the spring. Then he would run it south along the divider fence, to whatever hole or break it had come through.

But swamp underfoot, as Fritchey's pa or granddad would affirm, is always more laborious than swamp on the map. It was its own kind of jungle and, like any jungle, better suited to evasion than pursuit. The reeds turned out to be taller and denser than they looked from higher ground. Just like elephant grass. Besides obscuring visibility, the tangled stalks hobbled movement, which made for a lot of tripping and stumbling. Factor in the clumsiness of the flapping denim coat and last season's cattail sausages, broken and ablated atop their stems, and Jim looked as if he were threshing old mattress filling.

Nor did a distant surveying afford any appreciation of what the cattails grew *out of*—a mire of decaying stalks and roots surrounding peat hummocks the size of barrelheads. And mud. Black mud.

Pickled mud. Mud that had never not been mud. Every other step between hummocks sunk to ankle depth. The difficulty of the extraction was complicated by the ease of leaving the boot behind. It was faster to hop-trot one hummock to another—until a boot sole slipped off the slush-covered crown and plunged even deeper than it would have plunged in normal slogging.

Jim stopped. From somewhere between the swamp and the hazy base of the notch floated snatches of yelling, of Rickett's calling and whistling to the dogs. From such a distance in falling snow, the yelling was muted, almost conversational. And it was comforting. Surely, Jim thought, he wasn't chasing the dun bull alone. Surely one or two others had followed him into the swamp—if only for fellowship. When he turned his head just right, he even thought he heard movement nearby in the reeds.

But what if the source of movement and fellowship was the bull and the scimitar horns? The prospect made stealth an ambiguous achievement. "Ain't nothing can find nothing in monster grass like this," Fritchey had whispered less than ten minutes before the sniper's round found him.

"He-ey, bu-ull!" Jim yelled with more bravado than he felt. Big, wet, wind-driven flakes muffled his volume. "Hey, bullie, bullie!" he yelled at the top of his lungs. "Where *are* you, bull?"

A dozen more hummocks—and three or four near-slips—and Jim stopped again. Sooner than expected, the wide arc of his path had brought him back to the divider fence. It stood just a couple of rods away through the falling snow. Already each post was topped with a neat little dollop of cream frosting. His path also had brought him just below the spring's biggest oxbow. With its closed end next to the fence, the bow encompassed a kind of glade in the cattails. The little glade was only sparsely pimpled with hummocks, and these only the size of medicine balls. Maybe it offered firmer footing.

For a minute or so, Jim stood watching the snow fall, and listening. He couldn't hear anything now. Maybe the bull had doubled back and was hiding in the trees at the base of the bluff. Maybe he had headed up the notch toward the corrals, seeking the company of his kind. Maybe he had gone home.

Beyond the open end of the oxbow came a rustle, then snapping, then splashing and crackling. In a blur, the dun bull burst from the cattails, followed at the hind dewclaws by the dogs. After one hurried nod in Jim's direction, the bull swung the opposite way and set a course down the center of the glade, toward the fence. But it wasn't so much the fence that stopped him. Or the spring. Even a spring which, up close, looked a lot wider and deeper than a hair-part. No, the bull seemed to think it over for a moment before deciding he *wanted* to fight. That's when he wheeled, head down, to face the dogs. At the very instant of the wheeling, Jim saw, bobbing through reed stalks toward the glade, a flicker of red bandanna.

Jim's arc through the swamp had put him south of the bull, not north. And north was where he needed to be. If he hadn't been standing where he was standing, the dun bull likely would have cut downstream, wide of the spring's meandering oxbow loops, and paralleled the fence all the way to his hole. But now, as things stood, he had been inconvenienced and was sore about it. And in much less than a minute, the red bandanna would clear the reeds, no great distance from the gracefully curved horns.

Jim Ray was running. Or trying to run. Every few steps, it was sinking, lunging, flailing, righting, pulling free, staggering ahead. Between him and the point where any yelling and arm waving would drive the bull *away* from the red bandanna lay a patch of swamp no wider than a street crossing. But with the bandanna coming so fast, the crossing seemed to stretch.

The closed end of an oxbow fits the animal's under-neck; the two tips of the open end fit the yoke. Only after a contracted moment to cover a protracted distance did Jim finally round this oxbow's downstream tip and gain the open end—a broad, hoof-pocked margin between swamp and glade.

At last he could actually run. Bull and dogs to the right. Red bandanna to the left. Here there was a some sort of bottom. Here boots splashed without sinking.

The bull's head came up. His attention had suddenly shifted from the barking dogs to the red bandanna beyond. His tail swished.

Jim was frantic to intervene. The flapping denim coat hung heavy as an X-ray apron. Almost, almost, almost. The slap-splash of boots seemed to outstrip leg movement, as if the rubber soles were going to go on ahead and wait for everything else to catch up. Beneath his sternum Jim Ray felt the sweeping, hammering hand of every stopwatch ever held on him.

You any better at long distance?

Then abruptly one boot did not catch up with the splash.

It was the most peculiar sensation. Just like that, the sound ceased, and up rushed the glade's surface and everything with it: molded hoofprints and dwarf cattail stems and slush and swamp grass and the medicine-ball hummock that slugged him in the belly.

The suddenness was confounding, as when a sniper's round found Fritchey in grass ten feet tall. *Zi-iip!* As when Jerome Snow went from moving to not moving in that last half-second, as if the sole of his standard-issue jungle boot were nailed to the trail. As when the toe of one of Goss Harvey's misfitting gumboots snagged on something between medicine-ball hummocks.

Up.

Down.

That was it. Turf trod on the instant before, turf most recently perceived from five feet and ten inches of altitude, now confronted Jim within licking distance.

With a jarring of molars and neck vertebrae, he had grabbled face-down among reed stems. His lungs had flipped inside-out. His temples throbbed like a kinked water hose. Amid the tingling of nerves, he retched for breath. The whole world smelled like swamp grass. Even when he opened his eyes, he couldn't focus on anything.

But he heard it all.

Din of yapping and barking, then a mushy scuffle of hooves and a mean moan and snort and awful yowl, all mixed with a cry and shout from a voice just beginning to ripen with puberty. And such a commotion of crackling reeds and yelping and slush-splashing and then yelling.

Watch it, Hewell! Just stay there. Stand still!

Hyaa! Hyaa!

Get back! Stand back!

Let him go!

Cattail fluff tickled Jim's lips, nose, eyelashes. His respiratory system had it backwards—gagging and gasping to exhale when all the exhaling that could possibly be done had been done. What he needed was a few bubbles of oxygen *inhaled*, and they were hard to come by.

He was wet. And certain parts seemed to be getting wetter. He tried to get to his knees. But each kneecap felt like the end of a stick of cordwood that couldn't be made to stand upright. His thighs and hips wobbled, then collapsed.

Then came a brushing through and crunching of reeds, more footfall in slushy grass. It was taking a long time for his lungs to resume their natural shape.

Somebody was kneeling beside him.

"You okay, Jim?"

He wanted to nod.

"Just take it easy."

He tried to nod.

There were others, getting closer.

"That was some spectacular spill. I could see him running, and then his head went down like a drop hammer."

The worst of the tingle and throb had subsided. But until he could sit up or stand, he would have to settle for rolling over. And when he rolled over, he saw faces.

First, Rowe Sloan, kneeling, speaking.

"How you feeling?"

In a circle above and around Rowe stood Darl Sebright and Beeswax and Crue Penroy and Hewell. The red bandanna must have slipped off the ruddy ears again because Crue was fussing with it—again—as if he needed something to do with his hands after such a close call, as if his nervous fingers could untie the knot of fright and relief and gratitude choking him. Fussing and sniffing and blinking away tears, his voice hoarse with pretended casualness, Crue said to his son, "Your ma's not going to much like it if I bring you home with an earache."

"Do you think you can stand?" Rowe asked. "In this weather, you don't need to be any wetter than you are."

He and Beeswax offered a hand.

Being hauled to his feet felt like film run backwards. For a moment Jim stood dizzy and disoriented. He opened and closed his eyes, as if blinking would help him regain his equilibrium. Gradually the fuzziness cleared, and the world came into focus. Snow. Swamp. Fence. Cloud-shrouded bluff and notch. Then he looked down. His left foot was bare. Bare and wet and numb with cold. So cold the broken nail on the big toe was hardly bleeding. He saw, lying in slush a few feet away, the bunched sock, its folds full of cattail fluff. And beyond that, the boot.

Rowe leaned and picked up the sock. He wrung it out and handed it to Jim.

"Did he get away?" Jim asked.

Rowe nodded.

"Good riddance," said Beeswax Jones.

"That's some bull," Darl said. "You see that thing hop the spring? Like it was nothing. Looked like a darned mule deer."

Steadied by one of Rowe's hands on his shoulder, Jim held up the bare foot, pulled on the wet sock, then the boot. Whatever had tripped him had also punctured the rubber at the boot's toe.

Jim heard movement through the cattails. It occurred to him that Rickett wasn't here with the others. He was catching up. The sound was close.

During a lull in the wind, enormous wet snowflakes dropped straight down from the sky. For the first time Jim turned and looked toward the center of the glade. The others looked, too.

Crue Penroy put a hand on his son's shoulder. "Did you see it happen?" he asked, and he wasn't referring to Jim's fall or the bull's escape.

Hewell nodded, brushed a coat sleeve across his nose.

One of the dogs stood still as a sentinel. The other lay motionless, a dark lump on the turf. In the waning light, he could have passed for another hummock.

"I did what I could for him," Darl Sebright said.

"He's a goner," Rowe whispered. "Did you see how high it threw him?"

Jim started toward the center of the glade. The others let him take lead. He heard Rickett whistle, heard the hollering of a familiar command. He stopped. The command went unanswered. For the first time in a long acquaintance with the lawyer, the sentinel dog didn't budge.

Jim took a few more steps and at last stood over the lump in the swamp glade. It was not a hummock. The eyes were closed to slits; the ribcage trembled; the flews leaked bloody slaver. Another whistle and yell. With each sound, the tail tried to thump the slushy turf. Yet as Jim watched, even that response grew weaker. Despite a poultice of sod—clawed from the turf and hastily applied—there was no remedy for the gash in the underbelly made by the one horn in a thousand this dog hadn't dodged.

Late that night, warm in his bed in the single-wide trailer, Jim came awake. His mind swam with images. As he lay listening to the sough of storm wind, it was hard to distinguish between dream and memory.

His bandaged big toe throbbed. Unless he turned his foot just the right way, even the blankets' weight constituted a painful pressure.

You can't say I didn't warn you.

That, or something like it, was what he had hoped to hear when Rickett finally cleared the cattails at the edge of the glade. But when Rickett saw the dying dog and the puddled blood diluted in slush, he became blind to everything else. He circled, paused, circled some more. "My good little dog," he whispered at last, squatting, pulling off a glove to stroke the snout with the back of his hand.

But Jim *had* been warned. Months ago, before last November's round-up, Rickett had spoken of Goss Harvey's habit, in those final winters, of forgetting the location of his several dozen muskrat traps. He never retrieved in the spring as many as he set out in the winter. And, at the time of setting, the anchor chain of every trap ran to its own thin rebar stake driven almost its entire two-foot length into frozen peat or the closest hummock. So it should have been no real surprise, down in Goss's favorite trapping grounds, that the toe of the gumboot had found such a stake—or at least the three inches of it protruding above the peat's surface just at the edge of the glade. The stake passed through the chain's end ring and kept the trapped muskrat from crawling off into warrens unknown and, with the amazing strength of only three good paws, dragging the costly hardware along.

Just before the dog died, Rickett took off an inner coat and tried to bind the belly gash. After the dog died, he refused all offers to help carry the burden. Holding the limp body—and completely indifferent to the blood—he started to pick his way back along the trail most recently tromped through cattail reeds. As the others strung out behind him through the cattails, Jim hung back. Before he joined the cortege, he wanted to know what had split his toenail.

He returned to the spot where he had fallen. In the premature dusk, it took him a minute to find what he was looking for. He bent over, got a good grip just beneath the stake's head—mushroomed by countless blows from a hatchet butt—and heaved. He had expected the bar to be more solidly embedded. He had expected a chain tether braided into peat. He had expected the other end of that chain to be attached to a buried trap.

But he had expected wrong. The bar presented so little resistance that he stumbled backwards and almost went down again; the pulling up exposed no chain, drew no trap from the mire. Maybe Goss had never gotten around to setting a trap. Or maybe he had retrieved the trap and not the rebar stake. Or what if the trapped muskrat somehow escaped with the hardware after all? Once or twice, Rickett had accompanied his client on the trapping line, knew his methods, and had, over the last year, explained them to Jim.

Ordinarily, Goss didn't trust the end ring's attachment to the stake and reinforced it with a band of baling wire twisted tight. But what if, this one time, he forgot the baling wire? Or what if he remembered only to have it gnawed through by a pair of rodent incisors roughly the same color as Beeswax's and hard as a cold chisel. And after freeing itself from the stake, the muskrat might have freed itself from the trap. Any teeth capable of gnawing through baling wire were more than capable of amputating a paw. But probably not before dragging the trap to some remote point in the bog. There the trap would eventually sink and settle.

There, eons later, with the pickled limb still clamped in its jaws, it might constitute the crowning weekend discovery of a husband-wife team of biology teachers.

Now, many hours later, the bandaged toe still ached. Jim got out of bed and limped to the kitchen. He shook three aspirin from a bottle, washed them down with half a glass of water, then returned to his blankets. It could have been a lot worse. The gumboot could have found a trap still set. Unlike their larger cousins designed for beaver, the jaws of a muskrat trap wouldn't take off human toes. Or so said Rickett. But they wouldn't do them any good, either. The pan of a well-oiled trap could be sprung, Rickett claimed, by a BB dropped from less than two inches. If you couldn't remember exactly where a particular trap was set, how could you move anywhere in the vicinity with any confidence? The trap mislaid was every bit as worrisome as the trap unknown.

It was the second kind that got Private First Class Jerome Snow. When he took his last turn at point, he had no reason to suspect a wire stretched across the trail. In fact, it wasn't much of a place for a booby trap. The trail appeared little used, even by animals. And on such a faint trail in such a vast jungle, who would imagine that that *particular* span, between a tree and bush resembling any other tree and bush, posed any special danger? And even if there had been forewarning of trouble down *that* trail, did Jerome Snow really know what to look for?

Jim didn't. He remembered, twenty months into his hitch, sitting through a series of lectures on enemy tactics in jungle warfare. He remembered a black-and-white slide of a punji pit full of thin bamboo stakes. They looked like barbecue skewers. Maybe black-and-white captured the truer image with some things. But not with punji stakes. Black-and-white didn't show, for instance, the coating of pig excrement to encourage infection.

There *was* a lecture on tripwires, three weeks before they shipped out, but Jim missed it. That was the morning he finally reported to sick bay for the boil on his belt line. "We'd better lance that puppy," the doctor said. "Where you're going, anything like that could be bad news deluxe."

All these months later, it was embarrassing for Jim to admit his ignorance, even to himself, even in the middle of the night, in the middle of a spring snowstorm in Wyoming: before dreaming of a black Christmas, he had had things backwards: he assumed the *wire* tripped the *foot*.

After much encouragement during that last chow break, Private First Class Jerome Snow had agreed to deliver what had to be, under the circumstances, a very subdued rendition of Bing Crosby's carol.

May your days be mer-ry and bright.

And then he took his last turn at point. Not even boot camp, not even the caution required by that final duty, could *completely* tame his gangly skip-hop of a gait.

He never knew what hit him.

That's what everybody said after Fritchey, and it was true. His eyes had quit seeing even before he hit the ground. The same was said after Jerome Snow, too, during the sweat-bath huff-and-puff tote to get him to the closest landing zone, which, somebody ought to have told somebody, was in sore need of some attention with a bush axe. Of course, the sentiment was meant as it was always meant—as a kind of collective solace. Nevertheless, in Snow's case it wasn't true. For a split second, he *did* know. Too late, but he knew. Maybe he *smelled* it. In the endless conjecture afterward, that possibility was suggested because tripwires are pretty much imperceptible to eyes and ears. "That's the *point*," Ardizzoli said. And it was true that Private First Class Jerome Snow possessed what even Beeswax would have had to concede was a fantastically keen sniffer. In more than one test, Jerome

Snow proved he could distinguish flavors of Kool Aid powder or chewing gum from three or four feet away, blindfolded. Black cherry or strawberry? Doublemint or Juicy Fruit? Bingo.

"How'd he get it?" asked the door gunner of the chopper that came for the bag they'd carried over a lot of hard terrain. Even with handles, the bag presented a torturously unwieldy burden. When somebody said tripwire, the door gunner grimaced and shook his head.

For a long time, the other consuming speculation was exactly how far Jerome Snow's standard-issue jungle boot—and what it contained—had flown through the air. It seemed important to put a number to it. And when conjecture on the boot's travel distance finally had worn itself out, on a morning when they saddled up in a downpour, Ardizzoli reverted to his default debate: dry socks or sex? "You can vote, too, Utah. We'll just count yours as a guess."

Just before midnight after Jim Ray's second May Day as heir of Honey Spring, the wind eased a bit, and the big toe quit throbbing so badly. Soon enough drowsiness came. Dry socks or sex. He thought of Jocelyn Vanderfisk in her blouse and jacket. Maybe, if you made it home in something other than a bag or box, you could hope for both.

A year ago, Bishop Clive Sebright had asserted, with conviction, that the inheriting of Honey Spring confirmed God's hand in Jim's life. Most likely Minnie Ray would have agreed. She was a strong believer in divine destiny, had told Jim many times that he had a great work to do. But that's what mothers said. And somebody must have said the same thing to Fritchey and to Jerome Snow. Nobody could figure it—why one survived and one didn't. Except God. That was one of his mysteries, according to that chaplain in Da Nang.

All Jim knew was that he *had* survived. And that thanks to Rickett's letter, read in that sandbag bunker in Chu Lai, he had had a place to come after war. But nothing accomplished in his first year at Honey Spring seemed to qualify as the start of a great work.

After a while, in the nether-thought of near-sleep, all the pondering blurred. Only such blurring could make of riverbottom swamp a romantic tableau featuring the fair maiden Jocelyn. But the fair maiden was soon crowded offstage by a bull. Five or six hours earlier, Jim had finally emerged from the cattail reeds, crossed the bordering meadow to the tree line at the base of the bluff, and started back up the notch. The treading of the branding crew ahead of him had churned snow and trail dirt into gumbo. Jim remembered noting how dark the sky seemed, and how that darkness made the hour seem even later than it was.

So what a stunning surprise when, during a brief calm, he looked up the notch and saw in the western sky a glow in the clouds, like a lightbulb muffled in cotton. As he watched, the lightbulb made flame, and the cotton thinned and melted. Suddenly a ray of sun escaped the muffle and shone down at the only angle by which it could align, even momentarily, with the notch. In that moment, Jim had turned. The brief, brilliant glow illuminated the section of pasture with the divider fence running through it. And just before being swallowed again by clouds, the light revealed something else. There, staring up at him, stood the dun bull, its four hooves planted lordly and indisputably on the Vanderfisk side of the fence.

CHAPTER 13

WHEN GOSS HARVEY LEARNED THAT MUCH OF THE roadbed gravel for the Depression-era paving of the Balford-Cody Highway would come from property he had traded away, he at first blamed fate. "Seems I was *born* for the short end of the stick," he said. But fate makes a poor antagonist. Blame craves a *face*. Only with a face can rancor take root. For Goss, that face, over a period of years in the late Thirties and early Forties, became the face of Enoch Vanderfisk.

By the end of World War II, Goss had convinced himself that he was the victim of a swindle. Bitterness became the thorn in his soul. Its festering tainted every corner of his life, even memories of things long past and settled. He decided, for instance, that doctors hadn't tried hard enough to save his son or wife. In old and amiable relationships with church mates, he now detected malice and conspiracy. And despite the charred trunk of a lightning-blasted cottonwood as stark and constant proof to the contrary, he even nurtured suspicions of human mischief in the fire that took his house.

But the darkest of all the consequences of his rancor was the conclusion that his old friend's courting of Honey Utley, nearly half a century earlier, was a betrayal after all. Over and over, to himself and anyone who would listen, he repeated the refrain: "Those two sure enough played me for the dupe."

Then, in the early summer of 1950, at age seventy-one, he told Bishop Hardin Cottrell to burn his church membership record.

Bishop Cottrell of course tried to ease his feeling. War only begat more war, the bishop said, citing, as an analogy, recent troubling news from Korea. The only sane answer to war, said this man whose only son had perished during Pearl Harbor, the only antidote to the hate and aggression of nations—or individuals—was the peace made possible by Jesus' atonement.

Goss was unmoved. He said he could no longer abide attending sacrament meeting with a crook like Enoch Vanderfisk sitting on the stand fulfilling his duties as a member of the stake high council. That crook might fool everybody else with his moneybags generosity and righteous prominence, but not Goss Harvey. To emphasize his disaffection, Goss ripped up his last tithing check, with Bishop Cottrell as witness, and said the offerings of one old dirt farmer would not be much missed by a church that was so indifferent to his missionary sacrifices a half century earlier.

Over the next ten years, more than one church person visited Goss, asked after his welfare, invited him back. But any hope of his accepting that invitation evaporated when, in late March of 1961, he read the *Balford Clarion*'s headline story on what the governor touted as one of the biggest highway improvements in Wyoming history—a three-year project to raise and widen the corridor through the Bighorn Basin. A major portion of that corridor, of course, connected Balford and Cody. The project was to begin that very year, as soon as weather permitted. The story ran three days after Goss's eighty-second birthday and, as it happened, just a month after Honey Utley's death. So it managed to salt more than one old wound. But out of respect for the dead, and probably considerable weariness, Goss concentrated on the grievance of gravel. For the third time in his life, he was going to have to watch a neighbor profit, and profit handsomely, from a resource that could have been his.

Early one morning in the summer of 1962, while conversing with his fellow ditch-riders before the day's rounds, Eb Godwin told a story that would bear much retelling. The previous evening, he said, against the brilliant glare of sunset just after a rain shower, he had seen the figure of a man standing at the rim of the Vanderfisks' gravel pit. At that season in the construction of the new highway, the pit doubled as a parking yard for bulldozers, loaders, earthmovers, rock-crushing equipment, and a fleet of dump trucks—all idle after a long day. The next morning, several of the drivers of those trucks found flat tires and holes in their windshields, not to mention a dead cow. The relish of Eb's story depended on two assumptions—that the high-powered rifle responsible for the truck damage and the cow's death (a rifle Eb had *not* seen) was connected to the man above the gravel pit and that the man was Goss Harvey.

The haystack had dwindled. The only bales left were those in the first tier, the stack's foundation. Weight had compressed them. Their undersides were earthy and moldy, veined with mouse trails. The herd needed to go down on pasture. And after the May Day blizzard had blown over and the weather had warmed again almost overnight, there was no reason to delay the move.

No reason except Rickett. He wouldn't hear of throwing wide the gates in the corral fence along the bluff until the divider fence through the swamp was thoroughly checked for the havocking of the dun bull. That was the gist of the conversation on the morning of the third day of May, at the closest edge of the sagebrush forest, as one man dug a dog grave between fast-melting snowdrifts and the other held, alternately, the shovel and spud bar. Ten minutes into the job, both had hung their coats on sagebrush boughs.

So on the fourth day of May, Jim fed to the herd the last moldy, misshapen bales, then, despite more pressing chores—tilling, corn planting, ditching—spent the morning walking the segment of fence in question, from the base of the bluff to the river, and back. He found no havocking. No break or breach, not a downed post or wire anywhere. Not even a missing staple.

Rickett heard this report at noon while standing at the stove in the single-wide, stirring a saucepan of canned stew with a wooden spoon. He didn't say anything. When the stew was hot, he ladled half of it on one plate and half on another. Then he took from the refrigerator a pint carton of cottage cheese and removed the lid. Without using a spoon, and without any effort to keep stew and cheese separate, he dumped half the carton's contents on one plate and half on the other. Not until they had stepped outside onto the new stoop and sat down in the lawn chair and ladder back did he finally respond to the report, and then only to say, "Damn the luck."

He was spoiling for a confrontation with Bernene and had hoped to be able to add fence damage to the dun bull's offenses. For a moment he sat thinking and stirring the lump of curds into his stew, to cool it, or thin it, or both. To Jim, the swirl of white and brown was not appetizing. Finally Rickett said, "No matter. We still have a case, and you still need to talk to them."

"*Case?*" Jim asked, working *his* spoon to keep the stew and cottage cheese on his plate as separate as they could be kept. "About *what?*"

Rickett looked at him with disbelief. "You *want* a randy mongrel bull roaming your pasture all summer?"

"He didn't look very mongrel to me."

"Well, we sure got no idea what kind of calves he'd throw."

"Before he could throw calves from *my* cows," Jim said, "he'd need . . . access. And now that I've got juice on in that top strand, he's not going to have that. We won't have any more trouble from him."

"That's wishful thinking if I ever heard it."

"And what would I say anyway? That he *flew* over the fence?"

"We got half a dozen witnesses saw that bull on your side," Rickett said. "Doesn't matter how he got there."

"What does it matter now anyway?"

Rickett stared at him. "You haven't even told Bernene, have you?"

"I can't see what good it would do."

"It's called serving her and her old man notice."

"Notice of what?" Jim asked.

"Litigation, Sherlock!" Rickett said. "Big Bernene's so all-fired ready to go to court, we'll just beat her to it. Six witnesses carry a lot of weight in any kind of litigation I can think of."

"I don't want litigation," Jim said. "And I surely don't want those guys who were helping me just because they're decent guys to have to get involved with anything like that on my account."

"I don't think that's your reason." Rickett paused. "Not your *main* reason, anyway."

Jim waited for Rickett to put into words what he himself had not.

Rickett obliged. "Hard to woo the niece if you're at war with the aunt, huh?"

"I don't know if I'd go *that* far."

"Well," Rickett said, "however far you *would* go, you haven't denied the essential premise."

"I haven't confirmed it, either."

"*Qui tacet consentire,*" Rickett recited, holding his spoon like a xylophone mallet and tapping the air at every syllable.

It was easy, in that moment, to imagine him persuading a box full of jurors who didn't know Latin maxims any better than Jim knew them.

"In law," Rickett explained with great patience (and condescension), "it means 'silence gives consent.'"

"In lunch," Jim responded, "it means I'm trying to change the subject."

Rickett ignored the effort. "*Woo*, I grant you, is something of an exaggeration," he said. "As a verb, it implies action. And I haven't seen much of that on your part, Romeo. But war? With a lady like Bernene Maxwell, the metaphor is no exaggeration at all. And if that's what she's got in mind, it would be best to strike first."

After studying Rickett's face for a moment, Jim said, "I don't much want to strike at all."

"That boy Hewell could have been hurt or killed."

"But he wasn't."

"You're lucky *you* weren't hurt or killed."

"But I wasn't."

"That bull put you both in harm's way."

"I don't think this is about Hewell or me being in harm's way."

Now it was Rickett's turn to wait for the other man to express what he wouldn't. But he was not patient. "You have to admit he killed a darned good dog," he said, looking toward the edge of the sagebrush forest in the vicinity of the little grave mound. "I liked that dog. *You* liked that dog. He was good company, and a good worker."

"I liked the dog just fine," Jim said. "But this isn't about the dog, either."

They looked at each other.

"I think the dog or the bull or the bull's trespassing just gives you an excuse to scratch a deeper itch."

Now Rickett looked away.

For half a minute, Jim didn't say anything. He was grateful for Enid Cottrell's history and for Bishop Clive Sebright's insight into that history and even for Beeswax's supplementary details. But there were things he needed to know that only Rickett could tell him.

"You never have explained," Jim said, "why you stayed on here even after your client died—with no pay. What kind of guy does that? What kind of *lawyer* does that? Every time I ask, you clam up."

Rickett pointedly devoted his attention to his stew and cottage cheese.

Jim said, "When I first talked to Beeswax last winter—when you were gone south—some things he said made me think maybe Nolan Rickett has all along had more stake in this Honey Spring business than he's admitting to anybody, maybe even himself."

Rickett looked down at his remaining quantity of stew and cottage cheese. "That's what you think, huh?" He scraped up a spoonful, put it in his mouth, chewed, swallowed. Two repetitions of that same sequence, and that part of lunch was over. He said, "Well, maybe you're right." He set the plate down on the porch stoop, leaned back in his folding chair, looked up at the sky. His deliberate drawing of breath into lungs long affected by tobacco sounded vaguely like a wad of cellophane wrap unfisted.

"You've never said a pious word about my smoking," Rickett said, burping. "How come?"

"I got my own vices to worry about."

"So you're saying it *is* a vice?"

"Would you be asking if it wasn't?"

The lawyer looked at Jim. For once, he didn't fish for a cigarette or raise a grievance about the Latter-day Saint faith. Then he looked across the yard toward the grain bin and loading chute. Somehow the set of his eyebrows and mouth and chin made it clear that, on the matter of his stake in Honey Spring, he had decided not to stay clammed up any longer.

Without preface or disclaimer, Rickett started the story that he had, for over a year, refused to tell.

"The one thing I have told you," he ventured as a first line, "is that Goss and I were not what you'd call close. Even after knowing him these last ten years and being around him all the time.

I didn't have much use for a cranky old Jack Mormon, and he didn't have much use for a lawyer. But from the get-go, I think he felt obligated to *try* to trust me. And I felt obligated to try to be worth it. How's that for a basis for a relationship?"

It didn't take long for Rickett to warm to his narrative.

"After defending a lot of dubious causes in my time—and being ridiculously overpaid for it, when I think of what so many folks I knew growing up did to earn their bread—I got to wondering would it be such a bad idea, before I got lung cancer or run over or struck by lightning, to defend one not so dubious."

"And litigation over a neighbor bull in my pasture *isn't* dubious?" Jim asked.

"Hear me out," Rickett said. "And remember, you asked for it."

"Okay, okay," Jim said, pumping his hands, spread-fingered, in a gesture of concession.

Rickett looked over the corrals, toward the sagebrush forest. Then he went on:

"Somewhere around the mid-Fifties, the Vanderfisks suddenly hatched a plan to claim rights to Honey Spring. I should say it was Big Bernene who hatched the plan. Honey Spring has really always been her baby. Why the interest right then, I don't know. But from what I could see, Big Frett was supportive. Maybe just to keep the marital peace—who knows? And Enoch? I heard somewhere he had mixed emotions on the matter. Bad as he felt for Goss's hard luck, he more than likely didn't take too kindly to being blamed for it. He wasn't pushing Bernene, I don't think, but he didn't fight her on it, either.

"Anyway, you need to understand that no is not a word Bernene Maxwell née Vanderfisk is used to hearing from anybody. And here's a guy like Goss Harvey doing his best to give her some practice. You have to admire that, don't you?" Rickett expected no answer and waited for none. "The spring itself is what she was after—the water. In dry country, it's always the water people fight over. It was like that down in Luna Valley. I knew neighbors, in some cases *brothers,* to fall out over who got how much irrigation water, and not speak to each other the rest of their lives."

The old lawyer shook his head in wonder.

"Over water?"

"You better believe it," Rickett said. "The Vanderfisks wanted that spring. As you know, Bernene has long had it in her head to build some sort of Vanderfisk tourist stop with the main draw being natural spring water—sparkling, salubrious, etcetera. Nutty idea, if you ask me. But who knows? Maybe a lady like Bernene could make it fly." He shrugged and rubbed his palm along the arm of his lawn chair. After a moment, he continued: "Anyway, they offered Goss, as a swap, other property elsewhere. They offered favors. And of course they offered money—and quite a bit of it. The answer was always the same. The harder they came after it, the harder Goss held on.

"So the Vanderfisk side finally filed a suit going all the way back to the original agreement. The suit claimed that any equitable split of the property implied an equitable split of the ground water.

"That's when I came into the picture. I still don't know how Goss found me. I hadn't been living up at North Fork much more than a year, wasn't even in the phone book yet. I was moping around all by myself in that giant fancy log house we had built to retire in, my wife and I. Barely got it finished, and the very next month *she* was the one diagnosed with cancer. This lady who didn't *have* any vices, she's the one with a tumor in her colon the size of a grapefruit." Rickett stared unblinking at the sagebrush forest. "She didn't make it six months. The truth is, after all those years in Denver, she wanted to go back to Luna Valley, where she had family. Married nieces and nephews, fertile as rabbits, lots of kids around."

Rickett stopped and worked his jaw for several moments. He kneaded his forehead with the fingertips of one hand, then brought his palm down along his face and rubbed his chin.

"My wife liked kids, would've loved to have some of her own. But we were never able. And not for lack of trying, I assure you. From the one doctor we asked, we never got much of an answer as to why. My problem? Her problem? Would it have made any difference to know?

"But being around all those grandnieces and nephews would've made her happy. And what did I do? I nagged and whined until finally I talked her into moving five hundred miles the opposite direction. North Fork! I'd been elk hunting up there *one* time and made it out to be paradise. The plain truth is, it was lonesome up there for her. And you better believe it was lonesome for me after she was gone You're married to a woman that long, she's half your habits.

"So when this old junker of a pickup pulls in at the cabin one morning, uninvited, I'm actually glad for the company. But for a long time it just sits there. Five, maybe ten minutes. Finally the driver realizes I can see him through the window the whole time because now he gets out fast, looking around, self-conscious, as if the trees have eyes. Then he climbs the porch steps and knocks. I'm standing right there with my hand on the knob, but I waited a bit to make it seem otherwise. Finally I open the door, and there he stands, Goss Harvey in the flesh. And that flesh looked rough, I tell you. He could've passed for a wino—hadn't slept in a week, hadn't bathed or combed or shaved, either.

"Of course I was curious who he was and what he wanted, but I never got to either question. Without a syllable of introduction or preliminary, he says—just like this: 'I've got a spring running along the edge of my place, and my neighbor and his daughter are trying to take it from me.'

"I have stood before many a judge who would have acclaimed such succinctness. And he was sincere. Do you have any idea how precious sincerity gets to be in a business that attracts pissant grifters and shysters like a dung wagon attracts flies? I didn't know the guy from Adam, but the way he stood there on the front porch of my big empty cabin, looking me in the eye, I knew he was telling the truth—or at least not trying to whitewash or inflate it. The way he said it, the Vanderfisks might as well have been after his soul."

For several seconds, Rickett didn't say a word. Across the little porch he looked at Jim. Then he looked far away, toward the McCoullough Peaks.

"Up to that point, I didn't think I wanted to fool with the law ever again. But after I listened to his case, what was I going to do—rot away lonely and idle in a cabin, burping and farting with impunity? Retirement sounds a lot more appealing than it really is, and living alone after a lot of years with a good woman is its own kind of hell. Goss's problems gave me a reason to wake up, keep a schedule, come and go like I had a purpose, step back into the land of the living. I looked at all his documents, all the records, every slip of paper in every shoebox, looked up the deed and all that. Then I got interested in the property itself, made reasons to walk every inch of it. Coming down here got to be pretty regular. In fact, I started coming when I didn't need to come, not for any lawyering purposes anyway. By then I think Goss was on to me.

"One day he said, as long as I was here, why didn't I make myself useful *for real*. He put me on a tractor, and the next thing I knew, I was half the crew. The thing is, he didn't have to coax. I was willing. There was, as you have so astutely ascertained, no money in any of it, not even farmhand wages; I knew that going in, before he told me. But it wasn't exactly pro bono, either.

"There *was* compensation, after a fashion. Tomatoes, for instance. And green beans and potatoes and corn and Swiss chard. And the sweetest little cantaloupes I've ever tasted; he called them muskmelons. The only thing I didn't care for was the zucchini. The truth is, he didn't, either. Why he grew the stuff by the truckful, I don't know. Maybe just because he could." After a pause, Rickett went on: "The point is, the man could raise a garden. He was *too* good at it. It was like he was overcompensating. Which meant he had to give most of it away."

"I thought he was a hermit," Jim said.

"He was," Rickett said. "His largesse wasn't just anonymous; it was sneaky. Of a night he'd drive around leaving grocery bags of garden stuff on the doorsteps of houses and hoods of cars that looked hard-luck. I don't think anybody ever suspected it was him.

"And in my case, at least, he went beyond vegetables. There was beef. There was bacon and sausage—right up until the last couple of years, when he quit keeping a pair of hogs. And plenty of honey, courtesy of you know who. I accepted all of it gratefully and enjoyed it—except the zucchini. I don't know what his other zucchini recipients did with theirs, but some of mine, I admit, wound up in the tumbling waters of the North Fork."

"All of which was okay. I didn't need money. What this jaded old hack needed was a reason to get out of bed every morning. He needed a reason not to torment himself about his wife spending her last days in a place other than where she really wanted to be. He needed a reason not to drink so much. And I admit, I kind of liked it. Showed up early, stayed late. Come breakfast or lunch time, I was actually hungry. Food started having some flavor again."

"Except zucchini," Jim said.

"Right," Rickett said. "But it doesn't have any to begin with."

They both smiled. For half a minute, the far treeless peaks of the McCoulloughs held Rickett's gaze. He cleared his throat, hawked, and spat off to the side of the stoop.

"As it turned out, there *was* some lawyering to do. Bernene and her husband hired a horn-rimmed local, at least twenty-five years younger than me. And one smart cookie. And being from here gave him the advantage. He knew the lay of the land, and I didn't. Oh, I knew plenty about politics in a little Mormon town, but I needed to know the kind of particulars about *here* that a stranger can't know.

"That's another reason I needed to work with Goss—I mean *really* work. I needed *not* to be a stranger to at least one person. And, frankly, there was something about him—not so much pitiful or desperate, but just one guy in a clunker pickup truck and single-wide against a pretty big family power, for these parts, coming after his sweet little no-account spring. And Bernene was so sure she was going to get it—without having any grounds at all—just by her brand of righteous indignation, which in her case is nine parts bullying. I think that's what swayed me."

Rickett paused. After a moment or two, he went on:

"And we won. A deal was a deal, the judge said. As he pointed out, the original proviso made it clear that the spring went with the west parcel and that Goss had to die *before* any reversion of deed could take place. I remember he looked at Goss, with all of us standing there, and said, 'And this gentleman appears to be very much alive.'"

Rickett shook his head, almost chuckled. Then he did chuckle.

"So they let it go—or so I thought. Right about that time, Big Frett and his big wife had other worries. That's when their youngest, the daughter with the funny name—"

"Patty Dew?"

"—have I told you about her?"

Jim nodded. "Pregnant and jilted—in that order."

"That's the one," Rickett said, for a moment appearing uncertain whether Jim was honoring or poking fun at his storytelling powers. "Anyhow, after that scandal, the Honey Spring affair stayed quiet for several years. I thought maybe we'd heard the last of it. But Bernene Vanderfisk Maxwell is a stubborn woman. She had never abandoned her plan for one moment, was just biding her time until another angle presented itself. And inevitably one did."

"The flat tires and broken windshields and dead cow?" Jim asked.

For a moment, the expression on the lawyer's face was a compound of surprise and begrudging admiration. "You get that from Beeswax or your Sister Cottrell's history?"

"Mostly Beeswax."

"Anyway," Rickett continued, "Goss was worried. Wyoming law doesn't much like vandals, and it takes its bovine population pretty seriously. But the plaintiffs still had the burden of proof. And a trained baboon could see they didn't *have* any proof. Opportunity? Okay. Maybe even motive: Goss *was* bitter, about the gravel and a lot else. But if we jailed everybody who was bitter about something, there wouldn't be many people left walking the streets. Bitterness was not evidence, not for *their* case. And means? As I pointed out in court, the slug that killed the cow— the same caliber as shot out the tires and windshields—was from a .270. On that point we had the testimony of the man who dug it out of the dead cow, a local veterinarian named Amos Lowe. No question it was a .270, he said. And a .270 is a caliber of rifle that, to my knowledge, Goss never owned. His rifle, which is now your rifle, is a .30/06.

"Nobody appreciated Goss's bitterness—certainly nobody grieved over it—more keenly than Enoch, but even he didn't think his old friend would *borrow* a gun to do such a thing. No, if Goss wanted to kill a neighbor's cow, he would do it with his own. That's when Enoch said enough was enough. And since he's the one person with courage or clout enough to put the brakes on Bernene, that was it. The charges were dropped."

The silence this time lasted so long that it made the next part, when it came, seem like an epilogue.

"But the law is not without its ironies," Rickett said finally. "Two summers ago, while you were off gallivanting in steamy jungle and verdant paddy, Goss went off his feed. By winter, he was bedridden. This turn of events was a windfall for Bernene. All that fighting before when the only thing she had to do now was bide her time and let Goss die a natural death. The same proviso by which she had so long been thwarted was now going to reward her! Absent an identified heir on the side of the deceased—who, I need not remind you, was harder to locate than any other person in my long and illustrious legal career— the very same legal system that had found in Goss's favor would now find against him, would, in fact, hand his place over to Enoch gift-wrapped." Rickett looked at Jim. "You pretty well know the story from there."

Out in the corral, a cow lowed. From the high branches of one of the cottonwoods, a magpie squawked. Then everything was still again.

"So that's how I came to be here," said Nolan Rickett. With a brisk back-and-forth motion of his palm, he dusted the knees of his trousers. "And I have stayed," he said, more to himself than to Jim, "because, when it comes right down to it, I don't really have any better place to go."

For a long time both men were quiet.

At last Jim said, "Ever thought about Vegas?"

Rickett looked at him.

"Or Atlantic City? Ardizzoli says those casinos love retired professionals with money. And they don't care *how* it was earned."

"Is that your idea of a noble end—to have me croak playing slots?"

"I was thinking something more for your social benefit," Jim said. "Craps maybe. You could throw in with the geezers in plaid shorts."

"Well, now, *that's* a different matter," Rickett said. Then, after a pause, he said, "Thanks just the same, Brother Jim Ray, but I think I'll stay here and keep an eye on the one dog I have left— and on you."

CHAPTER 14

ON HER SIDE OF THE FAMILY, HONEY UTLEY HAD A nephew named Clark. When this nephew came of age in the late nineteen twenties, he went off to a university in the east. After nine years and three different academic degrees, he packed up his books and diplomas, his wife and two small children, and bought train passage back to the west. But why so *deep* into the hinterland, his bow-tied mentor asked one last time in an effort to avert what he considered professional suicide. With several promising offers from places with libraries and museums and theaters, what could possibly be the draw of this backwater called Balford?

"It's where I'm from," Clark Utley said.

In those days, it was rare for a young man from Balford to get to any university at all—let alone one on the intellectual side of the country—even rarer to graduate from such a place with his religious faith intact, rarer still to go home to make his career. But so it was with Clark Utley. Through the end of the Depression, this scholar nephew of Honey Utley's taught language arts to the sons and daughters of farmers, stockmen, tradesmen, laborers. At the outbreak of the Second World War, still in his early thirties, Professor U., as he was now known locally, was appointed principal. By the end of the war, he had adopted his old mentor's preference for bow ties and was superintending all the schools in the county. Along with his school duties, he sat on boards, chaired committees, and regularly contributed to the op-ed page of the *Balford Clarion*. In all his associations, he was

appreciated for his fair-mindedness, his measured logic, his con-
ciliatory approach to any dispute. But perhaps his greatest gift
was an eloquence that welded grammar and goodness. He was
incapable of triteness or bombast, and he never talked down.

His many gifts, which he consecrated as fully to his religion
as to his profession, made Professor U. especially effective in
church work. In late November of 1953, at the age of forty-five,
he was called to succeed Hardin Cottrell as bishop of the Balford Ward. In the early fall of 1957, after less than four years of
bishoping—"Hardly enough to dull the shine," according to *his*
successor, Clive Sebright, who went on to serve three times that
long—Professor (now Bishop) U. was called as stake president.

But he put his less than four years to good use. For one thing,
he visited scores of disaffected ward members and invited them,
as circumstance warranted, to repent or forgive or simply bestir
themselves spiritually. Somehow his eloquence invited, in the
individual as well as the group, a spirit of softening and healing,
of recommitment and resolve. That spirit remedied almost all
the ailments bishops run into—the too-shamed penitence, the
too-proud *im*penitence, the petty grievance, the justified offense,
the awkward and poignant hanging back and standing off. And
it helped make bearable the many adversities that defy remedy.
Perhaps most notably, the spirit he invited acted as a balm for
even the most hard-bitten backslider.

The success of Bishop U.'s home visits, as they had come to be
known, was remarkable. In less than four years, sacrament meeting attendance tripled. Such results attracted the attention of local
and visiting Church authorities and served as the model in lead-
ership training meetings. Again and again, Bishop U. was asked
to explain his secret. Again and again, he modestly insisted there
was no secret beyond sitting down with people one on one and
speaking honestly to them in a way that allowed the Spirit of the
Lord to do the rest. And, as he always pointed out at that juncture

in the discussion, his approach did not *invariably* work. Little did he know, when he repeated this demurral during his last weeks as bishop, that his most memorable failure still awaited him.

The final home visit of his bishoping tenure took him, on a pleasant Thursday evening in early September of 1957, down the narrow dirt road that curved around a little orchard encircling a pond full of Honey Spring water. Construction of the new Balford-Cody highway would not begin for several years, so there was not yet a new right-of-way fence to fortify with electric strands, nor was there a gate with a top spar resembling a small-scale abatis. Yet as his car followed the narrow track between Honey Spring and a field of ripening pinto beans, Clark Utley was filled with uncharacteristic misgiving. As the car crossed into the slab-fenced yard and drew up to the single-wide, misgiving became foreboding. The history of the place and its inhabitant, all the disappointment and grief and bitterness, was like a pall. So when Bishop U.'s knock at the door went unanswered, he was greatly relieved. He was too good a man and bishop and too stalwart a Latter-day Saint not to feel *some* shame for such relief. But that shame could be at least partially mitigated by checking behind the trailer house, by making one final token effort to find the most lost of Balford's lost sheep.

Unfortunately, that final token effort was enough. For there he was, Goss Harvey, planted at the edge of the bluff. The image would stay with Clark Utley forever—one lone man in a lawn chair sitting amid sagebrush at the brink of a riverbottom expanse spread out below him. In the pleasant evening haze of early autumn, he looked small. With one hand, he steadied a quart mason jar on one of the chair's flat aluminum arms. With the other hand, he held a pair of binoculars to his eyes. As Bishop Clark Utley closed the distance between them, he first assumed the big lenses of the binoculars were trained on the dormant gravel pit, located, in the softened evening light, at a distance both deceptively far and deceptively near. But then Clark Utley realized the focus of the binoculars was a closer subject. Goss was looking down the notch, toward swamp pasture and the divider fence that bisected it.

Bishop Utley called out and identified himself. But even after the several one-sided pleasantries accompanying his delicate crossing of the barbed-wire bluff fence—in well-shined shoes and dress trousers made of light wool—and the last leg of his approach, Goss said nothing, made no move to break off his study with the binoculars. Suddenly, with Clark Utley standing in sagebrush only three feet behind him and to one side, Goss let out one of the weirdest cries of celebration that his visitor had ever heard. It was whoop and shriek, bellow and guffaw all in one.

"*Yii-wooo-ee-HAW!*"

The cry was accompanied by a chorus of creaking from the lawn chair's aluminum frame as it rocked convulsively amid sagebrush plants ranked like spectators or sentinels—as if the rocking frame were responsible for Goss's squirming and twisting instead of the other way around.

"*Yii-wooo-ee-HAW! Yii-wooo-ee-HAW!*"

Full-throated and vigorous as it was, the chorus was muted and swallowed by the big autumn sky overhead.

At last, thrusting the binoculars skyward, Goss Harvey shouted, "Take that, you greedy brindle *bitch*!"

Then for a minute or so he just laughed. The sound was a medley of labored snorts and sniffs and wheezes. It was a laughter uncomfortable to listen to—not for its meanness or vindictiveness, though there was some of that, but for its note of resignation and despair. From behind a wall, from some distance, it would have been hard to distinguish from sobbing.

Finally the sound ebbed. Goss lowered the binoculars, wiped his eyes with a frayed shirt cuff, and took a celebratory drink from the mason jar. Against the pleasant evening stillness hanging over the expanse of the riverbottom pasture, the clink of ice cubes sounded tiny. At last Goss turned toward his visitor—not so much to acknowledge him as to size him up. His gaze climbed from the wool trousers to the white shirt, lingered on the bow tie. He took another drink from the mason jar, then rested it again on the chair's arm. He said, "Don't worry yourself, Brother Whoever-You-Are. It's just water."

That was the high point of the conversation. The gist of the rest of it, all three minutes' worth, could be easily represented in three lines roughly marking a beginning and middle, and definitely an end:

"Nephew, huh? Well, you sure didn't get her looks."

And:

"You came all the way out here to ask me *that*?"

And:

"Bishop or no bishop, it's a good thing for your scalp that you're not a Vanderfisk."

It was still early on the first Saturday after the May Day blizzard. Except in a few shaded nooks in Bishop Clive Sebright's machinery yard, Jim could see no evidence of the storm five days earlier.

"Darl told me about that," the bishop said, leaning against the rear tire of his plow tractor. He had just finished fueling and was on his way to the field. "I've had some jumpers, but that's got to be some kind of record to get over *that* fence." He paused and considered for a moment. "But maybe he's not jumping. Maybe he's swimming."

Jim smiled indulgently.

"No joke," Clive Sebright said. The words were so earnest they sounded almost like a rebuke. "I've seen it. Critter follows the fence right to the edge of the river and does an end-around, wading or swimming, depending on depth. Cattle are pretty good in the water."

Now Jim didn't smile. "So there's nothing to stop him from coming and going as he pleases?"

"Nope."

It was as good a time as any for Jim to ask what he had come to ask: "Do I tell Bernene?"

Bishop Clive Sebright sighed and toed one of the timbers of the frame elevating the big diesel tank from which he had just filled the plow tractor. "If it was my bull getting across the neighbor's fence by mysterious methods," he said, "I'd want to know." For a moment he seemed to weigh the wisdom of his counsel. "What's the lawyer say?"

"Take her to court."

For a fleeting moment, the expression on the bishop's face seemed to grant points to *that* argument for being, if nothing else, predictable. But then he shook his head. "Even if you didn't have to see her in church every week," he said, "in a setting where you're both supposed to be renewing your religious covenants, it's no good. Something like that knocks the scab right off an old feud, stirs everybody up, makes bad blood for the whole congregation, the whole darned town."

"Court is Rickett's idea," Jim clarified, "not mine. *I* don't really care *where* her bull spends his time. I just don't want something to happen to him on my side and be blamed for it."

Bishop Sebright looked at him. "No other reason?"

"Like what?"

"Like forcing family loyalties might get in the way of other important pursuits."

Jim didn't say anything.

"You know what I'm talking about."

Jim nodded.

"You interested in her?"

It was Jim's turn to kick the timbers.

"You could do worse," Clive Sebright said. "Jocelyn's a sharp kid and not nearly the rebel she'd like her aunt to think she is." After a pause he said, "Does Mr. Rickett have any advice on *that* matter?"

Jim gave the timbers a reprieve. "Put it like this," he said. "He doesn't think I'm doing a very good job wooing the niece of the woman he's urging me to sue. But he also thinks the reason I'm not suing is because I'm more interested in wooing."

"Is he right?"

Jim shrugged. "Even without Jocelyn in the picture," he said, "I still wouldn't want to fight Bernene, in court or anywhere else."

"But she *is* in the picture?" the bishop pressed.

"Look," Jim said, "I'm male, I'm twenty-three, I'm single. And I've probably got as many hormones as anybody else who fits that description. And, yes, as I have assured Rickett *and* Sister Cottrell—who both seem mighty interested in my love life—I do hope to find a wife someday. In the meantime, I just don't want to give Bernene any reason to sue *me*."

The bishop looked at him and smiled. "Fair enough," he said.

"So what do I tell her," Jim asked.

Bishop Clive Sebright pondered the question for quite a while. "I know Bernene Maxwell," he said at last. "Almost *too* well. And I'm pretty sure what would motivate her to keep her bull where he belongs."

"Fins *and* wings?" said Big Frett Maxwell after sacrament meeting the next day. He chuckled. "That's some bull we've got, Bernie. Triton and Pegasus all in one."

There were several important differences between this conversation with the Maxwells and the ones before it. For one thing, Jim had initiated it. For another, it was unfolding in a little Sunday school classroom in the Balford Ward meetinghouse, with the participants standing instead of sitting. And the most important difference of all? One of those participants—if only in the role of onlooker—was Jocelyn Vanderfisk. Neither her aunt or uncle introduced her.

For the second time since the beginning of the meeting—which had been underway for only two minutes, three at the most—Big Frett pulled a watch from the little pocket in the vest beneath his suit coat. He checked the time, then looked at Jocelyn. "Have *you* ever heard of a critter capable of an immaculate fence crossing?"

Jocelyn looked at her uncle, then her aunt, then Jim. She shrugged and smiled.

"I am sorry about the dog, Theron," Bernene said, searching her purse for a stick of gum or a tissue or perhaps a cosmetic of some sort. "I suggest you check Mr. Harvey's fence again. He did not consult my father concerning the design, so we can hardly be expected to take any responsibility for maintenance."

"Fair enough," Jim said, looking at Jocelyn out of the corner of his eye. Big Frett had slid the watch back in its pocket and was now playing with the fob, twisting it around his finger, then untwisting. "I just wanted to make sure you knew about this," Jim said. "And—to thank you."

The fob twisting and purse digging stopped. At last he, Jim Ray, had the full and genuine attention of Arthur "Frett" Maxwell and his wife. In saying what he wanted to say next, in accordance with the bishop's plan, Jim was both intimidated and encouraged by Jocelyn's presence.

"You see," he explained, "I've got this Angus bull. I call him Goliath"—a name brashly cooked up for this meeting—"on account of his size. He's a *big* animal. And a darned good sire. We've had some fine calves from him. There's not a thing wrong with his blood line." Jim met the gaze of Brother and Sister Maxwell. Jocelyn he had to look at more peripherally. "Of course, he's not as good as *your* bull, not by a long shot. But he's served just fine for Goss's little herd."

Here Jim hesitated, expressing with his face—he hoped—all the weightiness and solemnity of the disclosure to come. After a moment, he continued:

"The problem is, he's getting older and . . . *slower.* He just can't get around like he used to—can't *do* what he used to do, if you know what I mean. And with all the heifers I kept back last year . . ."

Jim paused, as if to suggest—he hoped—that he was weighing the propriety, in the present situation, of following the sentence to its conclusion. The Maxwells stared at him, unblinking. And Jocelyn? There was, in her eyes, the loveliest trace of humor.

"I don't know any other way to put it," Jim concluded with a compassionate grimace and a whisper: "Old Goliath can use all the help he can get."

CHAPTER 15

O N A M O N D A Y A F T E R N O O N E X A C T L Y S E V E N W E E K S
after the May Day blizzard, heat waves shimmered over the
stubble of a big hay field at the far edge of Goss Harvey's property. Across the corrugations at the top end of that field moved
a tractor-drawn flatbed wagon. In the middle of the bouncing,
hay-slicked wagon bed stood Jim Ray, approximating the stance
of a surfer. On the other side of the wagon's headboard, planted
comfortably on the tractor seat, Rickett turned the steering
wheel to bring the rig parallel to the corrugations, lined up on
the nearest row of bales, and nudged the throttle with the heel of
his hand. A cigarette bobbed in his lips. He allowed himself one
per load; this was his fourth of the afternoon.

Hitched alongside the wagon, just behind the headboard,
was a mechanical bale elevator. At the bottom end of the elevator chute, two metal fins funneled the first bale lengthwise onto
the fingers of the conveyor chain. At the top end of the chute, an
inward-cocked platform channeled that bale toward the center
of the wagon bed eight feet below it. Until the first tiers raised
the stacker closer to the platform, the only way to get a hold of a
pair of twines was to wait for the bale to be crowded off its perch.
After dodging its fall, the stacker had about five seconds to lug
and jockey and secure in place before the next one fell.

In due time, the load reached, then exceeded, the height of the
elevator platform. Building the load so as not to require straps or
tie-downs, required tapering the sides. With each new tier, that
tapering further restricted surface space for both bales and boots.

As the load grew toward its crowning ridge, footing and balance became more and more dear.

Complicating space restrictions up on the load was Rickett's clutch foot down in the tractor's cockpit. In a year's time, the foot had lost none of its fickleness, as always became clear when the load was near completion. Two or three times, the rig might begin to slow, smoothly and reassuringly, only to leap forward once again. Thanks to the considerable play in the coupling of wagon tongue and tractor hitch, such shifts in movement were accompanied by a tremendous clash and jolt. Only when there was *nowhere* to stack one more bale—and, even if there had been, no good place to stand so as to do the stacking—only when Jim added frantic hoots and whistles to his repeated shouts, only then did the slowing finally take. Just at that moment, however, Rickett might grow as impatient for stopping as he was for starting, and stomp on the brake pedals. The brake shoe for the right rear tire might take a notion to grab while its mate to the left didn't. Another clash of metal. Another jolt like an earth tremor. Had Jim not been clinging to the twines of a well-lodged bale, the physics of the moment would have pitched him headlong to the stubble below.

But the thrill of stopping was more than compensated for by what came next. After the dismounting (to unhitch the elevator chute) and remounting (with water bag in hand), the stacker's only duty was to ride the mile or so to home and hay yard. His perch put him high above the tractor driver, as if that topmost front bale were the howdah on a behemoth.

The ride on this behemoth was not *entirely* relaxing. Magnified by the load's height and weight, every lurch and sway and yaw—at furrow ridges and culvert crossings and puddle sinks— registered in Jim's stomach. And once the wagon gained the road, elevation forced a reckoning with things ordinarily inconsequential to a road traveler. Cottonwood branches, for example.

They always stood ready to sweep a high-rider from the saddle. If their sweeping failed, a power line, sagging between two poles, waited to relieve him of his head.

Still, this time between loading and unloading was something to savor. The howdah had no canopy, so the view atop the moving hay wagon was spectacular. The sky was blue beyond blue. Gliding through one of its gyres, a hawk scrutinized, from a thousand feet up, the seams of stacked bales for stowaway mice. Every few seconds brought breezes unknown at lower levels. From his vantage point, Jim could drink from the water bag and appreciate, as from no ground-level angle, the feat of the raised highway. Under the summer sun, a steady stream of vehicles flashed past the historic marker turn-out, westbound to Yellowstone, eastbound to the Bighorns. How many of those drivers knew anything of the road layers under their wheels?

The sweetest pleasure of the high ride, Jim decided, was a certain kind of removal. From atop the load, you could enumerate, from a comfortable distance, every strain and labor, every risk and discomfort and vexation. Heat radiating up from stubble. Hay chaff on sweaty skin. All kinds of irritants—brome seeds and foxtail and cockleburs and thistle buds—finding their way into boots and gloves, collars and waistbands. Swarms of deerflies. Machine racket. Grasshopper chirr so persuasively imitative of a rattlesnake. Stings and bites, nettling and chafing, itch and din—for a time it was all thought about instead of experienced. The difference was monumental.

For some, such removal was rest and refreshment. For others, it was repudiation.

Riding the hay wagon behemoth, Jim remembered two of the guys on the guardrail crew. One was the son of an affluent father who, despite his money, wanted that son to learn the value of honest physical labor. The other guy was a reform school dropout. The two formed an unlikely alliance, based mostly on their shared contempt for the value of physical labor and on their common goal of doing as little of it as possible. The foreman called them Laurel and Hardly. The best cover for their goldbricking was to chum with the DOT inspector. The chumming was not fraternal. They just liked his pickup's air-conditioning.

On paper it was all the same work site, between this or that pair of mile markers on some stretch of new pavement somewhere in unpeopled Utah. And on that site, the inspector's air-conditioned pickup was parked pretty close to the asphalt's edge, right behind the auger truck, where workmates with shovels and tamping bars and mauls and wrenches were actually *demonstrating* the value of physical labor. Still, the divide between the air-conditioned cab and the un-air-conditioned shoulder of the road was enormous. For three months, the *only* ambition discernible in Laurel and Hardly was to get from one side of that divide to the other and to malinger there as long as possible.

As Jim rode the hay wagon, one memory led to another. One day, working west, the guardrail crew met a chain gang working east. Under the glare of the afternoon sun, the inmates wielded sling blades. Sitting in a truck cab, two guards wielded rifles. Jim remembered the wave exchanged by the guards and the DOT man, who wielded a clipboard and pencil. Different as they were, their jobs had one thing in common—the status of removal. Had either guard ever swung a sling blade? Had the DOT guy ever hefted a tamping bar? Whatever the answer, the quality that most defined their jobs *now* was sitting away and apart from the work they watched hour after hour, day after day.

In war, however, the difference between rest and repudiation grew blurry. That last chopper ride back to base was the weirdest, sweetest, most longed-for removal of all. One minute you're on the ground; you're there; you're in it. The next, you're up and over and gone. Twenty minutes, maybe thirty, to fly over trees and terrain that had taken days and weeks to hump through. Even Fritchey—who, unlike Ardizzoli, did *not* forever barter, bribe, bootlick, and cadge to get out of work—even no less a man than Fritchey agreed that the absolute gold-standard granddaddy of suck-egg duty was combat. "I'd gladly take latrine-barrel duty at base camp every day for the rest of my life," he said, "if it meant not getting shot at." In war, removal was survival.

Atop the moving hay wagon, Jim uncorked the bag and took another drink. The water was cool. He liked the smell of wet canvas. He studied the wide blue sky and thought about the Maxwells' removal from the problem of the dun bull. He thought especially of Bernene, wondered if she'd ever stepped foot in the gravel pit that had accounted for so much wealth. He tried to conjure an image of her in hip waders, floundering through swamp mud, bouffant bobbing, desperate to keep her bull and his seed on the Vanderfisk side of the fence.

No, someone else would do Bernene Maxwell's swamp combing. Not twenty-four hours after the meeting in the little Sunday school classroom, she had dispatched Hap and Percy Croft to ride the Vanderfisk side of the riverbottom. For several days they criss-crossed the property. Whether or how often they spotted the dun bull in that time, Jim never knew. Then they spent another day walking the divider fence with a roll of rabbit-proof wire and a can of staples, now and again reinforcing a spot that didn't need reinforcing.

A few mornings later, standing before a swatch of rabbit wire, Jim saw a horse come over a rise in the alkali scrub on the Vanderfisk side. The rider was not Hap or Percy Croft because the rider was female. She rode closer, close enough for Jim to recognize Jocelyn Vanderfisk. She came to the edge of an impassible bog. If not for that bog, she might have come closer still.

They were fifty yards a apart. Jim raised a hand in greeting. She did the same. Rickett was right about Jim's wooing. Its high mark was a smile or wave at intervals that certainly didn't rush things.

The ride on the hay wagon neared its end. Approaching the gate in the farmyard's slab fence, Rickett throttled down. High on the behemoth, Jim had to duck, fast, beneath the gate's high cross-brace. Paying necessary attention to things earthbound, Rickett must have seen, before Jim, the trunk of a pea-green Rambler parked on the near side of the trailer's stoop. Then they both saw the driver of the Rambler, a lady, open its door and stand, waiting, as the hay rig rolled to its smoothest stop of the day. They both watched as the lady came toward the loaded wagon, using one hand to shield her eyes from the sun. It was Enid Cottrell. In the sudden quiet after the turning off of the tractor engine, they both listened as she passed on news of the biggest removal of all.

Enoch Vanderfisk was dead.

CHAPTER 16

B Y THE TIME GOSS HARVEY WENT DOWN WITH THE sickness that eventually killed him, his scalp had been bald for forty years. And, during his final months, he lost what little hair he had elsewhere. A combination of potent medicine and deficiencies of the blood somehow affected the follicles in every region of his body. So the corpse beneath the gurney shroud, besides being withered and pallid, was also, in the words of a rest home worker, hairless as a scalded hog. Details of Goss's final physical condition were known to very few people—that rest home worker and her colleagues, a doctor, and the Cody mortician found in the Yellow Pages of that city's telephone directory. ("I don't want *nobody* from Balford involved," Goss had insisted. "You understand? *Nobody*.") Out of a desperate dignity, Goss guarded the details of his death, pitiful as they were, as he had guarded the details of the last decade of his life. Such guarding represented the only sovereignty left to him. Thus his cultivated estrangement from human society endured to the very end.

He succeeded in making it to his grave unbeknownst to everyone in Balford except the owner and editor of the *Balford Clarion,* a man named Lewis Glenney. But Goss overestimated the significance of his cherished secrecy even if Lewis Glenney didn't. It was an irony typical of human beings. News of Goss's death, as reported in a two-and-a-half-inch obituary on the newspaper's back page, was indifferently received. It was, for those who read such things as a kind of hobby, little more than notice of another death in another nursing home. In fact, the only surprise for most readers who recognized his name at all was that Goss hadn't been dead longer.

Enoch's death, on the other hand, was met with widespread shock, disbelief, sorrow. Such sentiments inevitably crept into the *Clarion*'s account, this one on the front page. If journalism has an equivalent of sackcloth, it was that story and its headline:

BALFORD VALLEY MOURNS PASSING
OF BELOVED PIONEER

As the story pointed out, this beloved Balford Valley pioneer—*and* successful businessman *and* unifying community leader—had been widely and affectionately known as "Old Enoch." While the story didn't mention that the name had taken root when Enoch's hair turned a premature but lustrous silver—well before the age of seventy—it made clear that it was an honorific. If Balford had needed a tribal chief, Enoch would have won appointment. Ubiquitous, venerable, involved, influential, robust, august—he loomed, in the end, bigger than life. His death swelled the ranks of his supporters, and softened his few critics to a state of generous respect and fair-mindedness.

To use the name was to assume a familiarity not justified in most cases by actual acquaintance. "Old Enoch just *felt* like a grandpa to the whole town," the *Clarion* quoted one of the legion of mourners as saying. Familiarity, justified or not, gave the user of the name a kind of claim on the man. For those who pay any attention at all to aged public figures, each successive year is usually regarded—albeit privately, tacitly—as little more than another inevitable increment toward the coffin. Not so with the residents who saw Enoch as the town's grandfather. For them, each birthday, as heralded in the newspaper—*Long-Time Bank President Turns 80; Balford Business Leader Celebrates 83 Years; At 85, Town Founder Says "Best Is Yet to Come"*—constituted a defiance of incremental decline, or at the very least, a distraction and a denial. And if the name enabled people to distract from and deny the decline of another, it enabled them to distract from and deny their own.

For a man his age, Enoch *had* enjoyed remarkable health and vitality. In the days before his collapse, he had not been sick. He had not been weak or listless or without appetite. He had not been particularly tired. Except for some undeniable aging in the fourteen months since Goss's burial, particularly some dulling of the silver mane, he, of all Balford's remaining pioneer generation, had been considered the most likely to make it to a hundred. On the morning of the day of Enid Cottrell's hay-yard visit—the nineteenth of June, a Monday—Enoch had showed up at the bank as usual to pleasantly while away five or six hours doing whatever he did in his office by the vault. But when noon came and Big Frett Maxwell knocked on the half-closed office door to ask, with affectionate ritual, if his father-in-law was ready to strap on the feed bag, he got no answer. Opening the door more fully only confirmed what he suddenly and unaccountably feared. Old Enoch sat slumped over at his desk, in a posture unnatural to pencil work, reading, or even napping.

Before long, the puzzle came to revolve around what exactly he *was* doing when his heart stopped. Clutched in one hand was the saucer-sized frame bearing the black-and-white studio portrait of young Honey Utley. Clutched in the other was the black and white street photographer's rendering, removed from its bottom-corner spot in the wall gallery, of two friends in white shirts and ties, each with an arm around the other's shoulders. Penciled on the back of that second photo were words no one still living had ever seen:

Me and Goss
Trip to Cody for missionary suit
Oct. 19, 1900
(H. standing by photographer)

At nine-thirty-five on a Saturday morning almost sixty-seven years later, the pews of the Balford Ward chapel, at least the portion not reserved for family, were already filled with funeral attendees. And those in the chapel were just part of the crowd. Behind the chapel was an overflow area, and behind that, the combination gymnasium and ambitiously named cultural hall. On ordinary Sundays and Wednesday Mutual nights, the overflow was partitioned off from chapel and gym, sandwiched between two big meet-in-the-middle accordion curtains hung from a ceiling track. But on this day, the curtains stood wide open. The overflow, otherwise used only at Christmas, Easter, and missionary farewells and homecomings, held a hundred folding chairs. The gymnasium held three hundred more. Even with that number, open seats were disappearing fast.

In another wing of the building, at the front of the women's Relief Society room, the last of a long line was just now filing past the open casket, under the vigilant eye of Balford's mortician, a man by the name of Burl Bigler. He had owned and operated Bigler Funeral Home for so long that no townsman in need of a mortician's services had ever so much as thought about looking in the phone book's Yellow Pages. Everyone knew him by what he did for a living. And what he did for a living was to take care of the dead.

He was good at it. Since the beginning of the viewing, he had demonstrated the paradoxical skills required by the part of his trade practiced outside the embalming room. He attended without hovering, supported without intruding, remained readily available but out of the way. For the better part of an hour, he had stood with calm and apparently inexhaustible dignity. No indiscreet peeking at his watch, no amateurish foot shifting, no conspicuous yawns, burps, hiccups, no breaking wind, no scratching of itches in remote clefts and hollows.

Above all, the public part of the job required a keen sensitivity to an irony never admitted in the midst of this most somber of rituals. That irony was this: Receiving consolation for grief could tax the spirit as thoroughly as the grief itself. Because of that irony, *someone* had to serve as an anchor of stability and decorum. That duty fell to Burl Bigler. It was he who had to be the unobtrusive guardian of the whole affair. Efficient but not hurried. Composed but not stone-faced. Stationary but not static. At the appropriate moment, he didn't move. And at the appropriate moment, he did. There was a good deal more expertise to it than was commonly understood. Yet some people—including Bernene Maxwell—had the nerve to murmur about his fees! The only way he was appreciated was by *not* being appreciated. Fill another casket for six hundred people to peer into with a mixture of fear and sadness—and, it must be admitted, *some* morbid curiosity—and let Bernene Maxwell have a go at it. Let *her* try standing off to the side for minutes on end, taking questions, dispensing comfort, directing wanderers, all without flinching or flagging.

Besides being a mortician, Burl Bigler was also Sunday school superintendent of the Balford Ward and knew the clock in the Relief Society room to be five minutes slow. For the better part of fifty minutes straight he had stood motionless as a statue. But finally the minute hand of that laggard clock crept into alignment—*three, two, one*—with the hash mark indicating nine-forty-four . . .

And *now* he moved.

With practiced smoothness and solemnity, he moved.

With reliable and authoritative clairvoyance, he moved.

With condolence and solicitude in every gesture, every hushed step, he moved.

In the working of a funeral, this was the opening curtain of Act Two. As he threaded his way through the lingering viewers, he negotiated the most delicate paradox of all—fusing the needs of the living with the needs of the dead. Both required keeping to a schedule.

Bishop Clive Sebright's role in Enoch's final public appearance was every bit as integral. Less than an hour after Enoch had collapsed at his bank desk, the bishop's home telephone rang. The caller was Bernene Maxwell. As was her way, she more or less dictated a meeting the next morning—Tuesday, June twentieth—in the bishop's office at church (at an hour that couldn't possibly have been less convenient to a farmer's work day) to coordinate the particulars of the funeral service. The meeting, she informed Clive Sebright, would include her and her husband, of course, and the mortician Burl Bigler, and (*only* because of an official Church requirement) him. At that meeting, Bernene had not been timid about her expectations. Her father, she insisted, was to be honored in a manner befitting a man of his contributions and legacy. Her tone suggested that other funerals during Clive Sebright's bishoping tenure had been defective precedents.

Her father *would* be duly honored, the bishop assured Sister Bernene, but his funeral would include nothing extravagant or unorthodox or otherwise different from any other Latter-day Saint funeral. The Church published guidelines for such services, and, as bishop, he intended to follow them. About the eulogy, for instance. It had its place, but that place would be allotted about twenty minutes. Did that number come from the guidelines, Bernene wanted to know, or from Bishop Clive Sebright? The principle, the bishop said, was proportion. Remembrances of her father's long life, productive and righteous as it was, could

not be allowed to shortchange the other purpose of the occasion, which was to teach the bedrock doctrines of life's purpose,
of the hope, through Jesus Christ, of resurrection and eternal
life. As the bishop reminded Bernene, the biggest advocate of
teaching such doctrines in a funeral setting would have been her
father himself. And no one would have been more mindful of
the program's length. With hymns and prayers, the whole thing
shouldn't go much beyond an hour.

During that Tuesday morning planning meeting in his
cramped office, Clive Sebright had said all that he said with a
tact and sensitivity surpassing his natural gifts. (Later, with
nothing related to the immediate duties of his calling to supplement those gifts, he confided to his wife: "If all folks want out
of a funeral is nostalgia or embellishment, they're better off at a
class reunion—or a bar.") It happened that the seating arrangement for the planning meeting put Bernene next to the wall,
beside and a little beneath the Gethsemane painting. After the
bishop's kindly laying down of terms, she had sat silent for a long
moment, with the painting's olive tree branches as a backdrop
to a huge bouffant stiff with dried hair spray. As always, she was
impeccably groomed. But even impeccable grooming could not
completely mask the tension between her bereavement and the
persuasiveness of the appeal to her father's wisdom—a tension
flavored with smoldering discord.

She and Bishop Sebright had a rather rocky history. During
arrangements for her only daughter's necessarily rushed wedding nine years earlier, they had met in this same cramped office.
Then, as now, he had said no to any lavishness of decoration or
procedure within the walls of the church house, though he had
said it perhaps a little less sensitively. At the time, Clive Sebright

had been bishop only a few months. Since he was so new to the calling—and a bit rough around the edges, even for a farmer—Bernene thought he might be eager to please a congregant of her prominence. Or, failing that, she thought he might at least respond to subtle coercion or, failing that, genteel cowing. She was wrong. The wedding ceremony, as newly appointed Bishop Clive Sebright made clear, was to be small, simple, modest, frugal. Even apart from her daughter's special "circumstances," that was the policy. In the end, *only* to honor that daughter's wishes, Bernene had bitten her tongue and submitted to the bishop's conditions—insofar as the wedding was concerned.

The reception was another matter. She just moved it, in the dead of January, to her big house on Balford Hill, then did her best to make the food, music, dancing, gifts, cake, and newlyweds' send-off as lavish as her motives and means could make them. Indeed, the whole affair lived up to its billing as the "grand nuptial celebration" promised in each of several hundred ornately embossed invitations. To get these invitations out as speedily as possible (given the delicate urgency of the whole matter), Bernene put them in her big purse and snuck them into church on a Sunday not long before the date chosen for the reception. At the conclusion of sacrament meeting, this woman who was fond of dispatching, dispatched two of her nine grown sons, one to each of the chapel's rear doors, to hand out embossed invitations to exiting ward members. This plan was executed without the bishop's foreknowledge or permission.

On her own turf, the reception festivities could be as grand as Bernene wanted them to be, and it was the bishop who would have to do the tongue-biting. But exploiting the handy proximity of a mass of Sabbath worshippers for personal convenience? That crossed a line. And the worst of it wasn't the disrespect and presumption. Much to Clive Sebright's chagrin, the worst of it, from his perspective, was the defective precedent *it* set. From that day on, for most of the next decade, anyone organizing a wedding reception, a bridal or baby shower, a graduation or anniversary or birthday or Tupperware party could invoke Bernene's example. Whether the inviter meant to save the cost of postage or (as in Bernene's case) the delivery time, the practice was at best questionable. While the bishop had to admit it hardly rose to the level of money-changers in the temple, it *did* stray from the mark and take advantage and annoy. Yet every time he had to correct a guilty party—or on the far rarer occasions when he managed to thwart a schemer beforehand—he only further solidified his reputation as a hidebound killjoy ("But you let Sister Maxwell do it!"). He was just trying to fulfill the calling, as the phrase went—a calling he certainly hadn't asked for. Who needed the headache?

Bishop Clive Sebright tried not to let the weight of such history influence *too* much restriction in his overseeing of Enoch Vanderfisk's funeral arrangements. But he couldn't deny that the satisfaction of enforcing such restriction had a *little* less to do with honoring Church policy than with settling the score with Bernene Maxwell. Vanity of vanities.

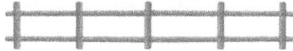

At ten to ten (the true time), on the morning of June 24, 1967—a Saturday—Burl Bigler gave himself over to instincts and habits honed from a quarter century of burying Balford's dead, including the bodies shipped home from three different wars. (Those were almost as hard as children.) It took only seconds to move from his post that couldn't *seem* like a post to the casket resting on its wheeled bier at the front of the Relief Society room. With one last scrutinizing of his handiwork (face skillfully flesh-toned and serene, hair restored to nearly life-like fullness and luster, arms and fingers positioned so as to appear *unstiff*), he soundlessly closed the lid. Then, with a subtle tilting of the head and a single blink, he cued an assistant. Together, they steered the bier through a sizeable population of Vanderfisks and out into the uncarpeted hall, to serve as vanguard of the chapel procession. With characteristic attention to detail, he had personally lubricated the bier's casters with a tiny flask of sewing machine oil kept in his suit pocket. And now—not a squeak.

At four minutes till, the bier glided across the carpeted foyer and over the threshold into the chapel. At the podium, Bishop Clive Sebright—who on this day had forgone corduroys and green jacket for an actual suit and his bolo for a regular Windsor-knotted tie—invited the many hundred people before him to stand. The casket rolled behind the rearmost pews and up the far aisle while a long line of family, led by Bernene's oldest brother, used the closer aisle. Household by household, person by person, the Vanderfisk clan took their reserved places.

In a back row of the gymnasium, Jim Ray and Rickett stood in front of their folding chairs. "Can you see her now?" Rickett asked with only the feeblest effort at whispering. Jim didn't answer.

"I just want to see what she looks like," Rickett said in a low, hoarse voice. This was the first time since Goss Harvey's graveside service that Jim had seen him in a suit and tie. "That's the only reason I came."

Jim didn't say anything.

"I couldn't tell which one she was in that other room. Was she even in there?"

Jim gave one stiff nod.

"Did you wink at her?"

Now Jim looked his way. In a clipped whisper, he said, "You do know we're standing in a church, right? And that this is a funeral?"

"Levity helps me cope."

"Well, cope a little more reverently."

With the rest of the crowd, they remained standing until ten o'clock sharp. That's when the bier's front casters arrived at their appointed place on the carpet, between the podium and the first pew. The fit would have been tight even without the flowers. Banked against the face of the podium wall was the largest quantity of floral arrangements ever amassed for a funeral in this chapel. It was a head-high mound of wreaths and sprays, a berm of greenery, of petals and stems, both natural and artificial. Such legroom as the flowers and casket left the occupants of the front pew had to be carefully navigated so as to make crowding seem like something other than it was. After double-checking the position of the well-oiled casters, the assistant nodded to Burl Bigler, who looked toward the pulpit and nodded to Bishop Clive Sebright, who took a breath and nodded to the hundreds of people assembled. Because people in such a setting often don't know what to make of an officiator's nod, the bishop supplemented his with the vocal instruction to "Please be seated."

It was a good service. Its hymns were drawn from a short list of the deceased's favorites. To open, the congregation sang, "Nearer My God to Thee." Halfway through, a choir composed of an army of great-grandchildren sang "Teach Me to Walk in the Light." And the service closed with "Sing We Now at Parting." Between hymns, Enoch Vanderfisk's identity and life, mortal and immortal, were well accounted for. Son-in-law Arthur (Big Frett) Maxwell delivered the eulogy, and the main talk was given by nephew (and stake president) Clark Utley. Yet, fitting as it was and had to be, nothing sung in the hymns, nothing said by way of condolence or eulogy or doctrinal affirmation or prayerful petition so much as hinted at the rift between Enoch and his Honey Spring neighbor.

Until the brief closing remarks of Bishop Clive Sebright. As was characteristic of the man, those remarks were without flourish or unction. Among other things, he said this:

"Not everything broken in this life can be made whole, and not everything lost can be restored—not in this world, anyway. But the hereafter is another matter. The forever unmendable is what the Savior saves us *from*."

That was all he said. But anyone with any sort of rend or scar or hurt—which was, of course, everyone in the crowd—listened with great attentiveness. And anyone old enough to remember remembered, with utter certainty, the one specific rend the bishop's statement alluded to.

After the bishop's words, a vast calm came over the chapel and overflow and the gym with the genuine hardwood floor. Blinking slowed. Eyes welled. Lips trembled. There were some six hundred living, breathing bodies assembled, yet for a remarkable interval, there was not a cough or sneeze or sniff. The quiet was sublime. Along each short pew and long pew, along the many rows of folding chairs, the faces of those in mourning, of those attending out of affection, loyalty, obligation, curiosity, were, all of them, for one rare moment, unitedly pensive, tender, hopeful. And for a time much too brief, during the strains of the closing hymn, during the earnest words of the benediction, during the recessional standing of the crowd, during the pallbearers' solemn taking up of their burden and their march toward the chapel's small side door used only for this purpose, during all that there were no rocky histories, no animosities, no scores to settle.

Funerals, Professor-Bishop-Stake President Clark Utley had noted in his talk, are for the living.

Long after the casket was loaded into the hearse, dozens of milling family members were still finding their way into the vehicles that would take them to the cemetery at the head of the cortege. Meanwhile, inside the church building, certain ward members—Jim among them, suit coat removed—had already begun clearing away the hundreds of folding chairs in the gymnasium. (Having some time ago surpassed his comfort threshold for mixing with this particular crowd—and for going without a cigarette—Rickett had escaped outside to wait in the truck.) Most of the chairs needed to be returned to classrooms throughout the building or collapsed flat and stacked on long, wheeled pallets. The remainder would stay with the folding tables being

set up for the customary family meal. That meal would commence immediately upon the family's return from the graveside
service.

Mystery for familiarity, silence for talk, gravity for cheer—honoring the dead had given way, once again, to tending to the living. It was an old and welcome transition, and it was underway
here in the gymnasium of a church house in Balford, Wyoming. In
the corner at one end of the basketball court, the well-varnished
hardwood came right up to a set of double-doors. Those doors
opened onto a long hall running perpendicular to the court. On
the other side of that hall, directly across from the double doors,
sat the kitchen. To the left of the kitchen, along the hall, were three
adjoining Sunday school classrooms. Then the hall bent ninety
degrees to the right and led to two or three more classrooms and
finally to one of the building's rear exits.

Bound for the farthest of those classrooms carrying his
third load of collapsed chairs—two for each hand—Jim went
through the gym's double doors and passed the kitchen's serving
counter. The counter's scroll-shutter was up, revealing a hive of
meal preparations. Amid the pleasant fellowship of collective
effort and the good smells of covered-dish bounty, a half dozen
women wearing aprons over funeral dresses were spooning,
slicing, warming, plattering. Among them, Artelle Darlington,
Mina Godwin, Ivy Teague. In any proximity to charitable church
service it was only natural to find Enid Cottrell. She saw Jim and
waved. Beside her, at the sink, a stout and cheerful soul named
Opal Renfro was emptying a big bag of ice into water pitchers.
Despite the rumble and clatter of an indiscriminate aim, Opal
Renfro's good-natured voice carried beyond the kitchen. First
she remarked on the biggest fruit medley she had ever seen sitting right there in the refrigerator. Then she asked the world at
large:

"What do you suppose it is about funerals that gives folks
such an appetite?"

Jim had about two seconds to contemplate the question. (Fear and danger had the same effect on Ardizzoli. In the most unlikely moments, he could be found finger-scooping turkey loaf or beenie weenie or date pudding from a C-ration can into his mouth.) Then it was time to contemplate other things. For Jim's rounding of the bend in the hall brought him face to face, body to body, with someone rounding the same bend from the opposite direction—at a run.

He hadn't heard footfalls.

In the flash-moment confusion of smell and sight, sound and touch—quite substantial contact, in fact—he knew that the other hall traveler was female. What he didn't know, until after the substantial contact, after smelling the perfume and shampoo and lip gloss, hearing the startled cry, feeling the reflexively upthrust hands against his shoulders—what he didn't know until *then* was that this particular female was Jocelyn Vanderfisk.

Finally. An interaction that was more than a wave.

In the half-second after the collision, her hands fell away, and she stumbled backwards and sideways. As he did.

Amid the clanking of the chairs—he didn't let go—Jim tripped, staggered, found his feet again. Up to the instant of collision, she had held her shoes in one hand. Now they lay asunder on the hard, artificial tile of the hall. Shocked and embarrassed, she looked at them, then at him, then broke out laughing.

He hurried to stand the four chairs upright against one wall and stooped to retrieve the shoes. The action gave him a good view of Jocelyn Vanderfisk's nylon-stockinged toes, ankles, lower legs. Their form and symmetry were exquisite. On the hall's smooth surface, nylon-stockinged feet would glide as if on a cloud and make no sound at all.

He stood with a shoe in each hand, extended them heel-first, said, "Now I know why Primary teachers make such a big deal about not running in church."

Taking the shoes as offered, one in each hand—still laughing—Jocelyn said, "First I take all the napkins at the A&W and now I try to plow you over."

She stood no more than two feet away. As they stood, she transferred both shoes to one hand. "I know you know my aunt and uncle," she said, extending her free hand, "but I'm not sure you know me."

Jim took her hand, let her guide the shaking.

"You're Jocelyn Vanderfisk," he said. "You ride motorcycles and horses."

She let go his hand, slowly. "And you're Jim Ray. You have a bull named Goliath, and you take your strolls in a swamp."

Even though her dress was chosen for the ceremonies of this day, it was wondrously flattering. For a moment, neither of them spoke. She looked down, shifted her lovely, symmetrical, nylonstockinged feet, then looked up again. Directing her gaze at the chairs leaning against the wall, she asked, "Were those for my grandpa's funeral?"

Jim nodded.

"Aunt Bernene said this was the biggest funeral ever held in this building.

"Four hundred people in the overflow and gym alone."

"You counted?"

"I heard it from a guy who did."

"You know," Jocelyn Vanderfisk said reflectively, "what Aunt Bernene *actually* said was that this was *by far* the biggest funeral ever."

"That sounds like her."

Jocelyn seemed to weigh his words—compliment or criticism? Noises from the gym and kitchen floated down the hall. They stood for a moment.

"Would you do me a favor?" she asked.

Scale mountains, ford rivers, cross deserts. Anything.

"Sure," he said.

"My mother and aunt are waiting for me—to go to the cemetery. Aunt Bernene sent me in here to give a message to whoever's in charge of setting up the meal."

Jim pointed toward the kitchen, toward the distinct tones of Opal Renfro's voice and the discussion of fruit medley.

"Aunt Bernene told them a hundred and twenty-five people. But now she thinks more like a hundred." She looked at him. "Will you do that for me?"

Jim nodded again.

"Thank you," she said. And as she said this, she touched his arm ever so briefly. She hesitated. "By the way," she said, "I think I saw my aunt's bull."

Jim was charmed almost as much by her volunteering of such information as by her eyes. "When?" he asked.

"Just a couple of days ago." Then she said, "All that time searching, and those Croft guys never found it. And I was just out riding again for fun, and I did."

They looked at each other.

"I haven't told Aunt Bernene," Jocelyn said, more serious now. "She probably wouldn't believe me anyway. Or she'd think your lawyer friend—that's what she calls him, *the lawyer friend*—has some kind of scheme going. Or maybe she even thinks you and I . . ." She stopped, more guarded now than she had been. After a moment she said, "Look, my aunt's a good woman, and she's been really good to me and my mother. But she doesn't always think the best of others. Plus, I'm not a *hundred* percent sure it was her bull. But if it *was* the bull you were talking about with my aunt and uncle that one Sunday"—she nodded toward one of the little classrooms along the hall—"it *was* on your side of the fence."

The meeting, however coincidental, had taken on an importance that went beyond an amended head count for the funeral meal. But now that the head-count message was delivered, Jocelyn said, "I better go. My mother and my aunt are waiting." But in making her retreat, she did not turn away from Jim. Nor did she end their conversation just yet. Walking backwards in her nylon-stockinged feet, she thanked him for helping with the chairs, suggested he find something to eat in the kitchen, countered his polite rejection of the idea, thanked him a second time, and a third. As she spoke, her backward-gliding feet took her ever closer to the little vestibule at the end of the hall. On one side of the vestibule hung a shelf above a row of coat hooks. On the other side sat a heating radiator at floor-level. On the hard, smooth tiles between them lay a rubber-bristled rug. Gliding backwards, her nylon-stockinged soles met the rug's rubber bristles. Jim felt the tickle in his stomach. With a beautiful hinging of the knee—and still facing him—she lifted one foot and slipped on a shoe. Then she did the same with the other foot. For a moment they looked at each other down the long hall.

"Next time I come around that corner," she said, smiling again, "I'll wear a cowbell." Then she turned and stepped out the door.

Forty-five minutes later—not long before the return of the Vanderfisk clan—all folding chairs and tables were in their proper places, and Jim went through the same vestibule, through the same door at the end of the hall, into the bright sunshine of mid-day. Angling across the parking lot toward his pickup, he caught a whiff of cigarette and smiled. He saw Rickett's elbow sticking out the truck's passenger window. He saw the hand emerge and the index finger tap ash into the hot air.

Then he saw something else. Parked on the other side of the lot, in the shade of one of the few trees on church property tall enough to provide it, was a big Harley-Davidson. He detoured far enough to confirm, on its gas tank, the decal that recommended making love, not war.

("Who *wouldn't* prefer it?" Ardizzoli had asked with scorn when a new guy reported the slogan's growing popularity back home. "That's like saying eat steak, not Spam; use TP, not leaves; drink your beer *cold.*")

Five minutes later the old pickup cleared the town limits and headed west on the Balford-Cody highway. It was very hot. Driver and passenger had hung their suit coats on the rubber-coated hooks of the gun rack and had loosened their ties extravagantly. Both windows gaped wide. Every exchange of words had to be loud to be heard above the rushing air. So far that requirement hadn't deterred Rickett.

"You sure it's him?"

"It's him," Jim said.

"Maybe he's just another mourner come to pay his respects," Rickett said.

"All the regular mourners have gone home," Jim said. "The only vehicles left in the parking lot belong to helpers and family, and there was no biker dude helping." For a quarter mile, Jim drove without speaking. Then, against the wind, he said, "She mentioned keeping her *family* waiting; she didn't mention anybody else. So the question is, Was he invited or just horning in?"

"The only people who horn in on a private graveside service are lawyers," Rickett said.

Jim looked at him. "So he had to be invited."

Rickett shrugged. Between every pair of sentences, the pickup covered a lot of ground, as if the speakers had to be more and more careful to pace their lungs.

"But," Jim said, "he wasn't with the family in the Relief Society room or the chapel."

"Are you sure you'd recognize him?"

"To tell you the truth, no," Jim said. "There were three that day at the A&W: a long hair with a beard, another without a beard, and a skinhead with a pirate bandanna. He's got to be one of those."

"Nobody would wear a pirate bandanna to a Mormon funeral," Rickett said.

"Whichever one he is, however he was dressed, he would've stood out in the funeral crowd. And if he was with *her,* I couldn't have missed him."

"I'd say not," Rickett said. "You were staring pretty hard."

"I wasn't staring; I was . . . paying attention."

"Well, you were paying attention pretty hard."

As the pickup passed through Ralston, Jim said, "So—what? He met her afterward just to go to the cemetery?"

"Could be."

"Because he's squeamish about funerals?"

"Or a chapel full of Mormons," Rickett said "Which, I got to tell you, I completely sympathize with."

As he drove the last leg of highway toward home, Jim glanced sideways at his passenger. He felt as if he were yelling into a wind tunnel. "Yeah, well, *I'm* getting kind of squeamish about *him.*"

"You think Niece Vanderfisk can do better?"

Staring straight ahead, Jim drove with both hands on the fissured steering wheel and gave his lungs and larynx a rest.

"Like maybe *you?*" In Rickett's case, it was as if a long inurement to tobacco had given his lungs and larynx even more stamina. "That's mighty chivalrous of you, Jim. But I told you last spring Big Bernene would beat you to the idea."

For the better part of a mile Jim stared through the bug-specked windshield at the ribbon of highway pavement shimmering in the sun.

"Your running into Miss Vanderfisk back there has Bernene's fingerprints all over it," Rickett said. "She orchestrated the whole thing. I'd bet money on it."

"Use her niece to angle for my half of Honey Spring—at her own dad's funeral?"

"It's not very romantic, I know," Rickett said, "but this *is* Bernene Maxwell you're dealing with."

Jim shook his head. "It wasn't orchestrated."

"With old Enoch being shoveled under even as we speak, who's going to put the brakes on Bernene's Honey Spring ambitions now? You think Big Frett's going to tell her no in her hour of grief?" Rickett paused. "And grief will not have dulled her thinking any. She's not any more partial to the mystery biker than you are."

"But," Jim said, "she's not any more partial to me than to him."

"Just because you told her about her bull's wandering ways?"

"Her opinion of me wasn't very high to begin with. Orphan drifter with no future, no career—"

"You've got a career."

"Yeah, okay," Jim said. "But I mean a career that counts for something with her."

"And what would that be?" Rickett asked. "Law?"

They both smiled.

"Well, anyway," Jim said, "I was too dumb to take her money and run back where I came from. That's how she sees Jim Ray."

At about that point in the conversation, the pickup passed the historic plaque, then, a short stretch after that, turned off the highway. Jim took the turn-off a little too fast. The front and rear tires bumped so hard off the unbeveled edge of the asphalt apron that every piece of irrigating gear in the pickup's bed jumped at the same time, then slammed back down with a tremendous clatter.

The last leg of the ride home, along Honey Creek, was made without wind and without words. But the conversation wasn't over. Back at the single-wide, after a final clutch-coast had brought the old pickup almost perfectly abreast of the front stoop, and after a turn of the key had killed the engine, Rickett lit a cigarette and made no move to exit the cab. After a moment, he turned in the seat, looked at Jim, and asked, "Is that how *you* see Jim Ray?"

"They offered me forty thousand dollars," Jim said, "and I turned it down." He shook his head in disbelief.

To dispose of his cigarette's ashes, Rickett alternated between the open passenger window and the rust hole in the floorboard. "But if you *had* taken the money . . ."

". . . I never would've met the girl," Jim said. Remembering that girl's hand on his shoulder and on his arm, he decided to disclose the one part of the story he hadn't yet disclosed. He looked at Rickett and said, "She saw the bull—on my side. And she hasn't told Bernene."

Rickett stared at him. Finally he conceded, "So maybe your encounter back there at the church *wasn't* orchestrated." Then, without a grain of his usual levity or wryness, he said, "Do you like this girl?"

Jim grabbed the bottom arc of the steering wheel. For several moments he studied one of the fissures in the steering wheel's hard plastic. He rubbed a thumb along it. Then he nodded.

"Okay," Rickett said, "that's good to know." Then he said, "But you do realize that any move on *your* part is for sure going to *look* orchestrated?"

Jim's hands came off the steering wheel. He shook his head, tried to formulate a protest.

"That's how feuds work," Rickett said. "You and the girl have both got to live with a history in this thing that neither of you had any part in making."

The Sabbath-like stillness hanging over the farmyard now thoroughly pervaded the cab of the old truck.

"So what do I do?" Jim asked finally.

Rickett stubbed his cigarette on the floorboard, then dropped the butt through the rust hole. "Well," he said with a lighter tone, "you *could* try another meeting with Bernene and Big Frett. You must have got through to her at the last one." When Jim didn't say anything, Rickett asked the question he had asked at least half a dozen times before: "And it was your Bishop Sebright's idea to put it to her like that? Like your bull could use all the help he could get?"

And for the half-dozenth time Jim confirmed the answer.

Rickett smiled and said, "Now *that* man could've been a lawyer."

CHAPTER 17

"I'M SORRY TO REPORT," ENID COTTRELL SAID ON THE second Sunday after the funeral, "that your Miss Vanderfisk has gone back to Bear Lake with her mother." She paused, then added with her usual coyness, "But only until Labor Day." Then, even more coyly: "Until then, until you can manage some proper billing and cooing, you'll just have to pine. Any romance worthy of the name requires a little pining."

His Miss Vanderfisk. But if Sister Cottrell's pronoun exaggerated matters, her verb didn't. Through late June and into July, Jim *did* pine. And dwell on. And moon. And fixate and regret and lament. In his mind he dissected and magnified each encounter, each *half* encounter—Jocelyn at the Valentine's dance, Jocelyn in the upstairs window, Jocelyn at the A&W. He marveled at how Jocelyn on horseback had transformed alkali scrub into the flora of Eden and an ordinary church corridor into a conduit of hope and possibility and desire. How many times did he recount to himself the after-funeral collision in minute detail? Every lovely curve and contour clothed by the silky dress, the whisk of that dress against his white shirt, the pressure of her palms against his shoulders, the handshake.

There was plenty of occasion for the pining and mooning and dwelling on—thanks to the solitary farm chores of midsummer. Thistle chopping, for example. As he waded from patch to patch in an ocean of waist-high barley beards, brandishing a de-clawed beet knife, Jim indulged, by turns, self-abasement, self-aggrandizement, and a maudlin romanticizing that made of every spiny stalk an obstacle to love.

Or cultivating. When Jim remembered his mother working a hoe in the corn and green beans of her little backyard garden in Mapleton, he had to admit the genius of machine weeding. But after only the first pass through the field in this second summer of farming, he again had to admit its tedium. Hour upon hour of creeping in low first gear, of looking left-then-right, left-then-right, to track the snail's progress of the frame assembly bolted to either side of the engine housing. The object of the tracking was to keep the rows of fragile new beans—six at a run—centered between closely set pairs of half-sweeps and to remain vigilant for a snagged rock or clod or alfalfa root that could plow out two dozen bean plants in a blink. But the enduring of tedium, like almost anything else in a long and lonely work day, could be made emblematic of romantic devotion. Every pass through the field stretched into a continent to be crawled across, on scarred hands and knees, in pursuit of the fair maiden.

But of all summer labors, none was more conducive to love-sick melancholy than irrigating, especially the first watering of beans in late June—which required more work than all the subsequent waterings. On every up-field run, the mechanical shovels that dug the watering corrugations—mounted as they were at the rear end of the cultivator rig—stopped a tractor's length short of the ditch. On that first irrigation, the shortage had to be made up, one corrugation at a time, with a non-mechanical shovel. The chore offered much time for thinking.

Thereafter, through the long month of July, irrigating was conducive to lovesickness three times a day with the moving and positioning of brace sticks, the resetting of checks and dams, the armloads of slimy-cold and sizzling-hot siphon tubes, and the constant, mostly futile quest to plug mole holes.

For several weeks after Enoch's funeral, Jim didn't see any of the bikers. Why they had hung around Balford in the first place remained a mystery. In their absence Jim began to wonder if, invited or otherwise, the owner of Harley-Davidson with the decal on its tank had followed (accompanied?) Jocelyn to Bear Lake. But then in the late afternoon of the fourth Sunday of her absence, Jim spotted a small convoy of motorcycles coming toward him on the four-lane through Balford. They were back from wherever they had gone. Riding in the lead was none other than the pirate bandanna skinhead. Seated on the pillion behind him was a girl Jim had never seen.

Through the rest of July, Jim saw the bandanna biker regularly—cruising the four-lane, or main street, or parked at the A&W. Each time, the same girl was warming the pillion. Then late in the month, he saw the pair again, this time much closer. Standing one afternoon by the inner-tube trough at the Ralston Texaco station, waiting for Bud to get to his flat tire, Jim saw, through one of the garage's open bay doors, the big Harley-Davidson approaching. It pulled off the highway and glided up to a gas pump.

The pirate declined Bud's help and began to fill the Harley's tank himself. As he held the nozzle, he said something. The girl on the pillion laughed. She wore a tube top and cutoffs. Nothing else. Even her bare feet were tanned. Under his sleeveless and unbuttoned denim jacket, the pirate himself was unencumbered with a shirt. He wore only a silver-dollar-size medallion hung from a leather thong around his neck. He was well-muscled. Standing beside the Harley-Davidson, rather than riding it, he looked bigger—and older. Late twenties, at least. Probably early thirties.

The pillion girl said something, then laughed and abruptly leaned forward to grab at the medallion. The pirate dodged out of reach without releasing the nozzle's valve lever. "You want gas all over you?" he scolded. Standing next to the inner-tube trough, half-full of water black as a lagoon, Jim heard the girl

say, "Come *on*, Dutch! I just want to see what it says." Still holding the nozzle, the bandanna skinhead leaned toward her and
spread his free hand on one of her legs, just above the tanned
knee. Then he slowly walked two fingers of that hand all the way
up the thigh. Only when the fingers got to the cutoffs' fringe did
the leg flinch. "In due time, girl," he said.

Make love, not war.

"I wish your father were here to explain these things to you,"
Minnie Ray had said when Jim was fourteen or fifteen. "But we
will just have to do the best we can." Her broaching of the subject was imbued with a modesty that seemed grave even for her,
a woman who had been a widow far longer than a wife. Because
of such modesty, Jim might have expected a vague and hesitant
preface. *You're growing up now, son, and you've probably noticed
changes in your body.* And so on. But such expectation sold her
short. With this particular lesson, she was neither vague nor hesitant. "No matter how enticing," she had said plainly and frankly,
"there are certain private places"—she discreetly indicated those
private places on her own well-clothed body—"where you may
not touch a young lady until marriage. Do you understand what
I am saying to you?"

He understood.

CHAPTER 18

FINISHING SUPPER ONE EVENING IN EARLY AUGUST, JIM and Rickett heard through the trailer's screen door the chug and fan-belt hiss of an engine, the creak of aged springs and shocks. The sounds grew closer. Then they glimpsed, through the screen door, the vehicle's lurching turn and the violently diminishing distance between its radiator grill and the porch stoop. When the driver finally stomped on the brakes, the front drums squeaked, and the engine coughed and died.

It was Beeswax Jones and his sheep wagon camper. When he made no move to roust himself out of the cab, Jim and Rickett felt obliged to roust themselves from the plywood table. They stepped through the screen door and onto the stoop. While Rickett sidled to the edge of the stoop's frame and studied the four-inch gap between it and the truck's bumper, Jim descended the steps. Because of the slenderness of the gap, he had to walk behind the sheep wagon camper to come around to the open window on the driver's side.

With no hat to contain it, Beeswax's gray-streaked hair stuck up wild and tangled. It was hard to imagine a comb equal to the task. Despite the heat of summer, the beard hadn't been trimmed for a long time. Beeswax's lips were drawn back from the saw-blade teeth. They were as stained and chinked and feral-looking as ever. And, as ever, he was chewing a wad of tobacco. Tiny trickles of dark juice leaked from the corners of his mouth into the beard's underhairs.

"Want to come in?" Jim asked. "We've got ice-cream bars."

"Watch yourself," Beeswax warned just before spitting out the window. Then, in an oblique response to the invitation, he said, "My hamstrings are hurting. That trail up from the river gets steeper every time."

"How's fishing?" Jim asked. Out of the corner of his eye, he saw Rickett ease himself down to sit at the corner of the stoop, which put him at a slight diagonal from Beeswax, with no windshield in between.

"Poor," Beeswax said. He hooked a thumb behind one shoulder strap of his bib overalls. "And I had my heart set on a mess of trout."

"For pit roasting?" Jim asked.

"No!" Beeswax said with a snort of disgust. "Pan-fried in cornmeal egg batter—that's the only way to do brown trout."

Jim waited to make sure the rebuke was finished. Seated at the edge of the stoop, Rickett had dug out a pocketknife and had begun whittling on the stick from an ice cream bar.

When Beeswax didn't elaborate on the art of trout cooking— or volunteer the purpose of his visit—Jim asked, "And how are the bees?"

"Fair to middling," Beeswax said. "They'd make better honey, you know, if you'd a let your clover blossom better back in June."

"That would've pushed our first cutting too far into July."

Beeswax shrugged and said, "It's your fodder."

He was a peculiar human being, but up to now in their acquaintance, his peculiarity had at least been marked by good cheer. For several long, sober moments he rolled his quid around in his mouth. Then he spat again—as some sort of cue to getting down to business—and said, "In my comings and goings, I mind my own business. But I also keep my eyes open. And there's something you need to know."

The whittling stopped. Rickett looked up.

"You've got yourself some trespassers," Beeswax said, "over below my hives."

"These trespassers," Rickett asked in his most lawyerly way, from his seat on the stoop—"human or bovine?"

"Human."

"You saw them?" Jim asked.

"I saw *tracks*."

"Tires or boots?" Rickett asked.

"Boots," Beeswax said, "just where my fishing trail starts up the bluff."

Jim glanced at Rickett: *my* bee boxes was one thing; *my* fishing trail was another. The irony of a half-authorized trespasser lamenting the encroachment of another had not gotten by the old lawyer.

"Where are they parking?" Jim asked.

"They're not," Beeswax said, "they're not driving at all, not coming from the highway."

"So locking my gate wouldn't help?" Jim asked. His use of *my* was deliberate.

"Not a bit," Beeswax said. He paused for a moment. "No, these are serious trespassers, Jim Ray. These are trespassers with vision. They're on foot, wading the river, crossing your west fence— which Goss didn't bother fortifying because it wasn't between him and the Vanderfisks. Never expected trouble from that side."

Jim tried not to stare at the saw-blade teeth. Finding another reason to throw in the pronoun, he said, "Doesn't seem like all that much trouble if all they want to do is fish the trout pools on my side." He looked Beeswax in the eye. "The more, the merrier."

For several moments, Beeswax chewed on his cud of tobacco, and on Jim's meaning. Finally, he spat a dark caramel stream and said, "These weren't fishermen."

"So who?" Jim asked with a laugh. "Asparagus lovers?"

For the first time in the conversation, Beeswax turned his head so as to look directly at Rickett, who had fashioned from the stick of his ice cream bar a magnificent toothpick.

"Remember a while back," Beeswax said, addressing Jim but staring at the sharpened stick with raw coveting, "when I told you how many deer there were getting to be in your pasture—and how sooner or later they'd get noticed?"

Though it was only early August, the imminence and inevitability of the changing season seemed to hang over the trailer and stoop and sheep wagon camper. Jim looked at the saw-blade teeth, then at the toothpick, then back at the teeth. He nodded.

"Well, sir," Beeswax said, "they've been noticed."

Less than an hour later, Jim found the kill himself. It was exactly where Beeswax had said—in the trees at the base of the bluff, a quarter mile from the river. And it looked exactly as Beeswax had described it—a big buck, skinned and gutted less than twenty-four hours earlier. Ribs, brisket, front quarters, hind quarters, every cut of meat, in fact, except the loin—all left to molder beneath the Russian olive tree from which the gambrel had hung. Jim could see where the gambrel's wire anchor had fretted the bark. The rear legs had been sawed off at the hock, the legs themselves flung into the grass. He crouched. For a moment, he stared at the dark eyes, glassy and opaque, as yet undisturbed by magpies. The only other parts taken were the antlers—sawed off at the skull—and certain organs picked from among the scattered entrails.

"The loin was an afterthought," Rickett explained the next morning over his coffee, "and anybody who wants horns for taxidermy display usually takes the skull, too." He held his thermos's metal cup a moment, took a sip, set it down on the plywood table. "This is parts poaching. I've seen it before, down in Colorado. Poacher works on commission for some low-life middleman agent with some low-life connection to the oriental market. There's a lot of money in it. For antlers, of course. And liver, heart, spleen, bladder. They dry what needs to be dried, grind it to powder, sell it by the ounce as a virility elixir." He pressed and twisted his cup on the table as if working a biscuit cutter. "But those aren't the real prize."

Jim waited.

"The *real* prize," Rickett said, studying the coffee ring just imprinted on the plywood, "is the reproductive apparatus—glands, gonads, the whole deal. That's why they want only bucks." He picked up his cup, took a drink, this time did not set it down. "Did you know," he asked offhandedly, "that some cultures consider the powdered sex glands of deer to be one of the world's most potent aphrodisiacs?" He paused and looked at Jim. "That means love potion."

"I know what aphrodisiac means," Jim said.

Rickett looked over the cup's rim. "You ever considered trying one?"

A week later, Jim came on a second kill, on the west side of the same riverward swale favored by the cattle.

"*Now* can I call the game warden?" Jim asked after his report to Rickett.

"I suppose," Rickett said. "I was just trying to spare you Big Bernene's wrath. When she gets wind of poaching on your side, she'll worry you to death about the possibility of poaching on her side."

"And what exactly would poachers poach on her side?" Jim asked. "Unless you know of some culture that values the aphrodisiac properties of gravel."

Rickett smiled. "She won't see it that way."

For a moment, neither spoke.

"What I can't figure out," Jim said, "is why I'm not hearing the shots."

"You sure there's shots to be heard?" Rickett asked. "Beeswax seems to think it could be a bow and arrow. Or something else."

"Like what? Crossbow? Blow dart? A real humdinger of a slingshot?"

"I'm just telling you what he said."

Jim shook his head. Nothing he had seen in the remnants gave credence to anything but a high-caliber round. He remembered how Ardizzoli liked to rank various ways of dying. It was his second favorite topic. "Sniper round wouldn't be so bad," he had said a day or so after Fritchey bought the farm, "except for the hole."

For a moment neither Jim nor Rickett spoke. Then, as if it had just occurred to him to ask, the old lawyer said, "Was there any thunder last night?"

"Mostly across the river," Jim said, "toward the Peaks."

"Wind?"

"Some."

Jim knew what the questions were getting at.

"How about the night of the first kill?" Rickett asked. "Do you remember?"

"Yeah," Jim said. "Not too much rain, but it boomed pretty good." He looked at Rickett, then said, "When it gets like that, especially with any wind in these trees by the trailer, I can't hear much of anything."

The truck was big, the sunglasses mirrored, and the uniform straight out of the dress and grooming guide of the Wyoming Game and Fish Commission: western-style felt hat on top, cowboy boots on bottom, and, in between, a rust-colored long-sleeve shirt and blue jeans. Nowhere did that guide or any of its companion literature specify a height requirement for the men aspiring to wear that uniform. Which was fortunate for the career ambitions of the guy driving the seldom-used road leading to the bee boxes. His name was Marty Overdale, and in his Game and Fish cowboy boots, he stood five and a half feet tall. If the dress and grooming guide had happened to prohibit facial hair, he could have complied for a month at a time without the bother of a razor. From a certain angle, the sunglasses gave him the look of a child aping a parent. At first Jim had a hard time believing that he was old enough to be a deputy warden or a graduate of Montana State University (an academic credential he found many ways to allude to) or even a holder of a driver's license. Yet he wore a badge.

"Well, I'll be golly-wogged," Deputy Warden Overdale muttered when the road ended at the bee boxes. "Looks like we've come to the edge of the world." For a long time the soles of his clean Game and Fish cowboy boots rested against the clutch and brake pedals. He seemed to be staring at a point in the air just beyond the bluff fence. He didn't much want to get out of the air-conditioned cab. When he finally killed the engine, his eyes went to Jim's heel-worn gumboots with a patch over one toe. "Is there anything else you didn't tell me about where we're going?"

Jim had said there wasn't any close road access, that there would be hiking, across riverbottom pasture and alkali scrub. Anybody who even pretended to know the Shoshone River Basin—beyond whatever was indicated by a map hanging on the wall of a government office—would not have been surprised at the likelihood of wet feet. So now he said nothing.

All the way down to the second kill, Overdale chided Jim for not reporting the first kill. The chiding started out pretty emphatic on the gopher trail, as the deputy warden yawed from zig to zag, but it got worse at the base of the bluff, where they ran into a boggy stretch first thing. To cross it, Overdale tried tiptoeing. He tried skipping. He tried hopping. But before they had gone thirty yards, his footwear was soaked clear through. Then they came to the first alkali sink. Plowing through the salty crust, Overdale's wet boots were soon coated white like a breaded fillet. With every step, bubbles oozed from the stitching between the uppers and the soles. By the time they got to the far edge of the sink and were ready for another boggy stretch, the white powder had crept all the way up to the knees of the dress-code blue jeans.

"In order for me to do my job," Deputy Overdale said as he marched across the second alkali sink, "I need to be kept informed. No secrets, okay? This property may be your responsibility, but these deer are mine. And it's my job to know when something like this happens."

The chiding became something more than chiding when the breeze carried to their nostrils the first whiff—ripened considerably by another morning of hot sun.

"Geez Louise and holy peas!" Overdale said, mopping his face with a forearm. "That is some kind of putrid." The tone blamed Jim not only for fouled boots and pants, but for stink, discomfort, inconvenience, maybe even for the sun's glare.

By the time Deputy Overdale actually stood over the kill, he had sweated through his reddish shirt at the armpits and belt line. He wiped his face again, this time with the other shirt sleeve, and then looked down. After a few seconds, he took off the sunglasses and folded them. The sight at his feet so fascinated him that it took half a minute for him to get around to sliding the glasses into his shirt pocket.

Beaks had found these eye sockets. Holding an arm to his nose and mouth, Overdale stooped as he no doubt hoped a seasoned game warden would stoop, to examine antler stumps, carcass cavity, meat left to rot, the pillaged guts. As he examined, he whistled lightly through his teeth and said, "This is some bad business."

That night, for the first time in months, Jim saw the making of a bullet hole.

In the dream, he watched Fritchey get hit and, despite the spreading stain, stood dumbly trying to factor the odd buckling of the legs. But then—this was the strangeness of dreams—the burden he ended up dragging through elephant grass, when he finally had leisure to check, had no helmet, no fatigues, no pack.

It wasn't Fritchey. It wasn't anybody. It was a deer carcass—or half of one. The hind quarters had been hacked away and the loin stripped from the spine. In the dream, Jim gripped one foreleg. As he lugged the carcass, the newly polled head flopped backwards at a hard angle. That position put the nostrils directly over the bullet hole. The only smell from such a wound was death.

Only then did Jim hear a shot.

His eyes opened. For an instant he still felt the tug of the burden, the tickle of hair in his palm. Slowly the feeling evaporated. He listened. He sat up in bed. It was hard to tell if the hour was closer to midnight or morning. He listened again. He felt none of the fuzziness of sleep. In his whole life, Jim had never dragged a deer in any manner, let alone by its foreleg. But waking in the early hours, the morning after Deputy Overdale's visit, he would have testified otherwise. He had felt the weight, the resistance, the hair soft as mink, the graceful concave of the bone between knee joint and dewclaws.

Already the images were fading. Had he heard what he heard in dream or wakefulness? He listened now for something else. There was no thunder, no wind.

Jim threw back his sheet and blanket and got out of bed. He pulled on pants, shirt, sweatshirt, splashed his face at the bathroom sink, stepped onto the stoop to put on his irrigating boots. He looked toward the bluff. Eastward, the sky over the Bighorns had already taken on the paleness of dawn. That was at least one answer: Midnight was long past.

From the stoop he crossed the yard, went through a barn door and out into the interior of the big north corral. He hadn't been in here since the cattle went down on summer pasture. Sun-crusted manure smelled different than fresh. Not so rank. Almost pleasant. Crossing the empty enclosure in the early light, ten days into August, Jim made out the pews wainscotting the far fence.

At the gate with the broken latch chain, Jim didn't fight the baling-wire bindings or a bottom spar lodged in sun-crusted manure. He climbed over. On the other side, he stood looking at the snubbing posts. Then he looked farther on, along the edge. After awaking with the feel of a foreleg in his hand, he had thought of this spot beyond the weathered ashes of the branding fire. It was an outcropping in the bluff backing Goss's farmyard, a kind of natural lookout. Of all the points along the bluff's edge, it afforded the fullest view of the riverbottom.

It was still early for such a view, but Jim was in no hurry. Any hurry would put more faith in the reality of the rifle shot than he wanted to put. As he stood listening to the day's first birdsong, he watched the sky. Especially at this hour, it was a splendor of immensity. The whole of it could be divided into the four cardinal directions—unless you counted straight up—and this eastward hatching of daylight was one of them.

And it was a splendor of variety—of shapes and colors. Just a moment ago, the sky above the dark bulk of the Bighorns had been solid slate. Then, without any cue or heralding, the slate broke into strips, stripes, shreds, wisps. All reconfigured, a minute later, into a thousand puzzle pieces shaped like Tennessee. The colors were just as mutable. Some whose names he knew: reddish gray, orange, yellow. Some whose names he didn't know: saffron, carmine, damask. All blends and variations and intensities, producing hues that *had* no name. Hues with no rival in the palette of land and water, of anything in or on the earth itself.

Then the sky was something else again. Great puffs and plumes and billows. It was stratosphere churned by a giant eggbeater into fluff, spume, meringue, white cotton candy.

Finally, the sky on this morning transformed into the underside of an immense domed roof arching down to its wall plate on the horizon. This roof's tiles rested on no rafter or stringer, yet were laid neatly imbricate in quantities beyond counting, with symmetry beyond comprehension. The lower edge of every single one of those tiles flamed pink.

Gradually, a glowing bulge appeared low in the skyline, right at the knob of a mountain peak. It shone brighter and brighter, radiating a light to be borne only with squinting. Now the pace of spectacle slowed. It seemed to take an inordinately long time for the sun's curved edge to actually pierce the horizon. But once it did, the ascension accelerated, like a hot air balloon snapping its last tether. With the ascension, a whole fresh cloud continent lit up in brilliant russets and yellows.

Jim remembered Enid Cottrell's comfort in sunrises. He thought of Wesley Hardin Cottrell, trapped with thousands of other sons of mothers in the bowels of the *Arizona* as it sank flaming into Pearl Harbor. He thought of his own father, killed somewhere in the Marshall Islands. He imagined Minnie Ray getting the news when she was eight months pregnant. *You've got the wrong house, the wrong wife, the wrong Garth Ray.* He thought of Agnes Vanderfisk, who, worrying over the first bodily irregularity, might also have been susceptible to denial. Yet both things were true: Garth Ray *had* left the world, and Jocelyn Vanderfisk was on *her* way into it. In the first mornings of their new knowledge, had either woman found any solace at all in the rising of the sun?

Jim stood for a long while. From somewhere in the trees below him came the successive murmurs of a mourning dove; then from the direction of the sagebrush forest, the crisp, sweet whistle of a meadow lark. Only gradually did he realize that he had heard both dove and lark against the noise of a thousand magpies. A congregation had roosted in one of the big cottonwoods on the other side of the trailer. Jim turned and listened. The sound was nothing close to song, for sure—nothing to rival a choir of robins or cardinals—but it was not nearly so raucous as the squawk and caw of a lone bird. It was background chatter and jabber. Magpies were the gossips of the bird world, and dawn was their social hour.

Hue by hue, shadow yielded to light. Detail by detail, the features of the pasture bottom took form—from the river to the base of the bluff. Now it was possible to distinguish, among clumps of brush and trees, scattered clusters of cattle. Among those clusters were some still bedded and some already up and grazing. It was even possible to make out, here and there, calves suckling. So went the illumination of the world every morning of every new day. And on this morning, in this little corner of the world, the illumination revealed nothing unusual or alarming.

Yet not a half hour later, weaving through clusters of Russian olives at the base of the bluff, Jim found a third kill. This one wasn't a deer. Nor was it skinned or gutted or deprived of its hind legs. What the poachers had mistaken for a buck was a big steer, well toned in its shoulders and haunches, sleek-coated from a diet of green grass. Glimpsing the movement of such an animal amid forked Russian olive branches, a poacher might understandably supply antlers where none existed. In its eagerness, the trigger finger would not be checked by other considerations. It would not be checked, for instance, by the incongruity of ears shaped nothing like the ears of a mule deer—ears shaped at birth by rude exposure to air thirty degrees below zero.

It was the Doberman calf. And the hole in his lower neck was a bullet hole, sure enough. Jim crouched. The hooves and dewclaws and underbelly seemed starkly familiar. The cod was well healed. From between the rigid parted jaws, the tongue protruded, dry and inert. If Jim *had* heard an actual gunshot an hour earlier—which seemed less and less likely—that shot hadn't killed this animal. This animal had been dead since at least late last evening. Jim had fallen asleep early, hardly remember going from rocking chair to bed. He didn't remember any thunder. But wind, maybe. And maybe he just didn't hear whatever there was to be heard.

He looked at the Doberman calf's eyes. *Light of the body, window of the soul,* Minnie Ray used to say whenever she suspected her son of playing loose with the truth. In the movies, as a show of respect, the eyes of the recent dead were already closed. But closed eyes, from what Jim had seen, were a nicety. He thought of the magpies, hungry after a night's roosting, all those craws and gullets and gabbling beaks.

Now his looking to the sky had a different purpose. A few ducks were winging toward the river. That was all. He stood and pulled off his sweatshirt. Then he unbuttoned and removed his shirt. It was short-sleeved, thin cotton, nearly worn out. In the cool air of early morning, it felt good to put the sweatshirt back on. He knelt beside the Doberman calf's head. He stared for a long time. He remembered the Doberman as a newborn on the coldest morning of the year. It had been no bigger than a fawn. He remembered the twirling of the docked tail as it suckled. He remembered the cavorting among the relaxed herd as they fed on frozen bean straw. He heard in his head the drumming of hooves on the corral pews, felt the snap and twang of the lariat, smelled the singed hide. It was a strange and melancholy thing to consider the remains of a creature who had so blithely defied death just by surviving birth.

Very gently, Jim spread the shirt over the calf's face, as a shroud, took special pains to cover the eyes. He remembered their impudent gleam daring him to cast the loop of the lariat. There was no gleam now. But perhaps if they were not noticed, the eyes would be spared the desecration of beaks. For a moment sunlight hit the shroud in such a way as to make it glow. In that moment, Jim felt with more weight than ever before the sorrow of casket and body bag, the sorrow of limbs and lungs and especially eyes rendered lifeless.

When at last he looked up from the faded glow of the shroud, from the stiff, sprawled legs and blood-spoiled coat, from the docked ears and tail, he realized that his sorrow had been witnessed. Standing and staring at him through low-hanging Russian olive branches, not twenty yards away, was the dun bull.

CHAPTER 19

GO TELL IT ON THE MOUNTAIN. THAT'S WHAT PRIVATE
First Class Jerome Snow would have recommended in song.

In this case, what there was to tell had two parts—the shooting of the calf and the sighting of the bull. To those he told—Rickett, Bishop Sebright, the sheriff and deputy game warden, Bernene and Big Frett—Jim reported only what he saw, only what he knew. But beyond those people, he couldn't control how anything got told on the mountain—or in the Balford Valley.

"By the time this story makes it rounds," said Sheriff Carl Sturgis with a chuckle, "people will have Martians and the Mafia both involved."

He wasn't far off in his prediction. From Beeswax Jones, who heard what he heard who knows where, the news carried, like whale sonar, to a very long list of Balford residents. Lewis Glenney, for example—owner and editor of the *Balford Clarion*. Dorcas O'Bannion, mail clerk and Sunday school chorister. Burl Bigler. Dairy farmer Jersey Teague. All of Warner Godwin's bunch—Eb and Gurn and Rector and Tolbert. Doc Lowe, the veterinarian. And, of course, Tom Criswall, the man who didn't like Mormons but had chosen to live all his life among them so as to guarantee constant nourishment for his contempt. Even a temporary resident like Dutch the skinhead biker heard the story.

To most, the greater interest lay in the sighting of the dun bull. Bernene Maxwell certainly fell into that category. At her direction, and with Jim's permission—only perfunctorily asked for—Hap and Percy Croft spent most of another week after the sheriff's investigation scouring Goss's side of the Honey Spring riverbottom. Time after time, they combed trees and bushes, swales and swamp—east to the divider fence, west to the river. All in vain. "If that animal wants to stay hid," Hap lamented on the evening they loaded their horses for the last time, "that river bottom's the place for it. All's he has to do is pick a spot anywhere in those fifty acres of cattails and stay still long enough for us to ride on by."

For a few, though, the more intriguing part of the story was the shooting of the Doberman calf. For professional reasons, that category included the sheriff and the good men of the local Game and Fish Commission. And, for no factorable reason whatsoever, it included Dutch the skinhead biker. The first actual words Dutch ever spoke to Jim, during another chance encounter at the service station, were condolences for the loss to his herd. Those condolences included these questions: "Who'd be shooting a rifle down there when it's not even hunting season?" And this one: "Did I hear right this wasn't the first time for something like this?"

Dutch had to mean the deer killed a few weeks earlier. He was from out of town, from parts unknown, wasn't even around when the tires and windshields of dump trucks were shot out and when a cow wound up dead. Unless he was tight with Eb Godwin the ditch-rider, which was unlikely, how would he know anything about what had happened six years earlier in the Vanderfisks' gravel pit?

Still, coming from a drifter like Dutch, during a rash of poaching, any such allusion was troubling. On his way back from town a day or so before the latest conversation at Bud's Texaco, Jim had seen the big Harley parked on the turnout above the pond and orchard. And he had seen Dutch and the pillion girl standing by the historic marker. No doubt both could have learned from the plaque many facts of great interest about the site of the first Mormon encampment in Wyoming's Bighorn Basin. But they weren't paying any attention to the plaque. They stood to one side of it, close to the guardrail, looking down at Honey Spring and pointing. By the time Jim's homegoing took him all the way to the property's far corner and the open abatis gate, then along the double-back of the old pavement, then across the cattle guard and around the cottonwoods and finally the orchard and pond, the Harley-Davidson was gone.

About the death of the Doberman calf and the sighting of the dun bull, there was one other person Jim told directly and one he intended to.

"Yes, I just heard about that," said Sister Enid Cottrell over the telephone. "I'm so sorry." Despite her considerable tact in not saying so, it was obviously old news to her. No one's sonar was keener than hers. And the blunder of his presumption served him right. Announcing the shooting and the sighting was only a pretext for the phone call. "I was wondering when you'd ask for it," said Enid Cottrell before giving him the mailing address in Bear Lake.

On a warm Saturday night two weeks after finding the dead calf, Jim sat down at the plywood table in the single-wide. On the table rested a pen, a yellow legal pad, and the box of stationery he had bought ten days earlier. For the fiftieth time he fingered the slip of paper on which he had written the Bear Lake mailing address. Finally he set the slip down, opened the box of stationery, took out the top sheet and elaborately centered it on the yellow pad, whose only purpose was to provide a smooth writing surface atop the plywood table's *un*smooth surface. At the top of the page of stationery, he finally wrote *August 26, 1967*. Beneath that, after another minute or two, he wrote *Balford, Wyoming.* Then he stared until the paper's cream color swam before his eyes, until filling that one page—one line at a time, with words laid end to end—seemed like the sum of all impossible goals.

It was late. He had to write something or give up.

Dear Jocelyn.

So he wrote that he was sitting at the homemade kitchen table of a single-wide trailer house perched at the edge of a river bluff, guyed to deadmen to keep it from blowing over that edge in a stiff wind. He wrote that it was ten o'clock, that only in the last hour had night air through open windows finally cooled the trailer's interior, which would have been even more of a hot-box without the shade of cottonwoods. They didn't make very good timber or firewood (an observation he attributed to his "lawyer friend"), but for the sheer audacity of their greenery (that phrase, too, had to be attributed to the same friend) in country that boasted less than ten inches of rainfall in a good year, for their knack of making the most out of the least, they were a pretty amazing tree. In fact, he wrote, at this very moment he was looking at the moon framed between the two of them growing just outside the closest window.

Unavoidably motivated by the poetic impulse motivated by romance, Jim expressed his desire to capture the beauty of that sight, of a remote—but still very bright—moon shining like a gem through a lattice of branches and leaves. Waning gibbous, he remembered—and wrote the words on the page. All these were *his* words. He thought of that same moon hanging over Bear Lake. The next thing he wrote was an apology for not having written a week earlier. He said he wasn't even sure she would get this letter before Labor Day, before she was due to return to Balford. He wrote that he nevertheless wanted her to know—from him—that her Aunt Bernene's bull had once again appeared on his side of the pasture fence and had once again eluded the Croft brothers' thorough search efforts. Whatever its other abilities, if that bull could do *that*, it must be a very special animal. Then, after long indecision, he added: *Maybe we can go riding on my side when you get back and look for it ourselves.*

Never mind that he had no horse or saddle or experience beyond one Boy Scout camp trail ride the summer of his fifteenth year. He had to ask.

Dear Jocelyn.

The same implement frame that supports six rows' worth of cultivating sweeps in June and July supports six bean knives in August and September. The knives, more than twice as long as plowshares and beveled thinner along the cutting edge, are arranged in three V-shaped pairs. Each knife, when lowered to its working position, slices beneath bean roots and, depending on its splay, lays the cut row left or right. The single row laid left by one V merges with the single row laid right by another to form a double row.

Mounted above the point of each V is a kind of prow, and attached to that prow, left and right, are sets of slender spring-metal rods that bring to mind catfish whiskers. The prow-and-whisker units—called dividers—part the thick vines ahead of each of the tractor's three tires. The middle unit, the one bolted to the yoke of the front tire, has the biggest prow and the shortest whiskers. The prow size owes to its position at the rig's forefront; the whisker length is curtailed so as not to interfere with the steering arc.

That's the half of the bean-cutting rig that bolts to either side of the engine housing. The other half mounts behind the tractor and is called a rod weeder. It is so named because a backward-turning rod—cast perfectly square at the foundry but soon enough worn almost round—comes along just under the soil's surface to ensure the complete detachment of all roots, weed and bean.

For Jim, after the death-crawl of cultivating beans two months earlier, the full-throttle speed of cutting them was tonic.

Not far behind came Rickett on the other tractor, pulling a side-rake—so named (by Mr. Deere or Mr. McCormick?) because the beans accumulated by the angled reel were left to lie at the side of the cleared swath. On the downfield pass, the swishing reel swept together two of the cutter's double rows; on the upfield pass, it added two more. So each complete windrow was a dense weave, eight rows' worth, of vines and mottled leaves heavy with plump, striped pods. At this stage, the pinto pods were still supple enough to withstand the buffeting and tumbling of being gathered. But it wouldn't take long, under a late-summer sun, for them to fully ripen and cure for combining.

At dusk on the last Monday in August, the twenty-eighth day of the month—exactly a week before Labor Day—Jim was cutting, and Rickett was raking in the field below the pond and orchard. Working west to east, toward the long, cattail-banked demarcation of Honey Spring, they had transformed the field's solid mat of crop into windrows. All day they had been at it, stopping only to fuel and grease. During the stop closest to noon, they sat on the pickup's tailgate to eat the lunch they had brought with them.

By early evening, only a thirty-yard strip of uncut beans stood between Jim and the field's side ditch. The side ditch paralleled the road; the road paralleled the spring. With twilight thickening around him, he thought again of the letter, mailed yesterday after church, wondered when Jocelyn would get it, tried to imagine her reaction. Then once again the prow of the front divider came to the grassy embankment marking the bottom of the field.

Clutch. Throttle down. Finger the knobs of hydraulic levers—knobs worn paintless and shiny from many seasons' worth of contact with fingers, gloved and ungloved. Listen to the whine of the hydraulic pump and creak of linkage to know when knives and rod weeder have been raised to height. Joggle gear-stick to reverse. Back up just enough for the rig's pivot to clear the rise of the embankment.

As Jim cranked the steering wheel and stomped on the left brake pedal, he happened to look toward the highway. At that moment he spotted, across the spring and fence, on Enoch's scanty cropland, a little cluster of deer. They were the first he had seen in several weeks, the first he had seen all season anywhere but the riverbottom. They didn't bolt. They didn't mill. They just stared—alert, attentive, vigilant. He counted nine.

Tuesday morning he and Rickett moved to another field. During the whole of another day, the cutting and raking tractors made their rounds. That evening the deer again revealed themselves, this time on Goss's side of the spring. Though Jim was acquainted with the mule deer's indifference to man-made barriers, though he had many times witnessed the ease with which its spring-steel muscles and tendons carried it over fences, the closer presence startled him. Standing at the edge of an adjoining corn field, the herd showed the calm wariness so characteristic of the species. Until the precise moment they were impelled to flee, they didn't. They had an instinct for weighing risk and threat, never seemed motivated by fear so much as by caution. Caution certainly marked the sentinels of this evening's group, which had, in a twenty-four-hour period, doubled in size. Heads high, they watched and listened and smelled. Then, between Jim's glances, they melted back into corn stalks.

"They're smart," Rickett said after the parking of the tractors in the growing darkness.

"I don't know about that," Jim said. "There they are, feeding in plain view of the highway. Now everybody and their dog is going to know where to come to get their buck. And like the apple and asparagus folks," he said, "I don't suppose they'll bother asking permission."

Rickett studied him. "*I'm* the jaded perspective in this partnership," he said. "Don't go reversing roles on me."

Jim didn't say anything.

"You could always lock the gate again."

"And let Bernene Maxwell think I've come around to her way of thinking?" Jim asked. "Not hardly."

Rickett shrugged. After a moment he said, "All I meant was the deer seem to know to stay clear of the riverbottom—where their mates were killed."

"And my calf."

For two more days the work went smoothly. At the end of each of those days, the deer came out, and they came out on Goss's side of Honey Spring. Then it was Friday, the first day of September, a demarcation whose importance would extend far beyond a change in months or seasons.

At five o'clock that morning, Rickett, who never in a year and a half had lost a day of work to sickness, called to apologize for having to lose this one to a bad stomach. "I'm camped by the toilet," he said.

"Seltzer and lime," Jim said. "That was Minnie Ray's remedy." Then he said, with more cheer than he felt, "Rest up. Get better."

Jim didn't begrudge the sickness. The truth was, he felt guilty—and a little incompetent—that Rickett saw rain and confining sickness as the only reasons for *not* showing up. Four months had passed since the noon meal back in early May when Rickett first told the full story of his involvement with Honey Spring. In that time, the old lawyer had several times repeated one of the themes from that long lunch story, namely how much he needed, and benefited from, his close involvement with the work of the farm. With each repetition, that involvement was made to sound more self-serving. And on certain days marked by fair breezes and blue skies, Jim could *almost* accept that profile of their arrangement. But on other days—and this first day of September was one of them—he knew better. Rickett's insistence on his own need was a tacit and generous downplaying of Jim's. Need on Jim's part included help with the work, of course, but even more important, it included teaching, correction, support, encouragement, confidence, companionship.

As Jim drove to the field they had moved into the previous evening, he felt the weight of the day's acres waiting to be cut and raked. And he felt the weight of the weather. It wasn't actually raining, but every so often the morning's cold fog distilled into little paw-print droplets on the windshield. From time to time, the accumulation urged Jim's hand toward the wiper switch. But a sweep or two with the same worn-out wiper blades—with the tiny black snake crawling up and down the glass—did little more than smear bug specks.

Though it was nearly seven-thirty in the morning, fog prolonged the night's darkness. With such poor visibility, Jim's bearings were off. This was the most remote and isolated field on the farm. Tucked into the farthest southwest corner of the property, a long way from Honey Spring, it was irregularly shaped, steeply sloped, and bordered all around with thick cover—willows and Russian olives, a long stand of cottonwood saplings, and, along the bluff, greasewood. Somewhere in the lower corner of this corner field stood Beeswax's honey boxes, but in the fog they were not visible. Traveling the track along a head ditch whose banks were thick with a summer's growth of brome, Jim drove right past the crossing. He had to back up, get out, and toe around in the tall grass to find the ends of the culvert. After crossing, he bumped blindly across corrugations until suddenly the tractors loomed in the mist.

He turned off the ignition switch, opened the door, and eased his feet to the ground. He thought he had parked well into the unplanted margin between ditch and beans, so he was surprised to find himself standing knee-deep in leaves and vines. The dew was so heavy it dripped. And on this morning, of all mornings, he had worn leather boots instead of rubber.

Even without Rickett to pronounce the verdict, Jim knew the beans were too wet to work. Leaves and vines burdened with such moisture would snag and bunch and drag along, and finally either slough off in straggly heaps or bog the tractor to a stop. And raking? You might as well try to rake soggy fishnet. Even if the rake teeth could manage the dense weight without snapping off, the leaves and vines, in their tumbling, would gather far more dirt and rocks than it was prudent to send through a combine.

For now, all he could do was fuel both tractors and grease the rake and the rod weeder. Fuel cans, funnel, grease gun and refill cartridges—everything was wet. His gloves were soon soaked. As were his boots and the denim of his jeans from cuff to knee. He shivered.

What he needed was a hot, dry, late-summer day.

What he needed was a lot of things, Rickett would have said.

Among them, a sun like an oven. Like a kiln. To warm joints and dry greenery and especially to cure the stalks of the ragweed and sunflowers that this field had produced with such abundance. When well cured, according to Rickett, they passed fairly harmlessly through the threshing cylinders, caused no more distress than a puff of dust from this or that clod still clinging to their roots. When not well cured, though, they were tough as cable. When they got tangled in the teeth of the flailing cylinder, they could choke the shaft to a stop. Which, in turn, stalled pulleys and sprockets. Which, in turn, burned belts and once in a while snapped chains.

If the weak, hazy glow in the east held any promise of becoming an oven sun today, the transformation was going to take a while. Only when he was sitting in the pickup and waiting did it occur to Jim that not quite a year ago, before he even knew there was a Jocelyn Vanderfisk, he was *praying* for fog and dew. It was October before he and Rickett finally got to the last ten acres of last year's bean crop. By then there were no leaves and vines to worry about.

They had long since withered and dropped off the standing plants. What remained was nothing but naked stalks hung with shriveled pods. Among pods so overripe and brittle, cutter knives and rake teeth left almost as many beans shattered on the ground as intact. The only way to prevent such waste was to cut and rake on mornings with a heavy dew. Dew made the pods limber.

So for several weeks he and Rickett had gone to the field at four a.m., which meant Rickett had had to leave his North Fork cabin at three. The McCormick had one functioning light; the Case—the raking tractor—had none. It was a victory, Rickett said, for the rake man (which was himself) just to get to the bottom of the field astraddle the same pair of double-rows he had started on at the top. Yet it was a victory persistently achieved. Always behind Jim in the chilly darkness came the steady engine throb of the raking tractor he couldn't see, except for a muffler spark now and again, and the reassuring *swish—swish—swish* of the rake reel.

And now, on a too-wet morning eleven months later, Jim remembered that his prayers during those weeks stipulated *dew*. Not rain. Rain would have been a hindrance, not a help. Yet during that same period in early October, rain *was* what someone in church had invited the congregation to stipulate in *their* prayers—for the farmers who had just planted winter wheat. Did one prayed stipulation cancel the other? Or trump it? Maybe their winter wheat, Jim remembered thinking, was more deserving than his beans. The wheat had been planted and tended on proper schedule. But if prayer was, as the hymn said, the soul's sincere desire, then the foolish and desperate could invoke it, too. Foolishness and desperation could make a desire *very* sincere.

That hymn was one of Minnie Ray's favorites. Jim remembered asking once before a football game if it was okay to pray for victory over an opponent who was also praying for victory. In response, his mother quoted the hymn's title line. But he wouldn't be satisfied. If winning was the sincere desire of *both* teams, he reasoned, how did the Lord decide which one to say yes to? She looked at him a long time. Then she took his chin between her thumb and forefinger and said, "He blesses us according to our needs. I believe that. But I also know," she said, "that his idea of what we need doesn't always match our own."

It was a better—and more reverent—answer than Coach Galloway's. With his crew cut and bubble of snuff in his bottom lip and the sweat pants cinched at the waist with a long, white shoelace, he espoused the philosophy that "God likes a good fight as much as the next guy." But Jim had to admit that Minnie Ray's quoting of the hymn wouldn't have worked as well as Major Reinhardt's for a send-off to war. "Let me put this whole business in Texas terms," said Reinhardt, who hailed from a place called Crystal City. "God ain't much interested in you dying for *your* country. What he *really* wants is for you to help the enemy die for his."

"It's called luck, Jim." That was Rickett's take on the matter. And though Jim found little comfort in life as a crapshoot, he knew as well as Rickett that even *with* prayer, one sick mother or wife gets better, and the other doesn't. Not long after Minnie Ray had breathed her last breath, Bishop O. Weldon Partridge wiped tears from his kind hound dog eyes and said, "I believe prayers are answered. I tell that to people all the time. But that doesn't make it any easier when the answer is no."

Jim stared at a windshield blurred with fog and paw-print droplets. Through such a lens, the world was easy to see as bleak. He remembered another bleak morning. Even though the absolute sincerest desire of every soul on patrol was *not* to get shot, the well-aimed sniper round still hit *somebody*. And one morning in the late fall of 1965, that somebody was Fritchey. Fritchey prayed more—more often, more sincerely, more selflessly—than any guy Jim ever knew in the Marines, including himself. Jim had seen him kneeling, had overheard him. On several occasions—at Fritchey's invitation—Jim had joined him. For Fritchey, prayer was the natural response to any problem anybody might be burdened with. Drought, flood, corn worm, leaky roof, grief, gout—the list was always long. And back home in Pea Ridge, Arkansas, he had two parents and a houseful of siblings probably praying the same way, praying especially for *him*. Yet what would Fritchey himself have said about the gap, in his case or any other, between what was prayed for and what actually happened?

"Must be God has his reasons."

Which amounted to about the same conclusion as Minnie Ray's.

On this first morning of September of 1967, the sun was in no hurry to be an answer to anybody's prayer. After a while Jim drove back to the yard and filled the morning working in front of the little tool shed. That's where the bean combine was parked—the long tongue of its hitch propped on an upright cinder block, its half-flat tires chocked with wood blocks. And beside the combine was the old truck used for crop hauling. Both needed to be readied for the harvest. "The first chance we get," Rickett had said.

This morning was that chance. On the combine, Jim greased joints and bearings, tightened belts, and replaced three pairs of teeth on the flailing cylinder. Then he climbed in the hopper. Wedging himself, back and feet, against two of the hopper's four funnel-sloped sides, he reached awkwardly down to clean, from the auger port, a dozen handfuls of moldered beans and a mouse's nest.

He saved for last the two chores that required compressed air because compressed air on this farm was an ordeal. Even more than most air compressors, this machine was brutal on

244   *Darin Cozzens*

eardrums. It clattered and hissed, clacked and snuffed. From moment to moment, the whole apparatus sounded as if it were about to fly apart. It occurred to Jim that, against such a racket, a whole platoon of poachers could fire M60s, and he would never hear a thing.

When finally the racket had gone on long enough for the building of sufficient pressure, Jim aired up both tires on the combine. Then he rerouted the hose and draped it over the truck's front bumper. Before he could blow out the truck's radiator (always half-clogged with chaff, thistle down, brome kernels), he would need to find the blow nozzle. He unplugged the compressor.

Starting with a shelf above the compressor, he searched benches, corners, cubbies. Then buckets, bins, trays. He checked pegs and spikes in the walls. He checked the narrow open tool box hung from the handles of the torch cart. He checked the board spines of two sawhorses and the angle-iron spines of the welding bucks. He checked everywhere. The blow nozzle was nowhere to be seen.

For a moment he stood thinking. Then, through the shed's side door, he stepped into a dirt-floored structure that was half lean-to and half awning. It was known as the grease shed. Here Goss stored, with no orderliness of arrangement, boxes full of grease cartridges and quarts of motor oil, and five-gallon buckets of hydraulic fluid and gear lube.

In the tight space, amid the boxes and buckets, stood a thirty-gallon drum long emptied of whatever lubricant it had held. Perched atop that too-little round drum was a too-big square of plywood. Brindled from spills and drips, the plywood served as a stand for funnels, spouts, dispensing pail, spare grease gun, filter wrench, rags. Also resting on that stand—slightly off-center and more precariously balanced than Jim could have known—was an old enamel-coated wash pan heaped with odds and ends. Crowning that heap was the compressor nozzle.

Step and lean and reach. But in the crowded space, the stepping and leaning bumped unevenly stacked boxes, which bumped the thirty-gallon drum. And the drum, as it happened, didn't require much disturbance at all to dump the piece of plywood and, with it, the heaped wash pan.

Down it all came, plywood and pan, and everything on and in. Spouts and funnels catapulted to far corners, and the upended wash pan strewed its contents like a sower strews seeds. Nuts, nails, screws, staples. Tacks, rivets, washers, pins. Stray sockets. Several Allen wrenches. Ball bearings of various sizes. Basting brush. Soup spoon. Marble. Stuff flew everywhere.

The compressor nozzle landed at the base of a wall. Only when Jim knelt to reach for it did he notice what had landed on the nearby lid of a bucket of gear lube. Scattered across the lid's surface were three or four rifle casings, all the same size. Jim stared and considered. The nozzle was forgotten. His hand went slowly to one of the casings. He picked it up. It had lain a long time buried among cotter pins and fence clips. Its brass was faded and tarnished. For a moment he rolled and twisted the casing in his fingers, then oriented it so he could see the primer end—the end with the stamped caliber marking. He brought it close and held it to the light.

It was a Winchester, and it was a .270.

It was afternoon before the sun finally burned the fog off and dried everything that needed to be dried. Once again Jim drove the roads leading to the bean field. Once again he bumped across culvert and corrugations and parked in the margin between ditch and tractor. Once again he climbed out of the pickup and leaned to swipe his hand through leaves and vines. That's when he saw the hoofprints. There were a lot of them, and they weren't all the small, toe-heavy crescents of deer. Whether they were made before or after his first arrival in the field, six hours earlier, Jim couldn't tell right away.

Then he could tell.

"You know it's fresh," Rickett had once said, explaining the stalking phase of an elk hunt, "when the pellets are still steaming." Jim had never felt any particular enthusiasm for scat. None of the pellets between the two tractors were steaming. But they weren't the only such sign. There was a long black-green splotch. And even eyes that had never eagerly studied elk scat for freshness could see that the splotch—from an abomasum much bigger than a deer's—had landed *on top of* his own boot prints, where he had stood earlier in the day to grease one end of the rake's reel.

With the fog gone and the afternoon sun bright in the sky, Jim looked all around. He felt watched. He needed to get going, needed to cut so he'd have something to rake. Yet only with great hesitancy and a strange self-consciousness did he climb into the seat of the cutting tractor and start the engine. As he maneuvered into position and palmed hydraulic levers to lower the knives and rod weeder, he kept looking around the field's perimeter. With each sweep, his gaze stopped at the far lower corner. From this distance and angle, Beeswax's honey boxes looked like headstones in a neglected grave lot.

This field's slope always felt steeper from a tractor seat. A wheeled rig gave gravity more to work with. Riding downfield, Jim only half-monitored the action of the cutting knives, took none of his usual pleasure in smooth mechanical function, was indifferent to each row's falling and folding into the one beside it.

Big hoofprints indicated a big bull.

"That's why they call it *sign*," Rickett once said. Where had the big hooves disappeared to in the last five hours?

And an empty .270 cartridge indicated a .270 rifle. Where was *it*? Dismantled? The pieces gathering moss at the bottom of the river? Entombed in swamp mud? Buried, in some sort of symbolic gesture, somewhere along Honey Spring?

If Goss did at some point own a rifle of that caliber, Rickett couldn't have known. Otherwise, he wouldn't have made the legal defense he made. Or he would have presented that defense differently. Yet Jim would have liked to feel more certain than he felt on any of those points.

Cut an acre, rake an acre. Cut another, rake another. Down the slope of the field, then up. Back and forth. So it went until late in the afternoon. Once again Jim was riding the cutting tractor. As it moved through the field, he monitored the action of dividers and knives and rod weeder—left and right, front and back. And, once again, between the different postures of his monitoring, between the leaning and swiveling, he regularly cast an eye toward the rain clouds massing over Carter Mountain.

All at once, forty yards into an upfield run, his attention was drawn to something else. There was a sudden oddity in the blurred rotation of the left rear tire. He clutched and braked and throttled down. Then he bumped the gear-stick to neutral and set the brakes. To supplement the braking against the field's incline, he left the knives and rod-weeder down.

Just before dismounting, he heard, above the low throb of the engine's idle, a steady fluid hiss. The hiss, he soon discovered, came from a six-inch gash in the tire. Besides puncturing the weathered rubber, whatever had made the gash had sliced beneath one of the tread ribs, left it hanging by a shred. It was the flopping tread rib that had caught his eye. Now, with the tractor at rest, the gash and flap stood just past bottom-center on the upward arc. From the gash bubbled a chalky white fluid. It ran to the low point between two cut double-rows, puddled between the tire and the rod weeder, then trickled downhill. The hiss smelled like flatus from a rubber intestine. Rickett had once mentioned this fluid. The tire shops filled the big ones with it, for extra weight and traction. It had something in it to resist freezing.

The tire was beyond patching. And it was too late on a Friday for the shop to send out a repair truck with a new one. With the prospect of a rainstorm, it would have been nice to finish the field, to have it done when Rickett returned. Jim looked over the two portions of the bean field, cut against uncut. He wasn't even close.

He began searching the herringbone track of the ruined tire. Mishaps always raised questions. And the answers never undid anything. But when finding an answer was the only thing that *could* be done, it was an itch and compensation both. What could make such a gash in a tractor tire? How far, *exactly*, did Jerome Snow's standard issue jungle boot fly through the air? What had become of the rifle that shot those .270 rounds whose casings he found in the grease shed?

The answer to one of the questions turned up a hundred feet downslope from the rod weeder. Protruding from the soil between corrugations, at a low angle, was a four-inch length of steel fence post. There was no way to have seen it, not from up on the tractor's seat, not under all those vines, all that mottled yellow-green foliage. With enough foliage, you could camouflage Times Square. That's what Ardizzoli said.

Jim knelt. The tip of the fence post was torch-cut. He gripped the four inches of shaft with one hand and pulled. It didn't budge. He tried two hands. He leaned and heaved and strained. Those four inches might as well have been the top end of a full-length post driven to the hilt. So when the piece suddenly broke loose, after much digging with a half-handled screwdriver scrounged from the McCormick's toolbox, Jim was surprised to see it was only fifteen inches long. And he was even more surprised to see, welded at the buried end, a circle of sheet metal the diameter of a tuna can. What a place for one of Goss's homemade fence-post extenders to turn up, here in the middle of a far field, in the far corner of the property. Cankered from its long burial, it looked harmless. Only in that particular path, from that particular angle, could it have done what it did to a tractor tire. A tire that was going to cost several hundred dollars to replace.

Jim stood. He was facing upfield, toward the cutting tractor. Holding a screwdriver in one hand and the fence extender in the other, he again weighed the two portions of the bean field, cut against uncut. Again he studied the rain clouds building to the northwest. Then, almost absently he turned and looked down-field toward the bee boxes.

At least thirty deer were running along the bluff fence, toward the distant sagebrush forest. And flowing among them was a pair of inward-curved scimitar horns that belonged to no buck of the muledeer species.

CHAPTER 20

J UST AFTER NINE O'CLOCK THAT NIGHT, RICKETT called to announce his recovery. "My bowels are valve-tight," he said. "I'll see you first thing tomorrow."

Of course Jim was made to report on the day's labors, every detail of progress and set-back, including the punctured tire. His long evening's fretting over Rickett's likely response was completely unwarranted. "I always did think those fence extenders were a damn jinx," Rickett said. "But a flat tire's nothing we can't fix. First thing tomorrow we'll call the tire shop. They're open till noon on Saturdays."

Then Jim reported the increasingly bold proximity of the deer herd and the early-evening sighting of the dun bull among them. He reported how he had followed the herd across the bottom of the bee-box field, across ditches and drains, across another field, then along the bluff fence all the way into the sagebrush forest. Still running, he bore the repeated pungent lashes of the big silvery boughs. Yet he lost them. The herd scattered, blended in, vanished. And among the mammoth plants, under gathering clouds, it had soon become too dark to keep looking.

"I'll be darned," Rickett said into the telephone receiver. He was not expressing doubt in either the report or the person making it when he added, "I've never heard of such a thing."

"Such a what thing?" Jim asked from his end.

"A domestic bull—and I use that adjective very loosely—running with a mob of deer this way. That's some animal."

Then Jim reported how, after giving up the search, he had retrieved the pickup and come back to the single-wide. After a pause he said, "I called the Maxwells."

"Oh?" Rickett said.

Bernene wasn't home. In her absence, it was Big Frett alone who had heard the explanation of their bull's most recent whereabouts and the company he was keeping. And this time, perhaps because he understood the legal burdens of ownership in a way his wife didn't, perhaps because news of the poaching was now widely known, Big Frett had given credence to the message. This time, he made no jokes about Triton and Pegasus. In fact, he pledged to dispatch not only Hap and Percy Croft, but as many other horsemen as he could line up. "Rain or shine, I'll have them there first thing tomorrow morning," Big Frett had said, "with instructions to comb every square inch of that river bottom, our side and yours. In the meantime, that bull won't roam anywhere tonight, not in this weather."

"About time," Rickett said. He had never accepted the argument that Big Frett Maxwell might have done more all along to stop the bull's wandering if the matter had been up to him alone.

What Jim didn't tell Rickett in *their* telephone conversation was how close he had come to calling the sheriff. (A call to Deputy Warden Overdale, on the other hand, never crossed his mind.) Rickett would have asked why the sheriff, and all Jim could have said was that he felt an odd foreboding, had felt it all day. And what could Sheriff Sturgis be expected to do about a foreboding?

Nor did he mention finding the rifle casing.

"You okay?" Rickett asked into the telephone receiver. "You went awful quiet on me."

"I'm okay," Jim said.

Now Rickett's end of the line went quiet. "Could it be," he said finally, "that it's Friday night and you're missing Miss You-Know-Who?"

"I'm okay," Jim said again.

Much later that night, after lying awake for an hour, listening to the first salvos of rain drops on the trailer's roof, Jim abandoned his bed. Without turning on any lights, he put on his shirt and pants and took a blanket out to the rocking chair in the living room. He positioned the chair in front of the window and sat down. This was the biggest window in the single-wide. It faced the haystack and corrals and, beyond that, the sagebrush forest. Jim looked through it now to keep watch on the darkness. That watch was accompanied by flashes and rumbles. Wind-blown rain streaked the glass. The little runnels forked, then forked again, like upside-down antlers.

Jim watched for a long time. As he watched, he thought about the ruined tractor tire. In his mind he saw again the gash and flapping tread and chalky fluid bleeding out and puddling and finally soaking away. And an hour later, when he had gone back for the pickup, things looked even more forlorn. Beneath the weight of the thick axle and hub and rim, the rubber of the ruined tired was mashed and deformed. Beneath a sky darkened with early autumn rain clouds, the whole rig sagged like a beast of burden gone lame in the hock.

Sitting in the rocking chair—but not rocking—Jim studied the runnels on the pane of the living room window. The timing of the tire puncture and the sighting of the deer mob was strange beyond strange. He thought of the gutted buck and the Doberman calf. After a while he got up from the chair and went to the window by the plywood eating table. Looking eastward into the night, he saw nothing. Then—flash and boom—and there were the trunks of the two big cottonwoods and the banks of Honey Spring and the divider fence. Another flash and boom—and there was the bluff fence and the dark line of the bluff's edge. And somewhere beyond all that, the great bowl of the river bottom and then the gravel pit.

He moved to the window over the kitchen sink. The next flash revealed only the lay of the notch. Beside the window, from the nail driven into the cupboard, hung Goss's binoculars. Jim left them hanging. In the flash-and-boom nighttime, they would enlarge no image, bring nothing closer to the eye. Back in the living room he stood again at the biggest window and looked out to the west. The rain had been a long time coming, but now it fell steadily.

After a little while longer, fatigue overcame restlessness. Jim shawled himself with the blanket and sat down again in the rocking chair. The thunder and lightning were close and constant. Before long his head drooped, and he dozed.

Sometime after midnight, he came awake. He raised his head and listened. And he heard, closer than highway traffic or a train whistle in the night, a noise that wasn't thunder. He stood and walked to the front door. He opened it and looked out into the rain and darkness. There was no eave on the single wide. He couldn't move onto the stoop, couldn't even lean beyond the threshold, without getting wet. For several minutes he listened and watched. Each flash illuminated, for just an instant, barns and corrals, sheds and haystacks. Then, just as suddenly, the curtain of darkness fell again. The effect was that of a flashbulb in the sky. It was vision and blindness at the same time.

Jim was about to close the door when, in the darkness between flashes, he glimpsed, out toward the middle of the sagebrush forest, in some sliver of open space between the big boughs, a wink of light, like a firefly.

Wyoming didn't have fireflies. Jim stood at the threshold of the single-wide's front door, just inside a scrim of rain streaming off the roof. He stared as hard as he could stare toward the center of the sagebrush forest. The wind had come up. A flare-flash of lightning illuminated stoop and yard, sheds and outbuildings, showed threads of rain coming down at a slant. Another boom and rumble. Another flare-flash.

And there! Another wink. Same firefly or a pair?

This one came from north of Goss's stockade fence, on the sagebrush-covered rise that concealed Goss's farmyard from the eyes of highway travelers. And again, wafting through the storm, that sound that was neither boom nor rumble.

Jim threw the blanket over the back of the rocking chair. Without turning on a light, he found socks and a sweatshirt. From the kitchen counter he grabbed a flashlight. He went to the closet. With his fingers he located the poncho. He pulled it on, slid the flashlight into one of its pockets, closed the closet door. He hesitated. Then he reopened the closet and felt along the shelf over the hanger bar, found the box of .30/06 shells. He opened it, emptied out a handful, put the handful in the pocket of his pants. Then he leaned down and groped until his hand encountered the solid stock of the rifle leaning upright in the corner.

Out on the trailer's stoop, holding the rifle under one arm, he used his free hand to pour water from his gumboots and tug them on. Dry socks, Ardizzoli. Then he was down the steps and at the pickup. Not until the moment he opened the truck's door was he reminded that his hinges creaked almost as loudly as Crue Penroy's. But at the same moment, Jim was also reminded that his cab light was defective. And light, on a night like tonight, was more apt to attract attention, anyway. He took the flashlight out of his pocket and tossed it on the seat. Then he leaned into the cab and set the rifle into the curved fingers of the gun rack.

After climbing in and latching the door softly, he found the ignition key, turned it to the *On* position. Pumping the gas pedal just once, he pressed the ignition button. When the engine started, he didn't turn on the headlights, didn't work the accelerator any more than just enough to initiate or sustain movement. Yet amid thunder claps and rumbles, he could hardly hear the pickup's engine himself. The cover-sound was to his advantage. But it was also to his disadvantage. The noise of any other engine, a noise he *wanted* to hear, was going to be equally muffled by the storm. He rolled down his window and cocked an ear.

He didn't need headlights. Flashes illuminated his way through the farmyard, through the stockade gateway, and along the narrow road between Honey Spring and the east edge of the sagebrush forest. But he did need the defroster. Even with the window down, the windshield was fogging. He flipped the fan's switch to the lowest speed. After a burst of chaff and dust from each defroster vent, the fan settled into its sputtering hum. In a dark cab on a dark road, the sound was oddly comforting.

The brilliance of the lightning flashes made the darkness in between even more profound. In those intervals, Jim couldn't see, close as they were, the big sage boughs brushing the driver's side of the pickup. For a moment it was his nose that did the perceiving. Through the open window, he smelled them, and once, as he turned his head and leaned to peer into the blackness, a bough licked his face.

Just beyond the sagebrush forest, the spring road widened at a junction. From that point, an access track branched off and ran west atop a low embankment dividing sagebrush from crop land. At the junction, Jim slowed to a crawl, clutched, and killed the engine. He let the truck coast to a stop, mindful to keep his foot away from the brake pedal. Only one of his brake lights worked, and that one only dimly. But under the circumstances, even one dim red glow was a risk.

Lightning flashed less frequently, and thunder rumbled more distantly. But the rain had settled in and was coming down hard. It drummed on the pickup's cab. Through the rolled-down window, Jim stared into the wet night. He was parked near the bottom corner of the bean field from which he had first seen the deer early in the week. But each of the now sporadic flashes revealed only neatly parallel windrows of pintos stretching away into the darkness.

He waited. After another flash, he saw what he had hoped to see. A firefly. And then, to its side, another. There *was* a pair. For half a minute Jim watched as they bobbed and winked, as they repeatedly diverged only to converge again.

It was a surprisingly long time before he heard, amid rumbles and pounding rain, snatches of revving and putting—like an outboard motor plying waves. Gradually the snatches fused into a steady sound, and gradually that sound aligned itself with the bobbing and winking of the lights. They were coming along the bottom of the bean field.

The lights again drew together. Then, according to pattern, they immediately drew apart, and more apart, and more. But this time, at the point of their greatest separation, they stopped. For a moment, they shone fixed and steady. What came next to Jim's hooded ears, after the lights had shone for that moment, was the sound of one of Minnie Ray's hair spray cans exploding deep in the trash barrel. The similarity was uncanny. And a second or two after that first muffled trash-barrel explosion sounded from deep in the bean field, it repeated, six or eight times in rapid succession.

Then the explosions ceased, and the fireflies resumed their pattern of movement. Jim waited.

In his teens, trash burning was his favorite chore, especially on evenings when an empty hair spray can tumbled into the barrel out behind the house in Mapleton. Contents under pressure. Do not expose to open flame. After putting a match to a newspaper or a corner of cardboard packaging, Jim used to linger. It took a while for the fire to get hot enough. He liked the thrill of waiting and waiting for the muffled bang. The thrill had something to do, naturally, with defying a printed warning. But it also made him feel heroic toward his mother—even if that feeling was arrived at through questionable logic. Widowed and poor and lonely, she could not possibly have soldiered on through bills and crab grass and heart trouble without the steadfastness of her noble son. And of the several fine examples of that quality, which stood out most prominently? What a burner of trash! After the bang in the burn barrel, that hair spray can was one less thing that could in any way go wrong in her life. After the explosion, it was as harmless as the charred pages of a *Reader's Digest* magazine.

The fireflies had converged and were again unconverging.

Adorn. That was her favorite brand. The cans were tall and thick-walled. How were the cans filled, Jim had once wondered out loud. "Well, I don't know," Minnie Ray had said, smiling. "Hair spray elves, I guess." Whatever the answer, those cans bottled a lot of pressure. He remembered the long hissing bursts of aerosol fogging the tiny bathroom or the little vanity in her bedroom. When his mother emerged, dressed for church or for her job at the library, she came trailing a cloud of mist and scent. Hair spray was her one indulgence.

The fireflies had stopped again. They hadn't been stopped very long when something whacked the pickup's rear fender. Then, lagging behind by a fraction of a second, came the muffled bang.

Intentional or accidental? Target or miss?

"Either way," Ardizzoli once said, "you're just as dead."

Get down. So as not to be just as dead. Get down. Be down. Stay down.

Jim pressed his face into the upholstery fabric of the pickup's seat. Passenger side. Hardly worn at all. There must not have been many passengers in Goss Harvey's life. What an odd thought to have, Jim admitted, even as his heart hammered its way up his throat.

Then this: The betraying of presence and position—which for the last half hour had been the thing most to be avoided in life—had now become its only point.

Headlights. They were the quickest answer. The switch was to the left of the steering wheel, on the far side of the dashboard.

He reared up, reached, fumbled for the knob, pulled, dropped back down.

He waited. He breathed. He listened.

Nothing else hit the pickup, but not because of any lull. Out in the field, hair spray cans were exploding like the Fourth of July. It took a moment to figure out why. The headlights were pointed up Honey Spring road and not across the field. Between road and field ran the border ditch, whose banks, like all the others on the property, were overgrown with late-summer brome. Road level and field level and ditch bank and grass made it so he could see the fireflies better than they could see him. The grass veiled all but the most directly pointed beams. But it wouldn't stop the next rifle round that happened to be sent in his direction.

Very fleetingly, Jim considered taking his own shot—out the open driver's window, into the sky—to betray presence and position *that* way. That was as good a purpose as any to put the rifle to. He could roll onto his back and reach it in the rack above his head. He could turn it end for end in the confines of the cab and dig under the poncho and into his pants pocket for bullets and load the magazine and work the bolt and point the barrel harmlessly and blast away.

But what if the fireflies misunderstood his intent and shot back?

It was simpler and safer just to point the headlights where they would be seen.

He took a fast breath and sat upright again. While his hands groped for the ignition key and button and gear-shift, his feet jigged with clutch, brake, gas, and the floorboard switch that ensured high beam. Then, cranking the steering wheel hard, he lurched backward in the wide spot of the junction, to position the pickup perpendicular to the road. With that movement his high beams pierced a stretch of thin ditch bank grass and swept across the acreage of the bean field like a pair of searchlights.

It worked. The popping of hair spray cans stopped. If time had been running normally enough for a count, the whole fusillade would have been found to take up about fifty seconds. So the ecstasy of a relief that would leave leg muscles jellied for three or four times that long seemed disproportionate.

Jim watched the fireflies. For just a moment they remained fixed points. Then one turned upfield, and the other followed. Now, the direction *they* pointed made *them* hard to see. They became dim flecks crawling fast toward the highway. Even as they evaporated in the darkness, their accompanying sound, the two strains of high-throttle scooter whine, merged into one steady hornet drone.

Against that far-away sound, Jim could barely hear the fan belt almost under his own nose. Dry bearings on several engine pulleys rasped with the rhythm of a pulse. Give chase, yes, but by which route? Field or road? He looked through the windshield, strained to see beyond the pale wash of his headlights, beyond such segments of bean windrows as were visible. He flipped on the wipers. At night, it was harder to see the wiper blade's little black snake. He looked through the passenger window, peered up Honey Spring road. When he turned back, he saw, by the light of his own high beams, what had eluded him earlier in the day.

It was the deer herd. At least two dozen animals had materialized in a rough semicircle around the pickup's front end. Through misty lines of illuminated rain, they stared. None of them seemed panicked or dazed or frightened. What they seemed was *intent*—on the raspy pulse of the fan belt, the hum of the defroster fan, the clock-tick steadiness of the wipers. And on Jim's presence. They stood very still. The little snake crawled up and down the windshield. Up and down. Once in a while the aged rubber squeaked faintly against glass. The deer didn't spook. In the foggy mist, two dozen pairs of eyes were riveted on him.

Jim moved his hand to the ignition key and turned it a quarter of a turn. All mechanical sounds stopped. The little black snake froze in its upward crawl. Though the headlights dimmed slightly, they still illuminated the deer herd congregated around the pickup's hood.

Jim never even considered the rifle. He had no interest in shooting at the animals looking at him. He wanted only to get out and stand among them.

With the gear-shift already locked in reverse, he didn't need the emergency brake, didn't need to risk the click of its pawl. He eased his feet off the clutch and brake pedals. With a groan in the driveline, the pickup's tires settled backward an inch or so. Still the deer didn't stir. The fingers of Jim's left hand pried the Vise-Grip lever of the door latch. The click evoked only ear twitches. He nudged the door. The hinges creaked. More twitches. When the rubber of his poncho chafed against the border seam of worn-out driver's-side upholstery, there were finally a few flinches. But still, very politely, the herd waited, waited, waited. And then, at the precise instant Jim's boot sole made contact with the wet surface of the road junction, they didn't wait anymore.

They bolted. They bolted as if goaded or summoned by a potent force. They bolted with purpose. They bolted as if they were born to bolt. To one side or the other, close enough to touch if Jim had thought to stretch out his arm, close enough to be heard—and deer were never heard—they rushed past the truck and into the darkness. Bounding over the spring. Over the divider fence. Over the moon, if there had been one. And they were gone.

For several moments, Jim stood by his open door looking after them. No one would ever believe it was possible to keep such close company with two dozen mule deer. Until tonight, he wouldn't have believed it himself.

He turned. The rainy darkness had swallowed the hornet drone of the scooters. Whatever their destination, they were long gone, too.

The rainy darkness had swallowed all urgency as well. It was the middle of the night, and Jim had no schedule to keep. He listened to the drops on his poncho hood. He reached into the pickup and retrieved the flashlight. He clicked it on and shined it along the fender. It didn't take long to find the bullet hole. The tip of his little finger fit the crater. He could feel the tiny doughnut of stripped paint. He turned and walked to the front of the pickup, stood between the headlights and peered out along the flare of the beams and into the darkness beyond.

Only as he happened to look down, at wet ground freshly imprinted by so many hooves, did it occur to him which set he wouldn't find. Among the audience of a moment ago, he had not seen the dun bull. And not for overlooking. Of course, even in full sunlight on a fair day, the bull's coat would have blended in. But close as the herd had stood, Jim couldn't have missed height and bulk. And surely not the horns.

Now he used the flashlight to comb the ground. Already the hoofprints were eroding under the pelting of raindrops. Even so, he would have recognized outlines and depressions of that size. And there were none. A full week (and probably more) running with the deer, feeding where they fed, sheltering where they sheltered, and Bernene's prize animal picked this night of storm and threat to go it alone? Jim felt again the foreboding from earlier in the evening.

After a moment he looked up the spring road toward pond and orchard, toward willow patch and cottonwood grove. Outside the narrow area lighted by the pickup's fading high beams—he needed to start the engine, replenish the battery— the darkness was different hues of obscurity. Those hues were relieved only infrequently now, and only very distantly and indirectly, by lightning flashes that had moved down the valley.

The rain had eased but not stopped. Jim walked up the road a ways. He stood listening to the splotches on his poncho hood. He directed the flashlight beam idly toward the highway, then clicked it off. He noted the quiet. Like the lightning, the rumbling of thunder had grown distant. Even on dry nights there was never much traffic at two a.m.

The sound of an engine (bigger than a scooter) was unmistakable. Any sound in the darkness of such a night was ventriloquism, but this one seemed pretty definitely to come from the other side of the cottonwood grove, from that short stretch of old highway—the one place on this property with close access to the new highway. That's when the realization came to him: the scooters weren't alone. To make their escape, they hadn't taken to the highway themselves, as he had assumed. They had rendezvoused with a truck or trailer or van, to be loaded up and carried away.

Then Jim was back in the pickup, scrambling again with key, start-button, pedals, steering wheel. Long minutes dawdled away while, not a half mile from where he stood, the poachers made ready for flight.

A road that was most sensibly traveled at ten miles an hour was, on this night, traveled at three times that speed. The old truck rattled and swayed, dipped and bounced. Amid the erratic probing of headlight beams, Jim took as his guide the tall, late-summer mane of grass between wheel tracks. All along that half mile of road, brome beards lashed the front bumper and scrubbed the truck's underside. Threshed kernels popped up through the rust hole in the floorboard.

At the bend by the apple trees, the pickup slewed right toward the pond. Rounding the cottonwood grove, it slewed left toward the ditch bank. All of a sudden, at a certain point in that rounding, sight confirmed sound. A pair of tail lights was just starting up the ramp to the abatis gate—a gate which, thanks to Jim Ray's largesse, stood wide open to the world, offering easy entrance and easy escape. To fossil diggers. To hay and apple thieves. To asparagus lovers.

And now poachers. They could go anywhere they wanted. East or west. Bighorns or Yellowstone. Atlantic or Pacific. Jim floored the gas pedal. To catch tail lights that bright, he would need all the speed and momentum he could muster. For the ramp and highway pursuit. And before that, to get up the incline to the stretch of old highway. But even before that, to get across the cattle guard, which in half an instant would appear before him to jolt the truck's axles and his spine, to afford the essential passage.

Right about *now*.

Jim's foot recoiled from the gas pedal and stomped the brake. The stiffening of the brake leg raised his rump off the seat. Skidding tires brought the front bumper right up to the cattle guard's edge. The stop killed the engine.

But it didn't kill the headlights. And what they now revealed confirmed why the heavy steel grating could afford no passage, at least not for anything with four wheels. Because anything with four wheels could not skirt the sizeable obstacle centered in that grating.

The sizeable obstacle was the dun bull.

In due time, daylight would confirm the bull's tracks on the far side of the cattle guard. But for now, Jim was left to surmise how an animal who could have confronted the cattle guard only while facing north was now planted in the middle of it facing south.

Fins and wings.

In the half instant before stomping the brake pedal, Jim had actually fancied—given the incline, a dip in the road, the rain-streaked windshield, the flap of the wipers, the weirdness of the night—that the bull was standing *on* the pipe spars or maybe even in the air above them, poised once more to elude, disappear, gallop into mist and fog.

But what he saw now through the windshield—an animal upright but seemingly legless—left no room in his mind for fins and wings. Nor what he heard. Thumping and thudding. Grunts and moans and snorts. A choked, abbreviated bellow.

Against such noises, Jim's own mattered not at all now—not setting the brake or unlatching the door or sliding off the seat. Even if every inch of movement between the pickup's door and the cattle guard had been marked with gong and trumpet blast, the bull wouldn't have taken notice. It was preoccupied with its own leaning and rocking and heaving and shuddering. The great horned head thrashed from side to side and up and down, in frenzied arcs. The horns themselves really did look like scimitars slashing through light and shadow. Twice the bull interrupted the slashing to grind its broad nose into the cleft between pipe spars and drag it back and forth, back and forth, with a terrible rubbery squeak.

With the flashlight, Jim probed for details which the already-dimming headlights could not unshroud. But even with the flashlight, he could not see, from the edge of the grating, all that had to be seen.

Staying well clear of the horns, he stepped onto the closest of the pipe spars. He had to move gingerly. The dark of the spars was indistinguishable from the dark of the spaces between them. Such surface as could support footholds was slick and curved. It was like stepping blindfolded onto mossy river rocks and greased ladder rounds.

And, as the bull's predicament soon witnessed, the penalty for a misstep would be steep. The pit beneath the cattle guard's pipe grating was just deep enough that the bull's trunk had hit the spars before the hooves made contact with the pit bottom. And now each of the mighty legs was wedged up to the shank. And they couldn't have been wedged between anything less yielding. Despite the striving, despite the muzzle-thrusting and head-swinging and heaving of massive brisket and shoulders and hams, the spars hardly trembled, hardly even creaked or murmured. And the bull's exertions, replayed a thousand times, would only tighten the entrapment.

Finally the throes subsided. Under the glare of the headlights the scimitar horns grew still, and the unblinking eyes stared at the pickup's front bumper. The rain and thunder had all but stopped, and there was no traffic on the highway. In the quiet, the bull's breathing sounded like the chuffing of a small steam engine at idle. Marking each chuff in the strange shadowed light were little plumes of vapor laced with silvery, web-thin strands of snot.

During the uneasy lull, the flashlight beam revealed that entrapment wasn't all. Where the bull's leap had failed, where hooves and limbs had plunged between pipe spars, certain bones had been made to curtail nineteen hundred pounds' worth of forward motion. Even the bones of the dun bull could not bear such strain. High on one foreleg—hard to see for being pinched between the spars and the chest—the raw end of a fracture had come through the hide.

As if offended by Jim's discovery, the bull groaned and began again to move the only parts of his body that were movable—the neck and head at one end and the tail at the other. The neck he strained and stretched as before. The head he tossed intermittently from side to side and up and down, as before. But this time, each downstroke ended with a sharp twisting of both neck and head, and a tremendous clashing of horn against pipe. The jarring cadence rang out in the darkness, and now, at last, the spars responded. The thick-walled pipe quivered. Jim felt as he felt the first time on ice skates. To stay upright, he had to sway and flail and lean and crouch.

For the better part of a minute these were his stances. Only gradually did the head-swinging slow. Only gradually did the heavy thuds and scrapes dwindle. And even then, even after the spars stopped vibrating, the tail kept writhing. At last it too stopped moving. After a moment, it curled to one side and rose almost mechanically to form a shepherd's crook held to one side. After another moment, several heavy, sodden lumps fell the abbreviated distance to the spars.

The lumps, fresh from the abomasum, were just perfuming the wet air when Jim happened to spot the other wound. Twice already the flashlight beam had swept the bull's lower left rib-cage and twice had missed it. Even now, under direct illumination, it didn't look like a bullet hole. Given the circumstances, there was nothing unusual about a patch of wet and matted hair.

Except this patch oozed. Like jam pulp through cheesecloth. And it had been oozing for quite some time. Probably ever since the dun bull's moment of separation from the fleeing mule deer and throughout his half mile of individual flight across the bean field, across two ditches, and (for some unaccountable reason) toward the highway. All at an upgrade. It had kept oozing right through a first leap—which had to have cleared the cattle guard; there was no other explanation—through the wholly unexpected encounter with the poachers' pick-up rig, through the turnabout and final dash and second leap. Ever since that doomed second leap, blood had oozed directly from the wound onto a pipe spar. From there it split into two thick beads, each following the pipe's curvature downward, to drip steadily into the gaping dark below.

Another grunt, another heave, another convulsion. But this convulsion ended almost as soon as it began. The spirit was willing, but the flesh was spent. Horn met pipe another two or three times, but only with the most inconsequential report, like a matchstick gnashed against an anvil. Brandished only moments before with menacing ease, the scimitar horns now seemed to weigh the head down. Boss and snout sagged. Breath went in and out of the open mouth in ragged gasps. Froth dripped from the lower jaw. The flashlight's beam, closely trained, showed the froth tinged with red.

After a time the breaths came at such long intervals that each was more surprise than expectation. This is it, Jim kept thinking. This is it. And though each successive gasp proved him wrong again, it proved him less wrong than the one before it.

So he was astonished when suddenly the bull shuddered and moaned and heaved his giant head upward; more astonished still when he tipped his muzzle to the sky and let out a long, deep, unbroken bellow. The sound carried into the night, over trees, over ditches and canals, over field and bluff and swamp, all the way to the river and beyond. It was defiant and resigned. It was eerie and reverent. It was anguish articulated.

Before the last echo had faded, the head came down again and for the last time. It came down in a free fall, as if detached from any vertebrae or muscle or tendon. The muzzle hit the pipe so hard the teeth clicked and the jaw joint popped. And there it stayed.

Against all odds, the bull was still breathing. Yet there was nothing to be done. The awfulness of the animal's predicament disallowed even the posture of death. No lying down, no stretching or shifting, no way to get easy, nothing like repose. "You sure you want it that deep?" Rickett had asked during the digging of the cattle guard's pit, seemingly unaware that, not a half hour earlier, he was the one who had also said, "You're going to want to go down farther than *that*." But it was Jim who had made the call. Whether out of stubborn independence or defiance or whimsy, he had gone a foot deeper.

Maybe if he hadn't, the bull might have had a chance. With his hooves in contact with the pit floor and—instead of hanging uselessly—bearing *some* of his weight, the bull could have at least eased the pressure on the fractured joint.

For one last moment Jim stood in guilt and helplessness and sympathy and grief. Then, without fear or caution, he knelt at the bull's head, reached and stroked the massive neck. The scim-itar horns didn't so much as twitch.

The pickup's engine had been off for quite some time; the headlights were dimming fast. What had to be done could not be competently done in darkness, nor would it leave a hand free for flashlight holding. So it had to be done now. Jim stood and, with surprisingly sure footholds, stepped backward off the cattle guard. With a reliable surface once again underfoot, he moved to the open door of the pickup. He switched off the flashlight and laid it on the seat. From the rack he lifted the rifle. From his pocket he dug one cartridge. Then he stepped between the pickup's front bumper and the edge of the grating. He opened the rifle's bolt, chambered the round, closed the bolt. Positioning himself had nothing to do with marksmanship, everything to do with tightness of space, closeness of target, oddness of angle. He brought the rifle to his shoulder, tried in the murky light to line up the sights, settled for looking down the barrel as he would have looked down a pointed stick. And hoping with all his heart that the dun bull was dreaming of harems of cows in lush pastures, he pulled the trigger.

CHAPTER 21

BEGINNING AT FIRST LIGHT THE NEXT MORNING, THEY arrived at the impassable cattle guard in this order:

Bishop Clive Sebright, who had answered before the telephone's second ring and, after listening for a moment, had asked, in a voice surprisingly alert for that hour, "Are you sure you don't want me to call them for you?"

Lawyer Nolan Rickett, who didn't hear the ringing of the phone mounted on the kitchen wall of his cabin in North Fork because he was already halfway to Honey Spring and who climbed out of his Chrysler a half hour after that missed call dressed in his farming clothes—frayed newsboy hat, faded and poorly patched coveralls, dingy high-top sneakers—with a cigarette in one hand and a jumbo bottle of Pepto-Bismol in the other.

A highway patrolman finishing a long night shift with what he had wrongly supposed would be a quiet run between Garland and Cody.

Hap and Percy Croft and their saddled but now unneeded horses (the entirety of the army of riders Big Frett had boldly pledged the night before).

Sheriff Carl Sturgis, who was summoned by the highway patrolman's radio.

Beeswax Jones, who, standing beside the gas pump at Bud's Texaco (Bud's first customer of the day), grew curious when the sheriff's eastbound car made a sharp U-turn in the middle of the highway through Ralston and then sped the other direction.

Doc Lowe, who for the better part of a decade had been threatening to retire and who sorely regretted not having acted on that threat when the sheriff's call woke him only a few hours after his (the veterinarian's) return from a midnight farrowing on a little farm way down past Greybull—where he had delivered a dozen healthy Duroc piglets only to lose the sow to hemorrhage following a prolapse of the uterus.

Winn Bingham, who had said, in a voice not so alert, "Give me a half hour," when the bishop stopped by en route to Honey Spring to enlist him and his big tractor loader.

Of course the bull's owners (and Winn's in-laws): Big Frett Maxwell, who, even with the bull's whereabouts now known at last, was chagrined to see that his envisioned search army consisted of only the two Croft brothers, and even more chagrined that he had left the organizing of the army to them. And Big Frett's wife, Bernene, who for very few other reasons—fire? flood? avalanche?—would have left the house without makeup and still in the hair curlers she wore to bed most nights (the secret of her gargantuan bouffant) and who ever thereafter would dispute her husband's claim that Jim Ray's call that morning had come before that of their daughter, Patty Dew (Winn's wife).

Lewis Glenney, who, thanks to a call from Dr. Amos Lowe's wife, would now have something for the *Clarion*'s next front page besides another story about the progress of this season's harvest accompanied by a big filler picture (above the fold) of a lone combine at work against a backdrop of majestic mountains and open sky.

And finally, Deputy Game Warden Marty Overdale, who wasn't called or summoned by anybody.

Thanks to a lot of well-defined tracks—and full daylight—it didn't take the sheriff long to arrive at official conclusions.

"Looks like three poachers and two scooters—"

"Tote-goats, they're called," Rickett said, between a drag on his cigarette and a swallow of Pepto-Bismol.

Studying the old lawyer, the sheriff couldn't decide whether the interruption was a correction or concurrence. And Rickett only complicated the question when he added, "The tractor tread on that wide rear tire—that's their signature."

It might have helped the sheriff to know that Rickett had uttered exactly the same lines at least a half hour before his (the sheriff's) arrival. But in the absence of that knowledge, the sheriff finally broke off studying the hat and coveralls and shoes, and resumed his summary. He said Poacher A, waiting just beyond the cattle guard, must've known the whole plan was foiled when he saw B and C skedaddling his way. This Poacher A would have followed his mates' progress by their headlights. He would have watched them come up through one field, somehow hop a ditch, come up through another, and then, at a far culvert, get on the irrigating road coming from the west side of the property and head toward the cottonwood grove and the junction with the Honey Spring road. And while Poacher A was concentrating on the approach of B and C from one direction, here came the bull from another.

"Put it this way," the sheriff said, "Poacher A and the bull weren't expecting each other."

That, along with the rest of the sheriff's conclusions, merely confirmed what Bishop Clive Sebright and Rickett had deduced first thing and what Jim had guessed in the night: the dun bull *had* jumped the cattle guard the first time, had cleared it clean and kept running, only to confront the poachers' rig parked along the flattest stretch of the old highway. And the meeting must indeed have been unexpected. What else would explain so stark a reversal? The skidding of the hind hooves had gouged two long grooves in the silt overlaying the old pavement.

The rest of the story could be read in the signature of the tote goats' rear tires. There were scooter-sized herringbone tracks braided all across the lower end of the bottom bean field. And the tracks weren't the only evidence. Everywhere the scooters had broken through a windrow, they had scattered pods and vines. From a distance, dozens of such breaks resembled the disheveling and desecration of a bad wind.

At a certain point, the tracks turned upfield. They stayed between windrows all the way to the head ditch. On the other side of that ditch, in road grit moistened and settled by rain, the herringbone tread pattern looked more creature than machine. If stared at long enough, it conjured the scales of a strange python.

Owing to the conditions of the previous night, the tote-goat tires even left their mark on the cattle guard itself. Each tread rib was a rubber stamp, and muddy grit made the ink. Despite contact surface limited by the curvature of the pipe spars, the ink was now dry and the tread marks clear. Thus they became the most damning detail of the investigation. At the sheriff's request, those rubber-stamp tracks (and many other crime-scene images) were captured by the camera hanging from a leather strap around Lewis Glenney's neck. The tracks' plain-to-see circumventing of the bull proved that he was already hurt and stuck when the scooter riders came on him, and that they left him that way.

Shortly after his nine o'clock arrival, with the on-site investigation all but finished, Deputy Warden Marty Overdale astutely observed that the conditions of the previous night were ideal for preserving tracks. If Sheriff Sturgis heard Overdale's astute observation, he paid it no mind. Along with the bishop and Rickett and Bernene and Big Frett, the sheriff was standing at the cattle guard's south edge, approximately where Jim's pickup (now parked at the fringe of the cottonwood grove) had slid to a stop last night. At the north edge of the cattle guard—and the bull's tail end—stood the others. Both groups were watching Doc Lowe work. The old veterinarian was stretched out prone on a sheet of plywood laid diagonally across the pipe spars. With a pair of instruments resembling awls, he was examining the bullet hole in the ribcage.

Even with Overdale's warden-come-lately arrival, the audience was smaller than it had been. With the sheriff in charge, the highway patrolman had slipped away more than an hour earlier. And at the bishop's request, Winn Bingham and Jim were gone in the bishop's truck back to Winn's place to fetch what couldn't have been found in Goss Harvey's tool shed—enough heavy rope and old harness straps to make a belly sling, several full lengths of chain (with end-hooks intact), and a functioning come-along.

"And bring a bone saw if you've got one," Amos Lowe had said in a private exchange. "I went off and forgot mine."

The reason for the privacy of that exchange was Bernene. She was in high dudgeon. On another woman, the neat ranks of lipstick-sized, chrome-colored hair curlers—still wound snug against the dome of the scalp, even after a night's sleep—would have been innocent enough. But on Bernene Maxwell they formed a helmet. On any other woman, the stark smallness of the curler helmet in contrast to the familiar and enormous bouffant would have called to mind the humbling reduction and exposure of a freshly sheared ewe. But the strange contrast only made Bernene more formidable.

"If that gate had been closed, Carl," she said for the second or third time, "this *never* would have happened. That's what gates are *for*. I repeatedly told him that."

Still watching Doc Lowe, the sheriff said, "We'll get it all sorted out, Bernene."

On the other side of the cattle guard, while Lewis Glenney took more pictures—some for the sheriff, some for the newspaper—the Croft brothers asked Overdale if a domestic bull stuck dead in a cattle guard on a Saturday morning fell under Game and Fish jurisdiction. Overdale's response sounded like someone reading from a policy manual. Meanwhile, tonguing and swishing and shifting his quid of tobacco, Beeswax studied the bull's loin and hind quarters with the eye of a butcher.

At last Doc Lowe finished. With a heave and grunt he drew himself into a kneeling position on the plywood mat, waited a moment as if to let his head square again with the world, then stood stiffly. To Sheriff Sturgis he said, "That's about everything there is to see until I can get Icarus here up on one of my tables at the clinic."

"You can find the slug for me?"

"I'll find your slug."

Sheriff Sturgis cast a quick sidelong glance at the curler helmet and immediately clarified his question: "The poacher's—not the boy's."

"I'll find your slug," Doc Lowe said.

"Anything you want to know about *Jim's* slug," Rickett offered, "just ask."

Bernene scrutinized the dirty hat, the patched coveralls, the stained sneakers. Then her gaze settled on the jumbo bottle of Pepto-Bismol, and she asked, "Are you not well, Mr. Rickett?"

"Fit as a fiddle," he said. "Heartburn, cramps, diarrhea, gas—this stuff does wonders for every symptom of dyspepsia." He offered the bottle and said, "Try a snort?"

To those who didn't know better, Rickett's age and dress spelled codger. Or tramp. But Bernene did know better, as did her husband and Doc Lowe and the bishop. And though the gravel pit shooting of a Vanderfisk cow, six years earlier, predated his first-term election, Sheriff Carl Sturgis, now already a year into his second term, had heard of the case and of the lawyer for the defendant. And on this morning in September of 1967, though Bernene did not welcome that lawyer's participation in any conversation about another of her dead bovines, the sheriff and vet and bishop did, if only because his participation buffered hers.

When it was clear that Bernene didn't want any of his Pepto-Bismol, Rickett shrugged and took another swig himself. Then, capping the bottle and using it as a pointer, he said, "Dig behind that hole *there,*" indicating the skull, "and you'll find a Winchester one hundred fifty-grain .30/06 hollow point."

"How can you be so sure?" the sheriff asked.

"You're looking at the guy who inventoried every jot and tittle of Goss Harvey's estate," Rickett said, "including several boxes of shells and the rifle to shoot them. You'll find the casing to one of those shells and the rifle both in that truck," he said, pointing over his shoulder to the 1941 Ford parked by the cottonwood grove.

"I wasn't doubting you," the sheriff said. "I'm just impressed with your recall."

"The Maxwells here can corroborate," Rickett said. "And Doc Lowe. The caliber of Goss's rifle was the subject of a legal inquiry with which they're well familiar."

The allusion hung heavy in the air. All conversation, on either side of the cattle guard, stopped. The five people standing at its north edge stared at the six people across from them. Under that scrutiny, most of the six took a renewed interest in the beautiful scimitar horns, the astonishingly long tongue hanging from the slack jaw, and the perfectly round hole centered between the half-open glassy eyes.

The sheriff studied the two-part crowd. "Well," he said after a careful interval, "that's good enough for me: One hundred and fifty-grain .30/06 hollow point it is."

The tension eased.

"That's what I'll put in my report," said Doc Lowe, picking up his bag of instruments. "Saves me opening the skull." Using the plywood mat as a bridge, he crossed to the cattle guard's north side and started a slow, upward trudge toward his truck, which was parked just off the pavement of the old highway, between Beeswax's sheep wagon camper and Lewis Glenney's Volkswagen Beetle.

The old veterinarian hadn't gone twenty feet before Bernene tiptoed across the mat herself, with surprising nimbleness, and hurried after him. Before she even caught up to him, she said, "And you're absolutely certain that animal *had* to be put down?"

Amos Lowe stopped and turned. The expression on his face bespoke weariness and grief and compassion—for all the dead bulls and motherless piglets in the world. "He was suffering, Bernene. The boy did exactly what I would've done."

To the bishop and sheriff, still standing at the cattle guard's south edge and thus out of Bernene's earshot, Big Frett said, "You can't blame her for being upset."

"Except for the poachers," said Sheriff Sturgis, "I'm not blaming anybody for anything."

"You wouldn't believe what that bull was worth," said Big Frett. "It had a heck of a pedigree, you know."

The remark was not out of earshot of at least two people on the other side of the cattle guard. Percy Croft leaned toward his brother and murmured, "Doesn't look like much of a pedigree now."

To which Hap responded, philosophically, "Took this to catch the old fence-hopping s.o.b., though." Then, after a pause, he said, "Tell the truth, Percy: Do you really think we would have had any better luck this time?"

Doc Lowe had resumed his upward trudge. This time Bernene didn't follow. As if unsure where to go, she started back down toward the sheriff, who crossed the plywood bridge and met her halfway. For just an instant her curler helmet caught the sun in such a way that her whole head glowed. And from the mouth amid that glow came these words: "So we've lost our bull, and that's that?"

"We'll get it all sorted out, Bernene."

Still standing on the lower side of the cattle guard, Big Frett said, "It's a bloody shame she had to see this. That bull was old Enoch's last gift to her."

Both Rickett and the bishop nodded commiseratingly.

Then Big Frett Maxwell, banker and Midas-touch business-man ever conscious of financial contingencies, said, "Fortunately, he was well insured."

The ambiguity—well-insured bull or well-insured father-in-law?—occurred to all three men at the same instant. When, as an intended clarification, Big Frett added, "There's some things money just can't compensate," he only compounded the muddling.

So it was a great relief when, at that very moment, someone yelled, "Here they come!"

All eyes turned to the opening in the highway fence unbarred these many months by the abatis gate. The bishop's pickup turned off the new highway and, with a jolt visible even from the cattle guard, came off the unbeveled edge of the asphalt apron. Then it cleared the gate opening and descended the ramp to the old highway. Using the plywood bridge, those on the south side of the cattle guard migrated to the north.

The only eyes that didn't follow the approaching pickup were those of Beeswax Jones. They stayed riveted on the dead bull. The person standing closest to Beeswax was Lewis Glenney, so it was Lewis Glenney who had to field the inevitable question: "You wouldn't happen to know," Beeswax asked, "if anybody has given any thought to the meat?"

On any other morning, one of the first pairs of hands to make contact with the actual work of the extraction would have belonged to Clive Sebright. His would have taken their turn with a long digging-bar lever and a series of inadequate fulcrums—stob, branch, rock—awkwardly set between spars, then willed not to slip or kick out just when enough space opened between body and pipe to thread a chain hook. His would have been among those fishing rope and old harness straps under and around the great barrel of the belly. Then his hands, in concert with a few other hands, would have taken up slack with the clinking of links and singing of hemp against pipe. His hands and others would have looped and knotted and fastened, securing rope and chain to the bucket frame of the big tractor loader. In this whole process, Clive Sebright the farmer would have joined Jim Ray and Winn and the Croft brothers, to grapple and heave, to strain and strive, to crouch and kneel and sprawl, all while listening to a constant patter of directions and suggestions from the cluster of onlookers.

But on this morning, Clive Sebright needed to be a bishop more than he needed to be a farmer. So he held back, mindful of Bernene's position at the forefront of the onlookers, alert to her expression and mood. In their dealings with one another, the best he and Bernene usually managed was a strained civility. But at this moment by the cattle guard, as often happened, his bishoping role somehow made him a better man, if only temporarily, than he felt himself to be. If only for this necessary moment, he felt, toward a woman he ordinarily didn't like very much, nothing but compassion.

Right away, for instance, he had noticed that Bernene Maxwell was the only woman in the group, a fact that couldn't have escaped the other eleven men. But what struck Clive Sebright now, with the hoisting of the dead bull about to commence, was how *little* that disproportion seemed to affect any of the eleven, including her own husband. With any other woman, the ratio would have occasioned a much more explicit awareness. The presence of any other woman—especially one younger and smaller, one more petite or curvaceous, one less helmeted—would have elicited deference, solicitude, bravado, maybe even chivalry. And however clumsy, however presumptuous and condescending and chauvinistic, the gestures motivated by those qualities would have been a response to the plain fact that the one among the eleven (twelve, counting himself) was female. Wherever she went, Bernene certainly commanded solicitude and deference. But not exactly for *that* reason. Would that distinction even matter to a woman like her? Until this moment the question had never occurred to Clive Sebright. Nor the answer: How could it *not* matter?

The realization was an indictment of his own petty narrow-mindedness, of his selling short of Bernene Maxwell. And it had to do with more than the lopsided ratio of the group. She had never impressed him as a woman given to sentiment for a barn-yard animal, yet here she was, genuinely distraught by the fate of the dun bull. And though her blame for that fate was misplaced and the logic behind it skewed, Clive Sebright the bishop felt compassion for her anyway.

So he watched her—watched and waited for a certain opportunity.

Soon enough it became clear that even Winn's big loader would have all it could do to lift *half* the body at one time. After a repositioning of the tractor, after some re-rigging of rope and chain, up the bucket went again. Again the lines tightened. Again the loader's frame groaned. But this time the massive hips began to rise from the pipe grating. Slowly each hind leg followed. Each inch of upward progress was hard-earned. Clamped as they were between pipe spars, the legs looked as if they were being extracted from a wringer whose rollers didn't roll. Up. Up a little more. And a little more. Every face showed wary and hopeful anticipation.

Just when it looked as if those hind legs were about to come free at last, something snagged. Hap, Big Frett, Deputy Warden Overdale, the sheriff, Jim Ray—they all stepped closer and peered hard at the grating, searching for the impediment. Several of them looked up at Winn Bingham, who was leaning left and right in the tractor seat, trying to see for himself what they couldn't see. Hap Croft looked at Winn and spread his hands in a gesture of helpless bafflement. Winn hit the up-down lever, then hit it again. The tractor's hydraulic pump whined, and the loader's frame shuddered. He shook his head.

Folks turned to get Doc Lowe's take on the matter, but Doc Lowe was trudging back up the sloped road. In his absence, it was Rickett who said, "The hooves are hung." He made this observation while studying, not the bull or cattle guard, but the level of the pink liquid remaining in his bottle of Pepto-Bismol. "I saw the same thing once with a draft horse," he said offhandedly. "Hooves'll make it in, but not back out. That's the way with a lot of things."

A closer search proved Rickett right: Given the thickness of a bull's pasterns and the shape and angle of dewclaws, the narrow spacing of the pipe spars never should have accommodated them in the first place. And given the dislocation and swelling, from injury and from death, the spacing certainly would not accommodate them now. There was some talk of going after the closest cutting torch, but such talk ended when it became clear why Doc Lowe had gone to the bishop's truck instead of his own. He came back carrying the commissioned bone saw. Without a word, he handed it to Jim Ray and pointed to the closest hind leg, to a level just below the hock.

Jim bent to his work. Just as the saw teeth made it through hide and into bone, Bernene Maxwell put a hand to her face. "I can't watch this," she said, backing away from the crowd. From her new position, trying in vain to avert her eyes, she said, "I just can't watch this."

She had separated herself far enough from the others that her second declaration was heard by only one person. That one person was Bishop Clive Sebright, who closed the distance between them so as to stand beside her. In a low voice he said, "I am sorry about this, Bernene." The curler helmet didn't turn. She stared toward the cattle guard, watching the movement of Jim's sawing arm, steady as a pitman.

Looks like a big hacksaw, somebody said.

But Bernene wasn't paying attention to the comments from the little crowd of onlookers. She was listening for whatever Clive Sebright might say next.

"This is raw deal for you and Jim both," he said. The curler helmet didn't turn. He said, "I wish it hadn't happened."

For both of them, the pronoun *it* inevitably encompassed more than the bull's death. Yet for now they let it mean that.

But bone sure cuts a lot easier than metal, somebody said.

"I know you're hurting," the bishop went on in a low voice, "but this isn't the boy's fault. And I think you know that."

They both watched as the saw blade, with a final stroke, severed the first leg. With that severing, that quarter of the bull's body, stretched between the pipe grating and the loader's bucket, jerked as if an anchoring peg had pulled loose. The severed leg—sawed bone at one end, hoof and pastern at the other—stayed right where it was, wedged between pipe spars.

That's because bone's mostly hollow, someone said.

Like your head, someone else said. There was good-natured laughter.

Without pause or rest, Jim repositioned to start on the second leg.

Bernene and the bishop watched him, saw stroke by saw stroke. "This is his place now," the bishop said in a low voice. "With half a chance, I think he'll settle here." He was quiet for a couple of saw strokes. Then he said, "For him, the war's over. Let's not put him in the middle of another one."

The curler helmet was very still.

Ask Jim *how easy it's cutting!* someone hollered good-naturedly. *He's the one sweating!*

More laughter radiated from the group. Even above the idling engine, even from the distance of the tractor seat—minding the height of the loader bucket and the tension of the rope and chain harness—Winn Bingham heard that laughter and smiled.

With one final stroke, the saw blade severed the second leg. Jerk of another anchor peg pulled loose, and the bull's body swung toward plumb, but only as far as the trapped front legs would allow—which wasn't all that far. Then Winn lowered the loader's bucket, and the men on the cattleguard began fashioning the lift-harness to manage the bull's front end.

"He just wants to live his life and be your neighbor," the bishop said. Then he added, in the lowest voice yet, "Especially if he can find the right girl to do all that with him."

Now Bernene turned her head and looked at Bishop Clive Sebright. She looked at him a long time. From the expression on her face, strangely unframed by the usual profusion of her bouffant, it was clear that, despite the astuteness of many of his surmisings, the lawyer Nolan Rickett was wrong about this one. It was clear, that is to say, that before now, Bernene Maxwell had never given a moment's thought, self-serving or otherwise, to a match between Jim Ray and her niece. But it was also quite clear that she was giving that match some thought now. If, on this morning, there was one thing she cared about more than her bull, that one thing was her niece.

Finally she asked, "Do you know something I don't?"

"Only that he's a good boy and he likes her is all," Clive Sebright said. He was quiet for a moment. Then he said, "How would you feel about giving things enough of a chance to see if she might like him back?"

The silver helmet still shone brightly. But some of the lipstick-sized curlers were no longer wound so tight. All around

Bernene's head, wisps of hair had come loose from their bindings, as if, on her, hair could be restrained for only so long. In
the morning light those wisps made a kind of frizzy nimbus. She
turned away, considering.

"Here in a bit," the sheriff could be heard to say, as the loader's
bucket started up, "we're going to need a truck to get this thing
over to Doc Lowe's."

"We can use ours," said the voice of Percy Croft. Without calling attention to the fact that the Crofts' rear bumper was already
sagging under the weight of the horse trailer, Sheriff Sturgis
replied: "I appreciate your civic-mindedness, boys. I truly do.
But I was thinking more along the lines of that big Game and
Fish rig, since it's evidently not doing anything else this morning." It was widely known that Deputy Warden Overdale prided
himself on a clean truck, inside and out. And it was going to be
hard to haul what had to be hauled without a little bit of mess.
"What do you say, Marty?" Whatever the deputy game warden's
response, it made the little crowd laugh again.

At last Bernene turned back to the bishop. They stood well
apart from the others. The combination of reason and feeling
were evident in every lineament of her face. Without the canopy
of the bouffant, her eyes seemed extraordinarily exposed.

"What I'm asking," the bishop said, looking into those
unblinking eyes, "is can you make peace with this?"

"With what's happened to my bull, you mean?"

"I mean all of it."

As Bishop Clive Sebright would often reflect long after his
bishoping tenure, Bernene Maxwell's answers to his questions
that morning by the cattle guard—could she give Jim a suitor's
chance and could she let go of all that needed to be let go of—
depended entirely on the scope of pronouns. On wishing *it*
hadn't happened. On making peace with *this*. Suddenly everything else going on—the low idle of the tractor engine, the work
of extraction, the chatter of the little crowd—seemed muted and

peripheral. The bishop and Bernene might as well have been sitting by themselves in an office improvised on this very spot, with the Gethsemane picture hanging from the nearest fence post.

Surely, in the long history of human folly in general, and Honey Spring in particular, granting a suitor's chance hardly rose to the same level of significance, spiritual or otherwise, as making peace—at least the kind of peace the bishop was asking Bernene to make. But the plain truth was that, as Bernene Maxwell stood at this particular juncture in her own history, her answer to one question very much depended on her answer to the other. With a slight reflexive twitching of her jaw, she pondered long and carefully. And by the time the bull's front end was hoisted and the sawing underway, it was clear that if she were going to say no to either proposition, she would have said it by now.

CHAPTER 22

I T'S NOT LIKELY THAT JIM RAY WOULD HAVE FORGOTTEN much about that first weekend in September of 1967. But Labor Day of that year gave him a marker that would resist the blurring and dimming of years. Ever thereafter he would be able to place, on the timeline of his life, the exact night of the dun bull's last leap, the exact morning of the extraction from the cattle guard. Why he felt at the time such guilt over the bull's death he could never understand. But as that guilt blurred and dimmed, it left a residue of empathy.

There was much more to be remembered. After that last day of August, a Thursday, Dutch and the other bikers were never seen again. And after Friday night, there was no more ant- ler poaching in the Balford Valley. Of course, those two facts spawned a great deal of conjecture as to the poachers' identities. But conjecture wasn't enough to warrant pursuit, especially since the Game and Fish folks were spread thin with the approach of hunting season and since half a dozen locals testified to the sher- iff that, as early as last April, they had heard Dutch and his mates declare their intention to be in San Diego *by* Labor Day—at least a three-day trip. And if they were the poachers, where did the tote-goats come from—and the rig to haul them? Doc Lowe did find, lodged in one of the bull's lungs, a poacher's rifle slug. But it was a caliber common to deer hunting and nothing to implicate the bikers, none of whom had been seen to carry anything big- ger than a pistol in their saddlebags.

In time, the much more momentous happening to remember from that weekend would be Jocelyn Vanderfisk's return from

Bear Lake. Because of her sometime acquaintance with Dutch, she was one of the half dozen people Sheriff Sturgis interviewed. The interview took place the Thursday morning after Labor Day. Thursday evening she had another appointment. That appointment (with preparations that would affect the day's quitting time, including the thorough cleaning, inside and out, of the 1941 Ford) was not made known to Rickett until Thursday's lunch in the single-wide: bologna sandwiches, potato chips, chocolate pudding, overripe bananas.

"So when was this arranged?" Rickett asked.

"Last Sunday."

"And you're just now telling me about it?"

Jim hesitated. Then, without much conviction, he said, "What if you're right about Bernene's meddling?"

Rickett, who would have liked to know what the bishop and Bernene had talked about for so long by the cattle guard, shook his head slowly. "I don't think so," he said. After a moment, he said, "And I don't think that's why you've kept quiet all week, either. Something's eating you."

The two men regarded each other for a long time.

Finally, Jim said what there was to say: "I found some old rifle casings in the grease shed." After a moment, he added, "They were .270s."

Rickett's face was hard to read. No smile, no frown; no shock, no expectation. Just a little paleness at the edge of his cheeks' coloring. After a long time, he fished a cigarette from his pocket, put it between his lips, and patted all around his plate. Jim slid the worn lighter from beneath the plate's blind-spot edge and handed it to him. Rickett took it, leaned his head—and the cigarette tip—toward it. But he didn't thumb the flint. Several seconds passed. He took the cigarette out of his mouth and placed it and the lighter on the table. He ran a hand through his thin hair. For the first time in a year and a half, he looked old and tired.

At last he met Jim's gaze across the plywood table and took a deep, wadded-cellophane breath. "If Goss did own a .270," he began, "I never saw it." Then, after a moment, he admitted, "But I never looked very hard. And, to show you just what kind of lawyer I am, what kind of man's been telling *you* how to do things all this time, I never asked him. TV lawyers always ask their clients, *Did you do it?* Not me. I didn't want to know. Knowing can be just as hard to live with as doing. After seventy-some years, my conscience is about evenly burdened by both. Whatever Goss had done, I didn't want to ask and make a lie his only way out. It isn't easy to get close to a guy like Goss, and, from his angle, maybe we were never friends. But I've told you what it came to mean after my wife's death to have someplace to go every day, something to do, somebody to talk to, even if our talk was half the time two gnawed old bones arguing. But that was better than sitting alone in a cabin and staring mortality in the face. If Goss shot one of Enoch's cows, the two of them are going to have to work it out in a better courtroom than I've ever been in." Rickett stopped. He focused carefully on the unlit cigarette beside his plate. "What you need to understand, Jim," he said, looking up, "is whatever Goss had done or not done, I felt for him. I honest-to-God felt genuine compassion. And that was almost worth forty years of lawyering."

Jim looked across the table. He studied Nolan Rickett for a long time. Then he said, "If Goss considered you half the friend I do, he was a lucky man."

Jim Ray and Jocelyn would end up keeping company, as Sister Enid Cottrell put it, through the fall and winter. The beginning of their keeping company was that first Thursday after Labor Day (the same day Jocelyn told the sheriff that, from what she'd seen, none of the bikers wanted to work hard enough to poach, not Dutch anyway). On that Thursday evening—at Rickett's sugges- tion and with his help (a twenty-dollar bill tucked into the cleft of the seat and found during the thorough cleaning of the 1941 Ford)—Jim took her to a certain restaurant in Cody. For the rest of his life, he would remember from their dinner conversation certain freely offered disclosures:

After the funeral, Dutch asked me to go to California with him, just for the ride.

And this:

Cool bike or not, I didn't want that kind of ride.

And this:

Going home to Bear Lake was a way to tell him no.

That conversation figured into the alchemy by which a human male and female decide or are moved or emotionally configured to like each other. Though they didn't plan the align- ment, they married exactly two years to the day after Rickett's letter arrived at the sandbag bunker in Chu Lai. As of the wed- ding date—March 15, 1968—Jim still hadn't made good on the promised horseback riding. ("You owe me," Jocelyn reminded him. "I've got it in writing.") The winter months had given him a ready excuse, but the weather wouldn't stay cold forever. Sev- eral times he had considered asking the Crofts for some basic riding lessons, but even if made under cloak of secrecy, such a request would inevitably reach the ears of Big Frett and Bern- ene, and out of an odd mix of vanity and insecurity, Jim didn't want them to know.

The wedding reception, planned with surprisingly little horn- locking between Bernene and Bishop Clive Sebright, was held in the church's cultural hall gymnasium with the genuine hard- wood floor. The basketball backboards were hung with crepe paper streamers. There were folding round tables covered with pretty cloths and decorated with carnation centerpieces. There was a table for gifts and another bearing refreshments. Crackers and cheese. Relish tray. Finger sandwiches. Butter mints and mixed nuts and punch. And of course a cake.

Guests got to the refreshments by way of the receiving line. The jewel in that line was the bride in her white dress. Standing with the bride was her mother, Miss Agnes Vanderfisk from Bear Lake, and beside the mother, the uncle and doting aunt. (The aunt's hair, incidentally, had never appeared more voluminous or more splendid.) The necessary appendage to the bride jewel was the groom. Standing with him was Mr. Nolan Rickett. Mr. Rickett was wearing a suit for only the third time since the groom had met him, the first time for an occasion other than a funeral. Over the course of the evening, the receiving line received everybody from the branding crew—Rowe Sloan, Darl Sebright, Crue Penroy and his son Hewell, even Beeswax Jones. With his hair slicked down and his beard rough-pruned, with a clean shirt and trousers and almost-clean suspenders, Beeswax hardly looked himself—except for his restless mouth. Even in the temporary absence of a quid of tobacco, his lips kept squinching and shifting, puckering and drawing back. And the teeth revealed by those movements were, as always, inimitable.

The last people to come through the line were not locals. The arrival of O. Weldon Partridge and his wife, after a ten-hour drive from central Utah, took the groom by surprise. During the earnest handshaking and embracing, O. Weldon Partridge's kindly hound dog eyes came about as close to buoyant joy as they could come, certainly closer than the groom remembered them ever coming when, five and seven and ten years back, this man was his bishop in the Mapleton Fifth Ward. After the warm greetings, those eyes looked from bride to groom with what could only be called somber happiness. "Theron Ray," the former bishop said as if to confirm his identity, "look at you." Then he said, "Your mother Minnie is smiling now."

After everyone had been received in the receiving line, there was cake cutting and, after that, singing by Patty Dew Bingham (née Maxwell), and after that, counsel to the couple by Sister Enid Cottrell. Sister Cottrell noted first how both bride and groom were from somewhere other than Balford but had, in the Lord's providence, found each other here. Then she noted how Jim's bachelor living conditions were at a blessed end, how curtains and tablecloths and flowers and matching dishes and a proper quilted bedspread would transform his life more than he could imagine. That observation drew approving nods and a ripple of laughter all around. Then she added, as a sort of aside (and to many knowing smiles), how the old pickup truck might have to give way to some other conveyance when the children started coming.

Sister Enid Cottrell stood for a moment in silence, her eyes slowly sweeping the crowd of reception guests. It took a moment to realize that she was hesitating. But after that moment, she ventured bravely into territory long avoided in any sort of public gathering in this town. She noted how the bride and groom represented two of the oldest families in the valley. She noted, with tears in her eyes, how human hurts, big or little, in marriage or elsewhere, can either fester or heal, depending on a willingness to forgive. Forgiveness, she said, is the great mender of rifts, not only in marriage and other private relationships, but in communities. "I know," she concluded with great conviction, "that Goss and Enoch would be sublimely happy for this young couple and for all their marriage represents. I know that with all my heart."

For several moments after Enid Cottrell had finished and taken her place beside her husband, people still sat in awed silence. They were so moved that they didn't go back to their refreshments right away. Seated between parents who could have passed for grandparents, even young Hewell Penroy waited a respectful interval before going back to the punch and butter mints and mixed nuts and ample slice of cake before him.

Early afternoon on a warm day in late April, a hawk soars in high gyres over the main canal and railroad and highway. Then, as if on some mysterious cue, it seems all at once to fix on a destination and to take as its guide to that destination the long, straight demarcation of Honey Spring. The newly committed-to direction carries the bird over the big plaque marking the first Mormon encampment in the Bighorn Basin and over the gap in the guardrail along the edge of the paved turn-out. Because of an understanding accompanying a marriage just six weeks old, the light chain strung across that opening will rust and the guardrail fade without the original purpose of the gap ever being realized. The hawk soars over all of it—over the willow patch at the spring's mouth, over currant bushes, over a slab of sandstone bearing (as of a week after the honeymoon) a newly etched pair of initials, over the half dozen blossoming apple trees encircling a pond glinting in the midday sun, and southward along the thin line of the spring's channel stretching toward the river bluff.

Just before the bluff's edge the hawk peers downward at the shiny rectangle of a single-wide trailer's roof. What the bird can't see, even with its remarkable acuity, is the interior of the dwelling, thoroughly scrubbed and transformed. Curtains and tablecloth (on a real eating table). Pictures on the wall. Clean second-hand couch with a lot of wear left in the upholstery. Throw rugs (over holes in the carpet). And stowed or hung or shelved in their assigned places, all the wedding gifts—silverware, tableware, kitchen utensils, samplers, hymnal, inspirational books, quart jar of *very* locally harvested clover honey. And, in the bedroom, a lovely quilted spread on a double bed.

High above the notch in the bluff, the hawk dips and swoops downward. With the slightest tilt of feathers and a flap or two, it could hold a southward course, cross the river, and within seconds begin espying rabbits or moles in the foothills of the McCullough Peaks. Instead, after flying over the trees at the base of the bluff, it levels off, banks east, circles back west, and commences climbing in lazy spirals. At a certain height, it levels off again and simply soars. One moment its gliding takes it over badlands and gravel pit; the next, over swamp and lush pasture.

Far below, a fringe of trees runs along the base of the bluff, from the river all the way to the notch down which Honey Spring flows. Where the fringe thins out, on the west bank of Honey Spring, stands a lone aspen. Spread out on the ground beneath its branches is one of the rectangles of canvas used to dam irrigation ditches. The canvas is clean and dry. On that piece of canvas, just six weeks married, Jim Ray and Jocelyn are finishing their lunch. Jim Ray lies on his back, eyes half closed, now and again bringing up a hand and taking a bite of cookie, then chewing drowsily. Jocelyn sits with her back against the tree trunk, resting, her eyes fully closed. The tree grows just up-slope from the gate they are making in the divider fence. They have worked all morning setting the H-braces for the gate's hinge and latch ends. Out away from the shade of the trees it is hot. But here, on the canvas beneath the tree, they feel the spring's coolness; from where they're resting, they can see the moving water. Where the water meets each bank, tufts of moss dance. The burble is pleasant.

After a time Jocelyn opens her eyes and leans forward. She folds a sandwich wrapping and drops it into their food basket.

She looks toward their morning's work and says, "Did you tell him this was my idea?"

"I did," Jim says, taking a last bite of cookie.

"What did he say?"

"He said you account for the looks *and* the brains in this relationship."

"He didn't say that."

"Ask him."

"I will," she says. Then she says, "When does he get back?"

"When Luna Valley has had its fill of his annual visit," Jim says, with his eyes still half closed. "*Or*," he announces slowly and with affected emphasis, "when we've had plenty of time to adjust to the pleasures of married life. Whichever comes first."

"I *know* he didn't say that."

Jim sits up. He and Jocelyn are shoulder to shoulder. He turns his head so as to study the fine profile of her eyes, nose, lips, and the collar of her shirt. "Every word of it," he says.

Jocelyn smiles and takes Jim's hand. "So," she asks, "are we adjusted yet?"

All along the fence line north of the new gate opening, asparagus spears are poking up from burned-off root mounds. East and west, the trees at the base of the bluff resound with birdsong. At the closest edge of the grassy swale between trees and swamp, a cluster of cattle are taking their midday rest. Some standing, most lying, cows chew their cuds with a sleepy rhythm. As if to scorn such lassitude, their calves look for reasons to frolic. Anything will do.

Suddenly, from behind one of the few cows standing, a baby calf steps into view. It is the smallest of the group, pasture-born in the week since spring branding. It is a beautiful little creature, in size and proportion—and color. Its coat is a lovely, glossy dun. For a long while after stepping away from its mother, the calf

stares at the two people beneath the aspen. Then it begins walking toward them. It stops and stares, unblinking, then comes on.
When it gets to the shade line of the trees, it stops again. It is less
than twenty yards away. For a moment it stands and looks at
the man and woman sitting shoulder to shoulder. Then, as if to
celebrate something known only to the three of them, it frisks in
a perfect little circle, bleating with delight.

ACKNOWLEDGMENTS

I AM GRATEFUL TO GREGG HEITSCHMIDT FOR READING and editing the manuscript for this book. Thanks to his help, this writing is less flawed than it would otherwise be. Many times his keen eye or ear has saved me from inaccuracy, excess, and infelicity. And that's just the short list of the faults he undoubtedly encountered. I am in his debt.

ABOUT THE AUTHOR

DARIN COZZENS GREW UP ON A FARM OUTSIDE RALSTON, Wyoming. After two years of missionary service in Ecuador, he earned degrees from Brigham Young University, the University of North Carolina–Greensboro, and Oklahoma State University. Author of two collections of short stories, he teaches at Surry Community College in Dobson, North Carolina. He and his wife are the parents of four children.